A Lady in Disguise

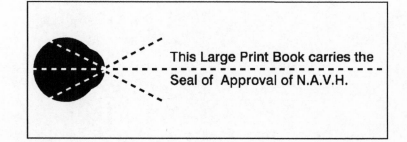

This Large Print Book carries the
Seal of Approval of N.A.V.H.

A LADY IN DISGUISE

LYNSAY SANDS

THORNDIKE PRESS
A part of Gale, a Cengage Company

Copyright © 2002 by Lynsay Sands.
This book was originally published as *The Reluctant Reformer* in 2002 by Dorchester Publishing Co., Inc.
Thorndike Press, a part of Gale, a Cengage Company.

ALL RIGHTS RESERVED
This is a work of fiction. Names, characters, places, and incidents are products of the author's imagination or are used fictitiously and are not to be construed as real. Any resemblance to actual events, locales, organizations, or persons, living or dead, is entirely coincidental.
The publisher is not responsible for websites (or their content) that are not owned by the publisher.
Thorndike Press® Large Print Romance.
The text of this Large Print edition is unabridged.
Other aspects of the book may vary from the original edition.
Set in 16 pt. Plantin.

LIBRARY OF CONGRESS CIP DATA ON FILE.
CATALOGUING IN PUBLICATION FOR THIS BOOK
IS AVAILABLE FROM THE LIBRARY OF CONGRESS

ISBN-13: 978-1-4328-7295-3 (hardcover alk. paper)

Published in 2020 by arrangement with Avon Books, an imprint of HarperCollins Publishers

Printed in Mexico
Print Number: 01   Print Year: 2020

A Lady in Disguise

CHAPTER ONE

London, March 1815

Maggie shifted her feet slightly, trying to ease the ache her cramped position was causing in her legs. The small movement was enough to cause her to bang her knees against the door of the armoire she presently sat in, making it rattle. Wincing at the pain that shot up her leg, Maggie was busily rubbing the appendage when the cupboard door opened and soft candlelight spilled in over her.

"Stop yer banging about, or ye'll be givin' away that ye're in there."

Ceasing her leg-rubbing, Maggie managed an apologetic smile for the scantily clad young woman glaring in at her. "I am sorry," she began in conciliatory tones, then paused and heaved out a breath. She straightened and began to step from the small closet. "No, actually, I am not. Er, Daisy, is it?"

"Maisey," the girl corrected.

"Yes, well . . . Maisey, then," Maggie said. The girl's put-upon air was irritating, as were the wrinkles that Maggie was futilely trying to brush out of her gown. "This is all really rather silly, and quite beyond the information for which I was looking. All I really wanted was to —"

The sound of a rap at the door made Maggie pause, alarmed. The young woman before her stiffened, then steel seemed to enter her eyes and she shoved Maggie firmly back into the armoire. Maggie landed on her behind with a grunt.

"It's too late to be changing yer mind now, milady," she announced, bending to shove Maggie's feet inside the closet before she could regain her balance. "Madame says ye're to watch, and watch you will. Now keep quiet," she said in a hiss. The door pushed closed with a decided snap.

"Damn," Maggie said under her breath, then struggled to a sitting position. The door rattled slightly, nearly covering the sound of a bolt being slid home. Pressing one eye to the crack where the doors did not quite meet, she saw Maisey nod with a grunt of satisfaction and whirl away to answer the door. Frowning, Maggie lifted a hand to push experimentally forward, but

8

the door stayed firmly shut. The girl had locked her in!

Well, this is just bloody beautiful, she thought irritably. *Brilliant! I do tend to get myself into fixes, don't I?*

Not that she could have gotten out now, anyway. Maggie considered herself a thoroughly modern young woman: highly intelligent, independent, and uncaring of what others thought of her — but only to a certain degree. Even she, thoroughly modern as she was, hesitated to deliberately draw the wrath and scorn of the ton down upon herself. Especially when she merely had to sit quietly for a short time to avoid scandal completely. Patience was not one of her natural virtues, but she had been attempting to cultivate it of late. Yes, she would simply have to look at this as a chance to develop herself. A learning experience, one might say.

She had barely finished that thought when it occurred to her that she was crouching down in a small armoire in one of the rooms of the infamous Madame Dubarry's — this was a brothel, for God's sake! What she would learn in this room . . . well, she just shouldn't know yet! What was more, she certainly couldn't write about it.

Good Lord, how had she ended up here?

9

Madame Dubarry, of course. The woman had been slow to warm to the idea of allowing Maggie to interview her and some of her girls for a story for the *Daily Express.* Once the madam had agreed to the undertaking, however, she had become quite enthusiastic. The older woman had bustled Maggie from girl to girl, attending the interviews to be sure each girl told the juiciest stories; then she had rounded off this most peculiar day by offering Maggie refreshment in her own private drawing room. It was while the two had chatted over tea that Madame Dubarry devised this harebrained scheme. Clattering her teacup down in its saucer, she had sat up abruptly, her eyes on the clock in the corner.

"What time is it, nearly seven? Oh, really, this is perfect timing! You *must* witness this, Lady Maggie. Really, you must. You shall thank me for it, I promise."

So saying, the woman had stood quickly, grasped Maggie's hand and dragged her from her chair, then hurried from the room and along the hall. Before Maggie could even collect herself enough to ask what she must see and why, they had reached this chamber. Madame Dubarry shoved her inside, installed her in the cupboard with admonishments to remain quiet and see, then had instructed young Maisey that Maggie was to witness the night's proceedings. She had fled the room nearly as hurriedly as she'd ushered Maggie into it.

Maggie, stunned by the abruptness of the event, had remained still and silent for a moment before the cramping of her muscles had forced her to shift positions and draw the wrath of the shapely young Maisey.

Really, had she been a bit quicker, Maggie might have managed to flee the room before Maisey's customer arrived. Now it appeared she was quite stuck. She sighed irritably and tried to ignore the murmur of voices from the room outside. Maggie had no desire to learn anything more than she'd learned in her interviews. And I won't, she assured herself. I simply will not look through the crack to see who Maisey's client is or what they are doing.

She frowned as the voices drew closer. The man's slightly deeper-timbered voice struck a chord of recognition within her. It sounded amazingly like . . . .

Her gaze slid to the crack despite her best intentions, and Maggie drew her breath in with a hiss. Good Lord, it *was* him: Pastor Frances. Her eyes narrowed on the man. She had just been discussing the fact that he was paying her court, and that she

11

thought he might soon propose, when Madame Dubarry had rushed her up here. Maggie was distracted from further thought by an odd question from Maisey.

"Who am I to be tonight, milord? Yer mother?"

Maggie's eyes widened in shocked dismay at that, but they nearly fell out of her head at Frances's answer.

"Nay. Tonight you shall be my dear Margaret."

"Sweet Lady Wentworth, is it?" Maggie was almost too shocked by Frances's presence to notice the irony in the young prostitute's voice. Almost. "The woman who personifies the very word 'lady'? The woman who never sets a foot wrong? Who is discretion herself?"

Maggie couldn't help but wince slightly at the pointy edges of Maisey's words. She also experienced a touch of alarm as she realized that, in her excitement, Madame Dubarry had addressed her by her real name when she'd brought her up to this room.

She forgot all such concerns when Frances answered, "Aye: my sweet Maggie. I have decided to propose to her. I arranged to take her to the Cousins' ball tonight. I shall propose to her afterward. I believe she will accept."

12

"Oh, 'course she will, guv'nor, a great, strapping man like yerself . . ." There was no missing the irony in Maisey's voice then. At least, Maggie caught it; the gibe seemed to slip right past the rather thin and emaciated Frances.

"Fine. You be Maggie then, and I shall practice on you." There was a moment of critical silence before he murmured, "You had best put something else on."

"Something else?"

"Well, Maggie would never greet me so scantily clad."

"Not even if the house were afire," Maggie agreed under her breath. Through the crack in the armoire doors, she took in Maisey's costume — what there was of it. Sheer silk and red, it covered absolutely nothing. It was scandalous.

There came a moment of uncertain silence; then Maisey heaved an impatient sigh. "Fine, then. Ye step on out into the hall, and I shall change. Give me five minutes; then knock."

"Why must I wait in the hall?" Frances whined.

"Well, ye want it to be as if ye were proposing to Lady Wentworth, don't ye? Would she dress in front of ye? Get on with ye. I'll only be a minute, and this will seem

13

more real."

Through the crack, Maggie saw Maisey usher Frances out of the room as firmly as she herself had been shoved into the armoire. The prostitute closed the door behind the pastor with a snap, then locked it. She was a no-nonsense type of woman, it seemed.

"Thank God." Maggie burst out of the armoire as Maisey unbolted it. "I thought I should suffocate in there. Now get me out of here."

"You know where the door is," came Maisey's unconcerned response. The young woman was digging through her clothing, picking up and discarding gown after gown.

Maggie frowned and glanced from the door to the girl. "I can hardly exit *that* way. Pastor Frances is out there."

"Then I guess ye'll just have to get back in the closet, won't ye?" Maisey snapped, discarding yet another gown.

"Get back in?" Maggie was confused. "Did you not let me out to slip me from the room?"

"No. I let you out so I could find a gown suitable enough to play the likes of ye. I could hardly dig about with you sitting in my armoire just waiting to be discovered by the pastor, could I? Damn! I ain't got a single dress as drab as the one ye're wearing." Throwing her last garment down in disgust, she glared at her as if the lack of wardrobe were somehow Maggie's fault. Then a catty look came over her face. "You wouldn't consider letting me borrow yer gown fer a bit, would ye?"

"Certainly not," Maggie snapped. She looked desperately around the room. "There simply has to be a way out of here."

"There isn't," the girl assured her. "Unless ye can fly out the window."

"The window!" Maggie hurried over to it, then pushed it open and leaned out. They were on the third floor. The ground was a long way down. She was about to give up on the idea when her gaze dropped to the wall, and she saw a ledge a couple of feet below the window. It was just wide enough that she could walk it — if she were careful.

She would be careful, she decided.

"Here!" Maisey grabbed her arm as Maggie sat on the sill and made to climb out. "What? Are ye daft? Ye'll break yer bones jumpin' from here."

"I am not going to jump," Maggie said with a hiss of exasperation, tugging her arm free. "I am going to walk that ledge to the next room, climb in through the window there, and get away."

15

Leaning out, Maisey peered down, her eyes widening slightly in surprise. "Oh . . . well." The girl hesitated slightly, her gaze calculating; then she announced, "Well, that would be nice, wouldn't it? Except that Lady X and Lord Hastings are in one of the rooms next door. Yer climbin' in on them would cause the scandal of the decade."

Maggie frowned at the news. Everyone, absolutely everyone, had heard of the infamous Lady X. She was the most famous of Agatha Dubarry's prostitutes, and as such, Maggie had not been allowed to speak to her — though she had caught a glimpse of the woman earlier while interviewing the others. From what she had spied, Lady X was a lovely blonde with a perfect figure, full lips, and deep, mysterious eyes. That was all she had seen.

Actually, it was all anyone ever saw. Her face was always covered by a blazing red mask that never came off. Men paid highly for the privilege of bedding her, each trying to discover her true identity, but no one had yet figured it out. It was rumored that the woman was actually a lady of nobility who worked thusly on the side to help shore her sagging family coffers. While many disputed the idea, claiming that surely no lady would risk being discovered in such an endeavor, there were enough men willing to dig deep into their pockets to try to find out, and Madame Dubarry was doing very well.

Maggie definitely did not need the scandal of walking in on the woman while she was entertaining — especially if she was with Lord Hastings, one of the most distinguished royal councilors.

"Which room are they in?" she asked.

Maisey smiled, the expression of a cat who has cornered a mouse. "Let me use your gown."

Maggie stiffened, then shook her head. "I shall find out for myself," she declared. Sliding her legs over onto the window ledge, she straightened slowly, clinging nervously to the sill as she fought to maintain her balance.

"Have it your way," Maisey said with amusement, watching. "But it does look a long way down. And I know I shouldn't like to make it all the way along that ledge to a window, simply to have to turn back and travel twice the distance to another." At Maggie's obvious uncertainty, Maisey pressed her advantage. " 'Tis just a gown. I'll give ye one o' me own to wear in its place. Then I'll send yers back to ye first thing on the morrow — once it's been cleaned."

17

Maggie took in the hopeful gaze of the prostitute, peered at the ground such a long way down, then shifted cautiously on the ledge. Her mind was made up by her jumping stomach. Cursing under her breath, she maneuvered back into the room and eyed Maisey unhappily. "The other room is empty, isn't it?"

The prostitute nodded solemnly.

"Fine. But —" A tap at the door cut her off, and both women glanced over sharply as the doorknob jiggled.

"Are you ready yet, my dear?" Frances cooed in a sickening tone. Maggie had never heard it from the usually dignified man.

"Oh, keep yer pants on. I'm hurryin' as fast as I can," Maisey snapped, then grimly turned to Maggie. "Well?"

"Oh . . . stuff!" Maggie huffed. She set to work disrobing as quickly as she could. Looking pleased, Maisey began to undress as well. The two worked in virtual silence until Maggie got her gown off. She handed it over, then crossed her arms, rubbing them as goose bumps began to form on her flesh.

"Yer shift and bloomers too."

"What?"

When Maggie stared at her in dismay, the prostitute rolled her eyes. "I'm supposed to be dressed like you. 'Sides, ye'll be caught fer sure if ye run around with those bloomers showing through my gown."

Maggie frowned at the transparent garment the girl held out, then shook her head in misery. "I will be recognized anyway if my face is seen. Oh, why did I leave my veil in Madame Dubarry's drawing room?"

Whirling, Maisey hurried to her armoire, returning a moment later with a plain red silk mask for Maggie to wear. "Here; put this on. With the mask, my clothes, and yer cloak, ye should escape all right."

Maggie glanced at it curiously. "Is this Lady X's mask?"

"Nay. Mine. Lady X's mask is far fancier." When Maggie continued to stare at her questioningly, the prostitute heaved a sigh. "Men like to play all sorts o' games. I . . ." She paused, scowling as there was another tap at the door, louder and more insistent this time.

"Maisey?" Frances sounded somewhat put out.

"Only just another moment, milord," Maisey called back. She shoved the mask at Maggie and said in a hiss, "Take it."

"Are you absolutely sure of this, Johnstone?" James Huttledon, Lord Ramsey, was finally moved to set aside the book he'd been reading when the Bow Street runner was announced. Carefully marking his spot with one of the many cloth bookmarks his aunt had made him over the years, he set the tome on a side table for later and sat up to give his full attention to this troubling turn of events.

"Aye, m'lord. I tried to find you right away. I knew you'd be wanting to know right prompt, but when I went by your town house, they told me you were at your club. By the time I got there, they said you'd left just moments earlier. I had to begin searching —"

"Yes, yes." James waved the explanation away and turned to stare out the window at the tranquil scene of the garden lining the back of his town house library.

Johnstone was silent for a moment, allowing Ramsey his thoughts, then pointed out gently, "It would explain where she's been getting the money to keep up the house and servants."

James jerked his head around to stare ferociously at the man. "You are not thinking that she *works* there?"

Johnstone appeared as surprised at the question as could be. "Well . . . what other business could a lady have at Madame Dubarry's?"

"For God's sake, Johnstone; she is a lady!"

"Aye, well, the claim is that Lady X is a woman of nobility."

James's mouth dropped open, but he quickly snapped it shut. "Good God," he got out between gritted teeth. He turned toward the window again.

They were both silent; then Johnstone said uncertainly, "I left Henries there to keep an eye out while I came to see what ye wanted me to do."

James remained quiet for a moment, then stood abruptly and strode toward the door of his library. "Hethers!" he bellowed as he stepped into the hall, relief filling him when he spied his valet approaching. "My coat. I am going out."

The servant hurriedly fetched his overcoat, hat, and gloves. As the man assisted him in donning them, James added, "Have some things packed. I am leaving tonight."

"Tonight, my lord?"

"Yes. I shall be staying at Ramsey for a while."

"Yes, my lord."

Maggie peered in at the scene taking place in the room next to Maisey's, and she groaned aloud. Her fingers tightening on the cold wall, she leaned her head unhap-

21

pily against it. After trading clothes, Maisey had helped her climb back out onto this ledge, hissing that Lady X and Lord Hastings were in the room on the left. She had then left and hurried to attend the impatiently pounding Frances.

Relieved to be out of her predicament Maggie had immediately inched along the ledge to the next window, expecting to find the room empty. Unfortunately, what she had not realized was that Maisey had been referring to her own left — which, of course, with Maggie clinging to the wall facing her, was Maggie's right. Which meant Maggie should have gone right. Which she hadn't. She had ended up coming all this way for nothing, for while curtains shrouded the window, making the images beyond blurred and foggy, the figures were discernible enough to see two people engaged in the most energetic round of ride-the-pony it had ever been Maggie's misfortune to witness.

Resignedly Maggie turned to glance back along the ledge, took a deep breath, then began the long return the way she had come, clinging like a limpet to the wall as she did. She was nearly back at Maisey's window before she realized that in her haste, the prostitute had neglected to close it.

Grimacing, she paused to the side and peered around its edge.

The time since she had crept from the room seemed like a century to Maggie, and while she knew that it was just the stress of the moment making it seem so, she was surprised to see that she must have indeed been gone for quite a length of time. A good ten minutes must have passed, at least, for Maisey — playing Maggie — had already served Frances a drink by a small table and chairs near the bed. Their refreshments finished and whatever passed for small talk between them done, Frances now knelt at Maisey's feet, the prostitute's hands clasped gently in his, heart-felt longing on the pastor's reverent face.

"I have known you for quite a while now, Margaret," he was saying. "Long enough to know that you are the woman for me. I would be most honored if you would consent to be my bride."

"Yes," Maisey agreed in a bored tone.

The pastor frowned. "Surely she wouldn't just say yes like that?"

"What would she say then?"

"Well, I don't know. Just . . . try to sound a bit more enthusiastic, please."

"Yes," the prostitute cooed.

Frances continued to frown, but apparently decided he wouldn't get much more out of the girl. Shrugging slightly, he surged to his feet, drawing Maisey up and into his arms with the same move. "You shan't be sorry, my dear. I shall make an outstanding husband — I promise you, we shall have a marvelous marriage." This he managed to gasp out between slobbery kisses across Maisey's cheeks and down her neck. When he reached the top of the prim black gown she now wore, he paused and pulled back to leer at her. "I love the proper little things you wear. They hide your lovely body from the eyes of other men, but there is no need to hide from me any longer." With that, he grasped the collar of the gown and ripped downward, rending it nearly to the waist before lifting wide eyes to Maisey's dismayed face. "Oops," he said lightly. "Now you shall have to punish me."

"Ye're damn right I will," the girl snapped irritably. "And ye'll be replacin' that gown, too. It weren't even mine."

"Then I, of course, shall replace it," Frances promised, unperturbed by her obvious anger. Releasing Maisey, he stepped back and began doffing his clothes.

Maggie turned away, unwilling to watch what would follow. She tried judging the space between where she stood and the other side of the window, wondering if she could traverse the distance quickly enough that she might not be detected. She supposed it depended on how distracted the two in the room were. Glancing back inside reluctantly, she saw Frances slide out of his top and drape it across the chair he had just vacated. Glimpsing welts on his back, Maggie paused in dismay, her gaze moving to Maisey to see that the girl had retrieved a long, wide leather belt from the armoire and was now eyeing Frances with a decidedly jaundiced eye. He continued stripping.

Staring in surprise at the pastor as he shed his trousers, Maggie saw that welts covered not just his back, but his buttocks and the rear of his upper thighs as well. She frowned in bewilderment. Was this what Madame Dubarry had wanted her to see? Did Frances really pay Maisey to beat him with a belt? Some of the girls had told her such tales in their interviews: stories of men who enjoyed odd or even unhealthy diversions during their sexual encounters. Was Frances one of those? It would seem so.

She shook her head with a sort of pity combined with disgust. What would make a man turn to such games? Frances had seemed such a normal, well-mannered, polite sort.

The first crack of the belt across Frances's back dragged Maggie from her ponderings to the realization that she was perched on a ledge outside the third-floor window of a brothel, balanced delicately between breaking her neck and being discovered and ruined. This was no time to be reflecting on Frances's foibles. She should just be grateful she had learned of them ere he proposed. Imagine if she had accepted, never knowing that just hours before the man had been whipped, among other things, by one of Madame Dubarry's girls.

Would he have expected her to beat him once they were married? Maggie immediately pushed the question out of her head with a shudder. She had no time for such thoughts. She would *not* be accepting his proposal. On that determined note, she peeked into the room once more, relieved to see that Pastor Frances and Maisey were suitably distracted, then forced herself to move past the window and continue on toward the next window along the wall.

James stood uncomfortably inside the foyer at Madame Dubarry's, waiting impatiently for Johnstone to conclude his whispered conversation with the madam herself. Ramsey had already been approached by, and turned down the offers of, three of the madam's girls, one of whom had offered to do a thing or two that he had never considered trying before. He certainly did not wish to attempt it now, here in this place.

"It's done, yer lordship. Madame says Lady X is with Lord Hastings now, but you can have a go at her next."

"I do not intend to 'have a go at her,' as you so delicately put it," James said in a hiss.

A flicker of irritation crossed Johnstone's face before the runner controlled it. "I didn't think you would, my lord. But I could hardly tell her ye wished to kidnap the girl, now, could I?"

"I am not kidnapping her. I am rescuing her."

"Aye. Well, I'd guess that there is a matter of perspective, ain't it?" Pausing, the man shook his head. "Either way, it'll cost ye deep," he announced, then mentioned a shocking sum.

"You must be joking."

"I never joke about money, m'lord. But ye'll either be paying that amount or waiting till a week from Sunday to lay hands on her. She's booked full for the night — a different man every half hour. Dubarry was willing to bump everyone back, but she

27

wants to be paid well for the trouble. What should I tell her?"

James considered walking out the door, getting in his carriage, and riding to Lady Wentworth's home to await her return there, but his conscience would not let him. He had made a promise to look after the girl — and looking after her did not mean glancing the other way while she bedded some two dozen or so men. Muttering under his breath, he pulled a bag of coins from his pocket and dropped it in the hand the Bow Street runner extended. "How long until Hastings's half hour is up?"

Johnstone's gaze slid to a clock in the hall. "About ten minutes. I'll just give Dubarry the money; then we'll go have a look around and see if there's another way out of here."

"Another way out?"

"Surely you didn't think to march out the front door with her, did ye? Dubarry ain't gonna like that. The girl is her golden goose."

"Ah, yes." James sighed; then he, too, stared at the clock on the wall. Ten minutes.

Maggie grabbed the edge of the window with relief and paused to rest her face on the cold glass. She was sweating. Amazingly enough, she was more terrified of falling than of discovery, which was surprising, because she could remember a time when the prospect of social ruin had been more frightful than anything. But that had been when she could afford such pretty concerns as her reputation, before she'd had the burden of so many lives piled on her shoulders.

"Damn you, Gerald, for dying, anyway," she cursed in a whisper, then immediately — if silently — apologized to her poor brother for cussing him so. Gerald had loved life. He had lived every moment of his short time on earth as if it might be his last. He had not complained when he was ordered off to fight Napoléon. And she had no doubt he had given his life in battle with as much passion and as little regret as with which he had lived. It was just too damn bad he'd been forced to leave her in such a fix.

As a woman, Maggie had been unable to inherit her brother's title and estates. While he had bequeathed her his town house in London — a purchase he had made with money from investments before inheriting his title and station from their father — everything else had been entailed to some blasted second or third cousin . . . if they had found the bloody man. The only money Maggie had to live off of was a small investment she had made with her own inheritance from their mother.

It wasn't really that small an investment. In fact, she could have lived quite comfortably off of it for her entire life — had she not been saddled with Gerald's property and servants. It was a town house fit for a duke, with lots of rooms, and nearly as many employees in attendance.

The practical side of Maggie had ordered her to release the servants, close the house, sell it, and move to a small cottage in the country. There she might have lived very comfortably with one or two hired hands. However, sentiment had not allowed her to sell the property. Gerald had loved the place. He had rarely even bothered to ride out to the estate he had inherited with his title, but his town house — there his spirit seemed to linger still. Maggie simply could not part with his home; it was her last link to her now all-but-deceased family. And as for the servants . . . faced with closing up part of the house and releasing a large portion of the staff, Maggie simply hadn't been able to do it. Gerald's staff were hardworking, cheerful individuals. She hadn't been able to look a single one of them in the face and tell him he was no longer wanted.

Such being the case, she had been forced

to find a way to support the large staff. The answer had come by chance. While sorting through her brother's papers, Maggie had come across the knowledge that her brother had led a double life. He'd been Lord Gerald Wentworth, Duke of Clarendon, and also G. W. Clark — the adventurist writer who wrote columns for the *Daily Express.* He'd provided articles about the seedier side of London life: rumors, truths, stories of gaming hells, fortunes won and lost, affairs, everything. From Gerald's papers Maggie had learned he had met with Mr. Hartwick — the editor of the *Express* — only once, and then he'd been in disguise to protect his identity. Members of the nobility did not do anything so crass as to work.

She had also learned that he wrote the articles and dispatched them via Banks, his butler. Which was when Maggie'd had her brilliant idea: she would become G. W. Clark. She could do it — and she had for the last three months. She had gone to great lengths to continue her brother's column, going so far as to dress up as a young buck and travel to the seedier sections of London with Banks in tow to protect her — for all the good the elderly butler was.

All that was how she had ended up standing here on the ledge outside the third-floor window of Madame Dubarry's. The woman had apparently been a great friend of her brother's, at least according to his notes. Certainly Madame Dubarry had been privy to the fact that her brother was G. W. Clark, for when the column had started up again three weeks after his death, she had paid a visit to Maggie.

With a sense of adventure equal to Maggie's and her brother's, Madame Dubarry had arrived on the Wentworth doorstep dressed as a poor fruitseller. On being shown in to see Maggie, the madame had announced her true identity, revealed that Gerald had been G. W. Clark, and complained that some "dastardly devil" had stolen his name. Maggie had been forced to confess herself the culprit. By the end of a pot of tea, she and Dubarry had struck up an unlikely friendship. They had been in cahoots ever since — although the woman had only recently given in to the interviews of her employees.

Amazing, Maggie thought. For the first time, she considered that perhaps Agatha Dubarry had been right when she had suggested Maggie come dressed as a man to this night's activities. Maggie had shrugged away the suggestion, thinking that the madam's girls might be more forthcoming with information while talking to another of their gender. It had worked, too. She had been introduced as the sister of G. W. Clark, sent to interview them, and the girls had responded very easily. And no one had known her true identity, not until Agatha had slipped up in Maisey's room. Maggie found she wasn't too concerned about Maisey, though. She had no doubt that Madame Dubarry could keep the girl quiet. Her real problem would be if some member of the ton saw her; then she would be recognized and ruined for sure. There was no way Agatha Dubarry could keep all of London quiet.

Yes, now would indeed be a beneficial time to be disguised as a man. And, she thought as she glanced down nervously past her long skirts, such a disguise would also have made climbing about on ledges more seemly.

"Lord Ramsey, we'll have to sneak her down the back stairs and smuggle her through the kitchen."

James nodded at Johnstone's suggestion. After he'd made a brief but thorough examination of the brothel, it indeed seemed the best bet to get the girl out. "Go have my driver move the carriage to the alley," he instructed, his eyes on the clock in the hall. "Hastings's time is up. I'll go see if he has left yet."

Nodding, Johnstone hurried away toward the front door, and James started upstairs. He was at the top of the steps before he realized that the runner hadn't told him in which room Lady X was supposed to be. He was about to return downstairs to ask Madame Dubarry when he changed his mind. He would recognize Hastings. Everyone knew of Hastings, if not in person, then by reputation. He was second only to the crown in power. Whichever room Hastings exited, James would enter.

He had just come to that conclusion when the thud of a door made him turn back around on the landing. A glance up the hall showed Hastings strolling jauntily toward him, whistling under his breath as he straightened his cravat. James almost cursed aloud. He had been too slow; he couldn't be sure from which room the man had come. There were several possibilities.

He would try them all, he decided resolutely. Giving Hastings a curt nod, he moved purposely past him to set about his work.

The thud of a closing door tore Maggie from her thoughts, and she glanced through the window into the empty room to which she had inched. If her thoughts had distracted her so long that this room was now occupied, too, she thought she might very well throw up. She did not think she had the stamina or nerve to traverse the length of the ledge again. It was with some relief that she saw that the room appeared empty. Letting her breath out, she reached down, opened the window, and silently slipped inside.

Now that they were on solid ground, her legs were more than just a bit rubbery. Ordering them to stand firm, Maggie strode quickly across the room, pausing at the door to take a breath and listen for sounds in the hallway. When she heard only silence, she eased the door open. About to step out of the room, Maggie recalled the mask Maisey had given her — she had shoved it into her pocket in her rush to finish dressing and escape. It would be better to wear the thing. So thinking, she turned back into the room and started to lift the flimsy red silk mask to her face. Her eyes fell on a bed and a woman gaping at her from the shadows within. The two females gaped at each other briefly; then the sound of footsteps in the hall reminded Maggie that she had to get out of here. She quickly finished raising the mask to her face, tied the strings of it in place, then slipped from the room without a murmur of apology.

She had just finished pulling the door closed when a hand slid around her from behind, covering her mouth and smothering her startled cry. She was lifted bodily, bundled in her cape, and carted swiftly down the hall.

CHAPTER TWO

"Any problems, m'lord?"

The words came muffled through her cape to Maggie some few minutes after she found herself so abruptly abducted — minutes during which she had struggled uselessly against the iron arms of her assailant and attempted to scream through the wide, firm hand that covered the lower half of her face. Her struggles ended rather quickly, though. The hand covering her face was not just over her mouth, but also rested along the bottom of her nose, and though she didn't think it was her abductor's intention, she was very close to fainting from lack of oxygen. Her ears were ringing.

For a moment when she heard the voice, Maggie felt hope that the hand across her face would be released and she would again be able to suck into her deprived body some much-needed air. But rather than let go, the hand shifted, covering her more firmly as she was jostled and dragged into what could only be the dark interior of a closed carriage. In the next moment, the clip-clop of horses' hooves on the cobbled London street, and a jolt as the conveyance started forward, told Maggie her guess was right.

Her ears ringing more loudly, she prayed that her suffocation would end before it was too late. The hand remained firmly in place. Glancing around wildly, Maggie realized that, rather than adjusting to the dimmer light, her sight seemed to be dimming further. She would not get air in time to prevent fainting; she could only hope that she would get it in time to stave off death. With that, she slipped into the dark, soft cushion of unconsciousness.

"She's gone limp," Johnstone announced, squinting through the dim light at the woman James held across his lap. "I think she's faint — Damn, Lord Ramsey! You've got both her nose and mouth covered! She can't breathe!"

James removed his hand at once. Turning the woman's limp form slightly in his arms, he peered at her in dismay. The pallor of her skin was obvious even in the dim light, and he cursed as he tugged aside her heavy cape and lowered his head to listen to her heart. It was a great relief to him when he heard its slow, steady thud. Sitting up with a sigh, he peered down at the gown she wore as they rode under a streetlamp. The creation of sheer red material was not made to cover anything; her nipples showed right through it! The carriage moved past the light and its interior returned to darkness, leaving Ramsey's captive nothing but a pale bundle of shadows on his lap. He hurriedly tugged her cape closed again and sank back on the seat.

"Is she all right?"

James frowned at the huskiness in the runner's voice. Suspecting the sight they had just beheld was the cause, and unaccountably annoyed at the fact, he was a bit snappish when he answered. "Yes. She's just fainted, and shall recover."

"Good," Johnstone answered.

They both fell silent as they rode beneath another streetlight. This time both men peered at their capture's face, taking in the delicate features visible below her mask. James stared at that pale visage, so innocent in repose, and he felt bewilderment overtake him.

He had seen Margaret from a distance several times during the months since his return from war, and each time he had been struck by the delicacy of her features, the refined air about her. Even having discovered her in Madame Dubarry's himself, masked and all, it was difficult to believe that the delicate creature he held was the notorious Lady X. The name had been bandied about his club for weeks, along with descriptions he could hardly forget. So lovely, what one could see of her. She had a figure more perfect than a doll's, lips made for the licentious joys of the bedroom, a body that didn't stop. . . . She was a tiger in bed, giving each patron his money's worth — and with seeming relish. It was said that Lady X, nobility or not, was no lady.

Clearing his throat, James forced the thoughts away and glanced at Johnstone. The man was staring at their captive from the opposite seat of the carriage. "Well, do not just sit there," he said. "Find something for us to tie her up with."

The Bow Street runner's eyebrows rose. "Do you really think that's necessary, m'lord?"

"I intend to take her to my country estate and keep her there until we find an alternate career for her. Do you think she will come willingly?"

"No, I suppose not," the runner admitted with a grimace; then he asked, "What of her

40

household?"

James's surprise showed in his voice as he asked, "What household?"

"Her servants. I realize she has no family left to be concerned about her disappearance, but her servants might raise a hue and cry when she doesn't return. What do you intend to do to prevent that?"

"Damn, I had not thought of it."

They were both silent for a moment; then the runner suggested, "Ye could write a letter. Tell them that you have invited Lady Margaret to the country to rusticate for a couple days and that she has taken you up on it."

"Do you think they would believe such tripe?" James asked dubiously.

"They are servants, m'lord. Servants don't question the word of the nobility — at least not out loud. Besides, you are a friend of the family. Well, at least you're a friend of her dead brother's. A letter should keep them quiet for a couple days at least, long enough for you to convince her to write something else to them, reassuring them she is fine."

James considered his suggestion for a minute, then sighed and nodded. "It will have to do. I will write a letter once we get back to my town house, and you can deliver it. In the meantime, we still need to tie her up." His gaze slid around the carriage, then to the runner again. "Perhaps we could use your cravat. Do you think it is long enough?"

Johnstone glanced down with surprise. "I think so, but . . . Oh, what the hell," he decided, setting to work on the garment, then he offered James a cheeky grin. "I'll just bill it to ye."

Maggie was slow to awaken. When she did, it was to find herself bundled in a darkened corner, her cape wrapped tightly around her — so tightly she couldn't move, she realized with dismay. *No, wait.* It was not her cape that restricted her movements, but her hands *were* bound. Her feet appeared to be as well. What the devil was going on?

Blinking in an effort to adjust to the blackness, she peered around at her surroundings. While she saw nothing, she could deduce that she was still in the carriage — the rocking motion of the seat she sat on and the steady clip-clop of horses' hooves made that obvious. Oddly, though, the noise of hooves was the only sound she could hear. The normal hustle and bustle of London's streets was missing. And she could still see nothing.

Then the darkness enveloping her was broken, the hood of her cape was tugged aside, revealing to her why it had been so dark. Without the material covering her face, Maggie could see the gray light of predawn creeping through the window.

Her gaze slid around the carriage, taking in the dark outline of a man seated across from her. He was the only other occupant of the conveyance. It was hard to see his features in the dim interior of the coach, but she could see his size, and that was enough to intimidate her.

"You are awake."

She blinked in surprise. His diction was perfect, his speech cultured. This was no street ruffian, but a gentleman. She had been abducted by a gentleman?

Abducted? Swallowing, she dropped her eyes to her lap to hide her confusion. She, Maggie Wentworth, had been abducted: dragged from Madame Dubarry's, suffocated to unconsciousness, and, apparently, carted off in a carriage. But why? For ransom? There was no money for which to ransom her, and even if there were, there certainly was no one from whom to demand it. Then, all at once, the answer seemed obvious. This was a mistake. She had been mistaken for someone else, one of Madame

43

Dubarry's girls, of course. Perhaps even the famed prostitute Lady X, she realized with dismay. She still wore the red mask Maisey had given her.

"Oh, dear," she murmured somewhat faintly, drawing her abductor's attention. Forcing a smile, though she wasn't at all sure that the man could see it, Maggie sat up as straight as she could. Attempting an air of confidence, she explained, "There has been a dreadful mistake."

"What mistake would that be, Lady Wentworth?"

His address managed to knock some of the wind out of her sails, and Maggie couldn't hide her surprise. "You know my name?"

"Of course."

Well, that blew her theory to kingdom come, Maggie realized with distress. Good Lord, he knew who she was. There was no mistake. She had been deliberately kidnapped. But why, for goodness' sake? Before she could ask, her kidnapper, apparently noting her fear, tried to reassure her.

"There is no need to be alarmed, my lady. The secret of your exploits shall remain safe with me. I have no more desire to unmask you to the world than you yourself must have to be unmasked. In fact, if I have my way, there shall be no chance of anyone ever finding out the games you have been playing. But understand: your alter ego dies this night. You shall not be returning to your previous employ."

Maggie bit her lip, holding back any protest she might have wished to make about her lucrative career as G. W. Clark. There was no sense in annoying her captor until she knew his identity and just how much of a threat he was.

"Now," the man went on gently, apparently pleased that she had made no argument. "You should rest. We shall be traveling for several more hours." Having given that order, he raised a cane to rap on the ceiling of the coach, which drew to an immediate halt. With a nod in her direction, he disembarked from the carriage. Seconds after the door closed, the carriage rocked slightly, as if he were mounting it to sit beside its driver; then the coach jolted back into motion.

Once the conveyance had settled back into its previous monotonous rhythm, Maggie let out a small moan. She had been kidnapped by some madman who knew of her secret doings as G. W. Clark! Of course, there had always been the chance that someone might discover those pursuits, but

45

she had never considered that upon discovering them, that someone might wish to kidnap her and force her to stop! Her real fear had been that they would reveal her and destroy her reputation.

She wearily leaned her head back against the cushioned seat. It seemed she had gotten into a true pickle this time. Not that such was strange for her; as a child her life had often seemed like one calamity after another. The fact had been something of a family joke. "Only you," her family had said. "Only you, Maggie, could end up in such a fix. Only you, Maggie, could land yourself in such a mess." And she had to agree. Just look at how she had ended up tucked into the armoire of a brothel. And how she'd been forced to climb out the window to escape an education she'd not been seeking. And now this kidnapping!

Maggie silently cursed herself for not allowing Banks to accompany her to Dubarry's. The butler often served as a bodyguard of sorts during her adventures, accompanying her and staying as near as he could without ruining her disguises. Old, thin, and fragile, the man wasn't really much of a deterrent to anyone wishing to do her serious harm, but his presence had always made her feel a little bit more secure — and she couldn't help now but wish he had been there tonight.

The butler had wished to accompany her, but Maggie had explained that, as she was simply going to interview women, she had no need of his protection. Madame Dubarry was a friend, she'd added, and thus Maggie would be perfectly safe. She found it ironic now that it had taken her some amount of persuasion before she had convinced him to stay behind.

"Idiot," she chided herself under her breath. Despite the fact that Banks probably would have been left to wait in the kitchens, and therefore would have been helpless to prevent her kidnapping, at least there would have been someone to notice her disappearance. Maggie wasn't at all certain that Madame Dubarry would think twice when she did not return. Men had already started arriving in search of evening entertainment when the brothel owner had hustled her up the back stairs to Maisey's room. The woman was likely now too busy tending to business to notice Maggie's absence. And who knew how long Banks would wait at the house before deciding to come in search of her?

Yes, she thought resignedly, she was in a fix all right. Now she just had to figure a way out of it. Getting untied would be a good start.

A new thought made her sit up abruptly. *Good Lord!* Her hands had been tied under the cape. Her captors would have had to open the cape to get to her hands. Which meant that they had seen the indecent scrap of red silk she was wearing! And what must they have thought of that? she wondered with dismay.

She peered around the dark interior of the carriage. Maybe they hadn't thought anything at all. Maybe it was dark enough here that they had not really seen what she was wearing. She had just started to nurture that hope when she realized that even if they had seen very little while binding her in the carriage, most likely they would get an eyeful when they arrived wherever they were going. With her luck, it would be bright as daylight when they decided to untie her, which would provide a lovely view of everything.

Damn Maisey, she thought irritably. If the girl hadn't insisted on the switch . . . *And damn Frances, too, for good measure,* she added, feeling peevish. *Heck,* she decided while she was at it, *damn Gerald as well!*

Groaning inwardly, Maggie let her head drop back again. This situation just got better and better. She really had to escape. Giving up relaxing on the cushioned seat, she began to struggle with her bindings. They were extremely well tied and very tight. They resisted being undone no matter how she tried.

All Maggie managed to do with her struggles was to tire herself out and rub her wrists raw. She gave up long before the first creeping fingers of dawn spread across the sky.

The carriage rolled to a stop in front of a manor house. Sitting up, Maggie winced at the pain the action sent through her now sensitive wrists and peered out the window, frowning at the immense structure. It was large — huge — obviously the home of a wealthy man, but the stone building looked awkward. It crouched rather than rose into the sky, and it cast dark shadows on the surrounding estate.

Frowning at the sight, Maggie tensed as the carriage rocked; someone was alighting from the driver's bench. She wasn't terribly surprised when the door opened and revealed the caped and hatted man who had been in the carriage with her when she had first awoken — not that she could see much more of him now than she had while he was in the dark carriage. While the sky was beginning to lighten, the coach now stood in the shadow of the mansion. She did, however, recognize the man's voice as he murmured an apology and leaned in toward her.

She understood the reason behind the polite apology as he quickly scooped her off the cushioned seat and out of the carriage. In the next moment she found herself hoisted like a sack of potatoes, the sudden impact of his shoulder in her stomach knocking the wind out of Maggie and effectively eliminating any possibility of her shrieking for help. Not that there appeared to be anyone about to offer that help, she saw with dismay. Turning her head to glance frantically one way, then the other, Maggie found there was no one in view but for the man presently carting her toward the estate's front door. Well, there was the driver of the coach, too, but one glimpse of the man's amused expression suggested that he would be of no assistance.

Deciding she had best save her strength, Maggie remained still in her undignified position, silently promising herself she would throttle her captor at the first opportunity for this humiliating ride. Then her attention was taken up by the interior of the house they entered. A marble floor flashed by beneath her head, the legs of a narrow table, too, then steps.

Maggie held her breath and remained as still as she could; if the last thing she wanted was to throw off her captor's balance as he ascended these stairs. She breathed a small sigh of relief once the steps were replaced by the flat floor of a wide hallway; then she was carted through a door and into and across a darkened room. The kidnapper's stride slowed, his hands shifted, and he bent forward, dropping Maggie indelicately on a soft surface in the still-dark room before turning and exiting.

It took her a moment to realize that the soft surface was a bed. Once she did, though, Maggie quickly tried to scramble off of it — forgetting that her ankles were bound together. She ended up crashing to her knees on the floor just as light flooded in around her. Lifting her head, she watched warily as her captor reentered with a taper from the hallway, which he used to set a fire going in the room's hearth. Then he carried the taper to the table on the opposite side of the bed from her, the one nearest the door. He set it down carefully, then turned to eye her where she knelt huddled against the bed.

She returned his inspection, but was quite

startled by the look of him. Her kidnapper was tall, with long, muscular legs and broader-than-average shoulders. His hair was dark and feathered, with gray at the temples, giving him a distinguished air. His face was handsome and strong, yet looked slightly hard, as if he didn't smile much.

The man gazed at her silently for a moment, taking in her wary state, then rubbed one hand wearily over the back of his neck and glanced fretfully around. "I am James Huttledon," he announced abruptly. When Maggie stared back blankly, he added, "I was a friend of your brother's. We fought side by side through most of the war."

Maggie felt surprise at this news, and some of her wariness dissipated as she made the connection in her head. Gerald had written to her often, long letters detailing his comrades, the battles they fought, the camaraderie they shared. There had been one man he had mentioned a great deal, and from his letters Maggie knew Gerald had respected and looked up to him. He had called the paragon James once or twice, but had most often referred to him as —

"Ramsey," she said a bit breathlessly.

"Yes. I am Lord Ramsey. Your brother died saving my life, and his last request to me was that I see after you."

Maggie was silent for a moment. She had known Gerald died bravely — his commanding officer had written the details of his leaping in front of a musket ball to save a comrade. However, she had never known whom he had died to save; the name had been left out. Now she stared at the man who had kidnapped her, the man her brother had saved, and felt only bitter disappointment. Gerald had died in this man's place?

She couldn't help her suddenly tight expression or the tone of her voice as she snapped, "I see. Well, forgive me for pointing out something you may not wish to hear, my lord, but I doubt very much if smothering, tying up, or kidnapping me is what Gerald had in mind."

Lord Ramsey grimaced, but after a moment said sternly, "It was not what I expected to be doing when I agreed. However, I doubt your brother expected you to get up to the things you have done."

Maggie stiffened at his tone, indignant. "And just what is *that* supposed to mean?"

His gaze slid downward, drawing her attention to the fact that by half rising, she had revealed a good portion of the flimsy red attire she had on beneath her cape, as well as all the things it did not hide. Flush-

53

ing bright pink at the view she was presenting, Maggie again hunched forward against the bed. Lord Ramsey's gaze immediately returned to her face. Feeling the mask she wore cold against her hot blush, Maggie felt an instant need to explain. Clearing her throat, she said, "This is just a disguise. I could hardly move about in there without one, could I?"

"Dear God, no!" the man agreed with sharp horror. Becoming stern again, he added, "You should not have been there at all. A lady of your standing has no business being in such a place, or working at such a . . ." When he paused, obviously in search of a suitable description, Maggie interrupted.

"Yes, well . . . I do have to earn a living, my lord. Someone must pay for the upkeep of that mausoleum my brother left me, keep the servants paid and fed." She pointed it out staunchly, but that only seemed to make the man's lips tighten with further displeasure.

Turning away, Lord Ramsey moved toward the door. "I am sure you did not rest much in the carriage. As for myself, I have not slept at all. We shall discuss alternate sources of income after we have both rested and refreshed ourselves."

"Just a moment!" Maggie cried in alarm. Her kidnapper stopped and looked back at her wearily, one brow arched in question. "My hands." She held them above the bed as if to show him the bindings. He hesitated, his eyes shifting warily to her face; then he shrugged and started back toward her.

"I suppose it will not hurt to untie you. There is nowhere for you to run, anyway. My servants are quite loyal to me." Moving around the side of the bed, Lord Ramsey dropped onto his haunches beside her and waited for her to turn so that he could reach her hands. When she hesitated, remaining positioned the way she was, the bed hiding her sheer gown, a crooked smile quirked his lips. "Suddenly shy? Is that not a bit like stirring the pot after the stew is burnt?"

Maggie felt her face flush but held her pose. He may well have seen all while she was unconscious in the carriage, but she was not offering any exhibitions now. Appearing to realize that, Lord Ramsey shifted to kneel closer to her and reached for her hands. Biting her lip, Maggie tried to ignore the way his shoulder and hip rubbed against hers as he worked on her bonds, and the musky scent of him as it wafted up to her nose. He smelled of fine brandy and expensive cigars — a scent she had always found pleasantly drifting around her father and brother when they had just returned from the clubs. She idly wondered if that had been where he was before kidnapping her.

"There we are," he said. "Now your ankles." He turned slightly, shifting back a bit so that she could turn and slide her legs out for him, but Maggie remained as she was, unwilling to risk giving him an indecent view.

"I-I can manage those, I think," she murmured huskily, avoiding his gaze. She sensed his hesitation, but after a moment he stood and moved away.

"Ring the bell by the bed when you wake, and a maid shall bring you something more comfortable to wear." The bedroom door closed behind him on Lord Ramsey's last word, and Maggie slowly relaxed, realizing only then how tense she had been. His close proximity had caused her to tighten up like a snail retreating into its shell.

Shaking her head at her behavior, she shifted her position and reached for her ankles, untying them much slower than he had done. But then, her hands were some-what numb from their confinement, and they gave her some trouble with the task.

Sighing in relief as the rope finally fell away, Maggie rose carefully and perched on the edge of the bed, then took stock of her prison. While the exterior of this estate had appeared stark and imposing, there was nothing of that inside. This bedroom was a cheerful light blue, its furnishings and coverings all nearly new, and expensive. Hardly reflective of its owner at all.

Grimacing to herself at the thought, Maggie glanced toward the door, briefly considering trying to leave, but just as quickly changed her mind. She could already hear the house stirring. There would be servants everywhere in no time. Besides, she had no way to return to town, or really even any idea which way London was from here. Nay, there was little sense in rushing off into the wilds of the country, especially dressed as she was.

Then, too, it didn't appear as if she were under any real threat here. If anything, it sounded as if Lord Ramsey were seriously trying to live up to his promise to her brother to keep her from harm. And apparently he felt her escapades under the name of G. W. Clark were too risky. Which they were, she had to admit. In fact, the whole situation had grown more and more precarious of late, for her readers were demanding more and more titillating articles. That was the reason she had risked entering the brothel — something she never would have considered ere circumstances had become so desperate, even with the heavy veil she had worn to hide her face.

Where was that veil now? Probably still sitting on the settee in Madame Dubarry's private drawing room. Maggie had taken it off after interviewing the last of Agatha's girls so that she and the madam might relax over tea. Both of them had quite forgotten it in the rush to Maisey's room. Which, in itself, showed the dangers of rushing about without planning. Nay, Maggie was best off sticking it out until she could convince Lord Ramsey to return her to her home, or think of a safe way to escape there on her own.

No doubt Lord Ramsey would offer her some sort of agreement when they met for their discussion later — a position as nanny to his children or some such thing. Yes, he looked the sort to be married with children. He was certainly old enough. Of course, she would have to refuse. Even if she dismissed the ignominy of being known to work for a living, no position as governess could pay as much as the *Daily Express*. No, when Lord Ramsey made the offer, she would be forced to regretfully refuse — then somehow had to convince him to return her to town.

Having settled the matter in her mind, Maggie stood and removed her cape and mask. She would have liked to remove her gown as well; it was terribly itchy. She didn't know if it was the material or a lack of cleanliness on Maisey's part, but the garment was insufferable. Unfortunately she had nothing to change into at the moment, and as indecent as the gown was, it was unthinkable to sleep in the nude.

Making a face, she crawled under the covers and settled herself in the center of the bed, unsurprised as she was overtaken by a yawn. Now that she believed she wasn't in any real danger, exhaustion was beginning to set in. This had been an incredibly eventful night, what with one thing after another. All she really wanted to do was rest.

Stifling yet another yawn, she glanced toward the bedroom door and frowned. It was all well and good that Lord Ramsey claimed a desire to honor her brother's last wishes, but really, she realized, she had no guarantee that such was the case. Actually, she had no guarantee he was even who he claimed. It was rather trusting of her to take the man's word for it like that. Naive and stupid, even.

"Oh, bother!" she muttered. Pushing the

covers aside, she crawled out of bed once more.

"Here you are, milord."

James turned from a contemplation of the fire in his library hearth and smiled a vague thank-you at an unusually rumpled Webster. His butler at Ramsey came forward with a tray bearing warmed milk with whiskey — James's own personal remedy for an inability to sleep. It was something James had not thought he would need as he rode here; he had nearly fallen asleep several times on the hard bench during the journey. Crowch, his driver, had actually nudged him a time or two to wake him before he could tumble right off.

But that had been before he had carried Margaret Wentworth to the blue room and dropped her on the bed. That was before he had seen her in the candlelight, on her knees, her golden hair tumbled about her heartshaped face, her soft green eyes glinting out from behind that damned red mask that lent such a seductive air of mystery to her and seemed to emphasize how sweet and soft were her lips. All that had been enough to give a man ideas. It had put images in his head: images of Margaret kneeling at his feet, her cape open to reveal all that blasted gown she wore revealed . . . her hands untied, reaching for the waist of his trousers, her glossy lips twisting as she pulled those trousers slowly down and . . .

Dear God! What was the matter with him? James gave his head a shake, relieved when the erotic imaginings dissolved. He could hardly believe he had been standing there fantasizing such things about a woman he was supposed to be helping. Hell, he could hardly believe he had been fantasizing at all. He just wasn't the sort to waste time on carnal pursuits. He prided himself on being a more intellectual sort. Oh, he had kept a mistress or two through the years, but it had always been more as a physical outlet — a sort of exercise, if you will — rather than from any real passion. In fact, James had always regarded the task as not dissimilar to boxing: Good for keeping the heart fit and the body in shape and a skill every man should have. And as with boxing, he had always considered the movements rather mechanical. In boxing it was jab, feint, uppercut as opposed to kiss, strip, fondle, and so on. Both were a step-by-step process leading to the final round and the ringing of the bell . . . so to speak.

Gerald and Robert had once claimed he was a bloodless sod when he'd revealed that philosophy. They had discussed many things while seated around the fire at night, and the subject of mistresses had invariably come up. Neither of his friends had understood, but James simply was not hampered by the carnal nature most men seemed led by. Or so he had thought. Yet here he was, lusting after the woman presently installed in a room upstairs, his mental processes as muddled as those of any brainless dog after a bitch in heat.

"Parliament canceled?"

James gave up berating himself as the last two words of Webster's question broke through his thoughts. Frowning, he glanced at his servant. "What was that?"

"I said you have quite taken us by surprise with this visit, milord. I did not expect you until the day after next at the least, after Parliament met. Was the meeting canceled?"

James stared blankly at the man for a moment, his brain slow to digest what he was saying, and slower still to accept that he had been so stupid. "Damn," he breathed at last, hardly able to believe that he had forgotten. He had long been a member of the House of Lords, and had made a concerted effort to attend each meeting. He had missed one or two, of course — illness, emergencies, life itself sometimes intervened — but just now there was a matter of some importance on the table and he really had wanted to be there. How could he have forgotten? Dear Lord, he had made a muff up this time.

Cursing, he set his untouched glass of warm milk and whiskey down with a clink and rose from his seat. "Tell Crowch to harness fresh horses to the carriage. We must head back at once. Then come to my room. I have to change, and I will give you instructions regarding Lady Wentworth while I do. Damn!" he added again.

"Lady Wentworth?" his butler asked in confusion as he followed James out of the library.

"She is in the blue room. A . . . guest. You are to be sure she remains one while I am gone."

CHAPTER THREE

Sighing, Maggie shifted in her seat and again glanced toward the door. It was past the supper hour. She had awoken around noon to find a new gown lying at the foot of the bed in which she had slept so poorly.

Her lack of rest was no fault of the bed's — it had been as comfortable as a mattress of clouds, which was the only reason she had eventually fallen asleep at all. Nay, her inability to sleep had been due purely to her anxiety and nerves about her host's intentions. He claimed to be Lord Ramsey, and that his intentions were to aid her, but . . . Well, how could she be sure he was who he claimed? Or if his intentions were pure? After all, he *had* kidnapped her.

She plucked fretfully at the soft skirt of the light blue gown she wore and grimaced. Despite Lord Ramsey's telling her to ring the bell when she awoke so that appropriate clothing could be brought to her, Maggie had not had to do so. She had risen to find this gown across the foot of the bed. Some-one must have slipped in while she slept. But who? Had it been the man calling himself her brother's friend or one of his servants?

One of his servants, she decided. Delivering gowns didn't seem a likely task for a lord. Besides, the idea of Ramsey slipping into the room while she slept was completely unnerving.

Maggie had checked the door this morning before she'd tried to sleep, only to find that there was no way to lock it. She had made a halfhearted attempt to barricade the portal with the chair she now sat in — the only one in the room — but its back was too short to be jammed under the doorknob. It was also too light to be any sort of bar to the door's opening. Every piece of furniture in the room had proven to be similarly too small or too large and heavy to be used in such a manner. Maggie had been forced to resign herself to the fact that there was no way to prevent anyone from entering. Which was why she'd had such trouble sleeping, despite her exhaustion. Her unconsciousness during the journey here had not, apparently, been restful. She was as weary when she awoke at noon as if she had never slept, and she'd spent the better part of this afternoon nodding in this chair, waiting to be retrieved.

It was evening and she was still waiting. Was Lord Ramsey never going to come? She shook her head and almost managed a smile. First she had been trying to find a way to barricade the door against his entry, and now she was impatient for the rascal to come around. Nonsensical, she supposed, but the waiting in itself was driving her mad. Besides, she was growing quite hungry. Nay, she corrected herself, she had *awakened* hungry; she was *growing famished.*

Her stomach rumbled as if in agreement, and Maggie suddenly thrust herself to her feet. Enough was enough! She could bear the waiting no longer. If the rude man had no intention of coming for her, she would go and confront him.

"He's probably a madman," she muttered under her breath as she crossed the room to the door. "Ready for Bedlam."

Such thoughts, she decided as she found herself standing before the bedroom door but hesitating to open it, were definitely not reassuring. She had just managed to shore her sagging courage and reach for the knob when a tap from the other side made her pull back with a squeak of dismay. Heart

66

racing and mouth dry, she stared at the blank surface of the door with apprehension until a second tap came; then she swallowed and called out in a voice so high and squeaky that she hardly recognized it as her own, "Yes?"

Maggie scooted back several steps as the doorknob turned and the door swung inward. Her alarm eased somewhat, however, when a petite young maid stepped in.

"Oh, ye're up." The girl beamed approvingly. "I said to Cook as how I thought ye'd be, but he was sure his work'd been for naught and the meal he'd prepared would go to waste."

When Maggie merely stared at her, concern clouded the girl's eyes and she tilted her head. "Are you feeling all right, m'lady? Lord Ramsey said as how ye were exhausted from the journey 'ere and might sleep the day away, but ye're looking a bit peaked, too. Ye're not coming down with the ague, are ye?"

Maggie managed to relax somewhat, and even felt a smile spread her lips slightly in answer. "Nay. I am fine, thank you."

The girl brightened at once, again beaming at Maggie. "Good. Then I am Annie. I'm to be your maid while ye're with us. Anything ye need, ye just ask me."

"Very well. Thank you, Annie," Maggie said after the girl paused expectantly.

Nodding, the girl smiled wider. "Shall I show you down to supper?"

"I . . . Yes, thank you," Maggie agreed, then straightened her shoulders as she followed the maid out of the room. Annie led her along the hall, then down the stairs to the main floor. Maggie spent most of the trip distracted by her first real tour of the house in which she was imprisoned. It had been dark and gloomy this morning when they had arrived. Aside from that, her undignified position — hanging down her captor's back — had not given her much opportunity to look around. She did so now curiously.

Much to her interest, it seemed villains did not live in villainous abodes. Ramsey's home was lovely. His maid led Maggie down a hallway of soothing grays with furnishings that were expensive and round-edged. The soft color scheme continued down the stairs to the entryway where it became more muted with dark blue. Annie then showed her through another hall of neutral colors and into a large chamber with a long, covered table — the dining room.

Lord Ramsey was conspicuous in his absence. Maggie felt her body relax slightly as she realized it, and thus took the time to appreciate the decor. The walls were painted a warm blue that could only encourage dallying over a meal. In the center of the room was a huge dining table covered with a pristine white cloth that barely allowed legs of a dark rich mahogany — matching the wood of the chairs surrounding it — to peek out from beneath. A sideboard of the same dark wood stood along the wall.

Maggie allowed herself to be seated, her gaze slow to move to the table itself. The maid had nearly left the room before Maggie took in the fact that hers was the only setting. "But . . ." she began, and Annie paused, peering back questioningly. Swallowing, Maggie managed a smile as she asked, "Is Lord Ramsey not to join me?"

The maid's eyes widened. "Nay, mum. He had to return to town. He left shortly after arriving and said — Oh!" She patted her skirts as if looking for something, then muttered fretfully, "He left a letter for ye. I was to give it to ye as soon as milady awoke. Now where did I — Oh, yes! Won't be a moment."

Whirling away, the girl fled the room, leaving Maggie to consider her words. Lord Ramsey wasn't here. He had returned to town. What did that mean? Well, she supposed that made it obvious he hadn't brought her here with the intention of ravishing her. *Not that I imagined for a moment that he did,* she assured herself. Though she did find herself feeling a touch deflated. There she had been hiding in her room all this time to avoid confronting a man who hadn't even been here. She sat up in her chair as the ramifications of that fact occurred to her. He wasn't here. Her captor wasn't around. There was no one to keep her here!

The thought brought her lunging excitedly to her feet, but before she could move away from the table, Annie came bustling back into the room with a self-satisfied smile on her face.

"Here it is." She presented a sealed message to Maggie in triumph.

Maggie hesitated, then accepted the note. She sank reluctantly back into her seat. Breaking the seal, she unfolded the missive and read, her consternation growing with every word.

Lady Wentworth —
My apologies, but I have to return to town to attend some business that could not be put off. Please consider yourself my guest for the next little while. Do

not bother the servants with requests to aid you in returning to London. You will find no quarter there. It would do you well to take this time to reconsider your previous choice of career. You shall need a new one, and we shall be discussing possible alternatives upon my return.

— Lord Ramsey

"Arrogant ass."

"What?"

The maid's gasp drew Maggie's attention to the fact that she had just muttered the irrepressible thought aloud. Her mouth tightening, she forced a smile. "Just a glass," she lied blithely. "One glass of wine is all I shall have with dinner, I think."

"Oh." The maid stared at her doubtfully, but didn't question her veracity, then she nodded and slipped from the room with a murmur that she would inform Cook that her ladyship was ready.

Maggie folded the letter again with agitation, the words *arrogant ass* running through her mind again. What did Lord Ramsey take her for? An idiot? Did he expect her to simply sit here sweetly awaiting his pleasure? He must be mad! He had said that the servants would not aid her, but would they actually stop her leaving? Well, it might be too far to walk to town, but there had to be a village or something nearer than that, somewhere where she could rent a carriage or . . .

Of course, she didn't have any money to rent a carriage, she realized with a frown. In fact, all she had was the gown on her back — and that wasn't even her own. She scowled, then sat up a little stiffer to assure herself there was yet something she could do. She had two strong legs, a fine mind, and determination. Those together should be enough to see her well away from this place.

With that thought Maggie stood, then paused to glance toward the windows that lined the western wall of the room. They gave a lovely view of the setting sun. It would be dark soon. Which gave her pause. Did she really wish to traipse through the countryside in the dark?

Her stomach growled, adding its own protest, and she decided she really should eat before she considered leaving. She would need her strength if she planned to walk in search of a town or neighboring estate where she might find help — if that was going to be her plan. She hadn't really considered the matter yet. Perhaps it behooved her to actually determine a specific plan of escape. Perhaps she should learn how near or far away help actually was. Perhaps she should —

Her thoughts were interrupted by the arrival of dinner. It came served on a parade of trays borne by solemn-faced servants. One might have thought they bore the queen's jewels on those trays instead of suckling pig, roast duck, or the various other dishes she saw. Letting her plans to escape fade away, Maggie sat silently and — she hoped — stoically as each servant approached her in turn to serve her a portion from his tray. Rather than set the platters on the table and leave her to her meal, as her own servants would have done, each man lined himself against the wall, gloved hands clasped loosely before him, eyes staring straight ahead and expression blank.

Maggie peered at the servers uncomfortably for a moment, then decided they weren't going anywhere; she had best get to it if she wished to eat. Picking up one of her forks, she set to work on the food. It was an extremely odd meal. Despite the fact that the men were all staring blankly at the opposite wall of the room, she felt as if they were staring at her. And they must have been watching her out of the corner of their eyes, for, the moment she finished her wine, the fellow who had carried it in and poured her first glass stepped silently and efficiently forward to refill it. When she finished off the portion of duck she had been served, another servant, he who had carried that in, promptly stepped up to retrieve the tray and offer her more. Maggie found the whole process most discomforting and ended up rushing, waving away offers of seconds in her eagerness to escape the staff's stifling presence.

It was a great relief when she finished the last scrap of food on her plate. Setting the dish aside she stood, abruptly waving off the servant who jumped forward to offer her one of the lovely-looking desserts that were his charge. Managing a pained smile to soften her dismissal, she moved swiftly around the table and fled. She was actually relieved to find Annie awaiting her in the hall. When the maid asked if she would prefer a drink in the salon, a visit to the library, or a return to her bedroom, Maggie opted for the last. It was time to plan her escape.

"Damn." Maggie tugged at her skirt irritably, trying to pull it free of the log on which it had caught. This was only about the hundredth time that it had happened.

The damn forest seemed inordinately full of fallen branches and the like, all catching at her gown and slowing her progress. It was as if the very woods themselves were trying to hinder her flight.

If one could really call it flight, she thought impatiently. This had started out as a grand escape, but it had foundered. Now she was merely lost in the woods. She managed to tug her gown free of its latest entanglement, then hesitated before dropping to sit wearily on the log that had previously been holding her back.

This was not going well at all. Oh, she had thought she was so clever with her plan. She had resolved to set out on the second day of her presence at Ramsey, directly after breakfast, but that had been before she realized that Annie was to be her "constant companion" — a much nicer description than the jailer that the girl really was. The wench hadn't left Maggie's side from the moment she arrived in her room the second morning to show her to breakfast.

Maggie had awoken that morning to find the blue gown gone and a yellow one in its place. Annie's work, no doubt, she had decided. Donning the gown, she'd found that it, like the first, was nearly a perfect fit. Nearly. Both gowns obviously belonged to someone who had a somewhat more generous bosom.

Maggie had no interest in deducing who the owner was. Probably a mistress of Lord Ramsey's, but Maggie didn't give two figs about that. Her mind had been solely occupied with her intention to escape.

She had followed Annie dutifully down to the dining room to eat, relieved to find that while supper had been solemn and attended by many servants, breakfast was a more relaxed affair. A selection of sausages, pastries, and such had been set out on the sideboard for her to serve herself. Maggie had taken that opportunity to store up on sustenance, eating a good deal, then slipping some serviette-wrapped goodies into her pocket for later, for her bid for freedom.

Once she was finished, she had exited the dining room to find Annie awaiting her. It was then she had realized that the woman would not be leaving her until she retired. It had been an unexpected crimp in her plan.

But Maggie had refused to give up easily. Pushing her irritation at this turn of events aside, she'd engaged the girl in conversation, trying to deduce the direction and whereabouts of the nearest village or neighboring estates, but Annie, while polite, had not been of much assistance.

"Oh, aye," the girl had assured her. "We have neighbors. Everyone has neighbors." But when asked how far away they might be, the girl had taken on a cagey look and shrugged. "I couldn't really say, m'lady. Not being nobility, I've never had much cause to visit them." She had been of equal use when it came to the direction and distance to the nearest village.

Given up on questioning the girl, Maggie had pretended to read a book, occasionally remembering to turn the pages as she pondered how to slip away. She had wasted the entire day that way and found herself subjected to another formal meal presided over by a bevy of servants that night, at last retreating to her room to consider and reject several other possibilities on how to escape.

In the end, it wasn't her own cleverness at all that had allowed her to flee. It was circumstance. Today had dawned gray and gloomy. Maggie had donned the rose-colored gown that had been silently set out overnight, followed Annie unhappily to the dining room to break her fast, then had opted for the library to glare blankly at another book and fret. Then, just before the noon meal, it had begun to rain — one of those slow yet steady, halfhearted drizzles that tended to last forever and cause a lassitude in everyone. Annie had yawned, and then Maggie had had her idea. She'd waited until after the noon meal, then had returned to the library, feigning a yawn or two to complement the real ones that were slipping from the maid. Then, as the girl had begun to nod in her seat, Maggie had closed her book with a snap that had startled the maid back to wakefulness.

"What a horrid and gloomy day," she had commented wearily, then added a yawn for good measure. "I think I should like a nap."

Much to her relief, rather than looking suspicious, the maid had appeared relieved at the announcement. Annie had escorted Maggie to her room without question, nodding when asked to wake her in time for dinner. After waiting what she considered a suitable amount of time for the servant to vacate the hall, Maggie had tiptoed over, grasped the doorknob, and slowly eased the door open enough to peer out. What she saw made her freeze at once. Annie had collected a chair from somewhere, positioned it to the side of her door, and settled in, looking as if nothing short of the Second Coming would move her.

Which verified her belief that the girl was a guard, Maggie supposed vexedly as she eased the door cautiously closed again and slowly turned the knob back before releasing it. Moving despondently away from the door, she had them peered about the room, stymied for a way to get rid of the girl. Something short of murder would be best.

Maggie considered sending the maid to fetch a beverage, or something to read or eat. But those options would have seen the girl return to find her missing, and Maggie wanted more time to get away before her absence was discovered. In her frustration, she started mumbling some not very nice words learned from her brother, before her gaze at last landed on the doors to the balcony.

Filled with hope, Maggie promptly hurried across the room and shoved outside. The balcony was on the second floor, of course, which was a problem in itself, but not one that was insurmountable. Maggie had been a rather adoring younger sister and had trailed her brother everywhere until he'd gone away to school. She had run with him, played games more fitting for boys, and had even climbed trees to keep up with Gerald. Which, she realized now, would come in quite handy. There was a lovely tree growing right off this balcony, one large, sturdy-looking branch even reaching accommodatingly over the railing. This will *be a breeze,* she'd thought with amusement.

Of course, she hadn't considered the fact that it had been many years since she'd climbed trees with Gerald. Nor had she considered the problem of her great, hampering skirts, or the rain that made everything slippery. She had barely managed to get out onto the branch and start her descent before she'd lost her footing and tumbled the rest of the way. She'd landed with an "oomph" in the bushes below. They softened her landing somewhat, but not completely. The fall had been enough to knock the air from her lungs, and she had lain there in the drizzle for several moments, aware of nothing but her body's desperate need for oxygen.

Once she'd regained her breath, Maggie had eased to her feet and peered about, unsure whether to be relieved or unhappy that no one was around to note her bravery or her near calamity. Pushing such foolishness aside, she had moved quickly to the cover of the surrounding woods and slipped into them.

Making her way through the woods along the laneway had seemed the safest bet. She hadn't wished to take the lane itself and risk being spotted, but she also had wanted to avoid finding herself lost in the woods —

keeping the lane in sight seemed the only option. Maggie had thought that as long as she kept the lane in sight, she would manage well enough.

"Ha!" she muttered now. Her plan had started out well enough, but then she had come across a river. There was a bridge over it on the lane that she had not realized they'd traversed. Worse, the bridge was still in plain view of the house, and her fear of being spotted had forced her to make her way deeper into the woods. Moving along the river in search of a place to cross, a shallow spot perhaps, she had not been concerned with getting wet. The constant drizzling rain and her fall into the damp bushes had already soaked her, so she had wandered along, moving farther and farther away from the lane, positive that soon she would find a safe spot to cross. Just a little farther. Just around this bend. Just around that curve.

A fallen oak had appeared across her path, reaching just to the river's edge, but not crossing it. She had been forced to make her way around, fighting with branches and brambles and moving deeper into the forest. Then she had pushed through a screen of underbrush . . . to find herself tumbling down an incline the foliage had hidden!

At the bottom, Maggie found herself not only wet, but mud-covered. She wasn't the sort to give up, though. *Stubborn* and *prideful* had been a couple of unattractive descriptions used for her in the past, and she admitted the designations were still true today. Determined to climb back up and continue on her way, she had found that the incline was impossible to scale. It was steep and slippery with mud from the rain, and her several attempts had only ended in lost footings and several behind-bruising falls. At last, she'd turned her determination to searching for an easier spot to climb. She had traveled an increasing distance from the river and the fallen tree, deeper into wilds, in search of that spot, following the curved and wending incline.

Maggie wasn't sure how far she'd journeyed before she discovered a place where the roots of a tree offered enough purchase to pull up out of the small ravine in which she found herself. She had barely reached the top when the snapping of a branch had alerted her to the presence of a nearby animal. Normally the stalwart, non-nervous type, Maggie had not been too alarmed at first, but slowly she became aware of the creepy silence of the rest of the woods. The hair prickled at the back of her neck as she stood listening to the sounds of something making its way through the underbrush from the way she had come. Finding her heart lodging itself in her throat, Maggie felt her body grow numb with fear. As she realized the sounds were drawing nearer, she broke, turning on her heel and making a mad dash in the other direction — running willy-nilly until her fear had eased enough to realize the mistake she'd made. The stupidity of running blindly in the wrong direction had been a hard enough admission, but the fact that she no longer knew the *right* direction was even more dismaying.

Maggie was now lost, completely and thoroughly. She was also soaking wet, muddy, cold, and miserable. Such were the results of her grand plan of escape.

Heaving out an irritated breath she peered at the surrounding woods, searching for something that might show her back the way she had come. Unfortunately, nothing looked familiar. She had not thought to note landmarks in her mad dash.

Her gaze rose to the trees surrounding her, and she briefly considered climbing one. Perhaps at its leafy summit she might glimpse the towers of Ramsey manor and, in that way, get her bearings. But the accident escaping her balcony was enough to change her mind; she was in no shape to climb trees anymore, was more likely to break her neck than anything.

She took a moment to wallow in self-pity, then forced herself to straighten her shoulders, stand, and get on with her escape. She had no intention of just sitting still until death by starvation or exposure overtook her. She wasn't the sort for such foolishness. Besides, wasn't she perfectly capable of taking care of herself? Else she would have sold off her brother's home and moved to the country, as any other woman would have done in her circumstances. Instead, she had taken up her brother's job and set about trying to support his home and servants. She could overcome any difficulty. She would simply head north until she came across something. But . . . which way was north?

Maggie pondered briefly, fairly sure she had heard that moss grew on the north side of trees . . . or was it the south? West? *Oh, dear.* Sighing, she decided she needed another manner of determining directions. Didn't the sun rise in the east and set in the west? Or was it the other way around? Oh, this was *damnably* irritating. She really should have paid more attention to such things.

At last, she simply decided that she would move toward the sun; in that way she could at least avoid walking in circles. The plan might have been a good one, if the combination of tree branches and gray clouds overhead had not obscured any possibility of finding the bloody sun.

It was beginning to appear that she was well and truly lost. Of course, it was all Lord Ramsey's fault. *The ass.* Had he not decided to stick his nose in her business and kidnap her . . . well, she wouldn't be *here!*

Satisfied that she had laid the blame firmly where it belonged, she wasted a moment attempting to shake some of the mud off her skirts, then straightened her shoulders and marched onward. If she simply kept moving, she would come across something. Eventually.

Much to Maggie's amazement, she hadn't been walking very long when the sound of rushing water caught her ear. Pausing, she listened to see which direction it came from, then moved toward it. Relief poured through her as she found herself stepping out onto the bank of the river. She had found it! Even better, she had come upon the waterway at a spot where it twisted and narrowed, one edge jutting out farther than normal and flat rocks making something of a path across. Some of her optimism returning, Maggie started over the stones, moving cautiously from rock to rock, until at last she leaped to the opposite side.

Buoyed by her success, she paused to debate her next move. Should she follow the river back to the land, back to where the Ramsey estate was in sight, then continue from there? Or should she simply move steadily away from the river and hope she came across the main road that led to Ramsey's drive?

The cautious side of her suggested that returning along the river was the smartest move, but that seemed to entail the loss of a great deal of time, and it was already beginning to grow darker. She had already wasted a good stretch.

The daring side of Maggie, that which had encouraged her to take such risks as donning the persona of G. W. Clark and visiting brothels or other unsavory spots in search of stories, was urging her to simply continue forward, away from the river.

She would likely come to the main road just as swiftly, but ages away from the Ramsey drive.

Maggie, as usual, found herself trusting

the less cautious part of her personality. She pushed determinedly onward. It was only a few moments later that she found herself stumbling out of the trees. She came out on the side of a laneway, this one wider and — judging by its rutted state — better traveled than the Ramsey drive. Maggie fought free of the bushes, pleasure and relief just starting to wash over her when a carriage trundled past.

Her first instinct was to flee for cover, lest it be Lord Ramsey. Maggie followed that instinct and whirled about to dart back into the underbrush. She knew, even as she did so, that the action came too late; she caught a glimpse of a man's face through the carriage window as she spun away. Maggie didn't recognize the man. She *was* sure it wasn't Lord Ramsey. She was also sure that she had been spotted. Still, her survival instinct sent her crashing into the woods to hide herself behind a handy tree.

Pausing with her back against the old oak's rough bark, she pressed a hand to her racing heart and tried to listen over the sound of her own heavy breathing. Her alarm increased as she heard the man call out, the carriage slow to a stop, and then the telltale sound of the coach door opening and closing.

Damn! The man was coming to investigate. Maggie's mind was suddenly crowded with possibilities. He could simply be a traveler on the road, curious about a woman dashing wildly about the woods. But then, he could also be Lord Ramsey's cohort in crime. Or, perhaps he was simply getting out to stretch his legs.

Maggie snorted aloud at the last possibility and glanced wildly around, seeking escape. She had not managed to escape her prison only to be caught now! She considered her options. Running was one, but she had already experienced the difficulties of racing about the muddy woods with tree branches and bushes snagging at her skirts. That was out. Which left hiding. Dropping to her knees, she scuttled into a bush next to the tree.

CHAPTER FOUR

"Yoo-hoo! Hello? Are you in some distress?"

Maggie scowled and pushed a bothersome branch away from her face as she listened to the man's calls from her cramped hiding space. Wonderful! A knight errant thinking to aid a damsel in distress. If only I could be sure that was all he is, she thought with a sigh, then wrinkled her nose. An unpleasant smell was wafting up to her. She wondered briefly at its source, but was then distracted by the sound of snapping branches and the crunch of dead leaves as her "rescuer" moved nearer.

"Yoo-hoo! Can I be of some assistance?"

The racket the man was making as he pushed his way through the bushes drew alongside her, then continued past. Maggie sagged in relief and released the breath she had been holding. It was when she inhaled again that she recalled the odor she'd noticed earlier. It appeared to be growing stronger. Dear God, what is it? she wondered and raised a hand to wave the smell away. The stink increased tenfold, and it was then that she noticed the muck on her hand. She stared at it, slowly coming to a realization.

Horror rushing over her, she set her one hand back to hold her weight as she lifted the other. It, too, bore the stuff. Dear God, she had crawled right into, or through, a pile of animal droppings! Shudders rolled through her, and she suffered a sort of squirmy fit, her body twitching and jerking with disgust as she began frantically wiping first one hand, then the other, on the ground and surrounding branches and leaves in an effort to remove the squishy substance.

"Er . . . excuse me. Hello?" The words, spoken directly behind her, made Maggie pause and turn her head. She peered back through the foliage, only then realizing that the bush wasn't wide enough to hide her. It ended at her hips. Her derriere — covered by the yellow gown she wore — was sticking out. No doubt it had been thrashing around like some ridiculously huge canary just now. Which must have been a sight for this man to come upon, Maggie thought wearily. This simply wasn't her day.

"Are you in some distress?"

Maggie almost laughed at his tentative question. Reassuring herself that the reaction wasn't one of hysteria but amusement, and that surely it was a good sign that her sense of humor was still intact, she answered politely. "Not at all, but thank you for asking."

"I see. Might I ask what are you doing in there, then?"

This had to be the most humiliating conversation she'd ever had, Maggie decided as she wracked her brain for an explanation that would both satisfy as well as get rid of the man. It was becoming unbearable to have him talk to her behind like this, trapped in the bush as she was.

"Only you, Maggie!" Her brother's amused voice echoed in her memory, and she silently cursed. She did not deliberately get herself into these messes. They just sort of . . . happened.

"I am bird-watching, and I fear your presence is scaring the birds away," she blurted.

"Er . . . might you not have more success with your bird-watching by looking *up*?" he asked.

Maggie promptly wished she could kick herself. It was obvious she did not think well under pressure. "Yes, of course. And I

91

was. However, I . . ." She searched her mind for an acceptable excuse for her position, and was quite pleased when she came up with: "Dropped something. My . . . er . . . a hairpin!" she announced with triumph. "Ah, there it is. Thank you. Everything is fine now. You may go." She waited hopefully but was disappointed by the silence that followed. He wasn't leaving.

"I should be happy to assist you back to your feet now that you have found your hairpin."

Maggie sighed and considered her options. She didn't think he believed a word she'd said, and he obviously wasn't going to simply go away. Crawling backward out of the bush and facing the man was her only option. The very idea made her cringe, but taking a deep breath, she began to scramble out . . . only to stop as her hair caught on a branch.

"Is there something wrong?" came the man's concerned voice when she paused and gave an exclamation of pain. "Are you caught?"

"Yes, I fear I am," she answered, leaning on one hand and using the other to try to untangle herself.

"Perhaps I can help." She heard the words, then felt him grasp her hips. Maggie barely managed a startled gasp before he seemed to realize the impropriety of such a choice, and clasped her by the ankles instead. Which was not a better option, in her opinion. Her feet were pulled out from beneath her as he attempted to drag her out of the bush. She screeched in pain as her hair pulled free of the branch — or perhaps was yanked out of her head, she wasn't sure which. Then she was traveling backward, her skirt — apparently also caught on a branch — staying in place so that she came out of the foliage flat on her belly with her gown forming a sort of tent over her head.

"Oh, dear!" Her feet were dropped and the man rushed to her side, pulling the material free for her as she struggled to get off her stomach. Dear God, it would be just her luck to have been dragged through the animal droppings! Maggie scrambled to her feet.

Once upright, she raised her hand, intending to push her now wild hair out of her face. The sight made her pause.

"Oh! You've mud on your hands." Retrieving a handkerchief, her "rescuer" began to clean her fingers.

Maggie's mouth opened, then closed. What could she say? It was too late to stop his ruining the bit of cloth, so she remained silent as he tidied her hands. Her gaze moved over him. She had only caught a glimpse of him earlier, so really wasn't prepared for his attractiveness. Tall and lean with sandy-colored hair and a charming — if, at the moment, somewhat alarmed — smile. She would place him at the same age Gerald would have been were he still alive. Which was, perhaps, two or three years younger than the man who had kidnapped her.

"I fear that is the best I can do," he announced apologetically, releasing her streaked hands and tucking the cloth back into his pocket. "Is there something wrong?"

Tearing her alarmed gaze from his pocket, she tried not to feel guilty about his waistcoat now needing cleaning. She was rather amazed that the man wasn't aware of what he had just wiped off of her, but then she couldn't smell it now so supposed he couldn't either. Likely, she had scraped the worst off so that what remained merely looked like mud.

Realizing that he was awaiting an answer to his question, Maggie shook her head. A clump of snarled hair immediately dropped into her eyes and reminded her of her ruined state. Having little choice, she pushed the tangled mess back from her face, then straightened with all the dignity she could muster.

"Thank you," she offered, then turned on her heel and pushed back through the bushes and out of the trees.

"Just a moment," he called, hurrying after her as she started up the road.

Maggie had taken several steps in her chosen direction before she realized that she should have gone the other way. She was now heading in the same direction that the carriage was traveling. This man was likely too polite not to offer her a ride.

"Might I assist you to where you are going? I should not like to be unchivalrous," he added as if he had somehow read her thoughts.

"I thank you for the offer, kind sir. However, that is not necessary." Maggie didn't slow her step, but she did roll her eyes. Why were people so predictable? He would have done her a great favor had he been a rude boor and simply returned to his carriage and his journey. It would have been an even greater favor had he not stopped at all, she thought, glancing down at her hands with disgust. She really needed to find some water to clean up. A glance down showed that she had truly crawled right through the muck. The knees of her skirt were brown.

Her mother — were she alive — would have been horrified. Maggie was horrified. Creeping about brothels, and crawling on her knees through the woods!

She sighed miserably as she considered how low she had allowed herself to fall. *I used to be such a proper lady, doing and saying the proper things* — she mourned, then admitted — *well, not always.* She hadn't earned the refrain "Only you, Maggie!" by never setting a *single* step wrong. Still, she'd managed only mild mishaps in the past, and most of them due to clumsiness or inattention. Since Gerald's death, she had taken risks she knew she shouldn't have and —

"You wouldn't be headed for the village, would you?"

"Yes," Maggie answered distractedly, then clucked her tongue in irritation. She was sure she should have kept that to herself. She had no idea who this man was. He could be a bounder, or a —

"Then, I fear you are headed in the wrong direction."

That made her pause. She turned to face him.

"It is back this way," he continued, gesturing in the direction from which he had come.

Maggie peered up the lane, then sighed. She started in this new direction.

He fell into step beside her. "I should probably introduce myself. Lord Mullin, at your service."

She stopped again and faced him sharply. "Robert?" His eyebrows raised at the familiar address and Maggie flushed. "I apologize for the familiarity, my lord, but Gerald usually referred to you as Robert in his letters."

"Gerald?"

"My brother. Gerald Wentworth," she explained with reluctance.

It was his turn to pause. "Maggie?" he finally gasped, then shook his head and corrected himself. "I mean Lady Margaret?" He grinned. "Gerald often spoke of you. He . . ." Lord Mullin paused and frowned up at the sky as it again began to rain. "Come."

Before she quite knew what was happening, he had taken her arm and hustled her to his carriage. Ignoring her protests, he ushered her inside, then went to have a word with his driver. Extremely self-conscious about her less-than-pristine state, Maggie folded the sides of her skirt over the front, tucking just a bit of each side panel between her knees to keep the cloth there. The action hid a good deal of her soiled skirt, but did little to hide the smell.

Groaning inwardly, she offered a nervous smile to Lord Mullin as he entered the carriage and pulled the door closed behind him. Settling on the opposite bench seat, he didn't seem to notice the smell. He was busy grinning. "Gerald's sister. I can hardly fathom it."

Maggie offered him a pained smile. She wasn't surprised he could "hardly fathom it." She wasn't exactly at her best. That thought decided her to make an effort to repair at least some of the damage, and she set to work trying to return some semblance of normalcy to her hair. Unfortunately, it appeared that her lie of having lost a hairpin had become a reality. Several of her hairpins had been lost during her sojourn into the bushes.

"Gerald, James, and I were in the same unit. Lord Ramsey," he added after a moment. "He is my neighbor. In fact, those were his woods you were mucking about in."

Maggie stilled under his speculative gaze. This man and Lord Ramsey were neighbors? He had been on his way home from the village when he'd come across her, and from his reaction, he had not yet conferred with her abductor . . . Which meant her host's claims were likely true. Her kidnapper was indeed James Huttledon, Mullin's neighbor, and the Lord Ramsey her brother had mentioned so frequently. Recalling her brother's adulation of the man in his letters, she also supposed that Ramsey had been telling the truth regarding his reasons for kidnapping her. He probably *had* had the best of intentions.

Not that any of them mattered, Maggie decided grimly. She had escaped those good intentions and intended to stay escaped. Banks and the rest of her staff must be quite upset by now. She had to get home and let them know she was all right. Besides, there was surely nothing Lord Ramsey could do. She had been over and over her situation. Carrying on with her journalistic career was the only acceptable way to make the money she needed.

Of course, it didn't bode well for her escape that she had ended in the carriage of a friend of the man who had kidnapped her. That was rather deucedly bad luck. She was just beginning to ponder what it could mean to her plans when Lord Mullin spoke again.

"What were you doing —"

"You said Gerald spoke of me?" Maggie interrupted to distract him. It worked.

"Spoke of you?" Robert chuckled. "Yes.

99

He spoke of you often. He, James, and I were thick as thieves, and he used to read your letters aloud to us around the fire at night. In fact, between his talking about you and our sharing your letters, I feel as if I already know you. Gerald was very proud of you," he added with a sad smile.

Maggie returned the expression. Her brother had always liked to talk. She had no doubt that he had regaled his friends with tales of their youth, and that he'd related them as vibrantly as he'd penned the articles for the *Express*. Gerald had always had a way with words. She hadn't been at all surprised to learn of his secret occupation; it had suited him.

Her gaze returned to Lord Mullin, and she stiffened. There was a perplexed look on his face, and he was turning his head slowly, sniffing as if seeking the source of some smell.

She flushed with embarrassment.

"I apologize for taking you out of your way," she said, hoping to divert him.

"Oh." He turned a distracted smile her way and shook his head. "Not at all. I am glad to have met you. I always hoped to. In fact, I have kept an eye out at the balls and routs, hoping to come across you."

"I haven't been attending many balls of

late," Maggie said quietly.

"Ah, yes, of course. I should have realized." Mullin pulled his sullied kerchief from his pocket and raised it toward his face.

"Oh —" Maggie began, but it was too late. She knew that it had probably been a pleasantly scented kerchief when he'd left home that day, and that he'd likely hoped to use it to filter the stink presently invading his carriage. Instead, he got a noseful of the very scent he was trying to escape.

"Agh!"

She watched in alarm as he began gagging violently and tore the kerchief away. His horrified gaze shot to her hands, then to her innocent expression, then back to her hands. "Your . . . you . . . eh . . ."

"Yes, my lord?" Maggie wasn't surprised when he sank helplessly back in his seat without comment. It simply wasn't polite to tell a lady that her hands were covered with animal excrement. Which was rather silly. If such rules were made to prevent embarrassment, they didn't at all work, Maggie thought; they simply made it so that people suffered their embarrassment in shared silence.

She peered at Lord Mullin's face. At first alarmed at the growing ruddiness of it, she quickly realized that he was turning red because he was holding his breath.

It is a terribly unpleasant stench, she thought and she promptly began to fan herself. "Is it growing warm in here?"

Lord Mullin was not slow-witted. Looking relieved, he sprang up on his seat and quickly set to work opening the carriage window, inhaling deeply of the fresh air that swept in when he succeeded.

Not immune to the stench, Maggie slid along her seat to enjoy the fresh air as well, exchanging a wry look with her host as she did. She knew that was as close as they were going to come to acknowledging any difficulty.

They were both extremely relieved when the village came into sight. By that time the rain had stopped, and she and Lord Mullin were half-hanging out the window in companionable silence. The aroma now permeated the carriage, and seemed to grow stronger and more overpowering with each passing moment.

The situation had been beneficial in at least one respect, Maggie decided. Forced to hang out of the carriage to avoid the stink, with the wind slapping their faces, ready to snatch any words they might say, conversation between she and Lord Mullin had been impossible. She had been saved from the possibility of any awkward questions regarding her tramping about Lord Ramsey's woods.

Unfortunately, now that they were entering the village, they were forced to settle back into their seats.

"Gerald was a good man," Mullin murmured into the silence as they faced each other across the carriage.

"Yes, he was," Maggie agreed. A sadness settled over her. Gerald *had* been a good man. A good brother. A good friend. A good employer to his servants. Why did it always seem that the good were taken from the earth while the rotten sorts were left behind to trouble others? As she wondered that, she stiffened; her gaze had dropped to the bench seat she occupied. Her face flushed with guilt and embarrassment once again, for she saw that Lord Mullin's carriage would not just need an airing. Some of the muck from her skirts had transferred to the seat.

Mullin cleared his throat, drawing Maggie's attention away from her crime. One look at the determined set of the man's shoulders hinted that he was going to ask one of those annoyingly uncomfortable questions like, *"What were you doing in the woods?*" that Maggie was not eager to answer. There was the risk that if Lord Mullin discovered she was escaping his friend, he might well take her back. Which would be most inconvenient.

She briefly considered lying herself silly, claiming that she had been traveling to Clarendon, the seat of the family's title, when her carriage broke down, but there were a couple problems with that lie. The first was that she had no idea where Ramsey manor lay in England, and whether it was in a position to be on her way to Clarendon. The second was that this Robert might insist on gathering her things from her imaginary carriage.

Maggie was saved from prevarication and the risk associated when Lord Mullin's carriage began to slow, distracting both occupants and delaying the man's interrogation. She and he nearly bumped heads trying to peer out the window at the same moment, exchanged a slight smile, then glanced out in turns to see that they had arrived in the village.

"We are here," her host announced unnecessarily, then looked at her in question. "Where did you wish to go?"

"This will do," Maggie announced abruptly. Unwilling to give him the opportunity to ask those questions she could see swimming in his eyes, she pushed the carriage door open then rushed clumsily out.

"Oh, but I cannot just leave you here," Mullin called to her, climbing down from the carriage as well. "Are you staying at Ramsey? Did you —"

"Thank you ever so much for bringing me here, my lord," Maggie interrupted determinedly. "I appreciate your assistance. Have a good day."

Turning on her heel, she then hurried off along the street, not caring at all where she was going as long as it was away from Lord Mullin and his questions. Fortunately, he did not pursue or try to stop her. Still, Maggie stepped into the first shop she came across. She had no idea where to rent a hack, and she would need directions.

"M'Lord?"

James glanced up from the ale he had been contemplating to find Crowch at his side, hat in hand. "Is it fixed?" he asked the driver mildly. They had hit a rock in the road, and it had cracked one of the carriage wheels. Fortunately, the accident had occurred just a mile short of the village, and the wheel had remained intact until they could reach a shop where it could be repaired. James had left the chore to Crowch and settled himself in the pub, somewhat exhausted by his travels between his country estate and London.

"Aye, m'lord."

"Good. Get yourself a drink; then we'll be off again." The fellow's weary smile of relief was enough to remind James that he was not the only one who had made this trip back and forth and back again. He felt a moment's guilt, which moved him to add, "I appreciate your efforts these last few days."

The words sounded as stiff as James felt. They were an apology of sorts, couched in a compliment. He was not used to having to give apologies, but then he rarely worked his servants as hard as this. Crowch had been asked to drive through the night to take Lady Margaret to Ramsey, then, after less than an hour's rest at Ramsey Castle, he'd had to turn around and drive James back to town for the meeting of the House of Lords. This morning, after the proceedings were finished, the man had been put upon for a return trip to the country. Last night's sleep was the only rest the man had had in two days. It was no wonder he was looking so weary. And the compliment was deserved, Crowch was a good man.

"We'll be staying in the country for a bit this time," James called as the driver settled with relief at a table for servants in the corner.

Crowch said little, but looked much happier at the news. He accepted the ale a wench set before him and drank thirstily. James waited as he did, idly pondering the arrangements he'd made regarding a Lady Margaret.

Lady. He grimaced slightly. Lady Margaret, Lady X — whichever she called herself, she wasn't deserving of the title. He could hardly believe she was the same woman that Gerald had prattled on about all those nights beside the fire. The Margaret Wentworth Gerald had described was brave, resourceful, smart, and beautiful. But above all, she was a lady. None of which seemed to match what James had learned about Lady X.

James had attended the meeting of the House of Lords that morning, but he had arrived back in London just before dinner last night. He had eaten, then found himself too wound up to sleep. Or perhaps he had been at that state of being overtired where sleep became elusive. Whatever the case, he had gone to his club to relax and await his weariness overtaking him. While there, he had sought out more information regarding the infamous Lady X. He had learned much. The courtesan was always a subject of gossip at the club, but James had paid very little attention ere now. Last night he had listened to the tales of her expertise with combined fascination and horror.

Lady X had arrived in London not long after Gerald's death. At least that seemed to prove it was circumstance that had led Margaret to take up such a disreputable career, James told himself. And yet, he had not been prepared for the degree of skill she was purported to have. Oh, he had heard before that the woman enjoyed her work, but until last night he had thought such words were simply the smitten boasts of her customers. But if half of what her marks claimed was true, she didn't just enjoy her work; she reveled in it like a pig rolling in muck.

From all he had learned, James was left wondering what on earth he was to do with the wench. Aside from the obvious, that was. He toyed briefly with the idea of offering her a position as his mistress. After all, he was between women at the moment; she was attractive and experienced, and might enjoy a break from her present position.

Perhaps she would prefer one lover. It would be much less demanding.

The scheme was the briefest of daydreams, however. James would have liked to be able to claim that it was his fond memory of Gerald, and the fact that this was hardly what his friend intended when he'd asked James — on his deathbed — to look after his sister, that turned him from the idea. But the truth was, it was his own responses to the woman that had quickly killed the fantasy. Just the thought of her had his body reacting like fire to an influx of oxygen. James was not used to, nor was he comfortable with, such passionate feelings in himself. He had always prided himself on his self-control and just thinking about Margaret shattered that. He did not know what it was about her. Perhaps it was the fact that she looked so sweetly innocent when he knew she was quite the opposite. Whatever the case, he had thought of little else but Maggie since taking her from Madame Dubarry's. And nothing he had heard during his visit to town had weakened his responses.

The girl was positively infamous. Every man in London was lusting after her. The only halfway sensible thing she had done was to wear her mask and insist on anonymity. But the game could not have continued for much longer. Sooner or later the girl's identity would have been revealed. Margaret was just lucky that he had been the first to discover it.

James was congratulating himself on that fact when the front door opened. He froze at the sight of Lord Mullin entering the inn. He'd bumped into his friend after leaving Crowch to see to the carriage repairs, and they had shared a drink together before Robert had left to continue home. The man's return now was wholly unexpected. Robert's troubled expression as he approached the table was concerning, too.

"Robert," James greeted his friend curiously. "To what do I owe your return?"

"You owe it to a certain lady of whose brother we are both acquainted," the man answered roughly. He settled on the bench next to James and said in a hiss, "What the bloody hell is going on?"

"What do you mean?" James asked warily, feeling himself tense. He had a bad feeling about this. "And which lady exactly?"

"Maggie."

"Maggie?"

Mullin made a face at his confusion. "Gerald's sister. Lady Margaret Wentworth."

James's eyes widened. "What of Gerald's sister?" he asked warily, already knowing he would not like the answer.

"What have you done to her?"

"Nothing. What would make you think I had *done* anything to her?" he asked, his mind beginning to work frantically. Had Robert stopped at Ramsey for some unknown reason on his way home? James hadn't considered that anyone might discover Margaret's presence in his home, or assume that . . . Good Lord, if she —

"Are you saying that she was at your estate without your knowledge?"

James winced. "You stopped at Ramsey?"

"Nay."

James was confused. "Then what would make you think —"

"I ran across her on my way home. There was nowhere else from which she might have come except your estate — and not by the normal route."

"What do you mean?" There was no mistaking the alarm he felt now.

"I mean, it was obvious she had left on foot and walked — or crawled, judging by the amount of . . . mud on her — through the woods to the road. So . . . Did you take her as your mistress? Have you had a lover's spat and she is now trying to run away on foot to teach you a lesson?"

"Of course not!" The fact that James had actually, however briefly, considered the idea of taking her as his mistress made his denial even more heated than it normally would have been. He saw the expression his emphatic denial inspired in his friend, and he scowled.

"Trust me, she is as pure now as she was when I met her." *Which isn't very pure at all,* he added to himself as he stood. "Come, Crowch," he called. "We must go collect Lady Margaret ere she stumbles into trouble on the road."

"I did not leave her there," Robert snapped, obviously insulted that James might think he had.

"You didn't?" James paused in his flight to glance back.

"Nay. Of course not. A gentleman would hardly leave a lady in the path of ruffians and ne'er-do-wells, even should it mean ruining the seats of his newly purchased carriage to whisk her to safety." The last was added on a somewhat pained note.

"I shall replace your seats," James said impatiently. "Where did you leave the wench? Is she in your carriage?"

"Wench?" Mullin echoed in dismay.

James gritted his teeth. "Where *is* she?"

112

Lord Mullin scowled, then said reluctantly, "Last I saw, she was headed for the livery stables. I think she meant to rent a hack." He paused. "Though she didn't appear to have a purse on her, so how she would pay for —"

James had heard enough. Turning on his heel, he burst out of the inn.

"Wait for me!" Lord Mullin cried, and James glanced back to see him nearly knock Crowch over in an effort to follow.

Shaking his head as he ran, James ordered, "Fetch the coach, Crowch, and meet us at the livery."

"Ye can't rent a carriage if ye don't have any coin."

"Yes, but you see, I do have coins — I mean funds," Maggie assured the surly, needle-thin man with whom she had been arguing.

"Well, then, show me the coins and we'll be off," the stableman said with obvious amusement.

Maggie ground her teeth with a frustration she tried not to let show. She reiterated: "I *do* have funds. Just not on me. I can pay you once I am returned to my home. My town house. In *London*." She added the last for good measure, hoping to impress the man, but knew at once that she'd had the opposite effect. His nose wrinkling with distaste, the man let his mean little eyes trail with disdain over her ragged and filthy form, then shook his head.

"Coin up front. 'At's how I do business. No coin, no carriage."

"But —"

"Margaret!"

That sharp call made Maggie turn in alarm to see whose voice it was. Her alarm did not lessen at the sight of Lord Ramsey striding forward, trailed by the younger Lord Mullin. James looked rather put out, she saw unhappily. As if *she* were the one who had done something wrong.

Silently cursing her luck, Maggie drew herself up and prepared to deal with this new problem. She had not walked, crawled, and fought through the rain and mud all day to be dragged back to Ramsey at its end. She would see herself to London or die trying. *Well, perhaps not die,* she allowed with a frown.

"Timmins!" Much to Maggie's irritation, at James Hattledon's brusque address, the stableman suddenly stood upright, a respectful expression covering his face that had been conspicuously absent throughout the duration of her conversation with him.

"M'lord." Mr. Timmins nodded at Lord Ramsey.

"My apologies if Maggie was bothering you," the nobleman said.

"Lady Margaret Wentworth," Maggie snapped, very aware that by calling her Maggie he was insinuating a lower station than she deserved.

"Oh, is it *that* game today?" Ramsey asked patronizingly.

Maggie whirled on him with dismay. Catching the meaningful glances he was throwing at Timmins, she snapped her mouth closed and turned to Lord Mullin. "I *am* Lady Margaret Wentworth. Tell him," she entreated, glaring.

When the younger noble hesitated, his gaze going to James, Maggie could have hit him. Any hesitation was enough to cast doubt, she was sure.

"I *am*," she repeated furiously. Then she added, "And this man has kidnapped me and is holding me against my will at his estate."

The move was risky. Her reputation would now be in ruins if this tale got out, but Maggie didn't see much choice. Besides, it wasn't as if she had any prospects to alienate. Frances had been the only man to show any interest in her since her brother's death, and she wouldn't marry him now if he were the last man on earth.

"Yes, and I have been ravishing you at every turn," Lord Ramsey said good-humoredly.

Maggie gasped. "You have not! He hasn't," she added for Timmins's and Mullin's benefit.

"Well, not recently, but I am sorry that I have neglected you so, my dear. I did have business to attend in town. I promise I shall be more attentive now that I am back."

Maggie was so confused by his words that it took a moment for her to realize that he had taken her arm and was leading her away from the livery. She recognized that fact at about the same moment she realized that his words would be construed as those of a man trying to soothe a neglected lover. She immediately tried to pull away from Lord Ramsey, but the arrival of his carriage right then aided him in preventing her escape; the way he bundled her up and thrust her inside could easily have been misconstrued as assistance rather than the brute force it was.

Unfortunately, while Mullin was close enough to tell the difference, his protest at such treatment was mild to say the least. Mentally Maggie named Robert a traitor as he murmured, "I say, Ramsey. Steady on. No need to manhandle her."

James's only response was to lunge up into the carriage behind Maggie and catch her as she tried to flee out the other door. He pulled her onto his lap, holding her firmly against his chest, trapping her arms with one of his own even as he covered her mouth with his hand when she opened it to scream. She was so busy struggling, she didn't even notice when Lord Mullin climbed into the carriage and took the opposite bench to glare at James.

"You had best explain this, my friend. I cannot allow you to treat a lady thusly. Especially not Wentworth's sister."

"I shall explain as soon as we arrive at Ramsey and she is dealt with," James snapped. He grunted as Maggie landed a healthy kick to his knee and bounced with restrained fury in his lap.

"For now, perhaps, you could just trust me?" he said in a hiss. Then his nose wrinkled and he glanced around with bewilderment. "What the Devil is that stench?"

Maggie paused in her struggles at the question and noted the way Lord Mullin's gaze slid to her.

"Dear God!" Lord Ramsey gasped. Bang-

ing on the wall of the carriage, he bellowed,
"Home, Crowch, and fast!"

CHAPTER FIVE

James had rather hoped that Maggie would wear herself out and give up her struggles by the time they reached his estate. Such was not the case. She was still wiggling, kicking, thrashing, and trying to bite his hand when the carriage rolled up before his manor and stopped. He didn't know where she got the energy. For his part, James was exhausted from trying to hold her still and prevent being neutered by her flailing legs and grinding bottom. He was also heartily sick of the stench permeating his carriage, as well as the growing anger and disgust on Lord Mullin's face.

With Maggie still clutched to his chest, James staggered out of the carriage and carted her through the front door that Mullin hurried to open for him. Pausing in the entry, he bellowed for his butler.

"Surely you can let her go now, James," Robert said impatiently, his gaze decidedly sympathetic for the hell-cat.

"I will, as soon as someone explains how she got away."

"You could just ask her," his friend suggested dryly.

James turned to snap something unpleasant at him, but paused, his attention drawn to the top of the stairs by a gasp.

"But she's asleep in her room!" A maid stood, gaping down at them, and cried out, "I have sat outside her door all afternoon."

"My lord?" Webster rushed up toward them, shock on his face. James Huttledon was not the sort to bellow and stamp about.

He glanced from one servant to the other, then released Maggie, giving her a less-than-gentle push that sent her into the startled butler's arms. "See that she is bathed and given fresh clothes."

"I do not want to bathe," Maggie snapped, regaining her balance and pulling away from Webster.

"You enjoy looking like you just crawled out of the stews, do you?" James asked coldly. Her eyes narrowed on him in displeasure.

"What I would *enjoy,*" she answered between gritted teeth, "is to go home. And if you will not take me, then I would appreciate Lord Mullin's assistance in the matter." She turned a stunning smile tinged with desperation on the other man. "Please, my lord. As a former friend of my brother's —"

"You can ask him after you bathe," James interrupted. He did not like the way Robert was swelling up in readiness to become the woman's protector. "Surely you have ruined his carriage seats enough for one day? Besides, you will have to wait for his carriage and driver to be fetched. Both are still in the village."

Maggie hesitated, obviously shamed by the reminder of what her befouled state had already done to Lord Mullin's seat. Then her shoulders bowed with resignation. James was grateful to see that the hoyden wasn't completely unreasonable.

"Very well. I shall take a bath," she announced, turning to start up the stairs. Her attempt at dignity was ruined when she suddenly whirled back, transfixing Lord Mullin with her eyes. "Please promise you will still be here when I finish? If not for my sake, then as a favor to my brother?"

"Of course," Robert said quickly, his shoulders drawn up. "I shall be here when you return, and I shall help you in any way I can."

Satisfied with that, she delayed only long

enough to toss a half-triumphant, half-furious glare in James's direction, then spun away to take her bath.

James watched her go, then glanced at Webster. The butler promptly straightened, a staunch look coming to his face. "Annie was told not to let Lady Margaret out of her sight until she retired. Also, the dogs were released at night as you requested."

"The dogs released?" Lord Mullin echoed in dismay.

Ignoring him, James rubbed his hands through the back of his hair with frustration. "If Annie was sitting outside her door, Margaret must have climbed off the balcony."

"The balcony?" Robert was goggling at the idea, but James continued to ignore him.

"Have the dogs released after you arrange for her bath, Webster. And tell Annie not to let her out of her sight for a minute."

"Yes, my lord. Shall I arrange a bath for you, as well?"

The butler's question drew James's attention to the fact that a good deal of the mud originally on Lady Margaret had rubbed off on him. He grimaced, but shook his head. "Not right away; I need to talk to Lord Mullin first. We will be in the library. Send Lady Margaret there when she is ready."

Gesturing for his friend to follow, James led the way into the study, heading first for the sideboard and the liquor that waited there; he had little doubt that this was going to be at least a two-drink conversation. Fortunately, Robert followed him in silence, accepting the drink James poured and taking a seat to patiently await an explanation.

James paced between the chair Robert had chosen and the fireplace, searching for a way to begin his exposition, but nothing came to mind. At last he paused, turned to face his friend, and blurted, "Gerald's sister is Lady X."

The silence that followed was complete. Robert gaped at him and James waited, silently counting to twenty-three before the other man blurted, *"Lady X?"*

He certainly understood his friend's horrified disbelief, for he had felt much the same way when Johnstone had revealed the information to him. It was unbelievable. Gerald's innocent little sister, a prostitute? If James were to be entirely honest, he hadn't even believed the runner until he had actually captured Margaret leaving that room in the brothel in a mask — and then he'd had to see her without the mask to be fully convinced it was the right woman. The idea of Gerald's sainted sister behaving so scandalously was untenable.

And yet he had seen the proof with his own eyes. Lady Margaret Wentworth, the sister of their late friend, was none other than Lady X. He doubted Lord Mullin would believe him out of hand any more than he himself had believed Johnstone.

"But —"

James raised a hand to interrupt his friend. "Let me explain before you start speaking your doubts — and I know you doubt me. I doubted this myself." Much to his relief the other lord fell silent and took a drink. Tugging at his cravat, James settled into the seat across from Robert, his gaze moving to the cold hearth before them. He supposed he should light a fire, or at least call a servant to do so, but he was feeling too weary at the moment to be bothered. Besides, the servants would be busy preparing Margaret's bath, not to mention preparing the evening meal. It was growing late in the day.

"As you know, Gerald's last request was that I watch after his sister," he finally began.

Lord Mullin nodded solemnly. "I was there both when he saved your life and when he gasped those words."

"Yes, well . . . as you remember, we were

not released from service right away."

Robert nodded. Just because Gerald had died did not mean the whole unit was released; they had continued to fight old Boney until just a month ago.

"Well, by the time I returned, Wentworth's estate had been settled. The title and castle are going to some cousin or other who went off to make his way in America. At the time of my return they had not yet found the fellow, though they probably have by now. At any rate, while the estate's solicitors could tell me that much, no one seemed able, or at least willing, to give me Gerald's sister's whereabouts since leaving Clarendon — the seat of the Wentworth title — or in aiding me to find her. I had to hire a Bow Street runner named Johnstone to locate the girl."

"And you found her at Dubarry's?" Robert interrupted in outrage. "My God, lawyers are such coldhearted bastards! To dump the woman out on the road without a second thought, leaving her to take up —"

"Nay," James interjected before Lord Mullin got too carried away. "Johnstone, the Bow Street runner I hired, did not find her at Dubarry's. Well, not at first." He heaved a sigh and shifted in his seat. "He found her at Gerald's town house in London. It seems that while he could not leave her the title and castle, he could and did leave her his personal property: his town house, a few small investments, his servants." James shifted again and took another drink. It gave Robert the opportunity to speak.

"But if she has the town house in London and money, why take up —"

"Greed, I suppose," James answered, staring into the swirling liquid in his glass with a morose expression. "Gerald's investments weren't enough to run the household for any length of time without the funds that are now going to Margaret's cousin. Had she sold the town house and purchased a small cottage in the country, then invested the money left over from the sale, she most likely would have been fine. But it seems such . . . rural living is not to her taste. Or at least that is what I must presume from the choices she has made. She settled in the London town house and, apparently, set to work at Madame Dubarry's to supplement her income."

"Good Lord," Robert murmured with consternation. "Who would have believed it of Gerald's sister? He always made her sound so sweet and naive."

"Yes, well, I could hardly believe it when Johnstone came to me with the news."

Robert's eyebrows rose slightly. "How did *he* find out?"

James shrugged. "He found her at the same time he learned the contents of the will. Which should have been the end of his investigation, I suppose, but it did not go unnoticed by me that financially she should be in a bad way and yet she had retained all the servants. I was . . . curious as to how she was managing, so I asked Johnstone to look into the matter."

"And he discovered she was Lady X," Lord Mullin finished.

"Aye." James took another drink. "I hadn't heard from him for a week or so; then he came to me the other night and announced, rather proudly, that he had sorted it all out. He'd had a man watching her, but the fellow hadn't come up with anything. Suspecting his comrade was slacking on the job, he had watched her himself and followed her to Dubarry's. I am ashamed to admit it was already his supposition that Margaret is Lady X, though he had no proof of it. Of course, the only way to find out if it was true was to unmask Lady X."

Robert stiffened. "You *didn't*!"

"What? Sample her favors and unmask her that way?" James asked sardonically, then shook his head. "Nay. I arranged a . . .

er . . . meeting. But I never intended to sample anything, just to get her out of there and unmask her. Which I did. We smuggled her out of Dubarry's, got her in my carriage, and brought her here. Unfortunately, they convened the House of Lords this morning, so I had to turn around and head right back to London. I left Margaret here while I did. I headed back again directly after."

"No wonder you look exhausted," his friend commented.

"Yes."

They were both quiet for a moment; then Robert asked, "Did you hire someone to guard her?"

James shook his head. "I didn't think it was necessary. I told the staff that no one was to aid her in leaving, and that I would return as soon as possible. I ordered Webster to have Annie stick with Margaret all day, not to let her out of her sight until she retired. And I assumed the dogs loosed at night would discourage her from trying anything then. I even wrote her a note explaining that no one would abet her escape, and that we would discuss alternate career choices when I returned. I thought such a note would assure her she would not be harmed. I never imagined for a moment that she would still run."

"No. Most ladies would simply have awaited your return," Robert sympathized. Then he added, "Of course, most women in her situation would never have taken up the career she did."

Ramsey frowned. "You sound almost admiring."

"Well . . ." The fellow shrugged and smiled slightly. "I guess I do admire her a bit. You have to give her credit for at least attempting to take care of matters rather than sit about and cry."

James was scandalized. "Taking up as Lady X is hardly an honorable way of 'taking care of matters,' " he snapped. He scowled at the other man for even suggesting the thought, but Lord Mullin merely shrugged.

"Well, it is better than the poorhouse perhaps. Anyway, what was she supposed to do — marry? Most marriages these days are a form of prostitution, anyway. At least she is honest about it." Robert laughed.

Though James shook his head at his friend's argument, he had to admit he'd indulged a thought or two along those lines himself. Certainly every mistress he'd ever had had been like a wife: he'd paid for her home, her clothes, her entertainment, and her servants — at least for as long as they've been involved. He supposed the only difference was that his mistresses were short-term. Of course, Lady X's customers did not bother with manors or servants; they had only to hand over cold, hard coin for services rendered.

He didn't admit any of this to Robert, though. He would never allude to anything but dismay at her profession. This was Gerald Wentworth's sister, after all!

"So? What do you plan to do with her?"

James glanced up at that question and grimaced. He had been pondering little else since smuggling her out of the brothel. What *was* he to do with her? His promise to her brother would not allow him simply to let her go about her business as a notorious demimondaine. At the very least he had to offer her options, to attempt to talk Margaret into giving up this life of shattered morals. But how?

He was saved from admitting his bafflement by the crash of the study door slamming open and banging against the wall. Both men glanced with startled surprise at the woman now standing in the doorway glaring at them. She was a sight to behold. Bathed, powdered, and dressed in a fresh gown that almost fit, her fiery eyes snapped from James to Lord Mullin and settled on the latter with relief. She promptly pushed away from the door and rushed to Robert as he stood.

"Thank God you are still here, my lord! I was so afraid that you might leave."

"Of course I am still here," Lord Mullin assured her, looking terribly uncomfortable as he did. "I said I would wait."

"Yes, you did." She beamed at him, then clasped his hands. "I wish to leave. Surely you will see me rid of this place? You will not let *him* hold me here against my will? He is a madman. He kidnapped me."

Lord Mullin's obvious discomfort grew; he avoided her eyes and looked everywhere in the room but at her. "Ah . . . well, as to that, my lady, Lord Ramsey merely wishes to help you. He wants to allow you time to consider your options for a better life."

"Options?" Margaret Wentworth scowled. "What options? I was doing well enough without his interference. Surely, as a friend of my late brother's, you will not leave me here?"

Robert straightened his shoulders. "It is precisely *because* I was a friend of your brother's that I have to agree with Ramsey. Surely you do not imagine that your brother

131

would approve of your present employment?"

She had the grace to look slightly ashamed at the question, but then her chin lifted defiantly. "He might not approve, but he would understand that under the circumstances —"

"And which circumstances would those be?" James interrupted. His dry words drew her irritated attention. "Your desire not to give up the excitement of life in town? I suspect your brother expected you to sell his town house, purchase a cottage, and live in the country off the proceeds."

"Oh?" She turned, her hands resting on her hips. Her pretty face twisted with derision. "So you knew my brother better than I, who knew him all his life, did you? *I* think my brother never expected to die so young. He planned to see me married and settled happily. Unfortunately, such was not the case. Instead he died and left the town house and the responsibility of those servants to me. I could hardly sell the house and leave them all unemployed."

Robert touched her arm, drawing her gaze back to his amazed face. "Are you saying that you took up as a pr — *that* career to keep your brother's servants employed?"

■ ■ ■ ■

Maggie scowled at Lord Mullin's shock. Writing articles for the *Daily Express* wasn't *that* shameful an occupation. The way these two were acting, one would think she had taken up prostitution! "What else was I to do? Every one of those servants was loyal to Gerald, and to my parents before him. Most of them have been in service to my family all of their lives. I could hardly see them on the street."

"Dear Lord," the younger nobleman said under his breath.

"You see?" Maggie smiled. He, too, was obviously horrified at the idea of such loyal men and women being left to fend for themselves. "I realize that it must seem a risky business, but it wasn't. Not really. I was always in disguise, or veiled, or masked — as I was when *he* grabbed me." She threw a disgusted look in Lord Ramsey's direction.

"Aye, but . . . I mean . . ." Lord Mullin gave a nervous laugh, then went on delicately: "Risk aside, surely you do not *enjoy* the work?"

She blinked in surprise at the question, then found herself reluctantly admitting what she had not yet admitted to herself. "Perhaps not always. At times . . ."

Both men leaned forward expectantly as she considered the matter, so consider it she did, forcing herself to be painfully honest about everything for a change — something she did not do often because she undoubtedly needed the money from her work. But if she were to be honest, she did not always enjoy being G. W. Clark. For instance, she had not liked climbing that ledge at the brothel. Though, now that it was over, it seemed just another adventure, at the time she had been nauseatingly terrified. And, in truth, she found some of the tales the women told her that night distressing. Some had even left her feeling tainted. The things those women did . . .

"Yes?" Lord Ramsey prompted, and Maggie met his gaze with some difficulty.

"Well, really," she admitted reluctantly, "sometimes it is frightening and unpleasant. But . . ."

"But?" Lord Mullin prompted when she hesitated.

Shrugging, she admitted, "But sometimes it is exciting, too."

"Exciting?" Both men echoed.

"Yes, of course." She shifted impatiently at their horrified expressions. Likely they were thinking of the gleaning of information for specific articles — such as the one about the gambling hells that cheated their customers, or the Four Horsemen's club, where young knobs went to race. She supposed those exposés had been a bit dangerous to write, but they had also been fun. Besides, both articles were about places these two had surely been a time or two themselves. Why should she be forced to remain ignorant of their particulars just because she was a woman? "Well, why should it be any different for me than for you?" she asked. "By all accounts you men certainly enjoy such pastimes. Why should I not?"

"Oh, dear." Lord Mullin tossed back the last of his brandy and set the glass down with a *thunk,* then he straightened and eyed Lord Ramsey meaningfully. "I wish you luck, my friend, but I fear you shall have a rough time rehabilitating her. Keep me posted on how you do." And with that the young noble rose to leave.

Maggie was horrified. Glancing at Lord Ramsey, she noted a similarly displeased look on his face. Why was *he* looking so resigned? *He* wasn't the one being left alone to deal with a situation with no way out!

"Surely you will not leave me here?" she

cried, following Lord Mullin to the door. "I really do have to return to London. And you promised to help me."

"Yes, I did," the young man agreed. "But that was before I understood all the particulars. Now I realize that James is only trying to help. You will not come to any harm in his care."

"Perhaps not," Maggie allowed, then shook her head miserably. "But I *do* have to return. If for no other reason than that my servants have no idea where I am. They must be greatly distressed by my disappearance."

Lord Mullin took her hands briefly, then dropped them as though they were hot. "It is my considered opinion, my lady, that you exert far too much energy on your servants' behalf," he said stiffly. At her bemused expression, he added, "Really, this is for the best, my lady. Let Ramsey aid you in this matter."

Then he walked out, pulling the door closed behind him and leaving her standing alone and bereft in the house of her captor.

Lord Ramsey was silent for a moment, watching her obvious unhappiness; then he downed his drink and stood. The movement drew her wary gaze to him. As she watched suspiciously, the man gave an expansive sigh. She didn't trust him, and she never would. Kidnapping her had not been a propitious start, no matter his oath to her brother. He didn't try to explain himself, though. Instead, he paused several feet away and gave a slight bow.

"Please make yourself comfortable in my home, my lady. As Robert said, you are perfectly safe here. I have only the best intentions toward you." He spoke sincerely, but what was that glinting in the depths of his dark eyes? Maggie was taken off guard by his next words. "And you really have nothing to be concerned about when it comes to your servants. I had a letter delivered to them the night I brought you here, stating that you were coming to my country home for several days' relaxation. If you are concerned, however, you are welcome to write a letter to them and I will see it delivered on the morrow."

Before Maggie could answer yea or nay to that, he gestured to his muddy person and went on. "In the meantime, I am going to clean up, then will most likely retire. It has been a rather wearying couple of days. You may take dinner in your room or the dining room — as you wish. I shall join you to break fast on the morrow, and we shall discuss then your situation and various ideas on how to improve it."

If he had hoped she would be seduced by his politeness, he was sadly mistaken. Maggie remained just as cold to him as before. She watched as he fought back an obviously annoyed expression; then she watched nonchalantly as he murmured good-night and left the room.

As he pulled the door shut behind him, Maggie felt frustration surge up within her like a fire. She could hardly believe this situation. Even more unbelievable was the fact that Lord Mullin had just left her here! Both of these men seemed to be of the opinion that they knew what was best for her. *Well, stuff that!*

Stomping to the library door, she tugged it open and stormed across the hall to the front entrance of the house. No one tried to stop her. No one even appeared. She should have taken it as a warning, but she was too swept up in her emotions. Pulling the front door open, Maggie stepped out on the front step with a feeling of triumph.

It died abruptly at the sound of barking. Turning her head, she glanced warily about until she spotted a pair of enormous dark-furred dogs racing toward her as if she were the fox in a hunt.

For a moment, Maggie couldn't move;

then she gathered herself enough to whirl back into the house. She slammed the door just as the beasts raced up the steps, and there was no mistaking the way the wood shuddered a moment later from the impact of the excited dogs' bodies. Now she knew why Annie was no longer trailing her about, why Ramsey felt comfortable leaving her unattended. He had released the dogs.

Surely they were not trained to attack just anyone on the grounds, she thought unhappily. Unfortunately, she wasn't about to pop outside to discover if they had been racing up eager for petting and attention, or eager to bite her.

Mouth tightening, she listened to the animals bark and leap at the door for a moment, then eased slowly away, half afraid that they would somehow work the door open and come after her. Maggie had backed all the way to the stairs before they began to quiet. Swallowing, she spun about and hurried up the steps to her room. Once in that chamber, she looked frantically around, then rushed to the archway to the balcony. Bursting outside, she immediately heard the barking start up again.

The dogs had heard the slight squeak of the doors opening, and they were racing to position themselves beneath her balcony.

Pacing back and forth beneath her, the beasts were leaping and barking excitedly. Maggie watched unhappily for a moment, then moved back into her room. Escape had been a foolish idea, anyway. She already knew she would never be able to rent a carriage to London; Timmins had proved less than helpful. And the chances of her coming across anyone willing to take her there themselves were slim. It appeared she was stuck.

As much as it galled her, she would have to see what her host had to say for himself at breakfast in the morning; then she would decide on her next move.

Closing the balcony doors on the still-barking dogs, she moved to the bed and lay down to rest until dinner was brought up.

CHAPTER SIX

"My lady, first I wish to say that I do understand the necessity that drove you to this career choice. Truly, I do."

Maggie set her tea aside and raised her gaze politely to Lord Ramsey, her eyes taking in his chiseled face. He really was a handsome man. It was a shame they hadn't met under different circumstances. She would be interested in knowing if the arrogance he had shown her was his normal attitude, or if it was merely a result of the unusual situation that had brought them together.

She had spent the better part of the night before reconsidering that situation — partially due to the reaction of Lord Mullin. After she calmed down, it had been obvious to her, from the short time she had spent with him, that young Robert was a good man, and that he had considered her brother a friend whom he'd held in much esteem.

She found that reassuring. After all, he would hardly leave the young, innocent sister of his friend in the care of a man who might possibly put her in danger. She had also decided that Ramsey's motives were likely just what he had stated; to look out for her, as Gerald had asked. Which meant that James Huttledon was misguided, but well-meaning, and also that she was perfectly safe.

Most important to her decision to tolerate Lord Ramsey was her brother's judgment; Gerald had written a lot about James in his letters, all of it good. He had considered him one of the most honorable men he had ever met and had given many examples: Tales of Lord Ramsey giving away his own food to starving women and children from destroyed villages they marched past, of risking his life to save others, of refusing advancement when it wasn't earned, but was offered because of his title. Gerald had admired, respected, and looked up to this man and — reading those letters — Maggie had come to feel much the same way. He was a good and honorable man trying to do his best for the sister of the man who had died saving his life. She would be patient with him and help him see that there was really very little he could do to help her.

Which didn't mean she didn't wish to get home. She had to get back eventually, and preferably sooner rather than later. She had things to do; she needed to return Maisey's horrid gown, and, more important, she had to finish her article on Madame Dubarry's brothel. Mr. Hartwick wouldn't pay her if she didn't get the article in soon. She had worked on it last night, and planned to finish it as quickly as possible.

She supposed that if she wasn't home by the time the article was done, she could always send it with her letter to Banks and have him turn it in. It wasn't imperative she be there; Banks turned her pieces in as he had done for her brother. She was rather hoping, though, that she could convince Lord Ramsey to return her before the article was finished.

Maggie very much suspected that the only way to convince her captor to return her to London was first to listen to what he had to say, then to explain in a logical, unemotional manner that while being G. W. Clark was risky, it was her only choice. He would be reasonable if she was reasonable; of that she was sure. After all, Gerald had never been one to suffer fools gladly. He wouldn't have considered James such a good friend or respected him nearly as much if he was as stupid as that ridiculous abduction of her from Madame Dubarry's had indicated.

Having decided all of this during the last restless night, Maggie had come down to breakfast fully expecting her host to start in at once. However, he had apparently thought it tactically preferable to wait until they finished eating. She could not say that it had been a poor choice. The delay had left her increasingly tense and unsettled as she had toyed with her food, waiting on pins and needles for just this subject to come up. Now she assumed an attentive pose, waiting to hear what Lord Ramsey had to say, prepared then to explain why he was wrong, in a calm and reasonable manner.

"I realize that there is very little for a woman, especially a lady of noble birth, to do to earn her way in the world," he continued, sounding quite reasonable. "But surely you see that what you are doing is not the answer? This profession will eat at your soul, steal your youth and your beauty. I have seen it many times."

Maggie felt her calm slip a bit and rolled her eyes at his dramatics. While it was true that researching her stories for the G. W. Clark articles sometimes saw her digging about in the underbelly of the beast that was society, the work was not as bad as all that. She didn't wish to argue, however, so she merely pointed out, "My lord, such worries are long past being a concern for me. I am five-and-twenty. What beauty and youth I had fled some time ago."

That put a frown on his face and had him observing her more carefully, at least what he could see of her from his position across the table. His eyes took in her golden hair in its prim style, then her face, her neck, and her breasts, covered as they were by her slightly oversized gown. The garment tended to sag a bit around her smallish bosom, Maggie saw with discomfort, and revealed more than she wished to display. She had to grit her teeth to keep from self-consciously tugging the neckline upward. When his eyes finally made their way back up to her face, she released a relieved breath.

"Why have you never married?" he asked abruptly.

"No one has asked me," she admitted through her teeth, feeling defensive. But her irritation immediately softened at his expression of patent disbelief. It was somewhat flattering that he did not believe her. "I am sure it is very kind of you to show yourself to be such a gentleman, but —"

"I will not allow you to return to your previous employment."

Maggie stiffened, the previous days' irritation at this pompous man returning in full force. "Unless you plan to hold me captive here forever, you really have no choice. You are not my father, brother, or guardian."

"Oh, but I am something of a guardian," he argued. "Your brother asked me to look out for you."

"I hardly think he meant for you to take me against my will and hold me captive in your home, my lord," she snapped with some asperity. The bolt struck home, and guilt covered his expression for a moment. She pressed her attack. "This is all really a dreadful mistake and waste of time. Please return me to my home and —"

"No." Lord Ramsey's discomfiture was gone at once, replaced with steely determination. "There are alternatives."

"Fine." She gave in gracefully. "Let us hear these alternatives."

"Well . . ." His expression showed that he had not expected her to be so open to discussion. Maggie waited patiently until the man had gathered himself together enough to plunge forward. She was not terribly surprised when he drew a piece of folded paper from an inner pocket of his morning coat, unfolded it carefully, then smoothed it out on the table. He looked over whatever he had written, then glanced up at her with a nod of apparent satisfaction. "I have taken the liberty of doing some figures, and, according to my inquiries, were you to sell the town house and add the proceeds to the monies you inherited from both your mother and the smaller sum from your brother, you should be able to purchase a good-sized house in the country and live quite comfortably for the rest of your days. That is, if you do not marry, of course. Should you marry, your investments will make a nice little nest egg, or be a supplement to your husband's income."

He glanced up from his notes, his pleased expression fading somewhat at the narrow-eyed look Maggie was giving him. Shifting uncomfortably under her cold stare, he asked cautiously, "Is there something amiss?"

"The money I inherited from both my brother and mother?"

"Aye." He frowned slightly, not understanding her displeasure.

"I suppose you have the exact sums there?"

"Well, yes. As far as I know. Are these not correct?"

He slid the piece of paper along the table until Maggie could reach it. She turned the sheet and scanned the figures. "Yes. These are correct. Might I ask how exactly you came by these numbers?"

"Johnstone — a runner — got them. Wills are a public record, you see."

"I do. Well, my lord. I am flattered beyond compare that you would take such trouble to dig out all my little secrets — my finances, my employment. My goodness, is there anything you do not know about me?" Folding the sheet of paper, she tossed it at him with an angry snap of her wrist.

Lord Ramsey caught the paper and set it carefully back on the tabletop, silent for a spell before carefully admitting, "I realize that you are not pleased by my having this knowledge, but your brother asked me to look after you. I did want to be sure you were doing all right financially."

Maggie felt herself soften again. As pompous as he could be, the man really was only trying to repay his debt to Gerald. "Yes, well," she allowed. "If you were able to find all this out, my lord, no doubt you also found that I am doing perfectly well on my own now. There is no need for your intervention."

"It would appear that you are handling your finances well enough," he agreed reluctantly. "The money you invested is paying well, and you have not withdrawn any large sums to buy extravagances. In fact, you appear to be making steady deposits while at the same time paying your living expenses. But you *must* agree that the way you are earning this money is of some concern." When Maggie's only response was a thinning of her lips, Lord Ramsey frowned and looked down at his notes. "If you would just sell the town house and purchase a less expensive country home —"

"I am not moving to the country, my lord," she insisted. "Perhaps you cannot understand this, still having family, but I have nobody left. Therefore, I depend rather heavily on the few friends I have in town. I will not deprive myself of them simply to satisfy your desire to see me live a more traditional lifestyle."

On that note Maggie stood, slapped her napkin onto the table, and turned to sail out of the room before she did something silly like get emotional. *So much for logic and reason,* she mourned as she left the room.

James watched Lady Margaret leave, his gaze dropping to the sway of her skirts as she went. She looked lovely in the deep green gown she wore today. The hue set off her coloring so nicely. Of course, the gown didn't fit as well as it might. His sister, Sophie, had left several garments behind when she'd married and moved away.

He had never noticed how generous Sophie's bosom was, but she was obviously larger in that area than Maggie. Overlarge, he decided, since Maggie's breasts had appeared perfect to him when he'd held her in his arms, the sheer, red gown of that first encounter revealing them fully to his startled eyes. Yes, they had appeared the perfect size and shape to him in that moment, so Sophie must be rather overendowed.

Grimacing at his less-than-gentlemanly thoughts, he peered down at the paper in his hand and the figures on it. He hadn't really expected her to agree to trading her brother's home for a less expensive life in the country. If that were an option, she would have done so long ago rather than resort to selling her body. He'd mentioned it only as the first of several ideas. Yet he hadn't considered the reason she was unwilling might be that she wished to stay near friends. He had rather assumed her reluctance was due to a wish to remain close to the excitement of city life. She had revealed a rather softer side of herself than he had expected. It was true, Gerald had been the last of her family. She had no one now but friends in the city. How could anyone expect her to give them up?

His eyes went to his notes, and he frowned slightly. He had one other option here that he would bring up at lunch. In the meantime, he really needed to try to come up with more. Which meant a visit to his library. James always found it easier to think surrounded by his beloved books. The very smell of the leather-bound volumes seemed to help him cogitate. Some time in the library, surrounded by the brilliance of countless ages, should help him find a solution that would please Margaret.

Maggie had just settled in a cozy corner chair in the library when her attention was caught by the sound of the door opening. Lifting her gaze from the book she had opened, she watched Lord Ramsey enter and close the door. The moment he did so, a change came over him. His very body language seemed to alter. The stiff, upright posture he generally practiced eased somewhat, allowing more graceful movement. His facial expression lost some of its severity, making him appear younger and more attractive.

Fascinated by this transition, Maggie was

reluctant to make her presence known. She found herself shrinking into her chair in an effort to avoid detection as he walked to the far wall and ran his hands lightly over the volumes there. He picked one off the shelf, leafed through it, then set it back and chose another. After a quick perusal through this book, he let the hand holding it drop and — now clasping it behind his back with both hands — moved to the glass doors to peer outside. He stood there a good while, staring — blindly, she suspected — out over the gardens. He was rocking lightly on his feet, still holding that book, and Maggie found herself unable to look away. The pose was one she recognized as a common stance she herself took. She often stood, gazing out of the window of her own library in just such a manner, a favorite book clasped behind her back — more for its comforting presence than any other real purpose — as she wrangled with some problem or other.

Maggie had no doubt the conundrum he was pondering. Hers, of course, and what to do with her. She found it rather sweet. Not since Gerald's death had anyone been so concerned about her. Despite grieving the loss of her brother, part of her had enjoyed her new autonomy — few women knew what it was like to be truly free of male intervention in their life. Another part, however, had not. It could be terribly wearying to bear the weight of so many livelihoods, and extremely lonely knowing that ultimately there was no loved-one to care. In truth, Maggie mattered only to her servants now.

Or so she'd supposed. She now appeared to matter to Lord Ramsey as well, if only due to the duty he felt he owed her brother.

Maggie observed his troubled expression, for the first time considering that she was an added burden on his shoulders. She felt sympathy overtake her, but knew from experience that telling him that he needn't worry about her would help little. His conscience would insist otherwise.

Closing the book in her lap, she gently asked, "Am I such a problem?"

The man nearly jumped out of his skin. When her voice pierced the silence he gave a violent start and whirled, the book dropping from his hand. His eyes fell on her with astonishment as she got to her feet and moved toward him.

"I am sorry. I did not mean to startle you so. Was it damaged?" she asked with concern as he knelt to pick up the fallen tome.

"No. It is fine, I'm sure." He brushed off the volume, then lifted a rather wary gaze

as she stopped before him. "I hadn't realized that there was anyone here. I shall
leave you to your —"

"Oh, no, please." She caught his arm
when he would have slipped past. "This is
your library, my lord. I should be the one to
leave."

"No. It's fine." He set the book on the
corner of a nearby table and gestured
vaguely toward the glass doors he had been
standing before. I just —"

"You came here to think," Maggie finished
for him. His eyes examined her curiously.
She felt moved to explain, "I recognized
your pose there at the window."

She turned to peer out over the gardens.
They were a far more lavish affair than
Gerald's in London.

Mine now, she reminded herself sadly,
then tried to distract herself from such
melancholy thoughts by admitting, "I do
the same thing at home. I tend to stand at
the window, book in hand, looking out over
the gardens as I ponder." She turned to
him, vague amusement curving her lips.
"Would I be vain in thinking that I am the
problem you were considering?"

"It would be unchivalrous of me to call
you a problem. A concern, perhaps."

"I see, well . . . ." Maggie's voice died as

her eyes landed on the book he held. *"Pride and Prejudice."*

"Yes." He lifted it for her to see.

"It is my favorite book in the whole world."

"Mine, too."

They shared a smile, then Maggie, finding herself oddly affected by his nearness, moved away to gesture around the library. "You have all of my favorites here, and many books I haven't yet read. This is a wonderful library, my lord. Gerald would be jealous. He prided himself on an extensive library, himself, but I think yours may surpass it."

"Do you think so?"

Something in his tone of voice brought her gaze back to James, and Maggie was astounded to find him grinning. She was helpless to prevent an answering smile as she nodded. "Yes. I do believe so."

He savored that for a passing moment, then his expression softened. "Books and our love of them are what first drew Gerald and I together. It was what we both missed most while at war. The two of us bragged endlessly about the libraries we had at home, arguing over whose was better." His gaze moved around the booklined room. "Being neighbors, Robert and I had been

155

friends for years, and he used to silence us both by pointing out that my uncle's library could easily beat both of ours. He was right, of course. Uncle Charles collected books all his life. He was forever enlarging his library to accommodate new acquisitions. It was three times the size of this one, and he was planning on enlarging it again . . . much to my Aunt Vivian's horror."

"Was?" Maggie asked.

"He died before getting to it," James explained, a new heartache entering his eyes.

Maggie was silent for a moment, respecting his grief, but he next blurted, "Uncle Charles instilled me with his love of reading. I . . ." He paused, looking suddenly embarrassed, as if uncomfortable at having revealed so much of himself.

Maggie regretted the end of these revelations; she had begun to feel that she was getting a glimpse of the real Lord Ramsey. Pretending not to notice his discomfort, she glanced around the room of books and said, "It was Gerald who taught *me* to love reading. It was the best gift he ever bestowed on me, I think. He used to say that books were treasures."

"And do you agree?" Lord Ramsey asked.

Maggie gave a laugh. "Of course. Books

can take you to far-off lands, occasion you to laugh or cry, and teach you much about the world that you would never otherwise learn. Books are quite simply wonderful. They even *smell* wonderful." She threw out her arms and turned in a slow circle, inhaling deeply of the scent with obvious relish.

James didn't smile. His thoughts were far too serious. He was thinking that here was a woman perfect for him. It wasn't her beauty, for there were countless beautiful women in the world, many of whom he had met. None of them had captured his attention for more than a moment, and certainly never to this degree. But here was a woman intelligent and with a passion for the written word equal to his own. He allowed himself to imagine a life with her; one where the winter evenings were spent with the two of them cozy before a burning fire, reading out loud to each other and laughing over an amusing phrase. But then their laughter faded, their eyes meeting and reflecting the fire from the hearth. He took the book from her hand, reaching for her even as he set it aside. Their lips met, their mutual passion for language taking a carnal turn. Then the door opened and they broke apart, their startled glances finding Lord Hastings in the doorway.

"Sorry, darling," his dream-Maggie said cheerfully. "Time to get back to work." And James was left seated on the sofa, watching his wife walk away on the arm of another man.

Groaning, James closed his eyes against this vision. Could a woman who had known the life Maggie had lived really settle for one man?

"Did you say something, my lord?"

James blinked his eyes open just as Maggie turned to him. Her hands fell back to her side, the tips of her fingers unintentionally catching the corner of the book he had set on the table mere moments ago, sending it spiraling once more to the floor.

"Oh no! I am sorry, I didn't mean . . ." Her voice faded away. They had both instinctively bent to rescue the volume, and now they knelt facing one another, each holding an edge of the book. As in his daydream their gazes met, and James fancied that he did see a hint of fire flickering in her eyes. He knew there was flame in his own. They rose as one, each still holding the book as if it were a conduit for the electricity sparking between them.

James felt himself leaning toward her, his body following its own edict. He was aware when her breathing became shallow, and she too inclined toward him. He felt her breath, whisper-soft, against his mouth. Her eyes slipped closed, her lips parting the tiniest bit, and James was about to claim them when the soft click of a door closing drew his head around to the entrance to the library.

There was no one there, no Lord Hastings waiting to whisk Maggie away. The sound must have come from somewhere out in the hallway. But it was enough to snap James back to his senses.

Straightening away from her, he cleared his throat and turned to replace the book on the table. He risked a glance Maggie's way to see the confusion reigning on her face, then searched for something to ease the discomfort of the moment. Reaching into his pocket for the slip of paper with his two suggestions for her future on it, he turned his back to her. He took a step away, then said, "It occurs to me that if you do not wish to move out of London and your brother's town house, another possibility is to close up the better part of the house and release most of the servants. You should be able to manage quite well with this reduced expense."

A long silence followed his words, but he

waited patiently for her to collect herself.

She sounded weary when she responded. "Impossible. I will not turn out servants who have served my family faithfully and well for years when all I need do to keep them is a little bit of work. I fear you shall have to come up with something else, my lord."

He considered her words during the following return to silence and still hadn't come up with a response when the click of the door made him turn to see that she had left the library. He was alone. Letting his breath out on a sigh, he moved to the nearest chair and dropped into it with relief.

There was no way he could ignore the fact that Maggie was going to be a terrible problem. He had felt sure when he had stolen her from Dubarry's that he could find an alternative to her lifestyle. Now, as he considered the matter, he seemed to be drawing a blank. Unfortunately, there simply were not many opportunities for women to make money in this man's world. Most women just married for it.

That was an option, he supposed. Her previous employment was still a secret — no one would know unless he told — so Maggie was still marriageable, but he found himself resisting the option. He simply could not imagine her wedding any of the eligible men of the ton. Or, to be more honest with himself, he didn't want to imagine her bedding any of them. Again.

He did seem to like to imagine her bedding *him,* however. He'd found himself rather distracted with such images ever since bringing her home. Every time he had paused to think of an alternate career for her, he found himself imagining her in that red gown of hers, doing one of those things that the girl at Dubarry's had whispered in his ear. Which was damned distracting. And damned discomforting, too. He had been walking awkwardly a lot of late.

He was finding it more and more difficult to control his physical response to her. Worse yet, his very mind was starting to follow his body's lead. For a man who prided himself on his self-control and who had spent some thirty years residing mostly in his head — with small safe forays into the occasional physical "bit of exercise" with his latest mistress — this was all rather disconcerting.

James had learned at an early age that loving people correlated with great pain when they were lost. He had done his best to avoid such grievous entanglements. It was safer to stick to more temperate emotions.

Affection rather than love. A mild desire rather than an all-consuming lust. Unfortunately, Maggie was bringing out intense carnal yearnings in him, and he feared he wouldn't be able to fight them much longer. Which was the problem. Had he kissed her just now, he very much suspected that it would not have ended with a simple kiss . . . or even just a passionate one. Even as he had bent toward her, his mind had been racing ahead to dragging her to the library floor and . . .

Feeling his manhood rise to make its presence known again, James killed his thoughts and closed his eyes. This was exactly the problem. The woman was driving him mad. His normally sane and controlled thinking was failing in the face of an almost continuous erection.

He considered his options desperately. Avoiding her cropped up in his mind, but he dismissed that at once. Avoiding her, while possible, was not likely to help. Her presence did not seem to be necessary to affect his libido, he merely needed to think of her — and he seemed to do *that* endlessly. Perhaps, instead, he should try working her out of his system: Take her upstairs and bed her over and over and over until his fascination with her eased.

162

That idea had merit, he decided. His body certainly seemed pleased with it.

Grimacing, James stood and moved toward the door of the library. He needed to get away for a bit to think. It was obvious his brain dropped into his drawers whenever he was anywhere near the woman. Even in separate rooms in the same house she affected his thinking. His only respite was to get away for a while and hope to come up with a solution more acceptable. Not that he minded the proposition of taking Maggie as his mistress. In fact, the more he thought about the idea, the more he liked it. Unfortunately, it was the last thing his honor would allow.

"Robert," he decided as he stepped out into the hall. He would go visit his friend and neighbor, and see if the other fellow could help him. Lord Mullin had proven a brilliant strategist during the war; he should prove able to assist in this battle. Or so James hoped.

"I suppose you suggested she sell —"

"The town house and purchase a country house." James finished for his friend, and nodded. "Yes. That was my first suggestion, of course."

"And she did not like that?"

"She refused it, as I expected." He paced the length of the other man's study. Lord Mullin had greeted him warmly on his arrival and agreed to lend his brainpower to the task. They were tossing ideas around now.

"What about closing up part of the house and releasing a portion of the staff?" Robert suggested.

"My second idea," James admitted wryly, "was shot down as quickly as the first."

"Hmm." The other man frowned. "I do not understand her refusing that. She hardly needs so many rooms for just herself. Or all those servants, for that matter."

"Don't you remember, Robert? She will not turn servants out who have 'served her family so faithfully,' " he quoted peevishly, and Lord Mullin gaped briefly before giving his head a befuddled shake.

"Well," the younger man said after a moment. "It would appear she suffers the same failing as most women. She is too soft-hearted for her own good."

"Too softhearted?" James spun on him in amazement. "The woman is bedding half of London rather than release some unneeded staff! That is a bit more than softhearted. Softheaded, more like."

"Well, surely not half of London?" Mullin

argued with a smile. "Half of London is women, which means the other half would be men — and since she has not slept with either you or I, she cannot have slept with that entire half, either. Perhaps half of half of London. Aye, she may have bedded a quarter of the town."

"I am not amused, Robert," James said tightly.

"Sorry. I was trying to lighten the mood."

James ignored his friend's shrug. "I do not need the mood lightened, I need resolution." He began pacing again.

"Well . . ." Robert mulled the matter over. "Kendricks mentioned that he is looking for a nanny. Perhaps —"

James stared at him in horror. "You are not suggesting that we allow her to take a position where she would actually have influence over children?"

"Oh. I see what you mean." Mullin grimaced.

"Besides, the Kendrickses are, at present, a very happily married couple. Her presence in their household would put an end to that within a week."

Robert frowned. "I do not know about that. She may be a prostitute, but that doesn't mean that she would attempt to disrupt a happy marriage."

"She would not have to try. Her very presence would be like tempting Adam with the apple."

Lord Mullin's eyes widened slightly and a faint laugh slipped past his lips. "Oh, now she is charming I am sure, but Kendricks is quite taken with his wife. I hardly think —"

"Taken with his wife he may be," James swore, "but I guarantee you that one week with Maggie, and Kendricks would be blind with lust."

"Blind with lust?" Robert appeared doubtful. "She is attractive, but —"

"Attractive?" James interrupted again. "The woman is temptation personified."

Robert pursed his lips, the image of a muddy and bedraggled Maggie stumbling out of the woods coming to his mind. That was followed by a more presentable vision, her still-damp and inglorious appearance after she had had her bath. She was attractive in a sweet, wet sort of way, he supposed. But he wasn't seeing what his friend was ranting on about.

"She has nice eyes," he said judiciously at last, and James gaped at him.

"Eyes? Forget her eyes! She has the most delectable body I have ever seen. The woman is perfect. Nay, Kendricks wouldn't be safe from her. Oh, at first he might barely

166

notice her, but then he would begin to notice her scent, become aware of it every time she entered or left a room, wafting around him, drowning his senses. Then every time her name was brought up, or he tried to think what to do with the woman, she would rise in his mind like Aphrodite, her lips full and sweet, her eyes mysterious behind that red mask, her skin pale and perfect in that see-through red silk gown she wears, the cinnamon-red of her nipples showing through its hazy gauze —"

"Cinnamon nipples!"

James stilled, blinking a time or two as Robert's exclamation recalled him to propriety. Just what had he been raving on about? Dear Lord, the woman was driving him mad! He despairingly quit his pacing to drop into a chair.

"What see-through red gown is this? And what the devil have you been doing over there at Ramsey with Gerald's sister? For God's sake, James! You are supposed to be reforming the wench, not —"

"Nothing. I have not been doing a damn thing." He bestowed a disgusted glare on his friend. "Get your head out of the gutter, Robert."

"Well, then, what is all this nonsense about a delectable body and see-through gowns?"

James shrugged unhappily. "She was wearing a see-through red gown when we snatched her from the brothel," he admitted. Then he shifted impatiently. "Enough about that! I came here today hoping you would have some helpful advice for me."

"Yes, yes, of course. I will try to do better," Robert assured him, but James was already off on another tirade.

"I have been racking my mind and coming up with very little!" he was saying.

"Well, you have been rather distracted, what with rushing back and forth from town."

"But all I could come up with were the same damn things you just brought up. The same things she discounted when we first talked to her. I even considered finding her a position with a family as a nanny, but I cannot, in good conscience, suggest her to anyone."

"No, I suppose not," Robert agreed. "If she would even consider it."

"Yes. That is the other thing, of course. I doubt she would agree."

"Hmm." They were both silent for a moment; then Lord Mullin asked, "What else is there for a woman?"

"Very little." James grunted. "Which is my

problem. But I cannot in good conscience allow her to return to Dubarry's either."

"No. That wouldn't do," Robert agreed.

"So, you see my problem?"

"Aye."

"That being the case, I have considered one last alternative," James admitted reluctantly. When his friend peered at him in polite inquiry, he hesitated, then added carefully, "Something more along the line of her previous employment, but not quite as disreputable."

"Her previous employment?" Robert frowned; then his eyes widened in incredulity. "Steady on! You are not thinking of taking her as a mistress?"

"Well, it would be a damn sight more respectable than working for Dubarry," James said defensively. "Besides, there is no sense in seeing her talents go to waste. And you yourself heard her say she liked the work."

"Dear God, James!" Robert's feet slammed to the floor with a crack. "That is hardly reforming her and seeing her out of the business!"

"She wouldn't be 'in the business.' And it would be a lot less risky. There would no longer be any worry of her identity being discovered."

"Oh no, everyone would *know* who she was — and that she was *your lover,*" the other man pointed out.

"We could be discreet."

"Discreet? James, do you hear yourself? Think of Gerald, man!"

That gave James pause. Gerald, with his sweet stories about his sweet sister. His little Maggie with her sharp mind and pretty face. Gerald had left out mention of her delectable body, he thought bitterly. Perhaps, had he prepared James for —

"Gerald saved your life."

James grimaced at Robert's condemnation. He could have done without the reminder of what he owed Wentworth.

"He wouldn't want his sister to be your mistress."

"Not even to get her out of Dubarry's?" he asked.

"Of course not," Robert said firmly. "Use your head, Ramsey. You are supposed to be finding a solution to this problem, not becoming a part of it."

James accepted that, then glared at the other man. "Well, then I suggest you come up with something, because I am at a loss as to what to do with the woman. All I can think about when she is around is —"

"Her cinnamon nipples?" Lord Mullin

inserted with dry amusement. "I shall give the matter serious consideration."

James grunted at the promise, but Robert ignored his pessimism.

"I will come up with something. In the meantime, it would appear that you are somewhat overly tempted by the girl. Therefore, you should avoid her as much as possible. In fact, why do you not stay for dinner? A little time and distance might help get her out of your system."

James hesitated, then nodded in agreement. It certainly sounded a better idea than sitting about gaping at Lady Margaret like some lovestruck pup.

CHAPTER SEVEN

Maggie stared out over the gardens. It was a lovely day. The sun was shining brightly on the multicolored roses along the path she was walking, but with her mind taken up with thoughts of her irritating host, she hardly noticed. She was beginning to believe another escape attempt would be necessary.

Unnaturally weary after their encounter in the library, Maggie had asked that her lunch be brought to her room. She'd wanted to avoid another tiring clash. Yet, by the time dinner rolled around, she'd recovered and been all girded for battle. The dratted man had muddled her plan by not showing up. She had eaten the meal alone — if one could call being surrounded by an army of servants, 'alone' — and, much to her alarm, Maggie had found herself missing the presence of the arrogant ass. Worse, assuring herself that her reaction was only due to restless boredom had not assuaged her fears.

172

The way her spirits had fallen this morning, when Annie announced Lord Ramsey would not be down to breakfast, had only exacerbated her annoyance. The maid had imparted, "his lordship returned quite late from Lord Mullin's estate." The girl hadn't said so, but the disapproving look she'd worn had made Maggie suspect the man had returned well sotted, which would explain his absence.

It did not, however, explain the unnatural attachment she seemed to be acquiring for her captor. She didn't understand it herself. She found James Huttledon irritating and arrogant. Yet there was no denying he was attractive, and there was a certain spice to sparring with him. Maggie felt alert and on edge whenever she was around him, much as she did during her escapades as G. W. Clark. It was as if she were indulging in something a little risky and dangerous just by being near him, and that sensation was intensely titillating. Which made her worry that her choice of employment was beginning to affect her adversely; perhaps she was becoming addicted to risk.

Maggie had found herself asking Annie questions about Lord Ramsey as the maid fixed her hair that morning. She'd learned that, much to her relief, the man was not married and never had been. He was the eldest of two children. His younger sister, Sophie, had been married two years earlier to Lord Prescott. Their parents had been lost at sea while both children were quite young, leaving them to be raised by their aunt and uncle. The uncle had died in his sleep while James was away at war, but his aunt Vivian, Lady Barlow, was still alive and well.

That had been the sum of what she had managed to learn, but the very fact that she had felt moved to ask was troublesome, to say the least. She didn't wish to like Lord Ramsey. Perhaps if he were not quite so obviously disapproving of her recent choices, if he weren't so stodgy and traditional, she would not mind so much. But there was really no sense in becoming attached to a man who looked down on her for working for a living. Once she convinced him that she did not need his interference in her life, Maggie doubted she would ever see the man again. They did not move in the same circles. Not anymore at least; she could no longer afford to.

Maggie wasn't one to yearn after things she couldn't have, so there was no sense at all in being the least bit interested in Lord Ramsey — she had repeated that to herself throughout her solitary breakfast. It was also what she was reminding herself of now as she wandered through Ramsey's gardens. She was a sensible girl and would behave accordingly.

Now all she needed was to convince the man to return her home so she could get on with her life.

"Would you care to break your fast now, my lord?"

James waved Webster's question away, continuing down the hall and out of the house, pausing only to snatch his hat and cape from the rack as he went. He had no interest in food this morning. All he truly wanted was some fresh air. He needed to clear his head. Avoiding his unhappy house-guest wasn't a bad idea, either. At least until Lord Mullin arrived with his promised solutions.

He recalled very little of the strategy session they had attempted last night after the fine meal Robert's staff had served. Most of what he remembered was that Lord Mullin still had the finest port in England. Unfortunately, that was mostly because it was having an unpleasant effect on him this morning. His hangover was the reason he felt a nice walk through the gardens was in order.

Such exercise would serve to remove the last of the effects of the port pounding at his head, as well as keep him out of Lady Margaret's way until reinforcements arrived.

He would also keep Gerald firmly in mind, James decided as he walked along the garden path. That should help keep him from being tempted to seek out the girl. Satisfied with his strategy, he nodded to himself, then lifted his head just in time to keep from crashing into the back of the very woman he was trying to avoid.

Damn, was his impotent thought as she turned with a start.

His second reaction was to reassure himself that he should remain calm. It was broad daylight. They were out in the open. All he had to do was keep Gerald in mind, and he could keep himself restrained. He had not acted on his rather lusty thoughts ere this, and there was no reason to think he might now. Somehow, though, it seemed harder not to act on such thoughts now that he was admitting having them.

It wasn't as if there was the usual invisible barrier of the girl being pure and untried, some dark part of his mind pointed out, weakening his resolve. And she did look lovely in that delicate little white gown. It emphasized her false air of innocence. It even almost made James forget how she had looked the night he had swept her from Madame Dubarry's: her hair had not been piled atop her head then as it was now, but had tumbled about her shoulders in golden disarray as if she were fresh from bed. Which she had been, of course. And her skin had seemed lustrous through the gauzy red material of —

Damn! He wasn't supposed to be thinking of such things, James reminded himself. He wouldn't think of such things!

Maggie was a bit disconcerted to find the focus of her contemplation appear before her as if conjured by her thoughts. Taking a deep breath, she straightened her shoulders and prepared for a continuation of their previous struggles. She had no doubt there would be a continuation, the man was like a dog with a bone when it came to the matter of her career. One would think she were prostituting herself, the way he carried on. However, despite her attraction to him — or perhaps because of it — Maggie was determined that today she would convince him to give up this ridiculous task he had set himself, and make him return her to her life and home.

She opened her mouth to fire the first salvo, only to pause as she noticed the way the man was staring at her. The oddest expressions were flitting across his face. She was becoming quite uncomfortable in her thin white gown when he seemed to realize that he was gaping. Forcing a smile, he straightened and offered a quiet "Good morning."

Gesturing for her to continue walking he fell into step, and they walked in silence for several moments before he attempted to break it. "It is a chill day," he murmured finally.

Maggie felt herself relax. It appeared they would discuss the weather and refrain from butting heads. Clearing her throat, she managed a smile and a nod. "Aye. It is a bit chilly today, my lord. It was lovely just a moment ago, but now a cloud seems to have appeared to hide the sun. Thus it is growing a bit chilly." She realized the truth of it even as she spoke. The sun was hidden behind a large, fluffy cloud and, without its warmth, the temperature had dropped several degrees. She began to wish that she had taken the cape Annie had offered her for this walk. Maggie had accepted the hat and gloves, but had thought a cape much too heavy for such a lovely morning. But then, the sun had still been shining.

"Hmm."

The sound drew her attention to her host. Noting the fretful expression on his face, she felt a smile curl her lip. That one comment on the weather appeared to be the extent of conversation that Lord Ramsey could manage this morning. The realization brought her some amusement as silence fell over them again. Crossing her arms and grimacing, she rubbed her hands lightly over her forearms in an effort to brush off the morning chill. It was a wholly unconscious movement, one she became aware of only when Lord Ramsey removed his cloak and draped it about her shoulders.

Maggie accepted the garment uncomfortably. When she then suggested they turn back to the house, he agreed in silence, taking her arm to lead her. They had nearly reached the doors to his library before he spoke again, the words bursting forth this time as if they simply could not be held in.

"How can you stand it?"

"Stand what, my lord?" she asked with bewilderment.

"What you do," he explained. "How can you *bear* it?"

Maggie turned to peer at him curiously, surprised at his true confusion and the almost pained expression on his face. He awaited her answer. Was he truly so perplexed that she could do what she did? She had to wonder a little impatiently what little lords were taught about women while growing up. Why was it so painful for him to consider that she willingly wrote articles for the *Daily Express*?

She forced herself to temper her irritation. After all, most of the ton would be shocked by a male member of the nobility writing such "rubbish." She supposed it was not so surprising that he would be horrified by the idea that a female member did. Sighing in acknowledgment of that, she turned to continue on toward the house. She had exited the manor via the doors to the salon, but he was steering her to the library, which was closer and more convenient.

"I can stand it because I quite like it, actually," she answered.

"You like it," he repeated not sounding at all happy. Maggie paused again to glance at him. He had stopped walking once more and was looking as miserable as he sounded. It was an exaggerated reaction, in her opinion, and she scowled before turning to stomp the last few steps to the glass doors.

"Aye. I *enjoy* it," she snapped. Tugging the door open with more force than was warranted, in her irritation, she strode inside and up to his desk. There she whirled to find him entering behind her, his expression verging on disgust. Maggie felt her chin lift defiantly as they faced each other. "I have always had a curious mind, and wondered about such things."

He continued to stare at her with that fascinated yet repulsed expression, and Maggie's mouth tightened. She would wager all the money she had been paid for her last article that he enjoyed pastimes like gambling and racing and such as well as talking about them afterward as G. W. Clark did in his article. Apparently a female such as herself admitting that she had enjoyed similar escapades was somehow grossly offensive to him however. *The hypocrite!*

"Oh, come now, my lord," she chided, tugging off her gloves with a series of impatient jerks on the fingertips. "I have heard a lot of puritanical types harp on about this, but I would never have taken you for a puritan or a prude. Surely you will not tell me that you have not had your own curiosities about such things? That you have secretly enjoyed —"

"I will not deny it," James interrupted quickly, unwilling to hear Maggie actually voice what she had done in that brothel. He

181

was already alarmingly excited at this vague discussion; should she start to describe the things she enjoyed in detail . . .

His gaze slipped over her figure in the soft white gown she wore beneath his open cloak. He had thought it very demure when his sister wore it. Unfortunately, on his guest it seemed subtly seductive. Or maybe that was the fault of the recurring images he kept having of her from the night he'd kidnapped her. It was hard to forget the curves he'd held in his arms, the breasts the gown had seemed only to emphasize in the gloom of the carriage. Even Margaret's innocent face had seemed seductive behind the red mask, framed as it was by her mussed flaxen hair. One's eyes had been forced to her sweet, swollen lips. While every single one of the borrowed gowns this woman had worn had only hinted at those charms, his mind filled in the blanks repeatedly and often, torturing him with that image and the knowledge of her lost virtue.

Feeling his sex harden at the thought, he straightened, his lips compressed. He forced out the words: "I realize that there is great pleasure to be found in such endeavors, but —"

"There, you see." She turned from setting her gloves on his desktop to beam at him.

Her delight in eliciting such a confession from him was obvious. "There is nothing to be ashamed of in admitting to it, my lord," she went on gently, turning to move behind his desk. "My brother enjoyed it a great deal, too. I begin to think there may be a bit of the adventurer in our family blood. He was quite taken with the entire thing. I know."

James was shocked, and he asked carefully, "You mean with the brothel?"

"Well, as a matter of fact, he was quite well acquainted with Madame Dubarry," she admitted. "It was through him, indirectly, that I met her."

"Through him?" James repeated in horror as he followed her around the desk.

Maggie turned, startled when she found him standing directly behind her. She frowned. "Well, yes. Not directly, you understand. But she came to see me after he died. They had been friends and she —"

"Suggested you go to her brothel?"

"No." Maggie's expression grew distracted as her eyes focused on his mouth. He felt her gaze there as an almost physical touch. They were only inches apart, and James became aware that he was crowding her, that she was leaning back slightly because of it, but he couldn't seem to move away.

Her chest was rising and falling at an accelerated rate. Her mouth parted, and he nearly groaned when her tongue slid out to wet her lips. It appeared a wholly unconscious action, but knowing her career, James found that difficult to credit. She was a skilled seductress, and there was no question in his mind that he would be easily seduced.

"Uh . . ." Maggie cleared her throat suddenly, and gave a little shake of her head as if to clear it. Then she said, "Nay. She did not wish me to visit the brothel. She thought it was terribly risky."

"The woman has more sense than I thought," James muttered as the tension eased between them.

Maggie rolled her eyes before rushing on, "But I assured her it would be fine, that I would wear a disguise. No one would ever find out."

"But they did," James argued.

"Yes, well, I suppose it was bound to happen eventually," she admitted with obvious resignation.

Taking a deep breath, Maggie forced a smile, then shrugged philosophically and raised her hands to remove the silly little feathered hat that matched her gown.

Lord Ramsey still stood distressingly

184

close, and showed no desire to move away as he asked, "And that is all you have to say? There is no shame?"

Maggie stiffened at the question, the hat half-off her head. "Why should I be ashamed? I realize that earning one's way in the world is frowned on by the ton, but then few of them *have* to earn their livelihoods. And many of them don't care what happens to their servants. Besides, I assure you my brother would not have been ashamed. I suspect the only reason he kept his own behavior secret was to protect me from any taint."

Lord Ramsey waved away her comment impatiently as he removed his hat and reached around to set it on the desk behind her. "It is different for a man," he said.

"Oh?" she asked archly. She drew her hands down between them, her hat clutched in her tense fingers. "How so?" Lord Ramsey frowned, but she continued, "You disappoint me, my lord. I hoped you would be different. That you would not hold men up to one standard and women to another. I thought you an intelligent man."

He squirmed at the rebuke, and Maggie was pleased to see indecision in his eyes, but then he gave a small shake of the head. "I am sorry, Margaret. I guess I find it hard

185

to believe that you actually enjoyed your foray into the brothel."

Maggie caught her breath in surprise. This was the first time that Lord Ramsey had called her by her given name and the tone he had used while addressing her was almost gentle. Biting her lip, she confessed what she would have refused to before. "I didn't. Well, perhaps I did at first. But by the end, I just wanted to get out."

Surprise spilled across his face at the confession; then his eyes softened and he raised a hand, startling her with the gentle caress of one rough finger down her cheek. "And now you are."

"Yes." She swallowed hard, her eyes focusing on his lips as they drew nearer. He was going to kiss her. She knew he was going to kiss her. She also knew that she should stop him. A proper lady would stop him, but Maggie didn't want to. It was that damned curiosity of hers. She wanted to know what it felt like to be kissed by a man like Lord Ramsey. Would his kiss be soft and wet, like Pastor Frances's tentative kisses had been? She didn't think so. She suspected they would be much different. They would not leave her wondering how to get the man out of the house without hurting his feelings. Maggie was positive they would make her toes curl. Actually, her toes were already curling in her slippers in anticipation, and her breath was coming in short, excited bursts. Yes, she was ripe for his kiss, so when she saw uncertainty flicker across his face and the way he hesitated, she took matters into her own hands. Stretching up on her curling toes, she pressed her lips to his.

Wham! She felt her heart slam into her rib cage, her body vibrating with excitement as she slid her lips uncertainly over his; then he took over the kiss with a sound somewhere between a moan and a curse. His mouth opened over hers, his head tilted and he began to devour her lips. Maggie's eyes popped open in surprise at the sudden hunger he showed. She saw that his own eyes were closed; then his hands slid up to cup the sides of her face, and he urged her mouth open. Maggie's eyes drifted closed again.

Pastor Frances had never kissed her like this! This was . . . carnal, sweetly sinful, and definitely delicious. Moaning into Lord Ramsey's mouth, Maggie inched closer, uncaring of the hat being crushed between them in her eagerness to feel his body pressed against her own.

Releasing her face, Ramsey slid his hands down to her arms and backed her around the chair until she bumped up against the desk; then he caught her in an embrace, drawing her close where his hands could slide down to curve over her bottom through her gown. He pressed her firmly against him and thrust forward. Maggie shuddered as she felt his hardness press into her; then she felt the first pangs of fear. She had instigated this kiss, had wanted it, but his arousal warned her she was playing with fire.

Raising her hands, she pressed gently against his chest, her face turning, but Lord Ramsey didn't appear to recognize it as an attempt to end their kiss. Instead, as she pulled away from him, his eyes opened and went to her chest. He raised a hand to cup one breast, and he spread his legs slightly, pressing her lower body more firmly between the desk and the proof of his arousal.

Maggie had begun to murmur an apology when his hand closed over her breast. Her mouth snapped closed, then a moan escaped as he brushed her borrowed cloak aside and lowered his mouth to the flesh revealed by the neckline of her gown. She felt his lips and tongue linger over the plump flesh there, then dip between her two breasts to lick that delicate skin. All at once, her breast was free of the gown and Lord Ramsey's mouth closed over the tender flesh of her nipple. Maggie experienced an immediate flood of fiery sensations pooling in her lower stomach.

Gasping for breath, she arched instinctively into his touch, her lower body grinding against his. Releasing her hold on her hat so that their bodies were all that held it between them, she reached back, pushing unknown items out of the way so that she could brace herself against the desk. She felt something warm and damp spread beneath her fingers, but cared little as he stirred her passions. Maggie let her head fall back, moans erupting from her throat as he tugged her gown down off her shoulders enough that her second breast spilled free. It was immediately enclosed in his warm hand, his thumb and forefinger replacing his lips on one nipple as he moved to lick and nip at the other.

Breathing something that might have been "Oh, God," Maggie lifted her head to peer down at him, her hands sliding into his hair and tugging unconsciously at the strands.

She wanted him to stop.

She wanted him to continue.

She wanted these feelings building in her to end.

She wanted the bliss they promised.

Her mind went fuzzy, confused by all her

conflicting wants. Had anyone suddenly asked, she might have had trouble remembering where she was. Perhaps even *who* she was. All she seemed to be was a bundle of desire. And she wasn't even quite sure just what it was she wanted, but she wanted it badly.

Responding to her tugging on his hair, Ramsey released her breast, then covered Maggie's disappointed moan with his mouth, catching and turning it into a groan of shared desperation. Where she'd been uncertain earlier, this time Maggie responded to his kiss with unadulterated hunger. Sucking his tongue into her mouth, she nipped it gently as she gripped blindly at his cravat with her free hand. Somehow she managed to get the cravat undone, and she pulled it off, releasing it in a flutter to the floor.

Maggie turned her attention to his shirt. She wanted to feel his bare skin under her hands. It was a desperate mindless want and she pushed herself off the desk so that she could use both hands. Unfortunately, Lord Ramsey's nearness hindered her attempt to straighten so that she lost her balance. She grabbed at him to keep from falling, one hand catching in his shirt, and the other — the one still down by her waist — landing quite a bit lower. His sharply indrawn breath and the sudden swelling of the body part she had unintentionally grabbed, told her what she held. Maggie broke their kiss, mortification rushing through her.

"My lord," she began, then paused when he covered her hand with his own. Maggie had been about to remove her hold on him and apologize for the embarrassing mistake, but was now unable to. He didn't seem to want her to.

"James," he gasped in a strangled voice. "Dear heavens, Maggie, I think you can call me James, now."

"James," she breathed, squeezing him curiously. He had been hard when she had grabbed him, and seemed to grow more rigid by the moment. Despite the fear caused by treading on this dangerous ground, she found herself curious about his body. He seemed extremely large to her inexperienced touch. Maggie tentatively followed the length of that hardness, amazed when he gasped and shuddered against her.

"Oh God, yes, Maggie. Touch me," he exclaimed. Then he turned his lips to her throat. He alternated kissing, licking, and nipping at the skin there, with whispering heated words against her warm flesh. Maggie adjusted the pressure she applied, and where she applied it, curiosity and uncertainty battling within her.

"Oh God, you're so talented," he groaned, surging against her hand. Maggie bit her lip. Some of her passion had faded under her curiosity and her head was beginning to clear. She didn't feel talented. She also didn't feel terribly comfortable. She shouldn't be doing this, any of it. Before she could remove her hand, however, Ramsey was brushing it away himself. Claiming her lips with his own, he once again thrust his hardness against the very center of her through their clothing. The double assault had her forgetting her fears in no time. Within moments, her legs were weak, and moist heat was pooling where Lord Ramsey was rubbing himself against her.

Maggie clutched at his upper arms, dazed by her body's reaction to him as he insinuated one leg between hers, rubbing the material gathered there against her suddenly exquisitely sensitive core. Breathing heavily, she clung to him with her lips and hands. She rode his thigh, her body moving with his, then she shuddered as a breeze whispered past the burning skin of her leg.

She pulled her head away then, glancing down distractedly to see her crushed hat lying abandoned on the floor at their feet.

Any guilt she felt at the abuse of the borrowed item was quickly displaced as she saw that one of Lord Ramsey's strong dark hands was tugging her skirt upward, his fingers sliding over the paler flesh of her thigh. A warning sounded in her head, but Ramsey's mouth had moved to her ear and was terribly distracting. It sent little tingles and shivers rippling through her. Maggie made little mewls of sound, then turned her head abruptly to catch his lips with her own.

His kiss this time was bruising in its intensity, but Maggie's response was just as passionate. Ramsey's fingers caressed their way onto her inner thigh. She cried out when they brushed against the swollen flesh of her excitement — more from the shocking tingling that shot through her at the caress than anything — then sucked desperately at his invading tongue, squeezing her legs around his caressing hand.

These delights were something Maggie had never experienced. She had never even imagined such waves of sensation as he was causing in her, and she was completely overwhelmed. Her chest heaving, her mind blank of all but wants, her body pressing closer, she rode the hand that promised such ecstasy. Then he ruined it by speaking. He dragged his lips from hers and nipped at her ear then moaned, "God in heaven, Maggie, you make me wild. I've tried to resist you but, God forgive me, I can't."

Maggie shook her head, his words piercing her passionate fog. He made it sound as if she were doing the seducing, but Maggie was quite certain it was the other way around. A good deal more of her ardor was snatched away in the face of sudden panic when she felt him invade her. She glanced down sharply, relief coursing through her when she saw that it was only his hand under her skirt, and she realized that it must be a finger he was inserting inside her. She wasn't certain she cared for the alien feeling, and certainly didn't like the panic it instilled in her. It suddenly came home to her that she was playing with a very dangerous fire.

"You're so tight," he breathed, sounding both awed and pleased.

Maggie wasn't sure what he was talking about, but did know she had to stop this. She squeezed her legs closed around his hand, trying to stop his movement. "My lord —"

"James," he reminded her, then silenced her with a kiss as he withdrew and inserted his finger again. The feeling was less alien this time, and he was again caressing her where it felt good — with his thumb, she thought — but Maggie resisted falling back into that mindless desire that had gripped her earlier.

"I want you to burn for me, too," he breathed against her lips, then licked her lower one and sucked it into his mouth.

"That is very nice, my lord," Maggie said a little breathlessly the moment her mouth was free again. "But . . ." She paused abruptly, because she had opened her eyes to find he had disappeared from view. She glanced down as his hands slid from between her legs and, instead, gripped her hips. He had dropped to his knees before her.

"Uh . . . yes. Well, I am quite flattered that youeeee!" She broke off on a squeal as his hands slid between her legs to caress her intimately once more. "Oh!" She swallowed, and tried to close her legs, but his body appeared to be in the way. "I . . . You really . . . Oh . . . It's nice that you want to make me . . . oh . . . yes . . . that *is* nice," she moaned.

"Yes. Burn for me, Maggie," he said. She shivered as his breath brushed against her thigh, her legs spreading farther of their own accord when he so urged. Then she went stiff as his head moved between her legs.

"What are you doing?" She jumped in alarm, nearly biting her tongue off as his mouth replaced his fingers. "Oh, no you mustn't!" Maggie grabbed at his hair and tried to tug him away. "You can't — You — Oh," she cried out as his teeth grazed her flesh, sending pleasure rippling through her. "Oh dear . . . that's . . . yes . . . I mean, no . . . no, you shouldn't . . . Oh, that . . . yes, that's nice too," she gasped. Giving up her hold on his locks, she curled her fingers around the edge of the desk and began to twist her head, her whole being centered on the sensations between her legs.

A knock at the door brought her back to earth with a thump. Stiffening and straightening, Maggie groaned as Ramsey again slid a finger into her. Legs trembling and chest heaving, she grabbed frantically at his head in a desperate bid to warn him, aware that he must not have heard the knock with her thighs pressed tightly to his ears. He ignored her panicked tug and grazed her again with his teeth. A gasp escaped her lips, for her body responded automatically with pleasure though her mind ballooned with horror as a second knock sounded at the door. Tugging viciously at his hair, she spread her legs farther to free his ears and opened her mouth to warn him.

Too late! She stiffened in horror at the sound of the door opening behind her. Panic like none she had ever before suffered raced through her, and Maggie abruptly released Lord Ramsey's hair. Brushing her skirts down to cover him, she quickly scooped the material of her gown back up over her shoulders, covering her breasts. Taking a deep breath, she turned to glance over her shoulder to discover who had entered.

CHAPTER EIGHT

"Lady Barlow," Lord Ramsey's butler announced, then blinked as he espied Maggie, seemingly alone. "I thought I heard voices. I just assumed Lord Ramsey was back from his walk and . . . in here," he said uncertainly. An elderly woman stepped into the room behind him.

"Ah . . . he, er, stepped out for a moment," Maggie murmured shakily. She straightened off the desk, and Ramsey, seeming finally to get the gist that they were no longer alone, eased away from her. He was still mostly under her skirts, and his position created an odd lump in the front of her gown, but Maggie was pretty sure that was hidden by the desk.

Glancing over to find the woman's eyes had narrowed on her, she raised a hand self-consciously toward her hair, freezing when it reached eye level and she saw that her right hand was completely black. Being a writer, she recognized at once what covered her hand, and her gaze shot to the desktop in alarm. The overset inkwell and the puddle of black ink surrounded by lighter hand-prints on the desk's surface told their own story. Maggie grimaced, then had a brilliant idea.

"He overset the ink and went to change," she said brightly, gesturing to the mess on the desk. "No doubt he shall return momentarily," she added, when Webster and the newly arrived woman continued to stare at her. Then, realizing that she was being extremely rude by keeping her back to them, Maggie eased her leg over Lord Ramsey's head and turned. A flush colored her face as she felt him shift behind her. He was still under her skirts, his body brushing against the backs of her legs, his breath blowing lightly against her bottom. Closing her eyes, Maggie tried to ignore the sensation, to forget that he was under there, with his cheek pressed against one of hers. She managed a strained smile.

"I am —"

"Margaret Wentworth," the other woman interrupted, and Maggie stiffened in surprise.

"You know who I am?"

"My nephew pointed you out when we

rode past in our carriage one day," the matron explained calmly. "It was your brother, Lord Wentworth, who saved my nephew during that nasty little war we had."

"Yes." Maggie yelped, kept by will alone from jumping as Lord Ramsey shifted behind her, his hands sliding up the backs of her thighs, grasping them lightly to help him keep his balance. She was quite positive he had not meant to reawaken the excitement he had been stoking earlier, but it happened anyway. The fires banked but not put entirely out by the arrival of Lady Barlow now danced once more along her nerve ends. Her nipples tingled.

Cursing her body for its complete indifference to the awkwardness of this situation, Maggie forced a smile, her mind working over the fix she and Ramsey were in. She had to get rid of the woman before James was discovered in this compromising position.

Dear God, what a scandalous discovery that would be! This woman would swoon, should she find her nephew under Maggie's skirts. Stuff it, Maggie felt rather like swooning herself. She could not believe she was in this fix. How had she got here?

Only you, Maggie. The words echoed through her mind and she groaned inwardly.

Then, her face began to redden at the vivid memory of James's head disappearing between her legs. Had she really allowed a man to do such disgraceful things to her?

Oh this was horrible! One visit to a brothel and she began behaving this way? This was too much even for her.

". . . and he died in so doing."

It took Maggie a moment to grasp what the woman was talking about. Oh, yes, her brother. His bravery. Gerald had always been a special . . .

Her thoughts died as she felt Lord Ramsey nudging at her legs, trying to urge them farther apart. Was the man insane? What the devil did he think he was doing? Surely he didn't think to continue their naughtiness with his aunt right here, crossing the room toward where Maggie stood! Fear of just that made Maggie's heart race in horror. Then her ankles were grasped firmly in two hands, and she gave a startled cry as she found herself slightly lifted, overbalanced, and dumped into the chair behind her. She caught a flash of Lord Ramsey's gray coat peeking out the front of her skirt; then the chair she sat in was tugged forward and she found herself tightly against the desk. Her skirt, with Ramsey still under it, was firmly under the desk.

201

"Are you all right?" Lady Barlow stared at her in amazement, and Maggie forced herself to smile.

"Yes. I, er, stumbled," she lied, then bit her lip as Lord Ramsey clasped her knees with his hands. She went still, waiting a moment before she was sure he had just been looking for a more comfortable position. No doubt it was crowded under there, and hot, and . . . She didn't even want to think about it.

"Where did my nephew go?"

Maggie blinked in answer to the question, then peered at Ramsey's aunt, her hands settling nervously on James's hat. "I am not sure, my lady. He did not say." Picking up the hat, she began to turn it slowly in her hand, then stilled as Ramsey gently pinched her calf. Apparently realizing he had her attention, he clasped her ankles and lifted and lowered her feet one after the other in a parody of walking. Obviously he was trying to tell her something.

Walking? she thought with a frown. *Walking. Moving.* "Leaving!" she cried.

"What?" Lady Ramsey regarded her blankly.

"I — It occurs to me that you must be weary and thirsty after your journey. Perhaps you would be more comfortable if we moved to the salon to await your nephew? We could have tea."

"That does sound lovely," Lady Barlow agreed. She turned toward the butler, who was already heading for the door.

"I shall arrange for it at once, my lady," Webster said.

Lady Barlow nodded, then turned back to Maggie. "Shall we?" she asked.

"Yes, of course." Pushing her chair back, Maggie stood, pulling her skirt with her away from Lord Ramsey. She didn't dare glance down at him, but simply started around the desk and across the room as Lady Barlow moved toward the door. The woman paused before opening it and glanced back, looking as if she were going to say something. She spoke then, amusement filling her eyes. "Did you intend to bring that with you?"

Glancing down, Maggie flushed. She still held Lord Ramsey's hat gripped in her hands. She was also still wearing his cloak clasped about her neck — which was probably the only thing that had saved her from being seen earlier tugging the top of her gown into place. "Nay. I shall just put it there on the desk," she agreed, turning to do so.

Hurrying back across the room, Maggie

started to set the hat on the desk, then reached to undo her cloak, only to pause when she caught sight of Ramsey's hand waving from beneath the desk. Peeking over her shoulder, she saw that Lady Barlow was waiting patiently beside the door. She knew the woman couldn't possibly have seen the waving male hand, but Maggie cast her a nervous smile anyway, then turned back toward the desk, "accidentally" knocking the hat as she did. It tumbled off the desk, landing on the floor behind it. Muttering something about being clumsy, Maggie hurried around to retrieve it, and knelt out of sight.

"You mustn't speak of your work to my aunt," Lord Ramsey whispered to her. "She has no idea what you do."

Maggie spared him an annoyed glance for thinking she would be foolish enough to mention any such thing. "Of course I won't," she whispered angrily, then snatched up the hat. Holding it up for Lady Barlow to see, she started to straighten. "Here it is. No harm done," she called. The last word came out as a gasp, for James had grabbed her hand and tugged her back behind the desk.

"And if she asks what you are doing here, simply tell her that I invited you for some rustication — a thank-you for your brother's sacrifice."

"That was my intention, my lord." Maggie seethed, tugging her hand free and raising the hat to set it on the desk. Straightening, she forced one last smile for Lady Barlow and hurried around the desk and across the room to join the other woman. "Shall we?"

She started to urge Lord Ramsey's aunt toward the door, but Lady Barlow stood firm and gave her a narrow look. For a moment Maggie thought the woman had determined something was afoot, but then she merely gestured to the garment Maggie wore around her shoulders.

Glancing down, Maggie gave a nervous laugh. "Oh, my, the cloak. No, I shan't need this indoors, shall I? I shall just leave it on the desk with the hat."

She turned away, but before she could cross the room, Lady Barlow caught her arm. Then she called out calmly in an overly loud voice, "I shall just wait in the salon."

Maggie glanced at her sharply, alarm coursing through her at Lady Barlow's crafty expression. Pulling the door open, the woman called out, "Do not be too long, dear." Then she slammed the door.

Eyes wide, Maggie opened her mouth to

say something, *anything* to warn Lord Ramsey of his aunt's trick, but Lady Barlow's hand was suddenly over her mouth. All Maggie could do was watch helplessly as the chair behind the desk screeched its way back across the floor.

"That was a close one," Ramsey murmured, brushing his suit jacket down as he straightened. Then he turned to look about for Maggie. He froze when he spied her and his aunt by the door. Maggie tried to convey her apologies with her eyes — just in case his aunt's hand over her mouth was not enough assurance that she had wished to warn him.

There was a bare moment of silence, then Lady Barlow removed her hand from Maggie's mouth. The woman propped both hands firmly on her hips and her disapproving eyes settled on her nephew. "I am shocked, James! Just shocked! And ashamed. How could you possibly take advantage of an innocent in your care? And she's the very sister of the man who saved your life then asked, with his dying breath, that you look after her. Is this how you repay his valiant act?"

"Oh, really, my lady, this is not all his fault," Maggie exclaimed, rushing to defend him. Lord Ramsey was presently squirming with guilt under his aunt's righteous indignation. Maggie's attempted defense obviously helped him past his finer feelings. Straightening, he nodded and said, "She's is right. This isn't as bad as it appears. She isn't as innocent as you may think."

Maggie's gasp was matched by Lady Barlow's. Both women gaped at Ramsey in horror at his unchivalrous words. He immediately attempted to soothe them. "I just mean that Maggie — er, Margaret — is not some young child who needs protecting," he said to his aunt, then started around the desk toward them. "She is a full grown —" He paused uncertainly when his aunt made a strangled sound.

Maggie glanced at the woman with concern, then followed her attention to James's fawn-colored trousers — mostly fawn-colored trousers, she corrected with mounting horror. Dear God! There was a very distinct handprint on his groin.

Glancing down, himself, James gave a choked gasp and promptly covered the spot with both hands. "I, er . . . ." His gaze shot to Maggie, then away. "I spilled the ink," he excused himself, backing around the desk until it hid that portion of his body from view. Clearing his voice then, he asked, "Now, where was I? Oh, yes. Maggie. She is a full . . . er . . . grown, red-blooded woman."

"Blue-blooded!" Lady Barlow snapped, apparently recovered from her shock. "She is a full grown lady of nobility. She deserves more respect than this. In fact, she *deserves* a proposal."

Maggie supposed she shouldn't have been stunned by those unexpected words, but she was. And James appeared to be, too. He also looked horrified. The man had turned a sickly shade of gray-green she had never seen before, and Maggie felt her heart slip down into the vicinity of her borrowed shoes. She had told herself not be attracted to him. She had known that there could be no future with a man who thought so poorly of her career choice. But that was before their shared passion here in the library. To see him cringe now in such blatant aversion at the very suggestion of marriage to her . . . She felt shame overwhelm her.

"Oh, now . . ." James held up his hands and gave an extremely nervous laugh. "There is no need to, er . . . You cannot expect me to . . ." He paused and turned to the door with relief as another knock sounded. "Yes?"

Lady Barlow's tug on her arm was the only thing that kept Maggie from being hit by the opening door. The older woman moved to the side, taking Maggie with her, then the butler addressed James from behind the door now hiding them from view.

"Oh, you are back, my lord. There is a man here to see you. He says it is quite urgent."

"Aye. It is," another voice interrupted shortly. "Very urgent, and very private."

"Johnstone!" James was shocked to see the man. And not entirely happy, either, Maggie noted with disinterest. He glanced from the visitor to Margaret and his aunt.

"Aye, m'lord," the other man said, then addressed Webster. "Ye see, he does know me, and he really needs to hear what I have to say, so ye can be back about yer business." A short, stout man's back appeared; apparently Johnstone was being forced to slide past the butler to get into the room.

"Very well," Webster said slowly, not sounding entirely sure of himself.

Sighing in relief as the door closed behind the butler, the other man turned to Lord Ramsey and promptly crossed the room. He obviously didn't see Maggie and Lady Barlow, and blurted, "We've made a terrible mistake, my lord. Just terrible."

"Johnstone, I do not think this is the time —" James began, furtively looking to where

209

his aunt and Maggie still stood by the door, but the man didn't let him finish.

"You will when you hear this. Lady Margaret isn't Lady X after all!"

"What?" Lord Ramsey's startled yelp evidently covered the gasps of both women, and Mr. Johnstone didn't hear them. The man stopped before the desk, nodding his head. "It's true. She isn't. Lady X is still at the brothel, working. Lady Margaret wasn't there to 'ply the trade.' She was —"

"You thought I was Lady X?" Maggie shrieked. Her pain of a moment before turned to outrage.

Ramsey's eyes shot to her and widened, but Maggie started furiously forward, his outraged aunt on her heels. Apparently Johnstone's announcement had scattered James's thoughts; he gave her a look as if he didn't know who she was. Mr. Johnstone, of course, hadn't known she was there. The man turned to gape at her in horror.

"Oh, now, Margaret," Lord Ramsey began apologetically.

"You thought I was a prostitute?" Maggie repeated coldly as she stopped before him.

"Well, you *were* in a brothel," he pointed out reasonably. Maggie stiffened. She narrowed her eyes, then offered James a rather empty smile.

"Oh, of course. Perfect reasoning, my lord. And so were you. Are you a prostitute, too, then?" she asked caustically. Widening her eyes as if in surprise she cried, "But wait! I was in a men's club last week. Does that make me a man? Oh! And I fell into the river once. Does that make me a fish? And what if I go into the stables, does that make me a horse? Or a stable-boy?" She screwed up her mouth with displeasure. It was the only warning she gave before she yanked her skirts up and kicked him in the shin. Hard.

Cursing, Ramsey grabbed for the injured appendage with one hand and began hopping up and down even as he reached out toward her with the other. "I —"

"I do not wish to hear it, my lord. There is nothing to say. This explains *everything.*" Turning on her heel, she sailed angrily across the library, only to pause abruptly at the door when Webster appeared there. Lord Mullin was at his side. Ignoring the butler, Maggie turned abruptly on Ramsey's unsuspecting neighbor.

"I suppose you thought I was Lady X, too?"

"Oh, well," Robert stammered, then fell into silent bewilderment as he realized the meaning behind her question. When Maggie propped her hands on her hips and began to angrily tap one foot, he managed to shake himself out of his stupefied state and ask, "You mean, you aren't?"

James could have told his friend that would be the wrong answer, but the other man learned soon enough; Maggie tugged up her skirts and kicked him in the shin. As she had done to him, she left Robert cursing and hopping about on one foot, then pushed past an amazed Webster to storm straight across the hall to the salon. She slammed its door behind her with a crack loud enough that James was sure it was heard in every corner of the manor.

He straightened slowly with a wince to stand on both legs again, and glanced at his aunt. She peered from him to the closed door across the hall, then back again, her expression one of gross disapproval.

"Now, Aunt Viv —" he began, determined to redeem himself in her eyes, but instead let out a curse as his relative, too, wrenched up her skirts and kicked him in the shin. Leaving him imitating a stork once more, the woman whooshed across the library to the door. Lord Mullin had learned his lesson by that point, and was quick to limp out of her way. She stormed out of the room.

"Are ye all right, m'lord?" Johnstone asked, moving to James's side with concern. James rubbed his abused shin in an effort to ease the pain there, then waved the man off. He limped around his desk to drop into his seat.

"Ye might want some ice on that, m'lord. They both gave ye quite a wollop. Shall I fetch yer butler back to find ye some?"

"Back?" James glanced up to see that Webster had apparently decided it behooved him to vacate the scene. Robert, on the other hand, had come up to the desk. He wasn't looking too pleased.

"No," James told Johnstone, waving away the suggestion of fetching Webster back with ice. Ignoring his friend's irritation for a minute, he felt below his kneecap with a wince. Damn; both women had managed to hit the exact same spot! And they hadn't held back in the kicking, either. He was definitely going to have a bruise from this business. Which reminded him of the matter in question.

He asked the runner, "If she isn't Lady X, what was she doing at the brothel?"

"She was there to interview Madame Dubarry's girls for an article," Johnstone explained. At Ramsey's sharp glance he added, "She is G. W. Clark."

"G. W. Clark!"

James gave up on his leg and sank back weakly in his seat. His eyes went to Lord Mullin, who had just spoken, then passed him to settle on the still-open door of the library. His aunt was standing outside the salon, apparently hesitating to intrude on an upset Maggie's flight. Her delay had allowed her to overhear Johnstone's announcement, and she was now gaping at them in shock. Realizing James had spotted her, she turned abruptly and entered the salon, banging the door shut behind her.

"Aye." Johnstone's voice drew James's attention back. The Bow Street runner was smiling crookedly. "It took me by surprise, too."

"Are you sure?" James asked with a frown. "I mean, there is no mistake? You were so sure before that she was Lady X."

The runner grimaced apologetically. "I know, m'lord, and I apologize for me error. However, all the facts did seem to point that way, if ye'll recall, and even you believed it. Then, when you found her in that sheer red gown, her full, round breasts visible right through it —"

"I recall, Johnstone," James interrupted curtly. He also recalled that the man had been taken with the gown and all it revealed.

"That did convince me she was Lady X. The mask didn't hurt, either."

"Aye. And she didn't even have any bloomers on. Her lower half was —"

"Johnstone!" James snapped, killing the gleam in the other man's eye. He then turned his wrath on a chuckling Robert, not appreciating his friend's amusement at all. Once the other man managed to curb his laughter, James turned back to the runner. "All of that being the case, how can you be so sure she is not Lady X now?"

The man shifted uncomfortably, then straightened his shoulders and reported, "Ah, well . . . the afternoon after you left for here with her, there was quite a titter about Lady X. It seems she had a rather nasty little tantrum and refused to see any more customers after Lord Hastings. I thought it was a cover for the fact that she was missing, thinking Lady Margaret was Lady X as I did. But then the news got out that Dubarry was able to soothe her by offering more money. X was back in business by that night.

"Well, I thought sure *that* news was wrong — since you were supposed to have her. So, I went to Dubarry's to see what was what." The runner grimaced. "The old broad wasn't pleased to see me, as you can imagine. It seems your not showing up for your allotted half hour was part of the reason for Lady X's snit. But I handed her some cash — it's in this bill here. . . ." He paused to retrieve a piece of paper and hand it to James, then quickly continued as James scowled at the amount in question. "Anyway, I greased old Dubarry's palm, and she let me talk to a couple of the girls. There was one named Maisey. I suspected she had some information I might use, and I took her up for a roundabout and learned from her that G. W. Clark had interviewed her and the other girls the night before.

"She was rather proud of the fact, really, eager to announce that G. W. Clark was a lady of the nobility. She said that a visit by the lady in question's betrothed made her sneak out the window in disguise, and that they had switched clothes. She showed me the gown Lady Margaret traded her, and I recognized it as the one Lady Margaret had been wearing when she entered the brothel. When I asked her what the lady had obtained of hers, she said one of her best sheer red nighties — and a red mask. Had anyone seen the lady, Maisey said, they would have been sure she was Lady X. She thought it a grand joke."

"You learned this last night?" James asked

sharply. "Why didn't you ride out here at once with the news?"

"Well, after the last debacle, I wanted to be right certain, didn't I?" Johnstone shifted uncomfortably. "So, after I finished with Maisey I hung about hoping to catch a glimpse of Miss X, herself. I stood in the shadows of the hall forever. It wasn't until her last client left that I caught a glimpse of her. She *was* wearing a red mask, but it weren't plain like that one Lady Wentworth had on. It had fancy feathers and whatnot all over it." He paused to shake his head dolefully.

"I should have realized that someone as successful as Lady X would have more expensive duds. I'm usually good with such details." He heaved a breath at missing what he considered to be a telling detail, then continued, "At any rate, with the mask and all, I couldn't see her features — but I *could* see that she was definitely shorter than Lady Wentworth. She is also a lot . . . fuller." He gestured to his chest area. "Up top. Cannonballs, m'lord — in comparison to Lady Wentworth's apples, if ye know what I mean."

James scowled. He didn't care for the lady's chest being referred to as apples.

217

Especially not when he'd had a taste of them.

"Apples with cinnamon, hmm?" Lord Mullin murmured with obvious amusement. It drew James's irritation away from the runner. He glared at his friend, greatly regretting the way he had ranted on about Maggie's nipples the night before. Dear Lord, he had been describing her in great detail, and she was a lady. *Oh, hell!*

Closing his eyes, he rubbed his forehead, frustration overwhelming him. This was the last thing he'd expected. It was bad enough when he'd thought he had promised to look after a lady of ill-repute, but now to have kidnapped, then ravished her, as he very nearly had, only to learn she wasn't a lady of ill repute at all . . . Why, it was scandalous! He had acted horribly. Gentlemen did not behave so.

"G. W. Clark," he muttered, his mind running over the conversations he'd had with Maggie earlier. Lady Margaret, he corrected himself sternly. She had said she'd met Lady Dubarry through her brother indirectly, that he himself had quite enjoyed the way she was now making her living.

At the time, James had thought she meant Gerald enjoyed the pleasures offered by the ladies of the brothel — just as he had thought she enjoyed plying the trade. This news cast a different color on things. He could recall that the man was forever writing letters, either to his sister or his man of affairs.

James had read G. W. Clark's articles with great interest and amusement before the war, but not during. He'd heard Clark had gone off to fight, too, and had continued writing, basing his articles on his wartime experiences. James had not been able to obtain those articles published while he was away, but he now suspected that if he had, he would have recognized many of the stories.

Maggie had obviously continued them after Gerald's death, effectively taking his place. What a clever little minx she was, he decided, his mind going over the scandalous articles of late. "A Night with the Rakehells," had been one of them. It had caused quite a stir among the men and women of the ton to have so many of their naughty little secrets published. How the devil had she managed that? Obviously she had either paid for the information, or she had disguised herself and infiltrated the clubs. The clever little puss.

Lord Mullin's sudden clearing of his throat reminded James that he had been seated, lost in thought, for a goodly portion of time. Gathering himself, he rose abruptly to his feet. Starting around his desk, he said, "I will settle your account in a moment, Johnstone. In the meantime, why don't you have a drink? You must be thirsty after your journey here. Robert, show him where the port is, please."

"Certainly," Robert answered. "But, James?"

Irritated with this delay, James paused in the door to glance back. "Yes? What is it?"

"I was just wondering why your aunt is angry? I realize Margaret is upset at our mistaking her for Lady X, but why did your aunt kick you? Could it be that you were caught red-handed . . . Or should I say black-handed?" he added, his gaze dropping.

James didn't bother to look down. He knew Robert was referring to the handprint on his groin and — despite the guilty flush now suffusing his face — he stood a little straighter. "I knocked the inkwell over."

"Did you?" Robert asked. For the first time, James realized Robert wasn't simply annoyed with him over the mistaken identity business; he was furious. Which became clear as the man continued, "I don't know, it looks like a handprint to me. A woman's hand. You are the investigator, Johnstone; what do you think?"

"I noticed Lady Margaret's hand was ink-covered," the runner answered quietly.

"So did I. She does seem to have a tendency to muck her hands up a bit, doesn't she, James? Oh! What is that I hear?"

James frowned at his friend's sarcastic tone. "I don't know. What is it?"

"Wedding bells, I should hope."

James winced at his friend's harsh tone, but merely turned away and crossed the hall to the library. It was the second mention of marriage in less than an hour. His aunt and Robert both seemed to think he should marry the girl. Marriage to Maggie.

He let that thought touch his mind, then quickly pushed it away to be considered later. First things first, he told himself. At the moment, he wasn't even sure she would speak to him. He suspected it was going to take a lot of swift talking to get her to that stage, and he supposed he had better get to it.

Straightening, he took a deep breath then opened the door and stepped into the salon. His mouth was already open, ready to spew the first "I'm sorry" as he glanced around the room in search of the two women. It closed just as quickly when he realized that

the salon was empty. Both women were
gone.

"Webster!" He called, turning away and
starting to the hall. "Webster!"

CHAPTER NINE

Maggie was muttering under her breath. Most of that muttering was about Lord Ramsey, of course. He had thought her a prostitute, for heaven's sake! And so had Lord Mullin. They had thought her Lady X!

Well, all right, so she had been wearing a red mask and that horrid see-through red gown on their first meeting. And, okay, so that first acquaintance had taken place in the hallway, outside a boudoir of a brothel. Still, did she look like a prostitute?

Apparently she did.

And, she supposed, she had behaved no better than one today, allowing him to take such scandalous liberties with her. It was no wonder he'd been horrified at the idea of marrying her. She'd behaved no better than a tart and who wanted a tart to wife?

She flushed with a combination of shame and remembered passion as she recalled those heated moments in the library. His caresses had been liquid fire on her skin, and his kisses . . . Maggie could almost feel his lips moving over her breasts now, closing over her nipples, brushing up her thighs, nibbling at —

"You have gone quite flushed. Are you overly warm?"

The question was as effective as a pail of icy water being poured over her head. Maggie sat upright at once. Her expression stiffened, her eyes shooting to the plump, elderly woman seated across from her. Lady Barlow. Lord Ramsey's aunt.

Maggie had sailed out of the library, into the salon, and straight through, using the glass doors that led out onto the terrace overlooking the gardens to exit the room and the house itself. She had hurried for the stables, then — with every intention of stealing a damn horse if she must — to make her escape from Ramsey. Her only thought had been to quickly get as far away as she could from the site of this humiliation.

She had been so furious and caught up in her scattered thoughts that she hadn't realized that Lady Barlow — noting her absence from the salon and espying her furious flight for the stables — was hurrying after her. The older woman had caught up halfway between the house and Maggie's destination. When the woman had grabbed her arm, drawing her to a halt and asking anxiously where she was going, Maggie had not even hesitated to admit her intention.

Lady Barlow had hesitated, her gaze moving between Maggie and the house; then her expression had firmed. She'd turned Maggie around, urging her back the way they had come. But instead of marching her back into the salon, she had urged her past the glass doors and around the building to a carriage parked in the drive of Ramsey mansion. The carriage they were sitting in now.

Lady Barlow's footmen had been in the process of unloading several large, ungainly chests from the top of her vehicle, but the woman had ordered them replaced, announcing that she would not be staying after all. They would return to London at once.

The panting, sweating men had goggled briefly between their mistress and the half dozen trunks they had just managed to heft down, then had grumbled as they set to replacing them. Satisfied, Lady Barlow had urged Maggie into the coach. The two had waited silently while the vehicle shook and rolled slightly as all the chests were returned to the top and strapped down. Neither relaxed until everything had been put back in place and the carriage set out, rolling away from Ramsey. They had ridden in silence until now.

"Thank you, no. I am quite comfortable, my lady." Maggie managed a smile for the old woman across from her. Lady Barlow *looked* like an aunt, she decided. One of those soft, round, sweet-faced older ladies who would spoil her nieces and nephews, children, and grandchildren equally. She was probably kind to everyone, Maggie thought and felt dismay rumble through her as she realized the woman had heard everything. Lady Barlow knew that James had mistaken Maggie for a prostitute, and not just any prostitute, but the infamous Lady X. It was anyone's guess what the older woman thought of this whole debacle.

Lord Ramsey's aunt cleared her throat. "Are you really G. W. Clark?"

Maggie gave a start. "What? How . . . did you know?"

"I overheard that Mr. Johnstone person tell my nephew so, just before I entered the salon and found you gone."

"I see." Maggie shrugged. She supposed Lady Barlow's knowing was no worse than James's knowing. "Yes. I am G. W. Clark."

"Oh," the older woman said happily, her face brightening. "I have read every one of your articles. They are marvelous. So interesting and entertaining and —" She shook her head. "I can hardly fathom that you are a woman."

Maggie's mouth quirked, though she told herself she wasn't offended by the comment. No doubt most people would be shocked to learn that the intrepid G. W. Clark was a woman. No one would expect the reporter who wrote exposés on several of the most popular men's clubs, gambling hells, and brothels to be a female.

"How do you get your information, my dear? My goodness, those articles on the experiences of war . . . Well, they were so detailed. So realistic. One would almost believe you had actually been there, in the midst of the madness and the fighting, smelling the stench of charred and rotting flesh, hearing the screams of the injured and the moans of the dying."

"Yes, well, my brother wrote those. He was the original G. W. Clark. I have only taken over since his death."

"Ah." Lady Barlow nodded. "You are quite good. I did not even notice a difference in the writing."

"I try to stay as close to my brother's style

227

as I can," Maggie explained. "I did not wish anyone to be aware of the fact that any sort of change had taken place, so I studied his work carefully before I attempted to draft my first article. I even had to write and rewrite it several times before it was quite perfect. Actually, maintaining his voice is the hardest part; gathering the information is a breeze in comparison."

"Really?" Lord Ramsey's aunt asked with fascination, then beamed. "I must say, I quite enjoy the articles. Everyone does. They are quite the talk of the ton."

"Thank you," Maggie said with real pleasure. This was the first time she had received comment on her work. It was one of the problems with writing incognito: one did not receive praise for one's endeavors. Oh certainly one heard others' thoughts in a secondhand sort of manner, when one came across the topic at teas or such, but . . .

"Good Lord!"

Maggie focused on the woman across from her in concern. The matron's eyes had widened in a sort of horror. "Is there something wrong, my lady?"

"No. Yes. I just realized . . . That article, my dear, on what men get up to in the lesser gambling establishments, exposing the tricks and traps Drummond was using to rob them blind? It was published after your brother's death, but surely you did not —"

"Yes," Maggie interrupted with a sigh. "I did visit Drummond's establishment a time or two."

"But . . . how?"

"I disguised myself as a servant and slipped inside."

"They have female servants in those . . . places?"

"Certainly," Maggie informed her promptly. Then, beginning to feel a bit uncertain, she added, "Well, the two I went to did, at any rate." It had never occurred to her that they might not, and things had gone without a hitch — other than an unpleasant moment or two where clients had been overly friendly to the servant they thought her. She'd had to be quick to avoid the gropings and such, but she had handled it well enough. Her surprise at the rudeness of men in such places had quickly faded.

"So . . . how did my nephew come to the mistaken conclusion that you are the infamous Lady X?"

"You know her?" Maggie asked.

"Of her, yes. Everyone in London has heard the whispers." The woman tilted her head. "Is that what your next article is about? Exposing Lady X?"

"No!"

"Whyever not, my dear? All of London is a-twitter about that woman. Exposing her would be quite a coup."

Maggie frowned at the suggestion. "I do not like to go after individuals. I do not wish to harm anyone."

Lady Barlow's eyebrows shot up. "But, my dear, what was that article on Drummond, if not an attack on an individual?"

"Yes," Maggie agreed. "But that was because he was ruining the unsuspecting. He served them alcohol with laudanum, then robbed them blind with his crooked tables. He had to be stopped. Men were losing whole fortunes. But Lady X . . . well, she is hurting no one except perhaps herself. Besides, having to make a living in a less-than-approved fashion myself, I cannot look down on how she does it. Nay." She shook her head firmly. "Even did I know her identity, it would be safe in my keeping."

"Oh." Lady Barlow looked terribly disappointed. She had apparently rather hoped for such an article. She got over it quickly, though, and sat up a little straighter, a determined expression entering her eyes. "So tell me then, if you are not investigating Lady X, how did my foolish nephew come to the mistaken conclusion that you were she?"

"Oh." Maggie flushed. "Well, while I was not investigating Lady X, I *was* investigating brothels in general — and Madame Dubarry's ladies in particular. I thought it would be interesting to find out what men sought there and how the girls themselves feel about it."

Amusement curved the older woman's face. "Well, my dear, what the men seek there is really rather obvious, is it not? My, you are naive, aren't you?" she added when Maggie became flustered. "Five minutes in your company should have been more than enough to disabuse my nephew of his foolishness. Unless . . ." Her eyes widened incredulously. "Never tell me that you dressed as a servant and went to Dubarry's."

"Nay," Maggie assured the matron quickly. "Actually, I wore a black gown and thick black veil to interview the, er, ladies. But I fear there was some small difficulty getting out." Then Maggie reluctantly explained about Maisey hiding her in the cupboard and her own attempt to escape, only to be forced to hide by Frances's arrival, then Maisey's extortion of her dress.

Lady Barlow was laughing so hard by the

231

time Maggie finished, there were tears in her eyes. "Oh dear. Well, I suppose James can be forgiven his initial mistake. Still, it should not have taken him long to sort it out once to Ramsey. And I must say, my dear, you took a horrible risk with your reputation."

"Yes," Maggie agreed. "I am always taking horrible risks with my reputation for these articles. However, I . . . ."

Lady Barlow seemed to guess her dilemma. "Surely your brother left you well settled?"

Maggie grimaced. "He willed me his town house in London and enough money that, combined with what my mother bequeathed me on her death, if invested carefully, I could live the rest of my life quite comfortably. Frugally, but comfortably. Unfortunately, it is not enough to keep all the staff, and when it comes to deciding who to let go, I simply cannot do it."

"Ah, yes, that can be difficult." Lady Barlow nodded sympathetically. "In the end, that sort of decision comes down to necessity."

"I rather thought so, too," Maggie admitted. "So I cannot get rid of any of them."

The older lady blinked. "How so, dear?"

"Well, Banks — he is the butler and man

of affairs, and he has served our family forever. He is too old to find work elsewhere, yet too young to retire. His job is very necessary to him, so I cannot release him. And Cook, well, she has children to support. She is a widow, you see, so I cannot put her out. The housekeeper is alone as well. Her job is very necessary to her well-being. Then there is Mary, my maid, and . . . Why, we grew up together! She is planning on marrying John, the stable lad. Well, I suppose he is too old now to call a lad, but they depend upon the wages, and as they plan to marry, I could not possibly put either of them out. And of course there are Mary's sisters, Joan and Nora. They are housemaids. I could hardly keep Mary but throw her sisters out! The three were orphaned around the same time as I was and must rely upon me now. Their little brother, Charles, works in the stables with John, and I can hardly release him and split up the family, you see? So it is all a matter of necessity. They all need their jobs. And it falls on me to be sure they each have one."

Lady Barlow stared, aghast, through her explanation, then blurted, "But, my dear, if you cannot afford them —"

"That isn't *their* fault, and they are all

excellent workers," Maggie announced firmly.

"Well, yes . . . But you could give them a good reference. Perhaps help them find alternate positions."

"Oh, I could not do that," Maggie exclaimed with horror. "It would be like splitting up a family. These servants were all originally at our country estate. When our parents died, Gerald purchased the town house and decided to spend most of his time there. He handpicked the staff he would take with him. I grew up with all these people. Why, Banks was our butler in the country. He used to trip over my toys when I was a tot. And Cook used to sneak me sweets. And . . . Well, I grew up with Mary. They are family."

"I see," Lady Barlow murmured. Her forehead crinkled in agitation.

"Yes. I must keep them all together. And writing for the *Express* has allowed me to do that. It is the only way," Maggie said with certainty.

Lord Ramsey's aunt eyed her consideringly, then asked in a gentle voice, "Your brother was the last of your family, my dear, wasn't he?"

"Aye. Other than my cousin."

"Your cousin?"

"Victor. He inherited Gerald's title and Clarendon, the country estate, since it was the seat of the title," Maggie explained.

"Ah." Lady Barlow nodded, then asked delicately, "Could he not assist you? Perhaps he could take some of the servants back to the estate."

"Hmmm. I have thought of that. And he might be able to help. If they ever find him."

"Find him? Is he lost?"

"He went to America to make his fortune. The solicitor has men out looking for him, but it takes a while, you understand."

"Ahhh," Lady Barlow mused. Then she asked curiously, "If he isn't found, or isn't interested, or is found to be dead, would you inherit?"

"I am not sure. The title has always gone to the next male."

"Yes, but that is rather antiquated, my dear. After all, Elizabeth ruled the English throne for fifty years some two hundred years ago."

"Aye, but she was an exception. She never married and so was able to keep her power. Had she married, most of the power would have gone to her husband."

"It didn't go to Mary's Philip."

"He was a foreigner. We could hardly have had a Spanish king of England," Maggie pointed out. "Had she married a solid English cousin, things would have been different."

"Well, perhaps," Lord Ramsey's aunt conceded. "Men are so foolish with their laws."

"Hmm. Terribly greedy about power, are they not? I often wonder what they fear will happen when we gain it."

"That we should prove ourselves smarter than them, of course."

Her eyes wide, Maggie swallowed a bubble of nervous laughter that Lady Barlow did not miss.

"You doubt me? It is true. God gifted men with greater physical strength, but balanced it out by granting us greater intelligence." Spotting Maggie's doubtful expression, she asked, "Which creature would you say is physically stronger — the cat or the dog?"

"The dog. Well, most dogs."

"Which is smarter?"

"The cat."

"Just so."

"Oh?" Maggie felt uncertain. "Are you saying that men are dogs and women are cats?"

"Basically, yes, dear. Men are big, dumb creatures who lope about with their tongues hanging out. Nothing more ambitious on their minds than sniffing any likely bitch's behind."

Choking with scandalized amusement, Maggie covered her mouth. "And women?" she got out after a moment of struggling with her intense need to laugh.

"Well, I don't know about you, but I have encountered some pretty catty women in my time," Lady Barlow confided.

They both burst out laughing. Their mutual amusement faded after a moment; then the two sank back in their respective seats with small sighs.

Maggie eyed the older woman with fascination for a moment, then asked, "Do you count your nephew as a stupid dog, too?"

Lady Barlow's mouth puckered sourly. "The man who thought you a prostitute?"

Maggie was silent for a moment, then, much to her own amazement, found herself defending him. "That was not entirely without good cause. I was rather dressed up as one, and in a brothel, when he met me."

Lady Barlow made a face. "Oh, yes. No doubt he could be excused for it at first, but you were in his home for . . . How long was it? Two days?"

"Four days, actually, but only two with him in attendance."

"Plenty long enough for him to have realized that there was something wrong with his assessment. Of course, he might have been investigating further from what I saw."

"You saw?" Maggie echoed in a squeak of alarm.

The older lady smiled wryly. "I saw enough to know what was going on. Your hair was disheveled, your lips swollen, your eyes slightly glazed, and your gown off your shoulder . . . It was gaping open in front when Webster opened the door to the library to announce me! You recovered with commendable aplomb, though," she added to ease Maggie's mortification. "But did you really think that I wouldn't notice that my nephew was skulking around under your skirts . . . Or that I might believe it was for some *good* purpose?"

"You knew that, too?" Maggie asked in horror. She had rather hoped the woman thought he'd been skulking under the desk, not her skirts.

"Your state of dishabille and horrified glance downward were rather telling, my dear. Then, of course, when he crawled under the desk, I could see his feet and ankles." There was a brief pause, then the old woman finished, "I won't even mention that you left your fingerprints behind . . . quite literally."

238

Maggie bit her lip and glanced down at her knotted hands. She glanced up again only when Lady Barlow reached over to pat those hands reassuringly. "There is nothing to be ashamed of, my dear. It is obvious to me that, despite your adventurous career as G. W. Clark, you are quite naive when it comes to men. Your reactions have convinced me that you are still quite innocent. James, on the other hand, is anything but. He is quite experienced, and old enough to know better. Then again, he is a man, and men, like dogs, are easily distracted."

"Distracted?" Maggie asked in confusion.

"Yes. They can be the best of guard dogs one moment; then a pussy goes streaking across the lawn and off they go — tongue hanging out, ears flopping, caught up in the chase."

Maggie was silent for a moment as the image of Lord Ramsey rose in her mind. He was on his knees before her, his head burrowed between her legs. Then he lifted his head and smiled up at her, his features pointed and canine, his tongue lolling, his ears suddenly floppy dog ears.

"Dear God," she said under her breath; blinking her eyes open to see Lady Barlow's amused expression.

"I can tell that you have noticed the

resemblance. Never mind, my dear. He shall behave himself from now on. I shall see to it. After all, I too am grateful to your brother for saving my nephew's sorry hide, and I feel I owe it to him to look out for you."

Maggie smiled a little uncertainly at those words. It seemed she suddenly had no end of people wanting to look out for her.

She wasn't at all sure that was a good thing.

"It would appear that your aunt decided not to stay after all," Webster announced, his face expressionless. "She had her trunks reloaded and left. Lady Margaret went with her."

"Damn." James plopped into his desk chair at his butler's announcement. He had set the servants to the task of finding Margaret as soon as he'd discovered her missing. He had not been as concerned with his aunt's whereabouts. Now he knew where they both were, and his heart sank. Either woman was trouble enough on her own; together, the Lord alone knew what they might get up to.

Wincing at the possibilities, he considered the matter briefly, then stood. "I am returning to the city, Webster. See to the arrangements," he ordered.

After the man left to do as he was told, James turned to Johnstone. "You had best tell me everything you have learned about Lady Margaret. And about her writing as G. W. Clark."

CHAPTER TEN

The day was gray and gloomy, the overcast skies threatening rain. *Suitable,* Maggie thought irritably. It matched her mood. She should have been rather pleased with herself. She had entrusted her article on the brothel to her butler, Banks. He had delivered it to the *Daily Express* the day after her return.

As usual, Mr. Hartwick had read the article at once so that any editorial comments or revision requests could be returned via Banks. Much to her pleasure, the butler arrived home with the news that Mr. Hartwick was well satisfied. No changes were necessary, and the article would be in the next installment of the *Express.* That did gladden Maggie; however, it was the only thing that was going right of late.

It had been four days since she had returned from her imprisonment at the Ramsey estate. Maggie had spent most of that time alternately doing her best to avoid Pastor Frances and visiting every dress shop in London in search of a replacement for the sheer red nightie that Maisey had loaned her.

Much to her consternation, Maggie had thoughtlessly left the item behind when she had fled Ramsey. This was the second fruitless day she had spent trying to replace it: a terribly embarrassing effort. Snickers and wide-eyed looks of disbelief had been the general reactions as Maggie had tried to describe the frilly see-through outfit to various modistes. With each shop she chose, she became more disheartened — and less sure that she would ever be able to succeed in the quest.

The shop she had just left, however, was the worst. The proprietress had at first been indignant upon hearing the description of the article of clothing; then she had become angry and rude. She had finally interrupted Maggie's stammerings to announce that she didn't need her "sort" in her store. The woman had then shown her out. Which was enough for Maggie. She was finally willing to concede defeat.

Perhaps it was for the best, she decided as she headed home; the garment would likely cost more to replace than she had readily available at the moment. With luck, Maisey would agree to call things even. Maggie would not request a replacement of her gown — the one Pastor Frances had torn off of the young prostitute — and she hoped that Maisey would forgo requesting the return of hers. She suspected Maisey would agree readily enough. The girl could use the money Pastor Frances had given for replacing Maggie's garment to replace her own!

Unless she's already used it to buy me a new gown.

The thought popped into her head from nowhere, and Maggie fretted over it. Maisey really was not asking too much to wish her garment returned. Surely there were special shops for such items, ones of which she was unaware.

Perhaps there was an article for G. W. Clark there, she considered as she began to cross the street. But on second thought, while she herself found the subject interesting, her readers were likely looking for subjects of a racier nature.

With her thoughts distracted as they were, Maggie didn't see the carriage coming at her. It was a shout from somewhere off to her right, toward her town house, a warning, that made her glance around. She froze in horror upon seeing the vehicle bearing down on her. Maggie could practically feel the hot breath from the horses' noses and mouths before she was grabbed forcibly and pulled out of the way.

"Are you all right?"

"Yes, yes. Thank you. I —" Maggie released a gusty breath as she turned to her rescuer, then froze. It was none other than Lord Ramsey. Wonderful!

She hadn't seen James since fleeing Ramsey manor. She had received several letters from him since her arrival home; each had been sent back unopened. She wasn't ready to read what he had to say. She could have forgiven James the insult of his mistaking her for a prostitute, after all, the circumstances surrounding their first meeting *had* been unusual. However, that humiliation had been compounded by shame at what she had let him do to her, and mortification over his reaction to the idea of marrying her. On top of that, while Maggie had defended him to his aunt during the journey to London, that was before she'd had the opportunity to mull the matter over. It had occurred to her, once home, that while Lord Ramsey had been spouting all those fine sentiments about finding her an alternate career, he hadn't passed up the opportunity to take advantage of the situation himself.

She may have behaved shamefully, but he had behaved no better.

And, why hadn't he realized his mistake in believing her to be Lady X once he'd spent some time with her? Lady Barlow seemed to think he should have, and now Maggie did, too. The worst part was, despite her anger with the man — despite the insult, the shame and humiliation — just thinking about him was enough to send her pulse racing. And she couldn't stop thinking about him. The things he had done to her had been like nothing she had ever experienced. Her body had tasted ecstasy, and wanted more . . . Maggie wanted a man who had insulted and humiliated her and who, she was sure, was only now attempting to apologize because it was the "proper" thing to do and he wished to please his aunt. Which simply engendered even more shame in her. At the moment, her overriding feeling for the man was a burning resentment.

Realizing that her mouth was hanging open, Maggie closed it with a snap. "Oh, it is *you.*" Turning on her heel, she rushed across the street, leaving Lord Ramsey staring after her. As she expected, it did not take long before he collected himself and hurried in pursuit.

"Maggie," he began, grabbing at her.

"I did not give you leave for such familiarity, sir," she snapped, tugging her arm loose and picking up her skirts so that she could hurry along without tripping.

"Very well, Lady Margaret, then." He sounded a bit impatient — or was it shortness of breath as he chased after her? Not that Maggie cared much.

"I fear we have not been properly introduced, my lord, and ladies do not speak to *gentlemen* to whom they have not been introduced."

James winced at the acidity of Margaret's tone as she said the word *gentlemen,* then realized that he'd paused and she was getting away. They had reached the town house she had inherited from her brother. Even now, she was pushing through the gate and starting up the short walk to the door. He rushed after her. "Very well, my lady. Please allow me to introduce myself and —"

He stopped abruptly as she sailed into her town house, slamming the door in his face with a resounding crash.

"Apologize," he finished softly. Straightening his shoulders, he rapped determinedly on the door.

It wasn't answered promptly, so he rapped

again, a bit harder, then forced a pleasant smile to his face. The door opened, and out peered an elderly gentleman — one with the arrogant look of inquiry that could only be mustered by a butler of many years' experience.

"Yes?"

"Lord Ramsey to see Lady Margaret Wentworth," he announced calmly, producing his card.

The butler accepted the token but smiled blandly and murmured, "Lady Margaret is not in." He started to close the door on Lord Ramsey then, but James stuck his foot in the door.

His smile slipping, James said, "You had best check again, my good man. I know she is home. I just followed her here."

The butler's eyes narrowed superciliously, and he shook his head. "Nevertheless, she is not *in,*" he insisted, glaring at James's offending foot.

James opened his mouth to force the issue, then decided against it. He removed his foot, allowing the door to again be closed in his face. Scowling, he turned away and was pleasantly surprised to find his carriage waiting on the street outside the Wentworth gate. He had been on his way to his club when he spotted Maggie. Ordering

248

the driver to stop, he had leaped out to approach and had nearly reached her when he noticed the runaway carriage headed her way. It was just a matter of good fortune that he'd been there at the exact moment needed to pull her out of its path. Not that she was appreciative of his saving her from being run down. The woman had made it more than clear since returning to London that she wanted nothing to do with him. She had rejected a plethora of invitations from both him and his aunt, and not responded at all to his letters.

It was obvious that Lady Maggie Wentworth had no intention of allowing him to apologize. At least not in a forthright manner, he amended, walking to his carriage.

Once there, James commended his driver for having the sense to follow him without being so ordered; then he directed him to his aunt's. As they drove away, his gaze moved over the Wentworth town house.

If she would not agree to speak to him and allow him to make amends in a forthright way, that meant he would have to use trickery. To get a few words with the woman, he would have to be devious. Much to James's amazement, he was looking forward to the challenge.

■ ■ ■ ■

Maggie paused impatiently on the corner to allow several hacks to pass, annoyed despite herself. The day was lovely. The sun was shining, flowers were blooming, and a gentle breeze was blowing away the generally unpleasant smells of London. All of which had combined to make her decide on walking to Lady Barlow's rather than waste the money on a hack. Fortunately, the older woman's home wasn't far from her own.

She'd been invited to a ladies tea party by Lord Ramsey's aunt. Maggie had agreed to this invitation after politely making excuses to avoid the others for three reasons. First, James Huttledon might be many things, but he was not a lady; so she could be pretty sure he would not be in attendance. The second reason was quite simply that Maggie rather liked Lady Barlow. Ramsey's aunt was a charming woman, with a wonderful sense of humor, and Maggie had felt quite bad refusing her earlier invitations. The third reason Maggie was attending — despite the small risk of running into James before or after the tea — was Lord Barlow's library. James had first mentioned this colossal collection to her, but Aunt Viv —

as the woman had insisted Maggie call her by the end of their journey together — had described it much more thoroughly when Maggie had shown an interest on the way back to London. The noblewoman was not as enamored of the written word as her husband had been, and still referred to it as "Lord Barlow's library," but had still shown a good deal of pride in the collection. She had described it in vivid enough detail that Maggie had been dying to see it ever since. And in a very few moments, she was going to get that opportunity.

Squelching down the excitement the thought raised in her, she glanced along the row of town houses, idly noting the house numbers. It was then Maggie realized that she couldn't recall Lady Barlow's address. Fortunately, she had thought to bring the invitation along. Lifting her bag, she pulled the folded piece of paper out to check. She had just started to refold the invitation when she felt a hard knock in her back.

A choked cry of surprise slipping from her lips, she threw her hands out, trying to regain her balance or grab at something to steady herself — but there was nothing there. She glanced around wildly as she found herself crashing forward into the road. Maggie spotted the oncoming track at the same moment that her foot twisted beneath her.

She fell forward and to the side, her fingers clenching instinctively around the invitation to Lady Barlow's as she thrust out her hands in an effort to break her fall. Those efforts were too slow and her fall was too hard; her head slammed down, cracking smartly on the road. Pain exploded in her head, almost but not quite blinding her to the fact that she was about to be trampled to death. As she tried to roll clear, the last thing Maggie saw were the oncoming horses rearing and kicking. The last thing she heard was their panicked screeches. Then she slid into darkness.

The murmur of voices drew Maggie from unconsciousness. Unable to understand what was being said, but vaguely recognizing that she knew at least one of the speakers, Maggie moaned and slowly opened her eyes. She winced against the pain the light caused her. Everything was blurry at first, and she closed her eyes again instinctively in an effort to clear her vision.

". . . She 'ad this 'ere invite clutched in her 'and, and I didn't know where else to take 'er. I figured leastwise you'd know 'er people and where she belonged." Maggie

252

didn't recognize the voice that was speaking.

"Yes, yes, you did the right thing," another voice said. There was no mistaking it, and Maggie opened her eyes again slowly, confusion clouding her mind as hands gently brushed her hair from her brow and a dark face came into focus above her.

"James?" she murmured, positive she was dreaming. Or perhaps having a nightmare, she decided as she became aware of the vicious pounding in her head. She was forced to close her eyes again, for the bright daylight pouring into the room was unbearable.

"Yes. It's me. Are you all right? How is your head? You appear to have taken an awful knock."

"I did?" She couldn't recall. Squinting up at the man, she noted the concern on his face with some surprise, then glanced around as another voice spoke up.

"Yep. Ye sure did, ma'am. Near to knocked yer good sense out all over the road."

Maggie grunted and wearily closed her eyes. The speaker was not within her present field of vision, and she really didn't have the energy to sit up and search him out.

"Here you are, my lord." Maggie started at this third voice, her gaze finding a new

253

figure looming anxiously at Lord Ramsey's side. A servant, she saw, for he wore a butler's vestments.

"Thank you, Meeks." She saw James take a cloth from the man, dip it in a small bowl, and wring it out. He turned toward Maggie. She instinctively closed her eyes as he reached to lay it gently on her forehead.

What had happened? Maggie wondered, her mind taken up with trying to understand her surroundings. *Near to knocked yer good sense all over the road,* the man had said. Reaching up worriedly, she attempted to feel her forehead, but her hand encountered only the cool, damp cloth, then was grasped in what she was sure was James's own large, warm hand. It pulled hers gently away. "Just rest for now."

"Am I bleeding?" she asked, feeling suddenly weak.

"No. But you have a nasty bump."

"What happened?"

"Do you not remember?"

"No."

"Oh, well . . . ." James hesitated long enough that Maggie squinted over at him with concern, only to find that he wasn't looking at her; he was exchanging glances with the man out of her sight. Maggie tried to see the room's other occupant, but the moment she moved her head, a stabbing pain shot through it. Lying still seemed a more intelligent present course of action.

"It seems you fell while crossing the street," James volunteered.

"I did?"

"Nay," the other man spoke up then. "She didn't fall. She was pushed, I think. Right out in front of me carriage. Struck 'er 'ead real good, too, when she 'it the road. Knocked 'er right out. It's just luck, m'lady, that I was able to stop me 'orses. You were a hair away from being trampled. Still and all, ye knocked yerself something nasty. Nothing was waking ye up, neither. 'Ad you not been clutching this invite 'ere," — he raised his hand slightly, and by tilting her head just a fraction Maggie was able to spot to her right a crumpled and muddy piece of paper: the remains of the tea invitation she had been reading when she'd been knocked into the road — "Well, if it weren't for this, I don't know what I would 'ave done with ye. Couldn't just leave you there like that. It's lucky the coal man can read and saw that you was 'eaded 'ere."

Maggie managed by several small twists of her head to peer at the man speaking, her eyes widening as she recognized him and remembered. "I fell into the road." She

255

gasped, trying to sit up, only to have another wave of pain convince her to lie still a bit longer.

"Just rest there, Maggie. It is better, I think," James said.

"Maybe for a moment or so," she agreed.

"So," James said, staring at the carriage driver. "Did you happen to see who pushed her?"

"Well . . ." The man's mouth twisted doubtfully. "It all 'appened right quick."

"You just said she was pushed. Surely you saw who pushed her?"

"Well, not really. It was the way she stumbled out into the road what made me think she was pushed. Her upper body sort of flew out, dragging her feet behind, and she looked startled and alarmed, like she wasn't happy to find herself there."

"Surely you saw something? Think, man," Lord Ramsey ordered impatiently.

The fellow's face crinkled, his eyes closing in concentration. "There were three or four people directly behind 'er, but there was one fella . . . sort of criminal-looking, if ye know what I mean. 'E had these mean eyes and a nasty scar on 'is cheek. 'E was big. Strong-looking. And 'e disappeared right quick, too. Didn't stay to 'elp me carry 'er 'ere, either."

"Big, strong, mean eyes, and a scar," James repeated with obvious dissatisfaction.

"Aye. 'E 'ad dark 'air, too. Needed a cut in my opinion."

"Do you know anyone like that, Maggie?"

"No," Maggie said, but couldn't keep the uncertainty from her voice. She *had* seen a man with a scar somewhere . . . perhaps at one of the gambling hells of which she had been writing the exposé? There were a lot of men with dark hair, though. And scarred faces were not so uncommon. . . .

"A scar on his cheek, you say?" she asked.

"Aye. A big, wide one. Looked like a burn, maybe. It was kind of a square patch a little smaller than me 'and. It covered a good portion of 'is cheek."

Maggie frowned as a face flashed in her memory: a laughing man, placing a bet, then turning so that she saw just such a puckered scar on his cheek.

"What is it?" James asked sharply, taking in her expression. "Do you know someone like that?"

"No . . . I know no one like that. But I have seen someone fitting that description before, I think."

"So have I." When Maggie turned to him questioningly, James added, "The man driving the carriage that nearly ran you down two days ago was rather large and had dark hair and a scar."

Maggie stiffened. "Surely you are not thinking it was the same man? That either incident was on purpose?" When Lord Ramsey merely frowned, avoiding her eyes, alarm made her sit up despite the pain that stabbed through her brain. "Why would anyone wish to do me harm?"

James hesitated briefly, then met her gaze. "You *have* exposed a rather dastardly character or two with your artic —" His mouth snapped closed as Maggie's horrified gaze shot to the curious hack driver. He cleared his throat, then smiled widely at the man.

"We would like to thank you for your assistance in this matter, Mr. Lawrence. It was kind of you to bring Maggie to us. I realize we are taking you away from your business though."

Gripping the hack driver's arm, he led him toward the door.

Maggie watched them go and was sure she saw Lord Ramsey hand the man some money as they went. Wondering how she was to find out how much and replace it — she didn't want to be beholden to James for any reason — she slid her feet to the floor and sat up gingerly.

"Oh, my lady, maybe you should stay lying down for now," the butler Lord Ramsey had called Meeks exclaimed, catching the damp cloth as it slid from her forehead.

Forcing a smile, she started to shake her head, then breathed in sharply and hesitated. Perhaps the man was right.

"That's it," the butler said with relief as she sank back down. She glimpsed him dipping the cloth in the bowl of water, then closed her eyes. She heard him wringing it out and raised a hand self-consciously to her forehead, wincing as she brushed the lump forming there. She had barely removed her hand when the cloth was laid in place.

Opening her eyes, she glanced at Meeks, noting that his gaze had moved down her body with a small frown. Lifting her head the tiniest bit, she followed his eyes the length of her gown. She, too, grimaced in dismay. Her head wasn't the only thing that had been damaged in the fall; her gown was ripped and covered with filth. It had been her best gown, but was now quite ruined. With the one Frances had ripped off of Maisey, her wardrobe was dwindling at a rather rapid rate.

"My lady has a tincture for headaches," the butler announced, drawing Maggie's attention away from her disrepair. "Would you take some if I got it for you?"

"I . . . Yes, I think I should be very grateful for it," she murmured. Her head really was throbbing rather fiercely. She could hardly think through the pain.

"I shall be right back, then," he assured her. She heard a rustle indicating he had left. In the quiet that closed in around her, Maggie could hear the murmur of voices from somewhere outside. She supposed it was Lord Ramsey talking to the coachman, grilling the man on every single detail of what had occurred. Concern drifted through her at the thought. As befuddled as she was, it was not very difficult to put together that he thought the other day's near-miss was connected to this accident. She personally found it a bit hard to believe. Accidents happened all the time. She, of all people, knew that.

Only you, Maggie. Only you could get yourself into such a fix.

A soft footfall warned her that she was no longer alone, and Maggie opened her eyes. Espying Meeks moving to her side with a bottle and spoon, she removed the cloth from her head and eased into a sitting position. The butler opened his bottle and poured a quantity of its contents into the spoon. When he moved it toward her lips, Maggie automatically opened her mouth, feeling like a child. A second spoonful of Lady Barlow's tincture followed, and Maggie took that as well, then offered a slightly embarrassed, if grateful, smile to the man. "Thank you," she said as he recapped the lid.

"You are more than welcome, my lady. Shall I freshen that cloth for you?" he asked, setting the tincture aside.

Maggie hesitated, then shook her head. "Thank you, no. I think it has done all it can."

For a moment she thought he would insist, but then he nodded and held out his hand. When Maggie handed over the cloth, he set it down beside the bowl, then looked toward the door. She suspected he didn't wish to leave her unattended, and was touched by his concern. It was surprising that Lady Barlow herself hadn't yet come to check on her, but Maggie supposed she was busy with the guests of her tea party.

She peered down at her ruined gown and sighed inwardly. A cup of tea would be heavenly now, something sweet to settle her nerves. She seemed to be all a-tremble after her calamity, and knew that chamomile with extra honey would help. However, she could hardly join Lady Barlow and the other guests looking the way she did at the moment.

"You said that you saw that man before. It wouldn't happen to have been at Drummond's gaming hell, would it?" Lord Ramsey's voice rang out.

Maggie turned her attention away from her ruined gown to watch as the man returned to the room, his expression grim.

"I am not sure," she admitted slowly. "It was at one of the gaming hells, I think."

He nodded, as if he had expected that answer, and she saw he was putting two and two together. From the look on his face, he was coming up with his own version of four. James certainly seemed to like to think the worst of her. First she was a prostitute, and now she was the sort to engender murder in the heart of some nasty scarred man.

Maggie scowled at him. Meeks's tincture was taking effect already, the ache in her head slowly receding, but unfortunately her irritation with the know-it-all before her was rising. What the devil was Lord Ramsey doing here, anyway? This was supposed to be a ladies' tea. And he was definitely no lady — the proof of which had been pressed against her quite intimately in his library in the country.

Grimacing at her thoughts, she turned abruptly to the butler. "Could you ask Lady Barlow to join us for a moment?"

Meeks turned a blank expression to her. "Lady Barlow?" he echoed.

"Aye. I should like to offer my apologies for having to miss her tea party before I leave."

"Tea party?" the man murmured, obviously at a loss.

"It is all right, Meeks. You may get back to your duties," Lord Ramsey butted in.

Maggie turned from the confused man to James, but waited until the servant had left before speaking again. "Lord Ramsey," she said shortly. "Where is your aunt?"

CHAPTER ELEVEN

"Lord Ramsey."

James didn't answer at once, but glanced a bit wildly around the room, wondering how he was going to get himself out of this one. It had seemed such a good idea to trick her into coming here with that fake invitation to a ladies tea. Unfortunately, he hadn't considered that Maggie would be no more pleased by his deception than she'd been with any of his past exploits involving her. Now that he had her here, what the devil was he to do with her? His intention had been to apologize for his past transgressions, but James somehow didn't think she would be any more willing to listen to him now than she'd been in the past.

"I understood I had been invited to a *ladies* tea," Margaret said, drawing his gaze reluctantly back to her face. Yes. She was angry.

"Aye, well . . ." Feeling the hot flush of

guilt creep up over his face, he grimaced, then confessed: "My aunt is not here. This is her bridge day. I took advantage of that to —"

"There is no tea party," she interrupted. It wasn't a question, but he answered it as if it were.

"Well, no. At least, not one others will be coming to attend . . . but I had to talk to you, and since you are never at home when I call . . ." He paused to glare at her — he was not at all used to anyone not being *in* to him — and could still hardly fathom that she had chosen to disregard his attempts at communication. She should be grateful that he had taken the trouble. Apparently she didn't see it that way, however. Even as he stood there, she was making impatient noises and getting to her feet. His eyes widened in alarm, and he rushed forward as she wavered unsteadily.

"You should not be up. You should be resting," he said firmly. She impatiently shook away the hand he used to try to steady her.

"I should not be *here*. And I am fine — that tincture has done wonders for me." She snatched up her crumpled and slightly muddy hat from where it lay on the floor beside the settee, and James admitted reluctantly to himself that it was true. His

aunt's remedy had apparently been effica-
cious; Maggie was no longer pale or frail-
looking. In fact, she had quite a bit of color
about her right now, though he suspected
some of it was due to temper. In fact, as he
watched he became more certain that her
quick recovery was due entirely to her building ire.

"I am leaving."

James watched helplessly as she arranged
her hat so that it would not irritate her head
wound, but when she started toward the
door, he was moved to action. Rushing
forward, he pushed it closed and then
positioned himself firmly in front of it, arms
crossed over his chest. "You can't. Not until
we talk."

"I have no interest in speaking with you,
my lord," she said stiffly, trying to grab at
the doorknob. James immediately shifted to
cover it, and she glared at him impatiently.
"Pray, stand aside."

He did not mistake the order as the
request it was couched as, but James shook
his head. "Not until you have heard me
out."

"I see." Her eyes narrowed on him. "Then
you are holding me against my will? *Again?*"

"No, of course not. But —"

"Then please stand aside," she repeated

pleasantly.

He glared at her in frustration, then stepped out of the way. She immediately moved to open the door. Desperate to make her listen, James blurted, "I will tell everyone that you are G. W. Clark if you do not at least give me a moment of your time." That threat made Maggie pause, so he pressed his advantage: "And I believe that my past behavior proves that I am the sort to do anything I must to get what I want."

Turning from the now open door, she sniffed and peered at him with distaste. "All your past behavior has proven is that you are a fool, my lord. I have no intention of talking to you."

She turned to flee, but he stopped her with a hand on her arm, demanding, "Do you not fear my revealing your secret?"

"Ha! Hardly, my lord! You are too much of a gentleman to do such a thing."

James felt a spontaneous smile burst out on his face. Despite his shabby treatment of her, Maggie still thought him a gentleman. It gave him hope that with a little time and the right words he could repair things between them.

Apparently reading the renewed confidence on his face, Maggie muttered in vexation and whirled away to storm out into the

267

hall. James followed on her heels. "Maggie, if you would just allow me a word with you . . ."

She paused at the front door and turned, a tight expression on her face. "And what exactly would you wish to say, my lord? That you are sorry that I am not Lady X?"

"Yes!" He started to smile, then saw her eyes narrow and — recognizing that he had said precisely the wrong thing — quickly shook his head. "I mean, nay! I —"

Maggie didn't listen to what he had to say. She'd heard enough of Lord Ramsey's nonsense. It had been humiliating enough to have the man take advantage of her while thinking she was a prostitute, and to know that she still recalled the way his arms encircled her, the way his lips pleasured her . . . Now, to listen to the man's attempts at explaining himself was unbearable.

Dragging the door open, she hurried out and down the front steps. She had walked here and would walk home if necessary, though she would have preferred hiring a hack. Anger was carrying her forward, but Maggie knew she couldn't count on it to get her all the way home — especially not after her injury. Unfortunately, there didn't appear to be any hacks about just then. She considered sending for one, but the sight of Lord Ramsey rushing down the steps after her changed Maggie's mind. She turned and started walking. It wasn't so far to home, really; if she cut through the park, she could be there in a trice.

Bolting across the street, she started along the tree-lined pathways, doing her best to ignore the curious stares of people gaping at her muddy and torn gown. Lord Ramsey's chasing after her like one of Lady Barlow's "dogs after a pussy" was not helping her to be inconspicuous, either, she suspected.

She hadn't gotten far into the park when a sharp cracking sound made her start and glance around. It sounded like a branch snapping — a heavy one.

She paused, a frown sliding over her face as she raised a hand to feel carefully at her hat. In the next moment, her headgear was forgotten and Maggie was squawking in amazement as she was tackled from behind and thrown to the ground. Before she could quite grasp what was happening, Ramsey had thrown himself atop her and was rolling them both under the bushes that lined the path. Finding herself clasped close in his arms, his body pressing intimately down into hers, Maggie had to brace herself

269

against her body's eager response.

"My lord!" she screeched in mingled embarrassment and anger. She pushed frantically at his chest in a vain effort to remove his bulk.

"I am not trying to attack you, Maggie," he said with annoyance. Leaning away, he peered back out through the bushes. "Someone took a shot at you."

"A likely story," Maggie snapped. "Gerald neglected to mention your penchant for prevarication, my lord. First the tea party. Now someone trying to shoot me. I think not!"

Taking him by surprise, she shoved him away and got quickly to her feet.

"Maggie!"

Margaret plunged back through the bushes, tugging at her skirt when he sat up and caught at her hem. Hearing the tearing material, she cursed impatiently and hurried onward, refusing to look down at the damage. Maggie's one thought was to escape the man now blundering out of the bushes after her, hissing her name in a voice she was sure people could hear at the other end of the park.

When he grasped her elbow and tried to drag her back to the bushes, she turned on him abruptly, swinging her bag and koshing him on the side of the head. Maggie knew she hadn't hurt him, but his surprise at the attack made him loosen his hold long enough for her to pull free. Before he could quite regain himself, she flew down the path and joined the throngs making their way on the London streets.

Maggie nearly convinced herself that she had lost him in the crowds as she hurried along, so when she reached her home and hurried inside, then turned to close the door, only to find him blocking her from doing so, she stepped back in surprise. That gave him the opportunity to slip inside. She glowered at him fiercely as he shut the door then moved to the window, shifting the curtains aside to peer out into the street.

Tapping her foot in a furious tempo, she propped her hands on her hips and tried to set him aflame with her eyes. When that didn't work — he didn't even turn to appreciate her wrath — she drew herself up and hissed. "You were not invited in, my lord. Pray, remove yourself ere I have to call my servants to help you on your way."

Turning, James goggled at her briefly in disbelief, then snatched her ruined bird's-nest hat from her head and shoved it under her nose. The feathers tickled. "There," he said. "See that? Someone took a shot at you."

Maggie opened her mouth to say something nasty, then paused, her mouth dropping to her chest. There was a round hole right through the center of her bird that she could have put a finger through.

"Well, finally! Something has left you speechless," he muttered.

Snapping her mouth closed, Maggie glared at her nemesis. "Did you hire someone to do this? To make me soften toward you? Because if you did, my lord, I can promise you that you will be replacing this hat!"

"What?" He was flabbergasted by the accusation. "Why the devil would I do a thing like that?"

"I do not know, my lord, but why would anyone shoot at me? No one has reason."

"So you assume that *I* set it up? To what purpose? To get into your good graces by saving your life? Fat chance, that!" He snorted, then drew himself up to peer down his nose at her. "How could you think such a thing of me?"

Maggie felt herself tensing as everything that had happened rushed over her. She felt herself adrift in emotion, and everything she'd bottled up inside her exploded outward. "How could I think such a thing of you? How could *you* think what *you* thought of me?"

James's indignity seeped away like water off fast-melting ice at her obvious pain and outrage. Regret flashed in his eyes, and she felt herself soften. Then he shifted uncomfortably and tried to explain: "Well, you must admit that what you were wearing that night —" He paused as she flushed, her cheeks burning almost as red as the gown in question. "And then you were at Madame Dubarry's," he added.

Maggie had heard enough. Turning abruptly away, she stomped into the parlor and directly to the bottles of liquor in the sideboard. She poured a generous quantity into a glass, downed it, then poured herself another full measure.

"May I have a glass as well?" James asked, joining her at the counter.

"Get your own," she barked testily, then relented. Pouring him a glass, she pushed it toward him along the counter, then turned and walked over to one of the two over-stuffed chairs by the fire. Dropping into it with relief, she stared bleakly down into the dark liquid in her glass for a moment. Then she glanced up into his wary face. "Why are you here? Why did you lie in wait at your aunt's? I presume you set this all up to see me?"

"Yes," he admitted slowly. Moving to sink onto the chair opposite her, he considered his own glass briefly, then admitted, "I wish to apologize —"

"Apology accepted," she interrupted. "You may leave now."

James's jaw dropped. He was not at all used to being dismissed. It didn't appear that he liked it much. "Your brother —" he began determinedly.

She interrupted again. "My brother is dead," she reminded him. Then, bluntly, she went on: "I release you from any promises or vows he elicited from you on his death-bed. You may go."

"I *do not wish* to go."

They both blinked at those blurted words. James looked both sheepish and horrified at the depth of emotion that had sounded in them. Maggie found herself feeling simply stunned. Swallowing nervously, she tore her gaze from his. "I think you had better —" she began.

"Please don't ask me to leave again." His voice was soft and weary and, despite herself, Maggie felt her anger begin to ease. She gave the barest of nods, but he saw it and relaxed in the chair as he confessed, "I quite enjoyed your company in the country."

She felt herself tensing again. "You mean, when you thought I was Lady X? When you thought I was a prostitute available to the highest bidder?"

"*Despite* thinking you a prostitute available to the highest bidder," he began carefully. "Yes. I enjoyed your company immensely, and that confused me. I felt it in my duty to reform you, but was also attracted to you physically," he admitted with a self-deprecating twist of his lips. "I found my honorable side constantly struggling against baser instincts. And then, as I came to know you, I found I actually liked you." He shrugged helplessly.

Maggie stared at him in wonder. She had known he was attracted to her. The little incident in the library had made that clear. She had never dared hope, however, that he might actually like her, too. Somehow, that seemed more important. Not that the other wasn't, but Lord Ramsey was the first man who had ever done more than kiss her. He was also the only one who'd ever inspired a desire in her to do more. . . .

Pastor Frances had never gone beyond a few sloppy swipes of his lips on hers, which had been just fine. She'd been more attracted to the idea of a solid, good man than by any overwhelming desire. No, that emotion was something she'd experienced with James alone.

"Is there anyone who may wish to do you harm?" she heard him ask.

Maggie stared blankly, confused by the sudden change in subject. Still, she tried to answer his question. As Frances had been the last thought to pop into her head before James had asked his question, Frances was the first person to pop into her head in answer to it.

She frowned as she thought of the other man, then winced as her furrowing brow caused pain to shoot from the bruise on her forehead. She forced herself to let the skin there smooth out again so that she could think.

The pastor had been someone she'd wanted to avoid as much as Lord Ramsey since returning, but, as he was the head of her church and Sunday was creeping closer, she had decided that it would do little good to continue avoiding him. Yesterday she'd invited him to dinner.

As expected, he'd proposed.

She, of course, had refused. What else could she do after witnessing that little scenario with Maisey? Frances hadn't accepted her refusal as gracefully as she'd hoped, and had pressed his suit. She had remained apologetic, yet firm. He'd appeared confused as she explained she did not harbor "wifely feelings" for him; then he had become cold. He'd even, before he left, pointed out that she was well beyond the age of youth and beauty, and that she was not likely to get a better offer. He'd even said she would regret her decision.

She considered now just how far he would go to ensure that she did regret it, then shook her head. *No.* Pastor Frances was not the sort to do her injury just because she refused to marry him. It would be silly and even egotistical to believe such might be the case. Still, she would be uncomfortable around the man until he found someone else to favor with his attentions. Which was terribly sad and unpleasant, but not deadly.

"No," she said at last, then shook her head. "I know of no one who would wish to harm me."

"The irate subject of one of your articles, perhaps?"

Maggie started shaking her head before he finished the question. "I thought of that, but no one knows who G. W. Clark is. Well, except you and your aunt, and Madame Dubarry."

"What of the women you interviewed?"

"I wore a very heavy veil during the interviews."

"What of the girl who gave you her mask?"

"Maisey?" Maggie opened her eyes wide with a mixture of surprise and amusement. "No. Maisey saw my face briefly, but" — she shook her head — "She is not the sort to be rushing about shooting at me. Besides, why would she? I did not even mention her name in the article. I didn't mention any names at all." She shook her head again. "No. There is no reason for anyone to wish me harm." When he frowned at her words, she shrugged. "Mayhap it was a stray bullet, James. Or a random act. I really do not feel I am under any threat. It is more likely that someone was aiming at you and missed."

"Me?" He looked insulted at the thought, and Maggie nearly laughed. *Good.* Now he knew what it felt like to be maligned.

"Well," she said mockingly. "Of course you are right, my lord. Why would anyone want you dead? After all, you are such a pleasant sort."

The man started to be offended, then he noticed the twinkle in her eye and seemed to realize she was teasing. He relaxed with a wry smile. They were both still for a moment; then he pursed his lips in thought. "I might be more willing to accept that it was an accident or some such thing if it weren't for the accident today — and for the other the last time we met. Those make me worry that bullet was aimed at you."

Maggie made a face. "On the other hand, one might consider the fact that all these things only ever occurred with you around. . . ." She paused at his dismayed expression, then rolled her eyes. With a sigh she said what she should have said before. "I must apologize for not thanking you for that, James. You may very well have saved my life that day."

He waved away her words, though he was obviously pleased by them. "The point is, if this were just a random shot, it would be one thing. But —"

"Oh, now you cannot truly imagine that wagon driver was deliberately attempting to run me down?" Maggie protested.

"Well, I had not considered the possibility at the time . . . but now that a similar-looking man pushed you out in front of another carriage, and someone is shooting at you —"

"We do not know it is the same man," Maggie protested. "You said the driver of the wagon was dark. Did you see a scar?" When James hesitated, obviously reluctant to admit that he had not, she added, "Besides, it was one stray shot in the park. Why did they not fire again if they were truly trying to kill me? I leaped back up and charged out of those bushes, making a perfect target of myself . . . yet a second shot never came."

He conceded that fact with a nod as he got to his feet. "I can see that I am wasting my time trying to convince you that you are in danger. At least promise me that you will take care in future?"

"I promise," she murmured, rising as well but feeling a trifle awkward. She wasn't sure where they stood anymore. Her animosity appeared to be gone, but where did that leave them? After what they'd done, what could they be? Friends? Acquaintances?

"I would also appreciate it if . . . I mean, now that we have reached something of a . . . Please stop refusing my aunt's invitations," he blurted at last. "She quite likes you and is holding me wholly responsible for your snubs."

Maggie nearly grinned, but caught the expression back and instead solemnly nodded. "I liked her as well. I would be pleased to accept any future invitations."

Sighing at Maggie's words, James exited the salon, aware that she was following as he moved to the front door. Opening it, he paused to glance back. "And do try to be careful. Make sure that the servants lock the doors at night, and take a carriage whenever possible."

"Aye, my lord," she murmured.

James frowned at her easy agreement, suspecting that it was given only to soothe him, but there was little he could do to make her listen without alienating her again. Nodding, he turned away and left the town house, his mind already working on ways for him to tend the matter as he pulled the door closed behind him.

He would hire Johnstone again to look out for her. The runner could also investigate whether the three incidents were linked attempts on Maggie's life or mere accidents. She wouldn't like it if she found out, but he *had* made a promise to her brother, to look after her. Which was the only interest he had in the girl, he told himself as he started toward the park. Margaret Wentworth was a respectable young woman, and what he'd done to — with — her was reprehensible. From now on he would treat her only with the respect that was her due.

He just had to push away his memories of her naked flesh, and the rest would be tea and crumpets.

CHAPTER TWELVE

Maggie cursed as her hair slid from where she had secured it atop her head and tumbled around her shoulders. Again. Heaving out her breath in irritation, she glared into the oval dressing table mirror she sat before.

"I should have asked Mary to fix my hair before she left," she admitted to the room. There was no one around to comment, no one at all; the entire house was empty. Which meant there was also no one to help her with this task, either. Worse yet, she had no one to blame but herself, she admitted in aggravation, making a face at her reflection in the mirror.

One of the fairs had come today. It was a much smaller fete than St. Bartholomew's, which was held in August, but it was one of the first of the season, so had caused a great deal of excitement among her staff. Their excitement had infected Maggie, too, and in a moment of largesse she had decided that every one of them should take the afternoon off.

At the time, she'd believed she wouldn't need them. As she was attending a ball this evening with James and his aunt, there was no need to make her meal, or clean up after her, and really there was little enough for the servants to do when she *was* around. With her plans to be out tonight, it had seemed silly to keep the servants in. She had convinced them all, against their somewhat meager protests, to take the afternoon off and enjoy the fair. Even Banks had gone, agreeing in his gruff old voice to Maggie's suggestion that an older, wiser influence might be for the best.

Of course, when she had given them all the day off, she had forgotten she would need assistance getting ready for the ball. Her maid Mary had brought it up and offered, with a pained smile, to stay behind and assist, but Maggie had not had the heart to keep her; it was hardly fair for everyone else to go while Mary alone had to stay behind and miss the fun. No, Maggie had refused to allow her to stay — despite her concerns about being able to do herself up properly.

It couldn't be that hard, surely? she'd thought. She could prepare herself. She was a perfectly intelligent young woman. She *had* managed to dress herself, though it hadn't been as easy as she'd expected, what with all the buttons in the back and such. Still, with some ingenuity and twisting and turning, she had mastered the situation.

Her hair was another matter entirely. Mary had always been swift and assured at the business, managing to perform miracles in moments with the unmanageable tresses. They seemed determined to defy Maggie's attempts. She was not feeling terribly intelligent or clever at the moment. In fact, she was feeling rather panicky and incompetent. The hour was growing late. James and his aunt would arrive any moment.

She felt herself blush. James and his aunt. She had seen quite a bit of the pair since the day of her injury. Lady Barlow had invited her to tea several times in the week since, and Maggie had accepted each invitation. James had been in attendance for all of them. He had behaved beautifully during each visit, a perfect gentleman. Nor had he brought up any nonsense about someone trying to kill her again, thank goodness. In fact, he had not tried to kiss her or do anything untoward — not even looking as if he had wanted to.

Maggie found herself looking rather purse-lipped at that thought, and she forced the lines out of her face. Surely she wasn't disappointed that he hadn't kissed her or anything else, was she? He was treating her like the lady she was, and that was only appropriate.

She wasn't fooling herself. Now that her fury at him had been resolved, she found herself recalling those decadent moments in his office. She had even relived them in a dream or two since, awakening as shaken and aroused as when it first happened.

Maggie's thoughts were interrupted by the sound of a door closing below, and she glanced abruptly toward the entrance to her room. Relief coursed through her. She hadn't expected the servants to return so early, but she was relieved that they had. Perhaps she could prevail upon Mary to help with her hair. She simply could not attend the Willans' ball with Lady Barlow and James if she did not look her best. She wouldn't want to embarrass them. They were taking her as their guest, after all.

Mary can fix my hair in a trice, Maggie thought with relief, standing and heading for the door. *If it is Mary,* she considered with a sudden frown. It could be that young Charlie had eaten too many sweets and one of his other sisters had returned with him.

That would be all right, though; both Joan and Nora knew how to do hair, each of them had stepped in to take their older sister's place as lady's maid a time or two. They practiced on each other and were quite skilled.

Or, she considered as she stepped out into the hall, if it was old Banks, weary and returning early alone, she would even be willing to let him have a go. Which showed the degree of her panic and frustration, she thought with amusement as she reached the landing and peered down into the dark and silent foyer below. There was no sign of movement or activity that she could see, but the servants would most likely stick to the kitchens or their own rooms. They would probably assume she had already left.

In fact, she decided as she noted the fact that night was falling, leaving the house shrouded in gloom, it appeared late enough that she should have already left. Lady Barlow and James were late. Picking up a three-tiered candelabra from the table at the top of the stairs, she lifted her skirt slightly and headed down. One of her servants had returned early; she had only to find out which.

Reaching the bottom of the stairs, Maggie walked along the hall toward the kitchen, her concentration taken up with doing her best to prevent the candles she carried from going out and leaving her in the dark. With her hand and arm out to shield their delicate flames, she opened the door to the kitchens by pushing against it with her hip. The action stirred a slight breeze that threatened to damp her candles, and, distracted by this concern, Maggie stepped into the kitchen before realizing that the room was in near darkness. Seeing that fact, she knew at once that no one had returned from the fair. Building a kitchen fire would have been the first act of any of her servants.

She stood, stymied for a moment by the realization, then stiffened. The hair at the nape of her neck was suddenly standing on end, prickles of electricity racing over her skin. Turning instinctively, she gaped in surprise as her candles illuminated a figure standing behind the door that had just swung shut.

Both of them froze for a moment as if posing for a portrait, the man blinking as his eyes strained to adjust to the candlelight splashing over him, and Maggie's breath catching in her throat as she absorbed the details of the intruder. He was tall and bulky, with wide shoulders and thick, strong arms. His hair was long and dark, his smile

287

cruel, and a square and puckered scar deformed his cheek. She took all that in, then felt horror race along her nerves as he started forward.

Crying out, Maggie rushed backward, but she jarred her hip against the table Cook used to prepare food. Instinctively she swung the candelabra at her attacker. The makeshift mace made a satisfying impact as it struck her assailant's head, stopping him briefly and sending the candles flying. Two of them flickered out as they fell, but one managed to remain lit as it rolled across the floor. Still, the room descended into the gloom of dusk, and Maggie spun away, stumbling through the near-darkness, knocking against unidentifiable objects as she sought escape.

She was in a panic at that point, her only thought to flee and get help. Maggie knew without a doubt that this man was the one who had nearly run her down with the wagon, and the one the hack driver had said had pushed her out before his carriage. There was no longer any possibility to deny that someone was after her. James's voice rang through her head, telling her not to go anywhere alone, to be sure that the servants always locked the doors.

Maggie cursed herself roundly for sending

the servants off and leaving herself alone and vulnerable. She hadn't given a single thought to his warnings, so sure she was that no one could be out to harm her. *I am an idiot and deserve whatever I get,* she thought viciously as she slammed into a counter, her hands knocking several items to the ground. A hand caught the back of her gown briefly as she tried to straighten, then released its hold to grasp her neck. Fingers closed around her throat from behind, squeezing viciously and cutting off her air.

Maggie's first instinct was to score the hands at her throat with her nails. When it had no effect, except to have the man slam her into the counter, his body pressing along the back of her own, she gave that up. Eyes closed and gasping for air, she felt frantically around for something, anything, to use as a weapon. Stars were starting to explode behind her eyelids when her hand fell on something hard. Fighting off the unconsciousness threatening to overwhelm her, she closed her fingers desperately around the handle of the heavy item — a pan, she thought — and, using all the strength she could muster, she swung it behind her, slamming it into her attacker.

A grunt by her ear and the loosening of

the man's fingers told Maggie that she had hit her mark. Coughing and sucking in air, she staggered blindly away, but managed only to take a very few steps before she was again grabbed. This time the man caught her by the shoulder. He whirled her around.

Maggie opened her eyes in time to see the room explode; a heavy object slammed into the side of her face. The world seemed to tip inside her head, and she knew she was falling. Something caught her temple as she fell — the corner of a table, perhaps? Maggie cried out at the sharp pain, but hardly felt the impact of the floor when she hit it.

Moaning at the agony in her head, she let it fall weakly to the side and found herself staring at the flames in the fireplace. At least, that was what she'd at first thought they were. Her eyes had started to close when some part of her brain told her she'd made a mistake. Forcing herself back to consciousness, she stared at the dancing flames, frowning when her attacker suddenly knelt before them. He picked something up, and Maggie frowned as she realized that the flames came from a candle. What she was looking at wasn't a fire in the fireplace at all. One of the candles from her candelabra, the only one that had stayed lit, had rolled up against a sack of grain that

Cook had left out and set it ablaze. Her house was now on fire, she realized.

Her attacker moved around the table and out of sight.

Alarm bells started tolling inside her head, and Maggie summoned strength enough to respond to them. Gasping in pain, she struggled to her hands and knees, swallowing the bile that rose in her throat as she did.

Getting to her feet seemed an insurmountable task, but she grabbed at the edge of the table beside her and managed to pull herself to her feet; her only clear thought was that she needed to find something with which to put out the fire. *Water,* she thought muzzily, leaning against the table. A sound drew her eyes to the opposite side of the room and her attacker. She frowned slightly, not sure at first what he was doing. He stood with his back to her, fiddling with something. Then light bloomed around him and he turned, a lit lamp in hand. The man seemed surprised to find her standing; then his mouth twisted and he hurled the lamp forward.

Crying out, Maggie threw herself to the side, tumbling to the floor as the lamp sailed past. She heard it smash against the wall, and a whooshing sound made her glance weakly over to see that oil had sprayed everywhere. The fire was quickly following.

The flames seemed alive, like fingers of some monster hungry to consume her. Her last thought before darkness claimed her was that she was going to die.

"We are late."

Lady Barlow peered at her nephew through the growing gloom inside the carriage and bit her lip to keep from smiling. The man was quite put out. He had arrived at her town house a good hour ago, earlier than she'd expected, and she hadn't been ready. Neither was she ready by the appointed hour, and she had left James cooling his heels in her salon while her maid had fussed over her. By the time she had made her grand entrance into the salon, the man was seething.

Far from being impressed with all the work her maid had put into her appearance, James had turned from his pacing with relief, snatched his aunt's hand, and nearly dragged her out of the house without her cloak or gloves. She had rebuked him quite firmly for the unseemly behavior, taken her time donning the items, then walked out to the carriage at a dignified pace. The whole while he'd pranced about her, almost begging her to move quicker.

Vivian had nearly burst into laughter at his antics, but she hadn't thought he would appreciate her amusement. She'd managed to stifle it behind a stern expression.

The boy was terribly eager to collect little Lady Margaret, which Vivian saw as terribly encouraging. James hadn't shown the least bit of interest in any of the other available ladies of the ton in years. She had despaired of his ever settling down and presenting her with a little grandniece or grandnephew.

She sighed to herself at the thought. *Babies.* She did love babies. Unfortunately she had not been blessed with any of her own. It had been both a tragedy and a blessing when her dear sister had died at sea and left her young children in Vivian's care. As much as she had grieved the loss of her sibling and brother-in-law, she had taken James and his sister to her bosom with love and devotion, treating them as her own. Without those two to look after and chase, she felt sure she would have grown into a bitter old woman. Any babies either child produced would be a further blessing. And now Vivian was becoming rather hopeful that Lady Margaret might be the one to lure James to the altar and begin producing such added wonders.

Her gaze slid to her nephew, and she smiled a little slyly at the normally calm and dignified man's fidgeting. Then, forcing her expression to a more serious mien, she murmured, "This shall be good for Margaret. Having the child at the opera with us should raise a lot of curiosity about her, and then the Willans always have a lot of eligible bachelors at their balls. Perhaps we can find her some suitable husband material."

She was not disappointed at the sharp way James glanced at her. "What?"

"Well," she murmured comfortably, "her brother *did* die saving your life. It does behoove us to find her a good, strong, well-set husband to take care of her."

"She doesn't need a husband," he protested at once, looking put out by the idea. "She can take care of herself."

"Nonsense. Once she is married she can give up writing those dangerous articles. She is taking too many chances, as it is."

James stared at her in horror for a moment. It had obviously not occurred to him that his aunt might take it into her head to see the girl settled. It was also obvious he didn't like the idea. At all. *Good,* she thought as she watched him shift. There was no reason for him not to want to marry the girl off unless he was interested himself. Oh, yes, she would see the stubborn cur married by the end of season, or her name wasn't Lady Vivian Jean Barlow.

"Dammit! I told Crowch to drive quickly. What is he doing?" James grumbled, drawing her attention. She glanced at him in time to see his head disappear out the window to address the driver. "Crowch? What is the holdup here? We are nearly at a standstill."

"Sorry, m'lord. There appears to be some problem up ahead. A fire, I think. There is smoke filling the road, and gawkers are holding up traffic."

"A fire?" Vivian asked, catching the man's explanation and leaning curiously toward the window.

Her nephew went as stiff as a board. "Can you see where it seems to be coming from?" he asked.

Vivian felt anxiety strike her at the dread in James's voice.

"I'm not sure, m'lord. It looks to be coming from somewhere near Lady Wentworth's. It could be one of her neighbor's homes, or hers. . . . I can't tell from here."

James was out of the carriage before Vivian had even digested Crowch's words. Leaning out the window of the door her nephew had just pushed closed, she peered up the street in concern. A black cloud of smoke was billowing up into the darkening sky.

James ran. He ran so fast his heart was thumping violently and loudly in his chest, deafening him to the startled gasps and complaints of the people he was pushing and shoving past in his desperate effort to reach Maggie. The fire couldn't be at the Wentworth town house. It couldn't be. But even as he tried to reassure himself, he knew that he was wrong, and cursed himself for not preventing this somehow — for not doing more about the danger she was in and seeing her safe.

He stumbled through the last of the onlookers, crashing against the gate separating the town house from the street. His hands clenched on the pointed metal spears as he gaped in horror at the burning building. Smoke was billowing out of several broken windows in the house and rising to merge into one large cloud that blackened the already inky sky.

"Maggie," he said under his breath. He had already started to pull the gate open when a hand settled on his shoulder.

"M'lord?"

James started to shake the hand off, but the man's next words made him pause.

"She ain't in there, m'lord. She's all right."

Turning sharply, James stared at the speaker, not recognizing him for a moment. "Johnstone?"

"Aye, m'lord." The man's expression showed some concern.

"Where is she?" he asked sharply, grabbing the man's coatfront in agitation.

"My man got her out." When James looked blank, the runner raised a soothing hand. "Ye remember? Ye said to put a man on her until we discovered whether someone were after her or not." His gaze slid grimly to the burning house and the brigade working to put it out. "Well, it looks like someone is after her after all."

"Where *is* she?" James repeated, his voice harsh. He didn't care about anything else at that point but seeing for himself that Maggie was safe. Seeming to finally realize that, Johnstone tugged free and started to lead his employer back through the crowd.

"This way, m'lord."

"James?" a voice called.

He hesitated in the street, then paused to rush back to meet his aunt. She was hurrying breathlessly through the crowd toward him. Frowning up the road, he saw that his carriage was still some distance back, and realized that his aunt had followed him on foot.

"Perhaps you should go back and wait in the carriage, Aunt Viv," he suggested as he reached her side.

"Is Maggie all right? Is that her town house?"

"Yes, it is hers."

"Is she all right?" his aunt asked again with growing alarm. James hesitated. He wanted to insist that his aunt return to his carriage and wait there, but he knew she would merely argue and delay him. Unwilling to waste time convincing her, he took her arm and hurried over to where Johnstone now stood leaning into a hack.

Reaching the runner's side, James released his aunt to step up and peer past the shorter man's shoulders into the carriage. It took a moment for his eyes to adjust to the dark interior. When they did, he found himself staring at a crumpled female form in the arms of a large, dark shadow.

"Jack says she was unconscious when he found and dragged her out of the house. He sent a lad to fetch me at the office and waited with her on the front lawn until the fire got too hot. When I got here, I had him get her in the carriage. I was going to take her to yer town house, but by that time the gawkers had clogged the road. We couldn't get out of here," Johnstone told him apologetically, stepping aside to allow James to fill the open door. Then he added, "She hasn't regained consciousness yet."

James didn't hesitate. Leaning into the hack, he lifted Maggie out of the other man's arms, then straightened with her. "Come," was all he said. It was enough; his aunt, Johnstone, and the man named Jack all trailed obediently back along the street to his carriage.

"Can you get us out of here, Crowch?" James asked grimly as the driver leaped down from his bench to open the carriage door.

The coachman hesitated, his gaze moving over the vehicles now ahead of and behind them, then he considered the empty half of the road where carriages should have been traveling in the opposite direction, but weren't. He nodded determinedly. "Aye, m'lord."

"Good man," James said. "Take us back home."

"Your home or Lady Barlow's?" the driver asked.

"My home," his aunt promptly answered.

299

When James frowned, she explained, "It is closer."

James's gaze dropped to the pale, smoke-smudged face of the woman he held; then he nodded and stepped up into his carriage. His aunt followed, settling on the bench seat across from him. James settled Maggie carefully in his lap, her head against his chest, her lower legs and feet taking up the rest of the seat. Johnstone paused long enough to order his man to join Crowch on the driver's bench, then clambered in as well, murmuring apologies as he settled next to Lady Barlow.

They were all silent as Crowch maneuvered the vehicle's horses, turned it on the lane, and headed them back the way they had come.

It was a very short ride back to his aunt's house, and James leaped out of the carriage — Maggie cradled to his chest — as soon as Crowch opened the door. He was grateful to see that Johnstone's man had already rushed ahead to announce their arrival. Meeks opened the door just as James reached the house, his eyes goggling at the sight of Lady Wentworth in James's arms.

"Another accident, my lord?" he asked in alarm, quickly stepping out of the way so that everyone could enter.

300

"*Another* one?" Lady Barlow echoed sharply.

James grimaced, but shook his head. "Not an accident, Meeks, and we will be needing a doctor this time. Send someone for Lord Mullin."

"Are you sure he is back?" Aunt Vivian asked with concern.

James nodded. "He returned yesterday," he responded, then breathed a heartfelt, "Thank God."

Robert had always been fascinated by medicine. That fascination had led the younger man to train in the field despite there being no necessity for him to work for a living. That training had been put to use when he was called to war. Robert had been the medic for their platoon, and James had watched him save many men he'd been sure were lost. James would trust no one else with Maggie's life.

"I shall see to it at once, my lord." The butler moved off down the hall to see to the matter as James carried Maggie into the salon. He laid her gently on the very same settee he had placed her on the day of the faux tea party. The room was dark for several moments, but then Johnstone thought to collect a candle from the hall. He used it to light several more tapers in the room, and within moments the salon was filled with a soft glow.

James almost wished it weren't. Up until that point he had thought her merely smoke-smudged; now that he was seeing her in the light, he could see that a good deal of what he'd thought were smudges were really bruises. The side of her face was one large welt, her lip was cut, one eye was blackened, and there were bruises around her throat.

"She fought," Johnstone commented approvingly, moving to peer over James's shoulder as his employer brushed the hair away from Maggie's forehead to reveal a nasty cut at her hairline. Then, apparently noting the blood that had soaked into her hair and ran back along her scalp, the runner added, "Landed on her back after the blow."

"I shall go fetch some water and a cloth, and be sure Meeks sent someone for the doctor," Lady Barlow hurried from the room.

"What happened?" James glanced toward the runner Johnstone had called Jack. The man stepped forward at once, his gaze going to Lady Margaret with a frown.

"I was watching from across the street. The servants all left in the early afternoon. She was alone in the house, far as I knew.

Then, just before sunset, I noticed a sort of glow coming from some of the windows on the lower floor. I knew it wasn't candlelight, and thought I smelled smoke." He shrugged, his expression grim. "Had a bad feeling. Decided I'd better take a look-see. I tried seeing in the front windows, but all I could learn was that the light was coming from the back of the house. She didn't come to the door when I knocked, so around I went. I saw someone runnin' out into the gardens as I came around the corner. I was gonna chase after him, then saw that the back door was partway open, and that the kitchens were on fire — so I headed for the house instead. She was lyin' in the center of the kitchen floor."

He shook his head. "Everything else in the room was afire, but it hadn't reached her yet. 'Twas just nipping at her skirts. I ran in and pulled her out, then carried her around to the front of the house. I stopped a passin' boy and gave him a couple coins to fetch Mr. Johnstone here." The man frowned, looking regretful. "I should have given him a couple more and had him fetch the fire brigade, too."

"Ye did fine," Johnstone said. He patted the larger man on the shoulder. "The brigade came right quick. How's ye hand?"

303

The question drew James's attention to the fact that Jack hadn't gotten away without injury. His right hand was red and blistered. He had rushed into a burning building, but James hadn't considered what that entailed.

"Oh, dear." The murmured words drew his attention to the fact that Lady Barlow had returned. How much of the man's words she had heard was anyone's guess, but now she rushed to Jack's side with the bowl of water and the cloth she had brought.

"Fetch more water and cloths, Meeks," she ordered, then urged the injured Jack to a nearby chair. Once she had cajoled him into sitting, she set the bowl on his leg, picked his arm up by the wrist, and plopped his hand into the water. Seeming to think that took care of the immediate problem, she turned to where James and Johnstone still hovered by Maggie and eyed them like two misbehaving children. "Now, you had better tell me about this previous incident Meeks mentioned . . . and why exactly you still have Mr. Johnstone in your employ . . . and why you had this poor man watching Maggie!"

"He was keeping an eye out — just in case something like this happened." James answered the last question first.

"And Mr. Johnstone?"

"Lord Ramsey asked me to look into who was causing all of these accidents," Johnstone answered with a shrug.

Lady Barlow nodded, then speared her nephew with her eyes. "What about this 'other incident' Meeks mentioned?"

James winced. It was a question he really would have preferred not to answer. He had sworn Meeks to silence about that day, so his aunt was not aware of the little incident at all. She knew nothing about the faux tea party, the invitation to which he had signed her name, or anything else about that day. Answering her now would definitely get him in hot water. She wouldn't be at all pleased to learn he had used her in such a way. Nor, probably, that he had used blackmail and lies to get Meeks to go along with him. Nor that he had put Maggie in a compromising position by tricking her into traveling somewhere to be alone with him.

Fortunately, he was saved from having to answer her immediately by the arrival of Lord Mullin. "Robert!" James said with relief. "Thank you for coming."

"Not at all." The younger man shed his overcoat as he crossed the room, Meeks on his heels. Pausing at James's side, he exchanged the garment for the bag Lady Barlow's butler had been holding for him, then turned his attention to Maggie. "What happened? I gather there was a fire? Was she burned?"

"I don't think so, but she has a nasty head wound," James said. "She's been unconscious for at least several minutes."

Nodding, his friend nudged him. "Let me have a look at her, then."

James stood at once and moved. He watched Robert poke at the wound on her forehead and lift her eyelids one after the other. When he started to look her over for other injuries, James turned away. Leaving his aunt and Robert to tend to the wounds of both Maggie and Jack, he urged Johnstone from the room.

"Have you come up with anything, yet?" James asked as he led the Bow Street runner into the library and closed the door.

Johnstone shook his head. "Not much," the man admitted regretfully. "I found a couple of people who witnessed the incident where she was pushed in front of the hack. A couple people remembered it happening, but couldn't say whether she had been pushed in front of the carriage or just bumped. No one remembered a scarred man being there except for that driver. I've nosed around to see if there's any ill will toward G. W. Clark, but no one's rushing forward with information. I'll keep at it, though."

"Aye. You do that," James murmured, rubbing a hand wearily along his neck. "This has to be connected to Lady Margaret's articles. There is no other reason for anyone to wish her harm."

Johnstone shrugged. "There doesn't appear to be. Usually such murderous attempts revolve around some sort o' monetary gain, but there doesn't appear to be anyone to gain from her death — except for her cousin, perhaps. He would probably inherit the town house and the money she invested if she died, but I looked into that and the lawyers still haven't located him. No, I believe ye're right, m'lord. It has to be connected to her articles."

"Did you look into Drummond?"

"Aye. It's not him. He's dead."

"Dead?" James glanced over in surprise and the runner nodded.

"Aye. Got his neck stretched. Rumor is that the judge who tried him was one of the victims of his flammery."

James frowned. "Then it must be because of one of her other articles."

Johnstone nodded. "Well that's the problem: it could be one of the articles she wrote, or one her brother wrote. Anyone who discovered Clark's identity now wouldn't necessarily know her brother was the writer before his death, and would blame *her* for it. Do you know how many articles they have done between them?" he asked in disgust. "The suspects are in the hundreds."

"Damn."

"Aye," Johnstone agreed.

"Well, my main concern is to keep her safe. Which might be easier now that her house is gone. She never would have agreed to leave it ere this, but now it shouldn't be too difficult to convince her to stay with me. I —"

"She will stay with me." A stern voice resounded through the room.

Both men turned to peer at Lady Barlow. She stood in the door to the room, and they had been so caught up in their discussion that neither man had heard her open it. They exchanged vexed glances.

"It would be improper for her to stay with you," Aunt Vivian pointed out. "She will stay with me. But someone must be sent to wait for and collect her staff. She says that they went to the fair. I imagine they should be returning soon. They won't have anywhere to go, and Margaret is quite worried about them."

"She is awake?" James started for the door, only to pause when his aunt remained blocking the entrance.

"Robert is still with her. He has finished with Jack, however." Her gaze slid to Johnstone. "I sent him to the kitchens for something to eat and drink."

"Thank you, ma'am. He is a good man."

"Yes, he is. He saved Lady Margaret's life. But he needs to rest for the remainder of the night, at least, before he will be any good as a guard again, so you may wish to arrange to send someone to relieve him."

"Yes, o' course. I shall see to it at once," Johnstone assured her. As he moved forward Lady Barlow stepped out of the way; then she closed the door behind his departing back and eyed James as she'd done when he was in trouble as a child.

"Now, James Matthew Huttledon, it's time you told me about this 'incident.' Meeks is looking bedeviled and guilty, and avoiding my questions. Obviously, whatever occurred includes your convincing him to behave against his instincts."

"Against his instincts?" James echoed with feigned surprise, trying to stall long enough to think of a way to explain without it sounding quite as bad as he knew it would. He already knew that his aunt wouldn't be pleased that he had used her name, her home, and her staff in an effort to get Maggie alone — even if his only intention had been to speak to her, not ravish her. His aunt wasn't of the belief that the end justified the means; he had learned that long ago. She preferred honest, aboveboard tactics in everything.

"Yes. Against his instincts. Even as a boy you were always able to twist that man about your finger. Meeks is as soft as pudding where you and Sophie are concerned. Now, tell. I am losing patience."

CHAPTER THIRTEEN

"Thank you, my lord." Maggie said, watching Lord Mullin return his implements to his bag.

"You are more than welcome. It's the least I could do for Gerald's sister." He closed his bag with a snap and stood. "Now, I had best go find James and Lady Barlow. I wish to have a word with them on your care. You just rest, Maggie. I know your head must be paining you. The tincture I gave you should help with that soon."

Maggie instinctively started to nod, then caught herself and merely watched him leave. He was right, of course, her head was pounding something awful, and her face felt as if someone had taken a cricket bat to it, but she was alive. That was something, she supposed. She wouldn't lay odds that she had much else left to be happy about. The last thing Maggie recalled before waking up here on Lady Barlow's settee, *again,* was lying helplessly on the floor of her kitchen as the fire spread around her.

Sighing, she closed her eyes and tried to get the image out of her head. The hum of voices from the hall told her that Robert had found James and his aunt, and was, no doubt, giving his diagnosis. Battered, bruised, and aching should about cover it, she thought wryly.

Reaching a hand up to feel her face, she found it swollen and deformed. Still, it was little enough to bear. Considering what might have happened . . . she'd been lucky and knew it. Maggie was not alive and well now due to any action on her own part. If anything, her foolish refusal to believe that someone might be out to do her harm had nearly cost her life. She should have listened to James. Any injury she had sustained was her own bloody fault. Even so, she could still hardly believe someone hated her enough to wish her dead.

A rustling made her start and peer around nervously, but she relaxed at the sight of Lady Barlow, Lord Mullin, and James entering the room.

"How are you feeling, dear?" the older woman asked, moving quickly to her side.

"Much better than I should, all things considered," Maggie admitted softly. She eased to a sitting position, ignoring the pain the action sent shooting through her.

"Are you sure you should sit up?" Lady Barlow asked, but her questioning gaze went to Robert.

"Yes," Maggie answered before Lord Mullin could comment. "If I continue to lie here, I will fall asleep . . . and I know I should tell what happened while it is fresh in my mind."

"Surely that can wait until morning . . ." the old woman began, but James interrupted.

"No, she is right. She may forget something important if we wait. Best to get this out of the way. If you feel up to it," he added gently, ignoring his aunt's narrow-eyed gaze.

She wasn't pleased with him at the moment. Aunt Viv had not taken the news of his faux tea party well. Fortunately, before she had been able to lambaste him about the ordeal, Meeks had tapped on the library door to let them know that Robert was finished with Maggie. James was rather hoping that tonight's events would see to it that his aunt never got around to that lambasting.

Aunt Vivian was the only one who could make him feel like a naughty five-year-old. He supposed it was a mother thing, and the woman had certainly filled that role for him.

A sound from Maggie drew James's gaze to her pale, battered face.

"Yes. I can manage," she assured them with quiet determination, then paused, seeming to try to organize her thought. Her eyelashes fluttered, and her eyes rose to him. "I suppose I should start with an apology." When he looked startled, she admitted, "You were right, of course, about the scarred man."

James's gaze sharpened with interest and he settled on the couch next to her, covering her hand where it rested in her lap with one of his own, he said, "Start at the beginning, Maggie."

She tried to nod, then paused abruptly, pain flashing across her face. She held still for a moment, then took a deep breath and began. "I let the servants go to the fair," she admitted regretfully. "It was opening day, and I was to attend the opera and then the Willans' ball with the two of you, so I saw no reason not to let them all go."

"Of course you didn't," Lady Barlow murmured soothingly, taking up a position on Maggie's other side. She reached out to squeeze her free hand. "It was kind of you to let them go."

"It was stupid of me, actually." A smile

that held little humor twisted her mouth as she admitted what James was thinking. It *had* been incredibly foolish of her. He had warned her not to go anywhere alone, and here she had released her entire staff and left herself vulnerable at home. At least she now realized the danger she had put herself in, he thought, gratefully. Then she spoke again.

"I neglected to consider that I would need help getting ready," she admitted to a sympathetic Lady Barlow. "With everyone gone, I had no one to help me with my hair or dress."

James rolled his eyes at the complaint. *This* was why she thought she had been stupid in releasing her staff? Never mind that it had left her vulnerable to attack; she'd had to dress herself! Dear Lord, wasn't it just like a woman to be more concerned with matters of vanity than her well-being. He exchanged a speaking look with Robert, who had taken a seat across from them.

"And then, too," Maggie continued, "had I kept someone behind I should not have been all alone when that man came. He might not have broken into the house had the servants been there."

Relieved that the fact had at least occurred to her, even if only as a secondary consideration, James nodded and prompted her to continue. "You let the staff go and were preparing for the ball . . ."

"Yes. I heard a noise below and thought one of the servants had returned early. Which I thought was grand. I was in terrible need of someone to aid me with my hair. I took a candelabra and went to find them." Maggie frowned as the memory washed over her, clearly frightening.

"He attacked me when I entered the kitchen. We struggled and . . . I lost." She sighed wearily.

"He set the fire after you were unconscious?" James asked.

"Yes. No. I was still conscious, and he didn't start the fire, but he did spread it."

"Spread it?" Robert echoed in surprise.

"Yes." Maggie explained, "When I hit him with the candelabra, the candles went flying. One landed against a sack of grain. It started a fire. He used the candle to light a lamp, then smashed it against the wall. I tried to stop him but . . ."

James's hand squeezed hers tighter.

"Who pulled me from the fire?" she asked after a moment. Her gaze went to him. "You?"

"No. You were already out by the time we got there."

"A fellow named Jack pulled you out," Lady Barlow added. "He had you in Mr. Johnstone's carriage when we got there."

"Johnstone?" Maggie murmured. She frowned.

"The Bow Street runner who thought you were Lady X," Lady Barlow reminded her. James didn't think his aunt sounded at all impressed with the man.

"I asked him to hire someone to keep an eye on you," he explained. "Jack was to watch over you — in case something like this happened. I knew you did not believe anyone would want to hurt you and wouldn't take the proper precautions. He smelled smoke and went around the back of the house just as your attacker fled."

"Did he catch him?" Maggie asked.

"No. He went into the house after you, instead," James explained.

She looked disappointed at the fact that her attacker had gotten away.

"He'll try again," she said faintly, then met James's concerned gaze. "Thank you. I really did not think anyone could be out to harm me, but I guess you were right."

"I wish I had not been," he assured her, concern eating at him as her shoulders sagged and her head drooped. Her eyes had grown sleepier and sleepier for the past

317

several minutes, and she looked quite done-in now.

"The draft I gave you is starting to take effect," Robert commented guiltily.

"Yes." Maggie roused herself enough to nod and say, "I should go home and . . ." She paused, a frown plucking at her brow as it occurred to her to wonder if she had a home anymore. She had no idea how much damage the fire had done.

"The servants are preparing a room for you here," Lady Barlow informed her.

Maggie glanced over with surprise. "But my staff —"

"I had Meeks send one of the footmen to wait for and collect your servants. When they return from the fair, they too will stay here tonight. If necessary, we can make alternate arrangements on the morrow, after we see what is what."

Maggie felt gratitude rush over her at the matron's firm announcement. Such decisions were quite beyond her at the moment; she was more than grateful to leave them up to someone else. It was nice not to be the responsible one for a change. She had missed that since Gerald's death. Responsibility could be a heavy weight when one was alone.

"I shall just go see if your room is ready;

318

then James can carry you up."

"There is no need. I am sure I can walk," Maggie protested.

"But why bother when I am here and can carry you?" James asked gently as his aunt left the room.

"James is right, you should save your strength for mending," Lord Mullin concurred, getting to his feet. "And I suppose I should let you all be and head home."

"No, don't leave, Robert," James said. "Johnstone should be returning shortly, and we are going to discuss . . . things. I'd appreciate your input."

The other man nodded and sank back in his seat.

Maggie knew she was the "things" James had alluded to; she hadn't missed the way his glance had dropped meaningfully to her as he'd said it. She supposed he wished to discuss how to find and capture the scarfaced man, but she remained silent, her gaze dropping to where her fingers were entwined with his. She was vaguely surprised at the sight, unsure when she had taken his hand, or if he had taken hers. She watched as his thumb brushed over her knuckles. Oddly, she felt safe and comforted.

"The room is all ready," Lady Barlow announced, returning.

Determined to get there on her own, Maggie quickly gained her feet, then paused, swallowing as bile rose in her throat. The room spun. She made no protest when James scooped her into his arms; instead she caught her arms around his neck and leaned her head wearily against his shoulders, breathing in the scent of him as he followed his aunt out into the hall.

Maggie stayed silent as he carried her up the stairs to the second level, the feel of his strong encircling arms reminding her of the intimacies they had shared that day in the country. Remembering his arms around her then, his hands moving cleverly over her body, his lips warm and demanding on hers . . .

Reaching the top of the stairs, James glanced down, his face lowering as he did, so that their lips were a bare breath away. For one brief moment, Maggie thought he might kiss her. She felt her heart speed up a bit, some of the weariness dropping away from her, but then he lifted his head again and nodded at a comment from his aunt.

Her breath coming out on a small sigh, Maggie turned to see that they had arrived. Lady Barlow was holding the door open for James to carry her into the room that was to be hers. He crossed the room to the bed

— pausing as his aunt rushed forward to pull the coverlets back — then bent to set her gently down on its soft surface. The moment he released her and stepped away, Maggie missed his arms around her.

"Out you go, James. Go talk with Robert," Lady Barlow ordered as he straightened. Lord Ramsey left the room without protest, pulling the door closed behind him. She turned back to Maggie and smiled. "He thinks I am put out with him and is walking softly now, else he would have resisted leaving."

"Why would he think you are angry at him?" Maggie asked curiously.

The older woman moved to the bedside and urged her to sit so that she could set to work at unfastening the back of her dress.

"Your buttons are mismatched," she announced with a chuckle, undoing them quickly. She helped Maggie to her feet to remove the gown, then answered her question. "He thinks I am angry about the faux tea party. I just learned of it tonight."

"You do not sound very angry with him," Maggie said when Lady Barlow paused to consider her in her shift. It had gone undamaged in the fire, but carried the distinct odor of smoke. Both women wrinkled their noses.

"I am not. In fact, I am delighted," Lady Barlow admitted, then she said, "I think we had best remove your shift as well, my dear. That smoky smell might give you nightmares."

When Maggie nodded in agreement, James's aunt helped her remove that last article. The older woman clucked in dismay as the various bruises Maggie had gained during her struggle were revealed. While her face had taken the worst damage, her hip was not far behind, and there were several other contusions across her body. The moment the shift was gone, Maggie slid into the bed, self-consciously pulling the sheets up to cover herself.

"Wait here, I shall fetch you something to wear," Lady Barlow began, then paused at Maggie's weary face and hesitated, before saying, "Well, perhaps you can do without tonight."

Maggie felt relief course through her. She didn't think she had the energy to don anything. She was having difficulty even keeping her eyes open. She watched the caring woman bustle about, collecting the discarded clothes, then asked the question that had been nagging her for several moments: "Why are you delighted that James tricked me into coming to tea?"

"Because I want grand-babies." Lord Ramsey's aunt frowned then added, "I mean grand-nieces and nephews."

Maggie stared at the woman, unsure what one thing had to do with the other. None of this was making sense to her, but she was far too weary to figure it out. She closed her aching eyes.

"My room is just next door," the older woman said quietly as she prepared to leave. "Just call out if you need anything."

"Thank you," Maggie whispered on a yawn.

"You are very welcome, dear. Sleep well."

Maggie didn't answer. She was already asleep.

It was an extremely rough night. Plagued by nightmares of being beaten and burned alive, Maggie struggled toward consciousness several times, only to relax as she dreamed she was held in strong, protective arms, and that James was murmuring comforting words to her.

A soft weeping drew her out of sleep the following morning. Opening her eyes slowly, she peered around the soothing green room she'd slept in until she spotted the source of the misery. Her maid Mary sat in a chair by the bedside. Obviously Lady Barlow's footman had brought her staff last night as promised, Maggie realized. But that didn't explain why the girl was sobbing.

Concern overtaking her, Maggie struggled to sit up, drawing the girl's attention. "Oh, m'lady, ye should rest," Mary cried, leaping from her seat at once and trying to force her mistress back down.

"Nay, let me up. What is the matter? Was someone hurt? James? Lady Barlow? Banks?" She started to run through the names of everyone on her staff, but Mary shook her head for each.

"Nay, m'lady. Everyone's fine. Except for you, o'course," she added, biting her lip and turning away.

Frowning in confusion, Maggie tried to understand what had the girl crying, then nearly kicked herself when she realized it must surely be the town house itself. It had been home to all of Maggie's servants too, of course, and every last possession they had had been destroyed in the fire along with her own. In fact, she realized as she noticed Mary wearing the same gown she'd donned for the fair yesterday, they had been left with only the clothes on their backs.

"Do not worry, Mary. There is no need to cry. I shall see that your clothes are replaced. In fact, you can all go today and purchase what you need. Just have everything put on my account."

"Thank ye, m'lady, but that isn't why I was crying."

"Then why *are* you crying?" she asked in exasperation.

The girl hesitated, her eyes returning reluctantly to Maggie's face. Then she cried mournfully, "Oh, m'lady, yer beautiful face!"

Fear touching her at the girl's horrified expression, Maggie struggled out of bed. Stumbling to the dressing table, she let a gasp slip from her lips as she saw herself. The entire right side of her face was a swollen mess of mottled red, black, and blue. If the left side of her face were not nearly untouched, she wasn't sure if she would have recognized herself. Her own eyes brimming with tears, she sank to sit on the dressing table chair.

She stared at herself for several minutes, her hands raising to touch her injured face, then Mary stepped up behind her holding out a robe. "Lady Barlow sent this up for you to use."

Maggie met the maid's reflected gaze in the mirror as she slipped the robe on. Her expression was pitying, her eyes full of sympathetic tears. The girl was about to burst into loud sobs again, Maggie realized and stiffened her spine.

"Well, that shall teach me to use my face for a club when next I fight off an attacker," she said with determined cheer. All it managed to do was cause Mary to lift the skirt of her apron to cry into it. Heaving herself up from the bench, Maggie moved to her side. She patted the girl's shoulder soothingly. "Oh, Mary, do not cry. It will heal in time."

For a moment, Maggie thought her words had worked. Mary paused and lifted wide eyes to her, but then she wailed, "Oh, m'lady, ye're so brave!" Then she set to sobbing even harder.

Maggie was still trying to soothe the girl a few moments later when the door opened and Joan and Nora entered carting a chest between them. Their sister's sobs brought them to an immediate halt, and they both stared with alarm.

"What's the matter with . . ." Nora paused mid-question as she spotted Maggie's face. Her eyes widened in horror, then, and she dropped her end of the chest with a thump. "Gor!"

"Blimey, he pummeled ye right ugly," Joan said as she, too, caught sight of her mistress. Letting the other end of the chest drop to the floor as well, she followed her sister over to get a better look.

Maggie shifted with irritation. There was just some bruising and swelling. It wasn't as if she were permanently disfigured. They were all overreacting terribly, she thought impatiently.

A rustling made all four women glance around.

"Is there something wrong, Banks?" Maggie asked with concern when she spotted the old retainer dithering in the doorway.

"No, my lady. I just thought to have a word with you . . . If you have a moment?"

"Of course." She glanced at the three maids who promptly started for the door. Maggie called out, "Collect the others together please, Mary. I should think the sooner you get the trip to the shops out of the way, the better."

"Aye, m'lady," the girl answered as she followed her sisters into the hall.

Banks waited until their voices had faded before crossing the room toward Maggie. "I wished . . ." He paused, wincing as he got near enough for his old eyes to focus on her brutalized face. Then, he drew himself up and said, "I wished to apologize."

"Apologize?" Maggie asked with confusion. "Whatever could you have to apologize for?"

"You. Your face." The butler's expression was tragic. "Your beautiful town house. All your —"

"Banks," Maggie interrupted gently, closing the last few feet between them to clasp his hands. "You have nothing for which to apologize. It is hardly your fault that someone broke in and —"

"But it is!" he protested. "I never should have left you alone. The only thing Master Gerald asked of me before he went bravely off to war was that I look after you, and —"

"You, too?" Maggie exclaimed, bringing confusion to the butler's wizened face. "Good Lord, Gerald put everyone in charge of me. He must have thought me a complete ninny . . . or dicked in the nob."

"My lady! Nay!" Banks cried. "Master Gerald did not think you crazy. He loved you and wished the best for you." The man's shoulders slumped, then he forced them back up. "I failed him, and I failed you. But I vow to you here and now, I shall not fail either of you again. I shall look after you as I promised."

"Banks," she began, torn between affection and concern. "I do not —"

"Maggie?"

328

Margaret stiffened at that voice. Banks stood between her and the door, but she didn't need to see James to know it was him; she would recognize that voice anywhere. Her stillness ended when Banks started to turn to face the door. Recalling Mary, Joan, Nora, and even Banks's reaction to the sight of her face, she turned the opposite way, instinctively hiding her hideous bruises.

"Maggie?" She could hear the concern in his voice as Lord Ramsey drew nearer, and found herself glancing around in a panicky fashion, seeking an escape. Her earlier thoughts that it was "just bruising" and that it would "mend with time" flew out the window at the idea of him seeing her. But there was nowhere to hide, even were there time to do so. Trapped, she dropped her head, letting her hair drape down to obscure her face, and waited.

Banks excused himself, and Maggie heard the soft rustle of clothing as he left the room. The quiet click of the door being pulled closed told Maggie that she and James were alone. Then, he touched her shoulder, urging her to turn.

"Are you all right?" he asked when she kept her head bowed. "I know you had some nasty nightmares."

Maggie glanced up, her eyes wide. "You

329

know . . . You mean I wasn't dreaming?" she asked in surprise.

Confusion covered his handsome face. "About what?"

"I was having nightmares, but I also dreamed that you were holding me," she admitted, before she could think better of it.

He smiled at her words. "Yes. For a little while. It seemed to soothe you."

She gave a shy nod, then stiffened as she realized he could see her face. She whirled away, ducking her head again. "Was there something you wanted?" she asked.

He was silent for a moment, then his feet came into view as he moved around to stand in front of her. "There is no reason to hide," he said quietly, forcing her face up with one finger.

"I look like a monster," she complained, trying to turn her back to him again. "Just the sight of me had Mary in tears."

"You do look pretty bad," he agreed honestly. When she lifted her face to glare at him for such an unchivalrous comment, she found his eyes twinkling.

"It will heal, Maggie," he assured her, then leaned forward to press a tender kiss to the corner of her lips.

Maggie inhaled, breathing in the scent of

him as his lips brushed hers. The smell and taste of this man were familiar and exciting and took her right back to their passionate moments in the library at Ramsey. It seemed like a century had passed since then, and Maggie couldn't hold back a moan of protest when he started to draw away. His mouth returned at once, and she could feel his smile before his tongue slid out to lave her lips.

Maggie moved closer, her arms creeping around James's neck as his slid around her waist. He pressed her tight against him until there was no space between their bodies, then he drove his tongue into the moist depths of her mouth. Pleasure rippled through her, and Maggie groaned. All her aches and pains, all her worries and fears dropped away. She felt safe and warm. She felt as if she had come home. Then he eased their embrace so that his hands could slip between them. He undid her robe with one tug at the sash and eased it open, then paused.

"Oh, Maggie," he breathed, and the regret in his voice made her peer down. She had been so horrified at the sight of her face, she had not even noticed her other bruises. Now she gazed at herself with amazement. There was one on the side of one breast, another on her ribs, and then a rather nasty one on her hip. There were more contusions on her legs, but Maggie was suddenly self-conscious standing there revealed and tried to draw her robe closed.

James caught her hands to stop her and bent to give her another kiss. It was unlike the ones they had shared in his library. Where those had been carnal, this one was sweet, slow and gentle; his lips and tongue were soothing her rather than invasive. The kiss stirred a lazy desire and sent a sluggish warmth flowing through her.

Maggie sighed into his mouth and relaxed in his embrace, then opened her eyes as his lips left hers. She watched his head duck, and caught her breath as he pressed a light kiss to the bruise on her injured breast — a feathery caress she barely felt as his hand closed over the other. Biting her lip, she watched him palm then squeeze that breast before shifting his hand to a more supportive hold as his mouth closed over her nipple.

"James," she breathed as he drew the cinnamon-colored flesh into his mouth and suckled. He barely seemed to have started, when he stopped and moved down to brush his lips over the angry discoloration on her upper ribs. The caress began as light as a butterfly's wings but ended with an erotic lick of the underside of her breast. Then James sank to his knees and his mouth whispered over the angry wound on her hip.

Maggie sighed again, then gasped when he moved his lips to the inner curve of her other hip. Her stomach jumped at the action, and she gripped the top of his head, as her legs went suddenly weak. His mouth moved to her stomach and he pressed a kiss there, his tongue delving briefly into her belly-button. He started to move lower, but his hands shifted to the back of her hips, and Maggie couldn't keep from crying out in pain.

James's head lifted at once, then he moved her robe aside and shifted on his knees to peer at her injury there. It was nearly as bad as her face, and she saw his sympathetic wince, then he stood, drew her robe closed and took her into his arms.

Holding her tenderly he said, "I am sorry. I didn't mean to add to your pain."

"You didn't. Well, I mean, I know you didn't," Maggie sighed.

Drawing back, James smiled at her, then pressed a quick kiss to her uninjured cheek. "I should go. I am meeting an agent from your insurer at the town house. He wishes to assess the damage and make arrangements for repairs."

Maggie opened her mouth to assure him that she could do that, then recalled her damaged face and changed her mind. She had almost forgotten how to accept aid since Gerald's death. This time she would take the offered help. "Thank you."

"You're welcome." James's smile widened, then he hugged her briefly and released her to cross the room. He paused when he came abreast of the chest Joan and Nora had carted in. "These are some of my sister's old gowns," he explained. "She and Aunt Viv are both pack rats. Neither of them ever throw anything out. See if you can't find something decent in here to wear, then come below. You can tell me what you wish me to say to the insurer before I leave."

Maggie nodded and watched him exit the room. Her body was still tingling. She also felt warm and . . . soothed. She had never felt like this before.

CHAPTER FOURTEEN

Maggie placed another stitch in the gown she was working on, then set it in her lap so that she could flex her hands and rub soothingly at her neck, which was beginning to crick. The last several days seemed made up of working endlessly at the task of altering James's sister's old gowns.

James and Lady Barlow had wanted to bring a dressmaker in to make new clothes for her — both of them offering to bear the expense of such an undertaking — but Maggie's pride would not allow her to accept such a generous gift. She was already terribly beholden to them, and she found it difficult to even accept these castoffs without some repayment. But neither Lady Barlow nor her nephew would hear of remuneration, so Maggie was forced to accept their generosity. She needed clothes, after all, and she was hoping that at some point she would be able to find a way to repay them.

Though, she supposed, she should be thinking of James's sister. It was that girl's old clothes being given away so freely.

Sighing, she picked up her needle and the green gown she was working on and again returned to her efforts. The day after the fire, Lady Barlow had spent a good deal of time helping her pin and sew the gowns so that the bodices fit. Maggie had sent her servants out to purchase clothes to replace their own lost wardrobes, and had appreciated the older woman's assistance, in their absence, but once the maids had returned and been available to help her, Maggie had convinced the older woman to return to her usual daytime activity of calling on friends.

While her female servants had assisted Maggie in sewing upon returning from their shopping trip, her male servants had gone with James to inspect the damage to the house, to see what — if anything — was salvageable. They had returned with the comforting news that the fire brigade her insurance company ran had arrived in time to ensure that most of the fire damage had been confined to the kitchens and the room above. The rest of the house had merely suffered smoke damage. While most of its furnishings needed reupholstering, and the linens and clothing needed replacing, the house itself was sound and would be quite inhabitable in no time. The work was, thank heavens, covered by the insurance Gerald had always insisted she keep.

Unfortunately, while James almost convinced her with his reassuring smiles, Maggie's butler, Banks, was a lousy liar. She had seen right through the tale. The way her butler had twisted his hat in his hands and avoided her gaze had made it clear that James was lying through his teeth. And the fact that, even several days later, the servants still returned each night to Lady Barlow's after spending the days helping to clear the town house seemed to confirm her fear.

At first it had just been the men leaving each morning to help out at the town house, but this morning Maggie had sent the women along, too, keeping only Mary back to help her with the last of her gowns. It had been cowardice that made her do so. With all of her maids sewing, they had been running through the gowns quite quickly, and Maggie had wanted to slow their progress. She was afraid that once she finished with all the alterations, Lady Barlow would insist on Maggie's accompanying her on social calls, and while Maggie's face was slowly returning to normal, it was still slightly swollen and an unattractive yellow. She was not vain by nature, but had no wish to be seen as she was.

Besides, she had some thinking to do. If, as she suspected, her brother's house was more damaged than James was letting on, she doubted if the insurance she'd purchased would cover the repairs. Which had her fretting. She needed money. Desperately. In fact, she had the gloomy feeling that her financial position was more precarious than ever.

Maggie scowled and jabbed her needle into the cloth she held, knowing that she shouldn't be wasting her time sewing extra garments. She should be out researching another story for the *Daily Express*.

Fortunately, Hartwick had long ago assured her he would take as many stories as she could write. Up until now, she had only ever supplied one article every two weeks; it wasn't so easy to keep coming up with fresh ideas, and biweekly articles had been enough to keep them afloat. Now she would have to squeeze out more. The only problem was, with her mind on all the many trials and tribulations in her life, she couldn't seem to think of anything good to write about.

Frowning, she considered the matter,

thinking up and discarding one story line after another. One was too boring, another too similar to an article she'd already done. She was almost relieved when Meeks coughed at the doorway, drawing her attention from her rather hopeless thoughts.

"Yes?" she asked as the man came forward. He held a small silver tray in his hand, bearing a folded piece of paper.

"A letter for you, my lady."

"For me?" Her eyebrows shot up in surprise, but she set her sewing aside and took the note. "Thank you." Nodding, the man turned and wordlessly left the room.

Maggie opened the unsealed note and read the letter with growing surprise and relief. It was from Maisey, an answer to the letter she had sent more than a week back about their traded gowns and the possibility of calling it even. The subject had quite slipped her mind, what with everything that had happened since. The delay was clarified at the beginning of the letter; the girl explained that she had been away at a private house party during the whole of this last week.

Maggie grimaced slightly, knowing as she did the girl's occupation, then read on, relieved to find that the girl thought it more than fair that they call it quits on the gowns.

She would keep the money Frances had offered to replace the ripped gown, and Maggie need not worry about replacing the red one.

It was one worry off her mind, but Maggie's relief knew no bounds when the young woman then mentioned that she had come across a certain club in which G. W. Clark might have some interest — a club in which it was said dastardly things took place. Maggie was to write back at once and let Maisey know if she was interested, then the girl could set up a time when it was convenient for Maggie to attend. The prostitute was even willing to go with her for a fee.

"Meeks," Maggie called, refolding the letter.

The man must have been waiting outside the door, because he stepped back into the room at once, not looking the least ruffled or surprised.

"It says here that the boy who brought the note would wait for a reply. Is there a —"

"I sent him to the kitchens to wait," Meeks answered calmly. Seeming to feel it necessary to explain, he added, "I could not leave the little urchin alone in the entry while I delivered the note; he might have pocketed something. And the neighbors would have complained had I left him on the stoop."

Maggie bit back an amused smile. She didn't believe his claim for a minute. The man was as soft as a raw egg. No doubt he had ordered the cook to find food and water for the "urchin." He had a kind heart.

"Yes, of course. I understand," she murmured, setting her sewing aside so that she could get up. "Do you think it would be all right if I used some of Lady Barlow's paper and ink to write a response?"

"Of course, my lady. Lady Barlow has said that I am to get you anything you require. If you follow me, I will show you to the library and supply you with all necessities for your correspondence."

"Thank you." Ignoring Mary's curious gaze, Maggie followed the man to the library, working out her answer in her head as she went. This was too perfect. She desperately needed a story, and Maisey, the dear girl, was giving her just that. It was the first stroke of good luck she'd had since that fateful night at Madame Dubarry's. Perhaps things were starting to look up.

James stepped down from his carriage and walked jauntily up to his aunt's house, a smile on his face. He had spent the day overseeing work on Maggie's town house and was pleased with how things were coming. The house had nearly been gutted before the fire brigade from the Union Assurance company — Maggie's insurance company — had arrived to put it out.

Of course, he hadn't told her that. The fuss she had raised over accepting a couple of cast-off gowns of his sister's, and her absolute refusal to allow him or his aunt to assist by purchasing her new gowns to replace the ones she had lost in the fire, had warned him she would be too proud to accept any help in repairing the town house. He had also realized, after a conversation with her insurer, that her coverage would not fund all of the necessary repairs, nor the replacement of her furnishings. So he had lied.

He knew without a doubt that Maggie wasn't completely fooled by his fabrications, but he was also quite sure that there was nothing she could do about them. He had brought in droves of workers and even her own people to ensure that the repairs and rebuilding were done quickly, and it was moving along nicely. Another day or so and her staff would even be able to move back in. By the time Maggie got to see it, she wouldn't be able to tell how much damage there had been or how costly it had been to set right. He would lie about the money, and she would not be able to prove otherwise. He was quite satisfied with his handling of the matter.

Reaching the door, James rapped lightly with his cane, then whistled lightly as he waited for it to be opened, enjoying the anticipation building within him. He had visited Maggie and his aunt often since the fire, usually playing cards with both ladies, though on occasion he had played chess alone with Maggie in the library while his aunt entertained friends in the salon. The doors had been left open on these occasions, of course, as was proper and expected.

James enjoyed those visits best. Maggie relaxed more around him when his aunt wasn't present, her smiles and soft laughter enchanting.

Tonight his aunt was having a small gathering of friends. James had not planned to attend — he'd expected to be meeting with Johnstone for an update on Maggie's attacker — but he had received a letter from the runner just moments ago and learned the man was rushing out of town tracking a clue and would miss their meeting. James had promptly ordered his carriage and headed for his aunt's — for Maggie.

He had no doubt she would be easily

culled from the herd of females and lured to the library. It had not escaped his notice that despite the fact that her bruises were nearly gone, she was still shy about displaying her face in public. He had every intention of taking advantage of that.

The door was opened by Meeks. The old man's eyes widened in surprise upon seeing him. "My lord, I thought you had a meeting and were not to be present tonight."

"My meeting was canceled," James announced cheerfully. He stepped inside.

"Oh, I am glad you are here, my lord."

"And I am glad to be here." James handed over his hat and cane to the man, his gaze straying to the salon door. He could hear the muffled murmur of female voices coming through it. "Is Maggie in there with the rest of the women?"

"Nay, my lord," Meeks answered grimly.

James paused on his way to the door to turn back questioningly. "Where is she then? Up in her room?"

"Nay, my lord. She is not here."

"What?" He stared at the butler, uncomprehending. "What do you mean, she is not here? Where *is* she?"

The servant hesitated briefly; then his mouth firmed with unhappiness. "She received a letter today, my lord. From someone named Maisey."

James's eyes widened in horror, and he snatched his hat and cane back. "Dear Lord, she has gone back to Dubarry's."

"Nay," Meeks said quickly, following him to the door. When James turned on him, the man seemed to struggle with his conscience, then admitted, "The letter was not sealed. A street urchin brought it. I dropped the note, it fell open, and I just happened to see —"

"You read it," James snapped, unwilling to waste time on the man's excuses. "What did it say?"

Meeks colored slightly, but he straightened and said with dignity, "This Maisey person claimed to know of a club she thought G. W. Clark might be interested in. A men's club."

"Which one?" James prompted.

"The letter did not say. It simply mentioned a club with dastardly goings-on and requested that her ladyship reply as to whether she was interested in the club and when might be a convenient time to investigate it."

"And what was Maggie's answer?" James asked impatiently.

Meeks drew himself up indignantly. "I

345

would not stoop to reading her ladyship's letters."

James frowned. No, he would not expect the man to be so impertinent as to open a sealed letter as Maggie's response clearly would have been.

"But," the butler went on. "A second missive to Lady Margaret also went unsealed. It simply said seven o'clock tonight, and an address. There was a mask with the letter."

"A mask?" James asked suspiciously. What was Maggie up to? "What kind of mask?"

"It was quite distinctive. A teal-and-gold feathered affair."

James digested that, then glanced up sharply. "Do you recall the address in the letter?"

"Of course."

"Good man," he said with relief.

Maggie leaned against the wall of the building, doing her best to look inconspicuous as she watched carriage after carriage stop and disgorge masked individuals and couples in front of the address across the street. The house looked completely normal, no different from any of the other town houses in this district, but if what Maisey hinted at was true, there was more going on than just a masked ball.

Shifting impatiently, she glanced nervously up the street, her eyes searching for any sign of Maisey. The problem was, Maggie wasn't sure for what she was supposed to be looking. Maisey was about Maggie's height, with dirty-blond hair, but if the girl came masked like the others, Maggie wasn't certain she would be able to spot her.

Worse, there was a good possibility that Maisey would not recognize her, either, despite the mask the other girl had sent to make the task easier. The young prostitute would be looking for that mask on a woman, and Maggie was not dressed as a female. She had decided at the last minute to go dressed as a man, an idea that had come to her while she searched the attic for shoes to match the gown she'd intended to wear.

Maggie had worn nothing but slippers around Lady Barlow's town house since the fire. She could hardly wear those out of the house, however, and Jean and Nora had mentioned while helping her sift through the chest of Sophie's gowns — retrieved under Lady Barlow's direction — that the attic was stuffed full of all sorts of things, including masks, fans, shoes, and the like. Searching through that treasure trove of stored items, Maggie had come upon a chest filled with male clothing.

The style and size of the boxed garments had convinced her that they were no doubt castoffs from James's youth, and the idea had struck like lightning that she should attend the men's club as a male. She'd had no problem finding appropriate garb in the chest for an evening at a men's club, not to mention a pair of old dress boots that fit nicely, and so her mind had been made up. She tied her hair at her nape, slid it down the back of her shirt, and donned the mask and a top hat. Fortunately, the mask was rather neutral in style, so it was not unlikely for a man to wear. It also boasted enough feathers and other trinkets to hide the fact that Maggie's hair was long and tied back.

Grimacing, she shifted her legs, glancing around to be sure no one was looking her way, then she gave the back of her breeches a brief tug. This was not the first time that Maggie had camouflaged herself in male dress, but it was not a disguise she often chose when she could avoid it. Binding her breasts was a rather painful procedure, and besides, she wasn't all that comfortable in these tight-fitting breeches. While James had been the same size in his youth, at least length-wise in the legs, he hadn't apparently had any hips. Maggie found the breeches far too snug for comfort across her bottom, especially when compared to the freedom of billowing bloomers and skirts. She found herself plagued by the constant and horrendous urge to tug at the behind of the trousers to draw them away from her skin.

It had not occurred to her while she had donned this brilliant disguise that she was just making matters more difficult, that Maisey would never think to look for a male. All she had been concerned with was that should the scarred man see her slipping away through the garden gate at the back of Lady Barlow's home, he would not recognize her — leaving her safe from that concern for a bit as she investigated this club where dastardly events took place.

Now she realized it had been an incredibly stupid idea. Maisey had sent the mask to aid in identifying Maggie, and she would hardly be looking for it on a man. She might very well not notice Maggie at all tonight.

Heaving out an impatient breath, she peered up the street, trying to work out how much time had passed since she had left Lady Barlow's. She had made her exit an hour before the appointed time, walking several blocks before feeling it was safe enough to hail a hack. She had planned to be here early. Maggie was always early for appointments. But it surely must be nearly seven o'clock by now. Where was Maisey?

"Lady Margaret."

Maggie gave a start at that hiss from behind her. Turning, she peered into the shadows cast by the awning of the building, barely able to discern a cloaked and masked figure several steps away. "Maisey?" she asked.

Nodding, the girl moved forward to the edge of the shadows. "Why are you dressed as a man? You should have worn a gown."

"I did not think it would matter. Does it?" Maggie asked worriedly.

Maisey hesitated, her eyes moving along the street, then across the road to the house, where yet another masked couple was spilling from their carriage; then she shifted impatiently. "It will have to do. Come."

Turning away, the prostitute led her across the street at a quick clip that didn't slow until they neared the door to the "club." Gesturing for Maggie to wait there, Maisey approached one of the two doorman standing on either side of the entrance a few steps away and held a brief, whispered conversation with him. It concluded with her dropping several coins into his open palm. Then, gesturing for Maggie to follow, the young woman entered the house, hardly glancing at the second doorman.

Offering a weak smile when the man turned his gaze on her, Maggie followed Maisey reluctantly into an entryway. There, another pair was handing over their cloaks to a servant. Maisey whipped off her own, tossed the expensive item onto the already weighed down man, then waited impatiently for Maggie to do the same. She removed her borrowed cape and handed it to the servant with an apologetic expression, then followed her guide and the other couple into a room filled with noise and color.

Maggie's eyes widened behind her mask as she absorbed the multitudes inside. The room was crammed to capacity, and she struggled to push her way through to keep up with Maisey. The masked occupants were both men and women, all talking and crowding together. There wasn't much out of the ordinary here that she could see, however. It was true that everyone seemed to be standing a bit closer than was absolutely proper, but space constraints dictated they had little choice in the matter.

Realizing that Maisey was outstripping her, and afraid she would lose the woman in the crowd, Maggie forced her way through the throng a bit faster, apologizing for her rudeness as she attempted to catch up. She did so just as Maisey started up a set of stairs to a second level, and caught at her arm anxiously. "Where are we going?"

"Upstairs is where all the action is," the girl paused to whisper, then continued on apparently confident Maggie would follow. Which she did, looking back over her shoulder as they went. From above, it was clear that everything wasn't as ordinary as she had first thought. While the majority of people were standing talking in the center of the room, there appeared to be a great deal of inappropriate touching going on. Scanning the edges of the crowd, Maggie discerned the true nature of this gathering. There were couples crammed into all manner of corners and recesses, indulging in the most improper behavior. She'd heard of members of the ton sneaking away into the gardens — shocking as that was! — but copulating against the wall was not acceptable at any of the balls she had ever attended.

"Come on!" Maisey called.

Realizing that she had stopped to gape down at the crowd below the stairs, Maggie turned to see her young guide moving off down the hall. Starting after her, Maggie did her best to ignore the lascivious couples lining the corridor, and hoped fervently that this article was worth this. She felt sullied just being in this place. Briefly she considered fleeing, but then she thought of the fire and the expenses incurred daily to repair her home, and she stiffened her spine. An hour — no, half an hour — and she would surely have the information she needed and be out of here. She assured herself of that with more hope than certainty and moved determinedly forward.

She hadn't taken more than a few steps when a scream from behind a door she was passing brought her to an abrupt halt. It had been a cry of agony, and Maggie felt chills run down her back. Was someone being murdered behind this wooden portal?

"Come on!" Maisey was suddenly at her side, taking her arm and dragging her forward again.

"But it sounded like someone was —"

"Games," the prostitute said in a hiss; then she showed Maggie the back of her head as she dragged her forward. For a moment Maggie felt trepidation race through her. Then, recalling some of the tales the prostitutes at Madame Dubarry's had told her, she forced herself to relax. She had seen for herself the games that Pastor Frances had enjoyed. They were just games, she assured herself silently. Then she frowned. If all this was just some sort of sex club . . . But Mai-

353

sey had said "dastardly things" happened here.

Confused and unhappy, Maggie sped up until she drew abreast of her short guide. "You said 'dastardly things' happened here. What —"

"You'll see soon enough," the other woman assured her, pausing near the door at the end of the hall and producing a key. After turning it in the lock, she pocketed the item and went through the now open door leaving Maggie to follow. After a quick glance down the hall, Maggie did so. Inside, her gaze moved over the room's odd trappings as Maisey lit a single candle by the bedside, then carried it to the window to stare at the street below.

"What — ?"

"Shh," Maisey hissed, then hesitated before setting the candle on the window ledge and walking to the door. "There is a peep hole in that painting on the wall. Through it, you can see the room next door. I'll return shortly."

"But . . ." Maggie started anxiously toward the prostitute, breaking into a run when the girl stepped out into the hall and pulled the door closed. She heard the lock click as she reached it, and she cursed. Maisey certainly liked to lock her in uncomfortable places, she thought with disgust. She twisted the doorknob futilely.

Giving the door an angry kick, she turned and surveyed the chamber. The bed was the only ordinary item in the room. An oddly angled bench with chains on it and an oddly shaped chair with wrist locks made her wonder just what went on here. Her second thought, as she peered at chains dangling from the ceiling and affixed to the walls, and a selection of whips and various other unpleasant-looking items along one wall, was that she probably didn't want to know.

Forcing herself to take a deep breath, she glanced at the painting Maisey said had a peep hole and moved for a better view. It didn't take long for her to realize that the eyes in the rather naughty portrait were hollowed out. Unfortunately, they were a good foot above her head. Moving to the chair with the wrist locks, she dragged it over to position it beneath the painting, then climbed onto it and peered through the eyeholes. A room similarly outfitted to the one she was in was all there was to see. It was empty.

Sighing, she stepped back down off the chair and glanced around, then paced the room, examining each various item therein. When she reached the door, she tried the doorknob again, but it was still locked. On impulse, she knelt and pressed her eye to the keyhole. Despite the fact that the room she was in was at the end of a hall and presented a clear view of its length, there wasn't much to see. The corridor was still crowded with couples indulging in libertine behavior she had barely touched on in those frantic moments in the Ramsey library. She supposed this was quite an education — and more like what she'd expected in Maisey's closet — but not one she really wanted. Maggie was about to straighten from the keyhole when a figure mounting the last few stairs at the end of the passage caught her attention. Surprised, she stared at the man as he moved up the hallway.

He wasn't wearing a mask.

That was what had originally caught her attention, but as he drew closer and his face came into better focus, her eyes froze on the scar. Sucking in her breath on an alarmed gasp and shoving instinctively back from the door, she tumbled from her knees onto her behind. She stared at the keyhole briefly, as if it were a snake, then just as quickly returned to her kneeling position. Much to her horror, she saw as she again peeked outside that the man was moving straight up the hallway. It seemed she hadn't given him the slip with her disguise after all. He must have followed her, had probably just been waiting for her to be alone! *Dammit!* Where was Maisey?

Realizing that the girl wouldn't return in time, and probably wouldn't be much help against the brute in any case, Maggie cursed and leaped to her feet. She searched frantically around the room for a weapon.

Her gaze flew over whips and chains in agitation; she somehow didn't see herself wielding any of them with much success. Still she grabbed the nearest one, then took an empty candleholder in her other hand for good measure. Turning grimly to face the door, she readied herself for battle. Her intrepid stance lasted until she heard the key in the lock; then Maggie's courage failed her and she scrambled in a panicked shuffle to the wall behind the door. Perhaps she might take him by surprise and bash him over the head as he entered.

The door opened, and Maggie reacted out of hysteria more than anything else. She leaped from her hiding place with a shriek, which made the intruder turn with a start. She brought the candleholder down on the side of his head with all her terrified strength. Much to her amazement, the man gaped at her, then went down like a felled tree.

Maggie stared uncomprehendingly at his unconscious form for a moment, hardly believing it had been so easy, then regained her scattered wits enough to drop her makeshift weapons and scramble over the man's legs and out the door. She was running at full-tilt, paying no attention to the startled reactions of the people in the hallway in her haste to flee the scene, so that when she suddenly found someone in her path, she smashed blindly into his bulk. With a moan of despair at the delay, she scrabbled to break free of the hands that rose automatically to restrain her.

"Maggie?"

Some of her hysteria slipping away, Maggie focused on the face of the man gawking down at her. Lord Ramsey's wonderfully familiar features took shape.

"James," she said with relief.

His expression immediately turned from shock to anger. Maggie bit her lip, then glanced back the way she had come.

"That man . . ." was as far as she got before she found herself being jerked along the hall by her arm. James was obviously furious, she realized, and peered over her shoulder toward the room where she'd left her attacker. He was beginning to stir. She considered telling James about the man, then decided against it. Scarface was a very strong man — bigger than Lord Ramsey — and she didn't want to see James hurt. Perhaps it was best all around if they simply left well enough alone and got out of there.

She made no protest as James jogged her down the stairs and dragged her through the crowded room to the exit. He had hauled her out of the house and crammed her into his carriage before she recalled that her borrowed cloak was still inside.

CHAPTER FIFTEEN

"I . . ." Maggie began in an effort to explain herself as soon as the carriage door shut, enclosing them in darkness and privacy, but James raised a hand to silence her.

"Not *one* word. Not one," he said in a furious hiss. "Or I might very well take you over my knee and . . ." His threat ended on a hiss of air.

Maggie stared, fascinated, at the tic of his eye for a moment, then, deciding she might do better to follow his advice, she turned her head to stare out the window. Neither of them said a word the entire ride back to Lady Barlow's. Maggie watched blindly out the window, her body stiff as she did her best to ignore the glare boring into her across the dark space between herself and Lord Ramsey.

When the carriage came to a halt, Maggie focused her eyes to see that they had arrived. She had hardly deduced their location when James thrust the door open, snatched her hand in his, and bounded out of the coach, hauling her after him. She was barely able to keep her feet as he dragged her to the door, his boots clacking angrily with each step. It was perhaps telling how angry he was that he did not knock or wait for anyone to open the front door of his aunt's town house, but thrust it aside as he had his carriage door. He pulled her inside.

Meeks rushed up as they entered, his eyes widening at the sight of them. He opened his mouth to speak, but James held up his hand as he had done with Maggie and merely sailed into the library with her.

The door slammed behind them as he tugged her across the room toward the fire. Then he paused and glanced around. Maggie wasn't sure what he was looking for, but she'd had just about enough of being lugged around like a horse by its reins. She pulled her hand free, the suddenness of the action probably the only reason she succeeded. James turned on her at once, and Maggie opened her mouth to go on the offensive, but she never managed a word. It seemed James had reached the end of his tether. Grabbing her by the upper arms, he pulled her abruptly against his chest. The action startled Maggie into closing her mouth, which was a darn good thing, since his lips then slammed onto hers with all the finesse of a charging bull. Had her mouth been open, she might have done him injury.

As it was, she winced as the inside of her lips were ground against her teeth in a brutal kiss. Then she began to struggle instinctively against his punishing grasp. James shifted his hold, wrapping one arm around her back, his other hand clasping her head and holding her in place as the kiss changed, becoming less harsh yet more demanding.

Maggie continued to struggle for a moment, then stopped, a gasp of shock escaping her as the arm around her waist shifted. One of James's hands slapped her bottom lightly through the pants she wore, then gently squeezed even as he urged her against him.

James took immediate advantage of her reaction. His tongue slipped inside her open mouth, but while she wasn't fighting him any longer, she didn't respond at once to his kiss. He pulled away and glared at her.

Maggie stared back, knowing that her confusion and a vague sense of hurt at his treatment were evident on her face. It took a moment before he seemed to see past his anger and notice; then he sighed and leaned his forehead against hers, still holding her tightly.

"I have never been so worried or frightened in my life as I was when I realized you were running about on your own. After those accidents, the fire . . . I was so afraid I was going to lose you."

His voice was low and husky. Maggie's eyes widened, her hands relaxing against his chest. The basis of this anger was fear. This was all because he feared losing her! And he had every right to that fear, she realized, recalling the man she'd left unconscious in that awful place. Her heart softening, Maggie slid her arms around James's waist, holding him.

"But you didn't. I am here. I am fine," she whispered.

His eyes opening, James pulled away enough that he could look at her again. Seeing her understanding expression, he managed a crooked smile. "I never want to feel like that again. Please don't go out again on your own like that. I will help you if you need to investigate a story. I —"

"Shhh." Maggie pressed a finger gently to his lips. "I promise never again to investigate a story without at least telling you. It was very foolish of me to go to meet Maisey alone. I should have known better after all that's happened, but I thought that I would be fine if I went in disguise. I was wrong," she added quickly when he would have interrupted. "I see that. And I am sorry I worried you. It will not happen again."

He remained speechless for a moment, staring into her face; then she felt the hand on her derriere move curiously against her bottom. A small smile crossed his lips. "You look rather delectable in men's clothing."

Maggie felt a blush rise from her chest to cover her throat and face, but she remained still in his arms, unresisting when he used the hand on her bottom to urge her lower body tighter against his. She could feel him growing hard against her. His gaze sought hers, and she met it unflinchingly; then his eyes dropped to her lips. She held her breath, letting it out on a disappointed sigh as his gaze traveled up over her face to her hair.

Smiling more devilishly, he reached behind her head and pulled her ponytail out of the back of her shirt, then removed the bit of ribbon she had used to tie it. The pale strands fell free, tumbling around her face and over her shoulders. Maggie remained still as he brushed his fingers through the tousled mane, smoothing it; then he caught her face in his hands and pressed a kiss to her lips.

The kiss started out gentle, James's lips soothing any hurt he might have caused with his earlier brutality, but it did not stay gentle for long. The moment Maggie opened her lips beneath his, kissing him back with innocent fervor, something seemed to ignite within them both. The embrace became consuming, his hands sliding away from her cheeks and beginning to explore her body, moving over the men's clothes she wore with curiosity and determination. One moment they were traveling over her breasts, through the shirt and binding that covered them; then his hands had slid back to her bottom, squeezing and lifting her against him so that his swollen arousal rubbed between her thighs.

Gasping, Maggie threw her arms around his shoulders and pressed herself tighter against him — eagerly, as he was pressing into her. He groaned into her mouth, then began to back her up until she felt the hard edge of Lady Barlow's desk pressing into her behind. Lifting her, gripping her buttocks, he sat her on the desk, then urged her legs apart so that he could step between them. He was still kissing her, his lips and tongue doing things that left her quivering and moaning into his mouth even as she kissed him in return. His hands were busy between them, working at her clothing.

She felt the cravat fall loose, then slide across the back of her neck as he drew it off her, but she hardly paid any attention, easing back slightly at his insistence, uncaring of the inappropriate nature of what he was doing as his hands moved over the front of her clothing. She hardly noticed when he pushed her waistcoat off her shoulders, or when her vest followed — except for a touch of impatience as her arms were briefly forced away from him. All she felt as the cloth slid off her to drop to the floor was relief that she could hold him again. She raised her hands at once to slide her fingers through his silky hair, thrusting her tongue out experimentally to tangle with his.

His fingers slid over her bound breasts, then dropped to tug at her linen shirt. She murmured encouraging sounds into his mouth as he freed her shirt and slid his fingers underneath running them lightly over the quivering muscles of her stomach, then the material she had used to bind her breasts.

Her arms tightened instinctively around him in protest when he suddenly broke away, but when his lips traveled down her throat she sighed gloriously and tipped her head back in delight. He nibbled and suck-led at her flesh. She noticed nothing as he found where she had fastened her bindings, undid them, then began to unravel them, drawing the wrap around and around under her loose linen shirt, easing her discomfort with every go.

She moaned her relief into his mouth as the last of the bindings fell away, freeing her tender breasts from their bondage. She almost reached down to rub herself sooth-ingly, but James took care of that, his hands cupping her gently and caressing the irrita-tion away. Her discomfort was quickly replaced by a different feeling entirely. Within moments, Maggie was pressing into his hands, encouraging him to a less sooth-ing touch.

James smiled against her lips, then pulled back and tugged her shirt quickly upward. Maggie felt herself blush as her breasts were entirely bared to him; then he pulled her forward until his lips closed around one erect nipple. She cried out, her modesty forgotten as he suckled and laved the sensi-tive tip.

Groaning in pleasure, Maggie pushed into the caress, her hands catching in James's hair, enjoying the soft textures as she pressed him closer. When she felt his hand slide down to cup her between the legs, she opened eyes she hadn't realized she'd closed.

Peering down at the cloth of her shirt, which he had let drop over his head to free his hands, she touched his hair through the linen with one trembling hand, then moaned in disappointment when he ducked out from beneath the material. His eyes met hers briefly; then he tugged her top away, attempting to lift it over her head and remove it entirely. The back of the shirt, though, was caught under her bottom where she sat on the desk.

James didn't hesitate; giving up his tugging, he reached for the collar and rent the shirt from collar to hem. Maggie gasped in shock as the garment came open; then she reached out to clasp him by the back of the neck and tug him forward to claim his lips with hers.

She kissed him in just as demanding and hungry a fashion as he usually kissed her, arching her back to thrust her breasts eagerly forward as his hands closed over them. It was madness, and it was delicious, and she ached to feel more of him. Releasing his neck, she felt her way to the front of his cravat, undoing and removing it with an ease that she could not duplicate with the buttons of his waistcoat. Much to her combined relief and disappointment, James's hands slid away from her breasts and moved to help, undoing and shedding first the waistcoat, then his vest with expedience.

Maggie didn't bother freeing his shirt from his breeches; reaching for the collar, she bit at his lower lip, holding him when he broke the kiss and tried to draw away. She slid her hands into the collar, pulling at the material. The garment did not rend as easily as her own, its material resisting, but with a little more force she heard the tear and felt the cloth give, splitting to James's waist. She promptly splayed her hands on his chest, her fingers spreading over his naked skin and nipples. Then she slid her hands around his waist and pressed forward to rub against him, shivering as the hair on his chest brushed her breasts.

He let her play that way briefly, then took over again, his lips mastering her as he urged her body forward slightly on the desk. As his hand slid down to press between her legs, Maggie felt the breath catch in her throat, her body freeze briefly with the shock of the sensations shooting through her. Liquid pooled in her lower abdomen; then James pulled away enough for his hands to work at her breeches.

It wasn't until the front flap of her breeches was undone and falling open, allowing air to brush against the skin of her stomach, that Maggie felt the first stirrings of the impropriety of all of this. His hand slid inside her breeches so swiftly, though, she couldn't catch his wrist in time to stop him. Then, as it brushed against her swollen flesh she wasn't sure she wanted him to stop.

"Oh," she moaned when he removed his hand from between her thighs. It was over, and, shameful as it was to admit, she didn't want it to be. Still she stood resignedly when he urged her to her feet.

Her eyes opened wide as James suddenly knelt before her, his hands catching the waist of her breeches and drawing them down. Maggie gave a strangled cry of embarrassment and instinctively tried to cover herself. James ignored this show of modesty, urging her to lift one leg, then the other so that he could remove the breeches from her legs entirely.

She expected him to stand again then, but he had other ideas. Pushing the trousers away, he glanced up at her with a devilish grin, then caught her by the ankles and tugged them swiftly apart — much as he had that day in his library when he'd dumped her in his chair. There was no chair this time, however, and Maggie was forced to stop trying to cover herself and grab the desk behind her for balance. Her alarm quickly turned to surprise, then trembling anticipation, as James's hands glided up the skin of her legs, tickling and tingling over the flesh of her calves, the backs of her knees, then up to her thighs, where they tightened and tugged, urging her lower body forward.

He pressed a kiss to her lower belly, leaned his forehead there and rubbed it once gently back and forth, then pressed a kiss to the hollow of her hip. Next came the top of her leg, as his hands slid to the inside of her thighs. The first brush of his fingers against her femininity made her buck like a wild horse; her body was assaulted by the same sharp sensations that had overwhelmed her in James's library. She'd forgotten how violent a reaction her body had to his touch. She remembered it quite clearly now. *This* was what had haunted her dreams. *This* had left her trembling and wanting in the mornings when she woke. This was . . .

"Oh, God." She gasped, closing her eyes tightly, her hands catching in James's hair. Her legs tried to close against the sensations he stirred as he probed the center of her excitement.

Apparently expecting that reaction, James caught her thighs. Instead of letting them close, he urged them farther apart. Catching her bottom lip between her teeth, Maggie leaned back, her thighs spread wide now of their own volition. Remembered anticipation flooded her as his head ducked between her legs.

Maggie stopped thinking. Thought was impossible under this assault to her senses. James's lips and teeth sucked and scraped over flesh burning with want. When he inserted one finger gently inside her, she was positive it was what her body was shrieking for. She shifted violently into the caress, her ability to speak reduced to grunts and groans and mindless begging. She wanted . . . She wanted . . .

She *wanted.*

She shifted and arched and ground mindlessly into his touch. As he straightened suddenly before her, his hand still manipulating her flesh, she pulled him to her by the hair, pressing upon him, an open-mouthed, desperate kiss. She raked at his shoulders until his upper body was pressed tightly against hers, naked flesh to naked flesh. Some vague memory of his guiding her hand to his arousal back at Ramsey rose in her mind, along with the feverish thought that perhaps, if she did it again, he might give her what she was aching for.

It was a purely selfish thought, but Maggie didn't particularly care. Sliding a hand between them, she sought and found the rigid length of him through his breeches. She smiled against his mouth when he stiffened. His mouth and hand froze until she squeezed, then ran her hand over the length of his hardness, then his kisses became more like her own desperate devouring.

Maggie didn't really have a clue what she was supposed to be doing, though, so relief washed through her when he brushed her hand aside. She felt his hand moving between them, but didn't realize what he was trying to do until he cursed against her lips, then tugged away to glance down. Following his gaze, she saw that he was trying to undo the buttons of his breeches. She started to reach down to aid him, but he didn't have any patience. Grasping the flap, he tugged violently, snapping most of the buttons and pulling the flap open so that his manhood sprang out.

Maggie's eyes widened incredulously at the size of the member pointing up at her, but then James moved closer, his lips gliding over her brow, down her cheek, and then to her lips. Her response to his kiss was a little less excited than it had previously been. Apparently noting this, James slipped one hand between her legs, obviously trying to rebuild some of that urgency. It didn't take much effort before Maggie was moaning and arching into his touch again. He left off his caresses to pull her a little further forward on the desk, and press her legs apart. Then, he paused.

Confused, Maggie glanced up to see the question in his eyes. He was awaiting permission. Biting her lower lip, she gave a slight nod. That was all he needed. Holding her firmly by the bottom, he plunged into her.

They both froze. For a moment the only sound was their labored breathing; then James lowered his head to glance at her uncertainly. "Are you all right?" he asked.

"Yes." Maggie's voice was slightly strangled, but understandable for all that. His penetration had caused a slight pinching sensation, but it was already gone. Feeling heat rise into her face, she cleared her throat. "You?"

A tiny laugh slipping from his lips, James leaned his forehead against hers and nodded. "Tell me when you are ready to continue."

Maggie hesitated, prepared to say, "Right away," then thought perhaps this would be terribly indelicate. She waited a twelve count before murmuring, "I think it would be all right to continue now, my lord."

She felt James begin to shake, and it took a moment to realize that he was laughing. Scowling, she drew back. "What is so funny?"

"You. Me," he admitted wryly — then all humor was gone from his face and his dark eyes seemed to swallow her. "God, you make me burn."

Maggie felt herself melt; then his mouth descended on hers. It was a hard, branding kiss, and he began to move out of her, then back in. Maggie wasn't impressed with the activity at first. It was pleasant enough, she supposed. At least, it wasn't *un*pleasant — but it did leave her wondering where all the fire and excitement had gone. That thought had barely crossed her mind when James used his hand on her bottom to change the angle of her hips, shifting himself at the same time to add a friction that had been absent.

Maggie gasped. Her earlier excitement returned in full force. Her nails dug unconsciously into the skin of James's shoulders as she arched into him, doing what she could to increase the fire that was building within her. Reaching and striving for the unnamed reward that awaited, Maggie instinctively closed her legs around his hips, her heels digging into his backside, urging him on.

"Oh, God, Maggie, I —" Breaking off that thought, whatever it had been, James reached between them, his hand searching the center of her desire, and Maggie cried out as his touch helped her finally find what she sought. She was so overtaken with the shattering discovery of her pleasure, she was barely aware of the way James suddenly thrust into her — or how he held still, his face contorted in what looked like pain as he gasped her name through gritted teeth.

Maggie was the first to recover. Aware of the echoes of a pulsing throb in her body, she turned her head against James's chest, her hands moving soothingly over his shoulders. He murmured something she couldn't understand where he slumped against her, then turned his head to press a kiss to the side of her throat, his arms tightening possessively around her.

Maggie was a little concerned to see the solemn expression on his face as he straightened. It rather pointed out just what they had indulged in and the possible ramifications. She knew instinctively she wasn't going to like what he said when he opened his mouth to speak, but wasn't any happier that he was cut off by the sudden opening of the library door.

"Really, my lady, I do not think —" Meeks's voice cried out in alarm. Maggie and James both watched in horror as the door opened.

"Nonsense, Meeks. I just want James to tell Lady Wingate here —" Lady Barlow's voice died abruptly as she stepped into the room and caught a glimpse of her nephew and her houseguest.

There was a moment of utter silence; then Lady Wingate — who — Maggie had unfortunately had the pleasure of meeting in previous, much more socially acceptable conditions — stepped around the frozen Lady Barlow and into view.

The old woman was a sweet, dear old friend of Lady Barlow's, one Vivian had known since her youth. She was also blind as a bat. Squinting at the tableau, she adjusted her glasses and tried to make out exactly what she was seeing. "What the devil? Is that you, James? Who is that with you? And what in heaven's name are you doing on Vivian's desk?"

The woman's screech set everyone in motion at once. James stepped around to try to shield Maggie from view: a poor choice that left him hanging out for the world to see, and left little doubt as to what had been going on. Meanwhile, Maggie had slithered off the desk. Well, once she unstuck her behind from the wooden surface to which she seemed to have become somehow adhered, she slithered off, dropping out of sight behind it.

Lady Barlow shook herself out of her own shocked state. She promptly turned to push her dear old friend out of the room. Meeks, always quick to help, muttered unintelligibly, grabbed the door, and tugged it abruptly closed behind himself as he followed the women out.

The room fell silent as James's aunt and her friend departed. James stood frozen for a moment, hands on his hips, his eyes closed against what had just happened, and a miserable sigh slipped from his lips. This was not what he had intended. Hell, he hadn't intended anything at all — but if he *had* planned anything, it would not have been this! He could hardly believe he had been caught in such a compromising position. *Dear God!* His brains had apparently gone a-begging. How had he been reduced to this? It was bad enough that he'd allowed his passions to overtake him and had taken Maggie on a writing desk like some rutting bull. But he had done so in his aunt's damned house, with her in the next room, where discovery was almost a certainty. What had he been thinking?

He knew what he had been thinking: he had been thinking of Maggie's silken thighs around him and her small, full breasts in his hands. He had been thinking of her lips soft and warm under his, and her warm, slick flesh wrapped around him. *Dear God, I'm thinking it again,* he realized with dismay, feeling himself swell with desire at the memories dancing through his poor beleaguered mind.

"James!"

Giving a start, he opened his eyes, guilt filling him as he met his aunt's furious gaze. She stood in the open doorway, obviously having returned to chastise him. Closing the door with a snap, she propped her hands on her hips and narrowed her eyes. "Put yourself away, young man, before I put that away for you!"

Brought to the realization that he was standing naked with a rather impressive — if he did say so, himself — erection in plain view, James turned quickly away. He tucked himself inside his breeches and did up the few buttons remaining after his earlier recklessness. That done, he started to turn back, then paused to tuck his shirt into his waistband and smooth his hair. He paused to take a long, deep, steadying breath, then turned to face his aunt's puckered expression.

"I . . ." he began, unsure what to say but ready to try. He needn't have bothered. Aunt Vivian wasn't up to listening to any of the nonsense he might have trotted out.

"I have managed to hustle every last one of my guests out. Where is Maggie?" she asked fiercely. James glanced over his shoulder, frowning when he saw the empty desk. A movement drew his gaze downward, and he spotted her barely covered derriere and ankles sticking out from beneath it. Knowing from experience how cramped and hot she would be, he sighed then stepped around the desk and bent forward to peer into the nook. Maggie sat curled inside, her knees up, covered by her shirt and her arms. Her head was bowed, her eyes pressed firmly into her linen-obscured knees.

"Maggie?" he called gently. Her only response was to curl up tighter, like a child hiding from an angry nanny. Biting back a smile, James dropped to his haunches and reached out to brush one hand over her elbow. "Come out, love," he said.

Her head shook violently.

James was about to try again when a rustle of material warned him of his aunt's approach. He glanced up to see her expression soften as she saw Maggie, and he felt relief. This was a bad enough situation; he really had no desire to see his aunt blame her for it. It was entirely his fault, after all. She'd been an innocent. He was experienced, skilled, had overwhelmed her with his passion. . . .

His smugness died an abrupt death when his aunt snapped at him. "Get out of the way, James. Leave the girl alone. Haven't you done enough to her?"

Wincing at her sharp tone, he straightened and moved around the desk. His aunt paused to murmur something to Maggie, then followed James, her expression becoming grimmer with each step. He was not at all surprised when she launched her attack.

"So *this* is how you repay her brother for saving your lecherous life?"

"I am marrying her," was all he said.

"I have never been so ashamed in all my born days. That poor — What did you say?"

James nearly smiled at her astonishment,

but managed to contain himself and repeated, "I shall marry Maggie, of course."

Aunt Vivian deflated like a sail losing its wind, then raised her head, her nose high. "Yes. Of course."

"A quick marriage would probably be best."

"Dear God, yes," she agreed. "Hazel Wingate is not known for her ability to keep a confidence." Moving toward the door, his aunt announced, "I shall start to make the arrangements. Perhaps you should coax Margaret out from under the desk. I will order a bath sent to her room . . . it should help her feel better."

Lady Barlow sailed out of the room, pulling the door closed behind her. Oddly, James would swear he had spotted a satisfied smile on her lips in that last moment. He frowned over it briefly, then turned to the desk as the chair squeaked, announcing Maggie's emergence from beneath.

Quickly rounding the desk, James took Maggie's hand to help her up, his heart aching when he spied the mortified expression on her face and the dark, rosy flush of humiliation on her skin. She ducked her head. This had been a lousy way to end her first experience in lovemaking, and he wouldn't have wished it on her for the world. She deserved better. The woman should have had a soft bed beneath her, a wedding ring on her finger, and a slow, passionate seduction. Instead she'd gotten a quick hump against his aunt's desk. He was an animal.

"This is awful."

Those muttered words from Maggie merely added to James's guilt. He pulled her body against his, a hug being the only thing he could think of to soothe her upset. It didn't appear to be working, he realized when she did not melt against him with relief, but stood stiff in his arms, her head shaking repeatedly in denial.

"Maggie," he murmured gently. " 'Tis not as bad as it seems. There will be some gossip, but once the marriage is accomplished, the rumors will die down and —"

"No."

"Yes, they will," he assured her, thinking she didn't believe him.

She pulled away and frowned at him. "I am not marrying you."

James blinked in amazement at her announcement, then, deciding she was too upset to think clearly, again tried to draw her into his arms. "Of course you are, my dear. We —"

"Nay, I am not," she argued, fighting her

way out of his embrace. Bending, she snatched up her breeches from where they lay crumpled on the floor. "When my brother asked you to look after me, he hardly meant for you to sacrifice your life to my honor."

"That is a bit melodramatic, is it not?" he chided gently, a touch embarrassed that he couldn't seem to get his eyes off her derriere as she tugged the breeches onto first one leg, then the other. "I am not sacrificing my life. I had to marry sometime, after all."

"Yes, but —"

"And there is always the possibility of a child." Much to his satisfaction, that thought seemed to give her pause. The horrified expression that suffused her face was almost gratifying. That last had definitely been a winning argument. Quite inspired really, he thought.

She turned on him pleadingly. "Can we not wait and see? Perhaps we will be lucky."

James gaped. He already *had* gotten lucky, as far as he was concerned. Glaring at her, he shook his head. "Honestly, Maggie, you are harder on my ego than any woman I have ever met! Most women would be leaping for joy at having to marry me. Hell, many women would have *arranged* for us to be caught as we were, but you —"

James paused, his mind suddenly stuttering over the idea of an arranged scandal. It occurred to him that making love to Maggie with a passel of women in the next room had been the height of stupidity. James was not generally a stupid man. One might almost think he had been hoping to get caught and forced into this marriage. Was it possible he had played such a trick on himself? he wondered in amazement. He shook such thoughts away as Maggie finished doing up her drawers and bent impatiently to collect her waistcoat.

"I do not care what most women would like or want, my lord. You should not be forced into an arrangement to save my reputation. I was hardly fighting you off or crying rape. I was a willing participant in this affair and shall suffer the consequences for it without regret."

"There is no need for anyone to suffer," James snapped. "Good Lord, woman, it is no sacrifice on my part. In case you missed the fact, I quite enjoyed ruining you. I already look forward to being able to enjoy you again, and on a regular basis. In fact, the idea of being able to do so in the comfort of a bed makes me quite eager."

To prove that fact, he grabbed her hand

as she tried to shrug into her waistcoat, and drew it down to press against the proof of his claim. Maggie stilled, her eyes widening, surprise on her face.

With her ripped linen shirt gaping open, James could hardly miss the way her nipples hardened. Releasing her hand, he lifted his fingers to catch one nipple between thumb and forefinger and pinched it gently. Maggie closed her eyes and swayed, her fingers tightening on his erection. It was enough to make James forget the situation and pull her into his arms. Catching her by the bottom, he pulled her forward, grinding himself against her.

If it weren't for a knock at the door right then, James very well might have taken her again — standing right there. But the knock made them draw apart.

"Yes?" James snapped as Maggie turned away to don her waistcoat. She began fastening the buttons to hide her torn top.

The door opened, and Meeks warily poked his head inside the room, relief on his face when he saw they were both dressed and behaving. "Lady Barlow asked that I tell you Lady Margaret's bath is ready, and that she would like to see you in the salon at once, my lord."

"Very well, Meeks. Tell her I shall be right there."

Nodding, the butler pulled the door closed, leaving him and Maggie alone again.

"I had best go above stairs," she murmured, moving to the door. James followed her, his eyebrows rising when she paused with her hand on the doorknob. Staring down at the floor, she asked, "Have you considered that you might find someone else you would rather marry? That if you marry me, you may come to regret it?"

"There is *no one* I would rather marry," James assured her with a smile.

She twitched impatiently, then said, "But what if you find someone you could truly love? What if —"

"Love?" James interrupted with a frown. "True love is a fairy tale for children, Maggie. We have friendship and mutual desire, which is the best anyone can realistically expect in a marriage. Actually, 'tis more than most people get. Do not trouble yourself about such nonsense. We will be married. We will get on famously. Now go take your bath."

Shoulders slumping, she opened the door and stepped out of the library. James watched her go with a frown. The woman looked terribly unhappy as she ascended the stairs to find her room and the waiting bath. He had to admit, it wasn't very flattering that the idea of marriage to him should be so unattractive to her.

CHAPTER SIXTEEN

Maggie chose the chair in the corner of the library. Cast in shadow, and out of immediate sight of the door, it looked to be a good place to curl up and hide a bit from the madness presently taking over Lady Barlow's home.

It had been a week since she and James had been caught with their drawers down . . . literally.

"Only you, Maggie." She whispered the familiar refrain to herself with a grimace, but had to admit she deserved it. She'd always gotten herself into trouble, and now she'd finally managed to get herself compromised and forced into marriage. She sighed dismally. The last seven days had felt like years. They had been filled with a whirl of fittings and planning: fitting the bridal gown, planning the rushed wedding.

The union was to take place in another two weeks. Lady Barlow had decided on the date. The woman was terribly concerned that their tryst in her library might bear fruit, so she said, and she insisted there be no scandal around the birth of any grand-niece or -nephew. As for the whispers such a rushed wedding would cause, those would die down quickly enough once the vows were said and done. They would be long forgotten by the baby's birth — if there was a baby.

It rankled Maggie that all of this was to protect a child that might not even exist. Well, she supposed, she was being unfair. They were also trying to salvage what they considered to be her endangered reputation. Yet Maggie wasn't as concerned with that as perhaps she should have been. After all, with Frances out of her life, she really hadn't had any prospects. Besides, it was not as if she went anywhere that she might be humiliated by overhearing the titters that being caught in flagrante delicto might cause.

Or, at least, she hadn't previous to this engagement. She thought with irritation about the last week since Lady Barlow and James had decided that he and Maggie should marry. She had found herself being dragged to ball after ball, party after party, as well as various operas and plays. Basically, they went anywhere they might be seen. Lady Barlow had said that it was to show that they had nothing to be ashamed of, as well as to allow the ton to see that she was now under her soon-to-be husband's protection. She would soon be Lady Ramsey.

Maggie's face puckered with annoyance. She could hardly believe that, in the space of such a short time, her life had been turned completely upside down. Everything was changing. Even her relationship with James was different than it had been before. For one thing, whereas he had often visited her and his aunt, spent hours talking, laughing, and playing cards with her before their engagement, since that fateful day they were caught in the library, she hardly saw him at all. She'd had only one chance even to talk to the man since that night, and it had not been about anything she herself had wanted to discuss.

He had started the talk by "requesting" that she discontinue her employment with the *Daily Express*. In fact, he had asked her to write a letter to Mr. Hartwick, informing him that G. W. Clark was retiring and would no longer be available to provide articles. He had then seen to it that Banks delivered the missive. When the butler returned with a rather alarmed note asking for an explanation, begging G. W. to reconsider, James had overseen her apologetic refusal to do either. The odious man had refrained from actually giving orders, but his requests had been little else. Was such the lot of a wife? she wondered miserably.

On the bright side, while they waited for Banks to return from his chore, James had mentioned that her servants would, of course, be incorporated into their household. He had told her that they would be her own private servants, that they would always have a home with them. In fact, he'd intended to move most of them into his town house right away, but Lady Barlow had argued against it. As they were Maggie's own private servants, the matron felt they should remain with their mistress, where they could assist with all the chores necessary for the wedding celebration. Aunt Vivian had told her privately that she knew Maggie's staff were like family to her, and thought she might enjoy the support until the wedding. Maggie was terribly grateful for that thoughtfulness. It comforted her to have Banks and Mary and the others nearby, and made her feel more at home.

The next subject he had brought up had been the town house of Gerald's. The repairs were nearly finished, he'd informed Maggie, causing a flash of guilt in her for not wondering about the matter herself. He had then suggested she sell the house and invest the proceeds in her own name, assuring her that he intended to leave her the freedom of those funds.

Which was very considerate, really. Maggie supposed she should be happy, or at least content. She knew very well that few women were as fortunate in their marriages as it appeared she was to be. But . . . But . . .

Maggie sighed miserably. She knew she had a lot to be grateful for, but, greedy woman that she was, she wanted more. She wanted a husband who would love and cherish her. She wanted *James* to love and cherish her. She made a face at such foolishness, wondering why the fact that he didn't bothered her so much. After all, it was not as if she loved him, was it? The very question made her tremble where she sat. *Did* she love him? Dear God, surely she hadn't been so foolish as to fall in love with the man?

Forcing herself to take a deep breath, Maggie tried to consider the matter sensibly. She *did like* him. She would admit to that. Even when he was being bossy and overbearing, as he'd been when he kidnapped

her, he had acted with the best of intentions
and had not been unkind. Then, too, while
having her in his power and thinking her a
fallen woman, he had not taken advantage
of the situation by using her to slake his
desires. Well . . . there was that time in the
Ramsey library, but that had hardly been
"using" her. Maggie herself had actually
initiated that kiss when James had hesitated.
Perhaps the truth of the matter was that she
had seduced him.

That thought gave her pause. Maggie had
never really thought of herself as a seductress, but she had pressed that first kiss to
his lips and set off that whole heated first
exchange. Aye, *she* had seduced *him.* And
wasn't that an interesting turn of events?
She had seduced him. *Aren't I a wicked girl?*
she thought with delight, finding the idea
terribly encouraging — in an odd way. If
she could seduce James, perhaps there was
the possibility that she could make him love
her, too.

She was still pondering that when the
library door opened, drawing her reluctant
attention. James stepped inside and glanced
around, and her heart tripped with surprise.
She had seen very little of him since the
night of their downfall. Lady Barlow, she
suspected, was doing her best to keep them

apart until they were safely married. Where before James had visited often and long, she'd hardly had a glimpse of him these last few days.

The day he had made her retire G. W. Clark was the only real time they had spent together, and that had been with Lady Barlow present the whole time, negating any possibility of a serious or intimate conversation. Seeing him here now, and without his aunt on his heels, was something of a surprise. Enough of a surprise that Maggie must have made a startled sound or movement, for he glanced her way, his eyes settling warmly upon her.

"There you are." Pushing the door closed, he crossed the room and caught her hand to draw her to her feet. Then he said, "Surely you have a welcoming kiss for the man soon to be your husband?" He didn't leave her time to answer, but instead lowered his head to cover her mouth with his.

It truly was little more than a welcoming kiss, though, a quick brush of his lips over hers, and Maggie felt disappointment rise within her as he started to pull away. She didn't pause to consider why she was disappointed, or admit that she enjoyed his kisses greatly and hungered for more of them, had hungered for them since their first one; she merely reminded herself that she was a seductress. Wasn't she? Hadn't she seduced James in the country — even if unintentionally? Couldn't she do so again?

Eager to test this new side of herself while she still had the courage, Maggie caught the back of James's head with one hand as he tried to pull away. Drawing him back to her, she again pressed her lips over his. James stiffened in surprise as Maggie brushed her mouth over his. Then, when she opened her mouth and ran her tongue along the seam of his closed lips, requesting entrance, he opened at once and the stiffness left him. He took over.

The stiffness in most of his body was gone, she amended with secret glee. The part of him pressing against her belly, however, grew noticeably stiffer, apparently excited by her aggression. He responded in kind.

When she broke the kiss to nip gently at his chin, then trailed little kisses along James's jaw to his ear, as he had done to her, her name slipped from his lips and his arms tightened around her. A moment later, his hands dropped to cup her bottom through her skirts. Maggie reciprocated by clasping his behind, then slid one hand between them and cupped his crotch.

"God, Maggie," he said under his breath, thrusting into her touch. He shook his head as if to clear it. "What are you doing? My sis—"

Maggie silenced him with another kiss, this one deep and passionate. She quickly undid the buttons of the front flap of his breeches, then slid her hand swiftly inside. She found and fondled his erection. He grew farther in her hand, bulging, throbbing, harder. Much to Maggie's surprise, her own excitement grew. She felt in control. Powerful. And she felt herself grow damp with arousal.

Recalling what he had done to her on two occasions now, she ended their kiss and dropped to her knees before him. Finding, licking, and pressing kisses along the length of his shaft, she began an effort to please him as he had done to her. She was kissing the tip of him when James unexpectedly thrust forward. Maggie started to pull back, her mouth opening in surprise, and found herself with a mouthful. The groan it elicited from him made her hesitate; then she drew her head back slightly, her teeth gently grazing the head of his member before she slid her lips forward again, taking in as much of the shaft as she could while she held its base.

The action appeared to have an electrifying effect. James bucked, the words "Maggie, oh, God!" torn from him in tortured gasps. Maggie managed the action two more times before he grasped her upper arms and dragged her back to her feet.

"Did I do something wrong?" she whispered in alarm. James shook his head violently, and she straightened before him.

"No. God, no," he muttered. "It is just that if you do not stop, I . . . I have been dreaming about you all week and I . . . ." Giving up his explanation, he peered about, then steered her behind the chair in which she had been sitting. Pausing there, he claimed her lips with something close to desperation.

Maggie kissed him back just as passionately. This time, when she felt the brush of air making its way up her legs, she didn't need to look down to know he was tugging her skirts up. The image she'd seen at Ramsey of James's dark hand against her pale flesh immediately rose in her mind, and she moaned into his mouth in anticipation, then bit his lower lip lightly in excitement. His hand slid between her thighs to work its magic.

Maggie was so wrapped up in what he was doing, it took her by surprise when his other hand reached down to stop hers as she tried to touch him again. Pulling it away at the same time as he broke their kiss, he grasped her by the waist and turned her to face the back of the chair in which she'd earlier sat. He then urged her to bend forward.

Lifting her skirts, he slid into her from behind. Maggie gasped in surprise. Eyes wide, she held her breath as he filled her, then let that breath out on a long, loud moan. One of his hands moved to cup her breast through her gown, and the other slid under the front of her upraised skirts. It found the center of her pleasure and continued caressing. Her moan turned into little mewls of pleasure and pleading as he began to slide in and out of her, his fingers moving in time with his thrusts.

Digging her fingernails into the upholstery of the chair over which she was bent, Maggie cried out; her body was beginning to shudder and shake. Pleasure exploded through her. She heard James cry out, too. After one last thrust, her body throbbing around him, he collapsed on her back with a groan.

The library door opened. One moment Maggie and James were hanging over the chair panting; the next they were both standing upright, guilt and alarm painting their flushed faces. James slid out of her, and her skirts fell back into place.

"James, where the devil have you gotten to?" Lady Barlow called irritably as she stepped into the room. There was an attractive brunette at her heels. Despite the fact that the woman was not the wizened Lady Wingate, Maggie suffered a definite sense of déjà vu at the situation. James's aunt looked about the room until she spotted them, standing one behind the other, half-hidden by the chair. "Oh, there you are. Sophie wants —"

Lady Barlow paused after only a few steps, her gaze narrowing at their flushed and breathless state. Her eyes widened, and she cried, "Good Lord, not again! What the devil is it with you and libraries that makes you unable to control yourself in them, James? You have always had a passion for books, but really!"

Groaning, Maggie closed her eyes and wished with all her heart that the floor would do her the inestimable favor of opening up and swallowing her whole. She was not at all appreciative of James's sense of humor when a small snort of laughter slid from his lips, blowing against the sensitive skin on the back of her neck. For a moment she considered sliding out from between him and the chair and making her escape, but she wasn't at all sure that the chair was high enough to hide his presently un-sheathed state — she was trapped where she was unless she wished it revealed.

Much to her relief, Lady Barlow did not leave her trapped for long. Giving a huff of disgust, the woman turned and made her way back to the door. "Sophie and I will be in the salon. I will expect you immediately, James. I do hope you can keep your hands off the poor girl long enough for her to meet your sister."

The door closed behind the two women with a soft thud, and James heaved a breath of relief. Sliding his arms around Maggie's waist from behind, he nuzzled the top of her head. "I fear she is right. I always have had a passion for libraries. Still, I never realized quite how much pleasure they could afford until I met you."

Caught off guard by the comment, Maggie found herself chuckling, her shoulders relaxing as the tension slipped from them. Covering his hands with her own, she leaned back and tipped her head to smile up at him crookedly. "I do not know if I can face them after getting caught like that again. Your aunt must think me the lowest of creatures."

"You?" He glanced at her with surprise,

then shook his head firmly. "Nay. She thinks the world of you. It is me of whom she thinks poorly. I am the seducer of innocents, you see."

"Oh, but I seduced you," Maggie protested earnestly, turning in his arms. James's gaze heated again. "So you did, you little minx." He rubbed his hands up and down her arms, his lips curving in an appreciative smile. "And rather thoroughly at that, too."

Rather pleased with herself, Maggie smiled and leaned against his chest, tucking her head under his chin to enjoy his simple caress. His hands moved over her back in a soothing rhythm. The two of them stood like that for a moment; then James chuckled.

"What a shame we were caught, however. I am quite certain Aunt Viv shall make sure we do not get any more such opportunities. We will be lucky if she doesn't raid the museum for a chastity belt and clap it on you until the wedding."

An amused giggle erupted from Maggie at the thought, and James's arms tightened around her. His voice was a bit irritated as he said, "There is nothing funny about it, madam. In case you hadn't noticed, just holding you like this has left me embarrassingly eager for more. The next two weeks are shaping up to be rather hellish."

Pulling back, Maggie peered down at his breeches, surprised to note that he was indeed bulging with interest. But that didn't surprise her as much as the fact that he was bulging against the cloth of his breeches. He was tucked in and buttoned up, and the only time he could possibly have done that without her noticing was while they had stood facing his aunt. It was no wonder she had worked out what they were doing if he had been busy putting himself away as she approached!

Maggie should have been annoyed with him, but he was gifting her with such a sweetly wry expression, she couldn't seem to muster any irritation.

"Come. My sister is going to love you, and you shall love her, too. The two of you shall no doubt become good friends."

"Your sister probably already hates me," Maggie muttered unhappily as he dragged her toward the door. "She probably thinks me a tart."

"Nonsense. She was caught in rather similar circumstances herself with her husband — before he was her husband," he confided with amusement. "Their wedding was rather rushed as well, you know. It would appear a bit of scandal runs in the family."

■ ■ ■ ■

A little more than an hour later, Maggie had to admit that James was right. She wouldn't have said that she and Sophie loved each other already, but they certainly got on well enough and had found several interests in common. Maggie rather liked her soon-to-be sister-in-law and hoped it might be mutual. Which was why it was such a shame that this was James's sister. Maggie felt rather in need of a friend just now.

Peering out the window of her room, she watched the activity on the street below with blind eyes. Maggie had enjoyed the visit, despite its embarrassing beginning, and had cut it short only out of consideration for Sophie and Lady Barlow. The two women had an obvious affection for each other, and Maggie had thought to let them visit privately after James excused himself. Maggie couldn't recall the evening's plans exactly at the moment, but supposed they would all either go to a play and a ball, an opera and a soiree, or some other similar combination. This would be another evening on display.

She twitched the drapes at her windows impatiently, her mind returning to the dilemma she'd been considering before her exciting little adventure in the library. Did she love James? The question left her with the beginnings of a headache. Normally she would have taken such a problem to her friend Charlotte to discuss. Unfortunately Charlotte hadn't ventured into London yet. It was early in the season still, and Charlotte's family tended to be one of the last to arrive each year.

Maggie had friends with whom she might have discussed other problems, but Charlotte was the only one with whom she would feel comfortable discussing this personal issue, and in this matter, Maggie wasn't at all sure she would even have felt thoroughly comfortable discussing it with her. Charlotte like Maggie was unmarried, but Charlotte was well-behaved — which Maggie could no longer claim. Nay, perhaps she couldn't have discussed this dilemma with her. What she needed was a more experienced woman, someone married, someone to whom she could talk. Like Sophie.

She discarded the thought as quickly as it came to her. While she hoped that she and Sophie might someday become close enough to discuss such things, it was too early in their friendship yet. Besides, the other girl would be biased in her opinions:

James was her brother.

Sighing, Maggie leaned her head against the window, her gaze focusing on an old woman peddling fruit on the street. The shawl covering her head and the hunched way she walked reminded her of the disguise Madame Dubarry had used when she'd come to tell Maggie that someone was impersonating her dead brother. Maggie smiled fondly at the thought of the woman. She supposed it was shocking that she enjoyed a friendship with the brothel owner, but Agatha was the only one who had seen both sides of her: what the world saw, and her secret identity as G. W. Clark. And the older woman never judged her. Which was not how the ton would have reacted, she knew.

"Oh, stuff!" she muttered suddenly, straightening by the window. She could talk to Agatha Dubarry. Aggie would neither be shocked nor biased. She would listen and offer advice born of years of experience. It was such a brilliant idea, and so obvious, that Maggie wondered why she hadn't thought of it before. She would invite Agatha to tea. She hadn't done that in ages — not since before her abduction to the country, anyway.

Moving to the bellpull in the corner, she

gave it a tug, knowing it would bring Mary immediately. She would send the girl for stationery and ink and invite Agatha here to Lady Bar—

"Oh," she murmured aloud as she realized that she couldn't possibly invite the woman here. This was not her home. It was one thing to invite the madam to her own house, but she could not possibly invite her here without Lady Barlow's permission. Maggie grimaced. She could just imagine Lady Barlow's reaction to a request to invite a brothel owner to tea. The woman would be scandalized.

Maybe, some part of her reasoned. *Then again, maybe not.* She hadn't been scandalized by Maggie's being G. W. Clark, she considered. Then she shook her head. Writing articles for the *Daily Express* and owning a brothel were not exactly similar degrees of scandal.

Sighing, she gave up the idea with regret, only to glance up in surprise when Mary rushed in. "Yes, m'lady?" the maid asked.

"Oh, never mind." Maggie started to wave the girl away, then paused as her gaze fell on the maid's serviceable gown and the shawl draped over her shoulders. Her cheeks were rosy, she noted, a telltale sign that she had been out to the stables to see her beau, but it was Mary's dress that caught Maggie's attention. The beginnings of an idea were taking root in her mind: perhaps Agatha could not come visit her, but might she possibly slip out to visit Agatha?

"M'lady?"

Maggie gave a start at the maid's uncertain murmur and stiffened. "It is all right, Mary. I was going to write a letter but changed my mind. I am sorry to have troubled you. You may go back to what you were doing."

"Yes, m'lady." The girl was gone as quickly as she had come — no doubt straight back to the stables, Maggie thought. She turned her mind back to her daring thoughts of moments before.

Dared she sneak out and visit Madame Dubarry? Lady Barlow and James would have a fit if she were caught. *If,* she argued with herself, and she had no intention of being caught. She would sneak out now, while James was gone and Lady Barlow was visiting with her niece. She would be back in plenty of time to prepare for their evening outing.

Yes, but there was her assailant to consider. She risked his harming her if he saw through her disguise. *But no one pays attention to servants,* she told herself. She could

408

dress as a servant, slip out the back, and carry a basket as if she were going to market. It was growing rather late for a trip to the market, but not so late that it wasn't possible. Then, too, no one would believe she would dare leave her guard behind and traipse about on her own. Not after the last attack.

Which brought her guard to mind. Maggie frowned. *Jack.* The man who had saved her from the fire was supposed to have taken time to recuperate, but he was . . . well, a man. And everyone knew that men could be stubborn to the point of stupidity when it came to their health. Good Lord, one could never expect them to admit to being human and needing to heal. Fortunately, nothing had arisen to call his claims of health into question. Not that she didn't feel safer with him around. She did, and she had no doubt at all that the man would do more damage to his own hands to protect her if the need arose. She simply didn't understand the male need to take such risks rather than admit to human frailties.

Ah, well, it didn't matter right now. What did was that originally Jack had merely been in the house. He'd been allowed to spend his time in the kitchen or wherever he would be available if there was trouble. But that had been before Maggie's jaunt to the men's club. After that, James had decided Jack needed to follow her around and keep a close eye on her. He now trailed her about like some hulking Cockney angel. Maggie had been forced to promise that she would sit still in the same chair in her room this afternoon simply to get a few minutes' peace and privacy — and she knew Jack had likely stood outside the door, anyway.

The thought made her groan aloud as she recalled what she and James had done earlier — and the noise they had no doubt made doing it. Dear Lord, seduce James she may have done, but she had also apparently given up her sense of decorum. Close proximity to the man obviously did things to her brain, else she would have recalled her guardian's embarrassing presence outside the door then, instead of now, when it was too late. . . .

"Only you, Maggie," she muttered then pushed those thoughts aside. Little could be done about it now, so Maggie considered the problem at hand: how to slip out without her guard knowing. After a moment's thought, she decided that simple prevarication would be easiest. Taking a deep breath, she gave her hands and arms a shake, then straightened her shoulders and walked calmly to the door. As expected, Jack stood in the hall looking solemn and immovable. Maggie smiled, hoping it was the same expression she usually used and didn't scream, *Hello! I'm about to lie to you!*

She forced herself to say, "I thought I should tell you that I am going to take a nap before tonight's entertainment. You might like to fetch a chair and something to entertain yourself — unless you'd rather go down to the kitchens for a bit of a snack and a beverage?"

"A chair'll do," the large man rumbled, as she expected; then he glanced up the hall with a frown.

"I think there is one in the gallery by the top of the stairs," Maggie suggested, hoping she didn't sound too sweet. She closed the door then, and quickly dropped to peer through the keyhole, relieved to see her guard move off down the hall. She hadn't expected him to take her suggestion of retiring to the kitchens, but his fetching a chair from the gallery also played right into her hands. He could see the top of the stairs from there and would think he could watch for her coming or going.

Of course, Maggie didn't plan to take those stairs. Easing the door open, she watched him walk down the hall. This was the tricky part, and luck would play a large part. She needed to slip out and make her way to the opposite end of the hall *before* he went into the room and returned, which meant she had to creep out into the hall while he was still in it. Fortunately, her room was only two doors from the attic, into which she planned to escape.

Maggie waited until he was halfway to the gallery, saw him glance back once, then decided it was now or never. She slipped out into the hall. She eased her bedchamber door silently closed, then made a quick dash on tiptoe for the end of the hall. She didn't look back until she had slid through the attic door, then she peered out as she eased it almost closed. Through the crack, she saw Jack glare back as he reached the gallery. Maggie waited until he stepped inside before easing the door shut and making her way up into the attic.

Her previous trip in search of a disguise to meet Maisey had revealed various other bits of clothing, some of which would aid her now. Sophie and James weren't the only ones who had cast-off clothing up here; there were also items of obvious servant quality. Maggie supposed the garments had been outgrown or left behind, but either way they would aid her now.

Once in the attic proper, Maggie cursed her own stupidity for not thinking to bring a candle. Opening the small window at the end of the packed room, allowing the gloomy late-afternoon light in, helped. The window was not very big and the light was rather poor, but it was enough. She was able to quickly find and don what she needed.

Locating a basket that had seen better days, Maggie tossed in some fabric and covered it with a linen shirt so that it appeared full. Next she made her way silently back down the stairs to the hall.

This was another tricky part, of course: getting out of the attic and slipping to the servants' stairs without Jack noticing. Pausing, Maggie eased the door open a crack and peered out into the hall. Her guardian had retrieved a chair, set it outside her door, and now sat twiddling his thumbs in a rather bored fashion. It did not look promising. In fact, as the minutes ticked by and Jack sat glancing alertly about, Maggie began to think she would be stuck on the stairwell forever.

At last, Jack stood, stretched, then walked toward the stairwell. Sucking in a breath, Maggie slid out of the attic stairwell, hurried the few steps to the servants' stairs, and eased through the door. As she carefully slid it closed, she saw Jack peer down the stairs, then turn back and start up the hall once more. Letting out her breath on a sigh, Maggie turned and started carefully down toward the first floor. Her ears straining for the sound of anyone approaching, she managed to make it all the way to the door leading into the kitchen undetected. Pausing there, she lifted the shawl hanging over her shoulders and rearranged it to cover her head and shadow her face; then she eased that door open to peek out.

She couldn't believe her luck when she saw how quiet the kitchen was. Lady Barlow's cook and another servant were standing in the cellar just off to the side, discussing something as they looked over the stock, but otherwise the room was momentarily empty. Deciding it was now or never, Maggie pulled her shawl closer around her face, pushed the basket up her arm, and moved quickly out of the stairwell. She was across the room and at the back door before she heard another door open behind her, but she didn't slow down or glance back. Counting on her servant's disguise to protect her, she slipped out of the house and straight through the gardens. She reached the back gate in a hurry, and a moment later she had passed through it to freedom.

CHAPTER SEVENTEEN

"Lady Margaret!"

"Good afternoon, Agatha." Maggie greeted the older woman with a smile of relief. It had taken a lot of talking to convince the brothel doorman to at least fetch his mistress out to her when he had refused her entrance at the door. She'd had to take on her snootiest attitude and order the man in her most cultured tones to ask Madame Dubarry to come outside.

At least, she thought happily, her disguise was working. This man had obviously been convinced that she was nothing more than a servant.

"Well, come in. . . . My goodness, come in," Madame Dubarry urged, turning to frown at her amazed doorman. "You must never again leave this young woman on the stoop, Ralph. She is always welcome."

"Yes, madame," the flustered man said, his gaze moving over Maggie's face as if he

415

were trying to memorize her as she entered. She offered him an apologetic smile, aware that her disguise had been the problem. No one paid much mind to servants. The fact that she had arrived here unmolested proved that.

"Well, what a delightful surprise," the brothel owner murmured, slipping her arm through Maggie's to steer her along the hall toward her private drawing room. "I haven't heard tell of you since you were here to interview the girls."

"Oh, er, well —"

"Speaking of which," Aggie interrupted Maggie's stammering, "I am sorry about that Frances business. The way you spoke about him led me to think that your emotions were not truly engaged, else I would never have let you find out that way. It wasn't until you disappeared without a word that I considered that you might have cared for him after all, that you'd been hurt by what you saw."

Maggie started to protest, eager to assure her friend that such hadn't been the case, but the older woman continued, "I went around to your house the day after — disguised, of course — but your butler said that you were not in. When I had no word from you after that, I assumed you were

416

angry at me."

The woman fell silent, an uncertain expression on her face as she urged Maggie into one of two chairs by the fire. She took the other for herself.

Once seated, Maggie quickly assured her that she wasn't angry or hurt. She told Agatha the tale of Lord Ramsey mistaking her for Lady X, kidnapping her, and taking her to the country for reformation then her return to London and her adventures since.

Knowing that the brothel owner could hardly be shocked by anything, Maggie didn't hold back; she revealed all, sometimes blushing and stammering, but continuing determinedly nonetheless.

Aggie listened enthralled, bursting out into gales of laughter at various points, and rolling her eyes or muttering at others.

When Maggie finally finished, both women fell silent, then Aggie sighed gustily. "So you are in love. I could not be happier for you. I really have to tell Lady X about Lord Ramsey thinking you were her — she will get a giggle out of it."

"Are you sure?" Maggie asked with alarm.

Dubarry smiled and nodded. "Yes, of course. It *is* funny, you know. An innocent like you being mistaken for —"

"Nay, not that," Maggie interrupted. "I

meant about the love part. Are you sure I am in love?"

Eyes widening, Agatha sat back and contemplated the question with surprise. "Aren't you?"

Maggie bit her lip, and Agatha's expression turned sympathetic. "Is that what is upsetting you? I could tell from your strained expression when I first saw you that something is. . . . I thought perhaps it was that Frances business, but —"

"I have never been in love before," Maggie broke in. "I am not sure if what I am feeling *is* love. And if it is, what should I do?"

"Let us deal with one question at a time," Aggie suggested soothingly. "And that first question would be, Is it love? What were your feelings upon first meeting Lord Ramsey?"

"Fear," Maggie answered honestly. "He was kidnapping me, after all."

Madame Dubarry grinned. "From what you said, you got over that fear in a hurry."

Maggie shrugged. "I learned he was a friend of my brother's. He explained —"

"And you believed him?" she asked with amusement.

Maggie blinked.

"My dear, I have known you since your

brother's death and been fortunate enough to have your confidence. In all your adventures as G. W. Clark, you were sharp and showed good instincts. You rarely accepted anyone's word for anything. You had sources willing to tell you all sorts of things going on here or there, but you didn't just write about any of those rumors and whispers; you investigated and researched each tale to find the truth for yourself."

"Well, of course I did. That is merely good sense; people lie all the time."

"And so . . . ? Did you investigate Ramsey's claim to be a friend of your brother's? Did you try to verify that he had only your good intentions in mind?"

"No. I tried to escape," Maggie countered.

"Yes, you did," Aggie agreed patiently, "but have you yet investigated whether Ramsey was telling the truth?"

Maggie found herself annoyed by the question. She knew what James was all about. "I didn't have to. Gerald had written about him often. He wrote about both James and Lord Mullin."

"Ah. So you knew of him before the two of you met?"

"Yes, I suppose."

"So what did you know? What did Gerald say?"

Maggie smiled. "Oh, various things. He mentioned that James liked to read and was teased by the others for always having his nose in a book. He said James was clever and honorable, and he told how, when they marched through decimated villages, James was always giving away his food to starving peasants."

"So you liked and respected Lord Ramsey from those tales even before you met the man?"

"Yes, I suppose I did," Maggie admitted.

"And then he kidnapped you and you were irritated with him" — the brothel owner grinned — "but you said you quite enjoyed the conversations and verbal battles the two of you shared."

"Yes."

"And when he kissed you? That first time?"

Maggie squirmed in her seat, her face flushing with embarrassment. "I . . . . He made me feel . . . Honestly, Aggie, I do not know if I could tell you my name if you asked right after one of his kisses," she admitted in a rush. "I am quite over-whelmed by passion just from his touch . . . or a light brush of his lips on mine."

"I see. And, liking and respecting him as you do, and as glorious as you find his physical attentions to be, why are you unhappy about marrying him?"

Maggie was silent for a moment, then admitted reluctantly, "I do not want him to marry me simply for honor's sake and later regret it. I do not want him to be unhappy."

"That *is* love, dear," Aggie said gently. "You are more concerned with his happiness than your own."

Maggie digested her friend's words briefly, then made a face. "I am not so altruistic, Agatha. I mean, I do care about his happiness, but it would also be a misery loving and being married to a man who did not love you back."

"What makes you think that he doesn't? It would appear to me he does." Madame Dubarry seemed slightly exasperated.

Maggie's eyes widened. "What makes you think that?"

"Well, my dear, unless the man is a complete idiot, he does seem to have taken an awful risk making love to you in his aunt's library. With a half a dozen guests in the next room, he was rather asking to be caught, wasn't he? And once caught, it was assured that there would be a wedding. . . ."

Rather than feeling pleased, Maggie felt disappointment drop over her. "Yes, but that was my fault. I *seduced* him."

Agatha burst into raucous laughter; then, seeing Maggie's injured expression, reached out to pat her hand. "I am sorry, my dear. I shouldn't laugh, but kissing the man hardly equates to seducing him."

"But —"

"Nay. Listen to me. I have a great deal of experience in these matters," the woman insisted. "The second time, in Lady Barlow's library . . . Well, perhaps *that* was seducing him. But a mere kiss isn't a seduction. Lord Ramsey knew exactly what he was doing that first time, I think. And it is very possible he was partially hoping to get caught."

"Hoping to get caught?" Maggie cried in disbelief. "But, why?"

"Perhaps he hoped for exactly what happened, that the two of you would be forced to marry." When Maggie looked doubtful, she asked, "What would you have said had he proposed?"

"No."

"Why?"

"Well, because I wouldn't want him to marry me simply to fulfill a promise to my brother."

"Of course not, and no intelligent man would expect you to. You see?"

"No."

"This way, you could not say no," Agatha pointed out. "And he was not forced to delve into anything as messy as his own emotions . . . or declarations of feeling that might not be reciprocated."

"You are saying" — Maggie tried to understand — "That you think he loves me but is unready to confess."

"I am saying that *he is a man.* He probably doesn't even know he is in love. By forcing a marriage this way, he delays having to discover it. Men often think that love will weaken them, that somehow the woman they care for has some power over them."

"But I don't," Maggie said.

Agatha smiled mysteriously. "No? And yet just last night, your touch made him entirely forget that his sister had arrived, that he had come to fetch you back to meet her!" The woman seemed amused by Maggie's blush. "You have a good deal of power with Lord Ramsey. But then, so does he with you."

"But if he loves me . . . I mean, my love makes me wary of marrying James. It makes me worry that this is all a mistake. I hesitate only because I wish him happiness. Why is it not affecting him in the same way? He seems quite content to marry me."

Agatha waved the question away. "Oh,

well, don't worry about that, my dear. No woman on earth will ever truly understand the way a man thinks. They simply react differently than we do." When Maggie didn't appear satisfied with that last answer, the woman sighed. "All right. If you wish my explanation on the matter, it is all a matter of confidence."

"Confidence?" Maggie echoed uncertainly.

"Aye. A woman may love, but if she fears the one she loves does not reciprocate her feelings — that perhaps she does not even deserve the gift of his love — she will let him go to another. Men, on the other hand, have more confidence. Should a man fall in love and fear the feeling is not reciprocated, he will tend to believe that he can *make* the woman love him . . . in time. So men hold on tighter. It all has to do with confidence. Have you never noticed that a man will think himself a catch no matter how little he has in the way of looks or wealth? And yet the loveliest woman often believes herself unattractive?"

When Maggie did not appear impressed by her argument, Agatha shook her head. "Never mind. Just trust me on the fact that Lord Ramsey has not reached his advanced age and remained single by giving in to impulse every time he was attracted to some young innocent. He has a reputation for being terribly proper . . . honorable and disciplined. And yet he gave in to you. And he sounds more than happy to marry you, Maggie. I believe he loves you. In time he will tell you so."

Maggie relaxed in her seat with a sigh. She wasn't sure she understood or even agreed with Agatha's opinions on love in general, or Ramsey in particular, but she did feel some of her misgivings replaced by hope. She let the conversation move on to other topics.

The two women enjoyed a companionable visit, but soon Maggie decided she had best return to Lady Barlow's. They were walking toward the front door when she suddenly thought of Maisey and what had happened the other night at the men's club. Pausing, she asked Madame Dubarry if the girl was around.

Agatha looked surprised by the question, but answered readily enough, "Aye. She is probably up in her room."

Maggie nodded, considering asking if the girl could be called down, then changed her mind. "Do you imagine it would be all right if I went up for a moment to speak with her?"

The madam's gaze narrowed on her considering; then she shrugged. "If you like. Though I could call her down here to talk if you wish."

Maggie shook her head; she didn't wish to speak to the younger girl in front of Agatha. "Nay. Thank you, but I will just go up to her room."

Nodding, Agatha turned them back toward the stairs. "I shall walk you up."

Much to her relief, Agatha did not stay when Maisey answered her knock, but left them alone to talk and moved up the hall.

"Could I come inside?" Maggie asked, smiling at the girl.

Shrugging, Maisey stepped aside to allow her entrance. "Ye can if'n ye like, miss, but I don't know what for. I thought we settled about the gowns."

"This isn't regarding the gowns," Maggie explained as she entered the room. The other woman closed the door behind her. "I wanted to explain about the other night."

Maisey looked at her blankly. "The other night?"

"At the club," Maggie prompted, frowning when the girl continued to look confused. "I just wanted to explain why I left without leaving word for you."

"Why ye left?"

Maggie hesitated. The girl truly didn't seem to know what she was talking about! "Why I left the club after you locked me in that room," she added.

Maisey shook her head. "I don't know what ye're talking about. I haven't seen ye since the night ye left through the window."

"What?" Maggie gasped, feeling the air knocked out of her. It was her turn to be left feeling bewildered. "But, you sent me a letter. About the gowns and calling it even."

"Yeah." Maisey nodded slowly, and Maggie felt some relief stretching through her. "Then you mentioned the men's club, offered to meet me. . . ." Maggie trailed off. The girl was shaking her head.

"I didn't say nothin' about no club."

"Yes, you did," Maggie insisted. "And then we met at the club, and you —"

"Ye're daft is what ye are," Maisey interrupted impatiently. "I didn't mention no club and didn't meet you at one."

"But —"

"I think it's time you left," Maisey decided abruptly, eyeing her as if she were mad.

Maggie opened her mouth to argue, but seeing the determined glint in the other woman's eyes, she decided that perhaps leaving was for the best. Maisey was apparently set upon lying, and the only reason she could think of for it was that the girl feared getting in trouble. Which would happen only if she were working with the man who had attacked her. That thought made Maggie remember that the man had unlocked the door. She'd heard him unlock it. Where else could he have gotten the key but from Maisey?

Eyes narrowing on the girl, Maggie decided she would give this information to James to pass on to Mr. Johnstone. He would get to the bottom of the matter. Deciding that the smartest move at that point was to leave, Maggie exited the room without further argument.

There was no sign of Agatha in the hall. Maggie didn't wish to leave without at least saying good-bye, but she had a sudden panicky desire to get back to Lady Barlow's. She was beginning to feel decidedly uneasy.

Hurrying to the stairs, she ran down them and straight for the front door, giving a start when Madame Dubarry's butler appeared to open it for her.

Mumbling her thanks, Maggie slid outside and hurried along the walkway, her feet moving faster with each step. She was in a frenzy to reach the Barlow town house and James. In her rush, Maggie didn't notice the carriage that kept pace with her or the footsteps echoing her own until it was too late. She was crossing the first intersecting street when a carriage turned abruptly before her, the door swung open, and she was grabbed from behind and bundled inside.

At first Maggie was too stunned to resist, but then she heard a shout and the pounding of someone running toward her. She began to struggle. The moment she did, something slammed into her head. She sank into unconsciousness.

James found himself hurrying as he leapt out of his carriage and made his way up the walk to his aunt's front door, and grimaced at his own eagerness. He had been distracted and a tad short-tempered for the last hour as he approved the repairs being done at Maggie's town house. If he were honest with himself, James would admit that he had been short-tempered ever since the night he and Maggie had been caught in the library. The *first* time.

Sighing, he paused and rapped on his aunt's door with his cane. There were several reasons for his moodiness. For one thing, he was a little less than pleased with Maggie's lack of enthusiasm for their upcoming nuptials. It was doing his ego little good. But he had adjusted to that, assuring himself it was caused by her fear of losing the autonomy she had enjoyed since her brother's death. She would relax and settle down with the idea once she realized that he didn't intend to smother her independent nature. He had no intention of doing that; her spirit was one of the things he admired most about her.

James *had* insisted that she give up writing for the *Express,* of course, but that had been out of necessity. Those damned articles were putting her life at risk, and while he had every hope that they would catch the scar-faced man presently trying to kill her, it was doubtful the fellow was the only one out there who would wish G. W. Clark ill. No, her articles were proving far too dangerous, and he was quite sure that her pride would have insisted she keep it up until the wedding had he not insisted straight off that she resign. Yet only pride would have kept her at it, he was sure. She had admitted, herself, that she didn't care for everything she had to do to get information for those articles. And, he rationalized, it was not as if she had a grand passion for the position. She had only been G. W. Clark for a couple months, and had only taken the position up to make extra money after Gerald's death.

Another reason for James's moodiness stemmed from his avoidance of Maggie in what he considered to be a terribly gallant effort to not toss up her skirt at every turn. James loved and respected his Aunt Viv dearly. She had raised him. He was now trying to behave as the gentlemen she'd raised him to be. But he could not do so with Maggie behaving as she had in their last encounter in the library. She easily brought an end to his good behavior with very little effort. So quickly he found his good intentions falling by the wayside. Even now, he couldn't wait to see her again, couldn't wait to be inside her again. To kiss her soft lips, lick her sweet skin, touch her round breasts and . . .

Feeling his body respond to his imaginings, James drew in his wayward thoughts. His concentration was most definitely shot. He had spent every moment since their last scandalous encounter either reliving those passionate moments, or imagining what he wanted to do to her next time. Which had made attending to the repairs of her town house and resolving what to do with her staff rather more difficult than it should have been.

He smiled at the thought of the Wentworth servants. He had spent more time with them than he had with Maggie, herself, of late. Most of her staff were helping out at the town house, and James had come to know them well. Enough to realize that her affection for them was returned tenfold. Every one of the servants was aware of the lengths she had gone to in her determination to keep them all on . . . and every one of them was as loyal as could be because of it. Which, when added to the fact that he knew Maggie would be miserable without them, had moved James to decide that — no matter what — he was going to see to it that they went wherever she did. It didn't matter if he already had a full staff. He was about to have a fuller one.

"My lord!"

He turned his attention from his thoughts to Meeks as the front door of his aunt's house was opened. The expression on the man's face echoed the relief that had been evident in his voice, causing an uneasiness in James.

"Good afternoon, Meeks," he greeted, stepping into the house.

"Good afternoon, my lord. Lady Barlow is waiting in the salon." The man took his hat, cape, and cane, waving him toward the room in question, and James felt his uneasiness increase. Refraining from questioning the man, he walked into the salon.

"James!" Lady Barlow turned from her anxious pacing, rushing to her nephew's side as he entered the room.

James's eyes widened in surprise at such a welcome, but he smiled and asked, "What is it?"

"Maggie is missing." The blunt announcement dropped into the silent room like a stone into a pond.

James's smile froze, his face blanching. "What?"

"She is *missing*. She claimed to want to rest before dinner, but I had a question about her preferences for the wedding meal, and went to see if she might be awake, and —" She shook her head unhappily. "She was not there."

"Where was Jack?" James asked sharply. "He was supposed to be protecting her."

"He was right there, standing guard at her door. He said that he stood outside it since she went in. She had to have left out of her window. It is the only way. I have had the servants search the entire house, but she simply isn't here."

"Isn't here?" James echoed with disbelief.

"No. I told Meeks to send servants to both you and Mr. Johnstone to make you aware

433

of the matter."

"I wasn't home. I just came from . . . I didn't get the message," James said dazedly.

"I did."

Lady Barlow and James both turned to the door as Johnstone strode forward, his expression grim.

"I have already put several men out to search for her," the runner announced. His gaze went to Lady Barlow and he added, "But it might help if we had some idea where to look. Did you question the servants, ask if she said anything to anyone about going somewhere?"

"Yes. No one seems to have any idea where she might be."

They were all speechless for a time, then James said in a bewildered voice, "She promised me that she would not go out alone again after the incident at the club."

Johnstone offered a sympathetic grimace. "Perhaps she didn't. Is anyone else missing?"

Lady Barlow's eyes widened at the question. "Banks!"

"Banks?" James repeated. His aunt nodded. "Meeks mentioned that he could not find Banks, either. And it seems to me that when we were riding back to town from Ramsey, Maggie mentioned that Banks often accompanied her when she investigated her stories."

James stiffened at the suggestion. "She does not do those anymore. She retired."

Before Lady Barlow could answer, Meeks appeared at the door to the salon, a concerned expression on his face.

"What is it, man?" she asked.

"A boy, my lady. At the door. He insists that he has a message for his lordship."

James hesitated briefly; thinking — hoping — that it might be from Maggie, he hurried out into the hall. A boy of perhaps five or six years waited nervously by the front door.

"Who is the message from, boy?" he barked, looming over the child.

The child's eyes widened fearfully, then darted nervously around as if in search of an escape route.

"Well? Have you been struck dumb? Who is the message from?" he snapped.

"I . . . I . . ." Dismay spread across his young face; then the boy wailed, "I can't remember."

"What? Look, lad, I do not have time to —"

"Perhaps if ye were not screaming at the lad, he could remember." Johnstone came up behind James. "Ye're scaring him."

435

Urging his employer to the side, the runner dropped to his haunches before the street urchin and offered him a warm smile. "Don't worry about him, lad. He's just a bit worried about his lady. Now, if ye can recall the message ye were to bring, ye can have this." Johnstone produced a shiny coin from a pocket and waved it. The boy watched it move from side to side before his eyes as if mesmerized, then blurted, "The lady. The bloke said to tell ye that 'e followed the lady."

"Who did?"

"Er." The boy frowned, his face screwing up as he tried to recall the name he had been given. "I can't remember, but 'e was a tall feller. Old. Stern-like."

"Banks?" James asked sharply.

"Aye, 'at's his name, guv'nor," the boy said, brightening. " 'E said as 'e 'ad followed the lady and sent me to get ye, and . . ." His face flushed slightly, and he admitted unhappily, "I can't remember the rest. . . . Somethin' about a man with a scar."

James paled, but asked, "Can you lead us back to him?"

"Sure, m'lord."

"Good lad." He sighed, patting the boy's shoulder, then turned him toward the door. Shouting for his driver, knowing the man would be in the kitchens, where he always waited while James visited his aunt and Maggie, James prepared to go and rescue Maggie.

CHAPTER EIGHTEEN

Only you, Maggie . . .

The words echoed through her head as Margaret touched a hand to her sore head and slowly sat up. It occurred to her that she found herself awakening with headaches a lot lately; it was becoming rather de rigueur. Frowning, she tried to see through the inky blackness surrounding her and determine where she was, but the darkness was absolute. She could not see a thing.

Lifting a hand, she felt her face, briefly hoping that her cape was covering it and blinding her as it had in James's carriage, but she was disappointed. Her hands and feet were unbound, her face uncovered. She was simply in a room devoid of light.

Or she had been hit so hard she was blinded, she considered. The thought scared her so much that when the door opened and light suddenly spilled into the room, she was almost grateful for it. Almost. The pain it elicited in her head was rather unbearable, however, so she was a little less thankful than she might have been. She scrambled to her feet and confronted the misshapen hulk that entered her prison, cast in shadow as he was by the light at his back.

At first, Maggie thought her poor eyes were playing tricks, for surely no one could be shaped that way. Then the hulk paused several feet away and bent at the waist. He hefted something off of what turned out to be his shoulders, and Maggie understood. Her gaze dropped to the burden the man had just deposited, and a gasp slipped from her lips at the sight. It was a bruised and unconscious Banks.

The hulk turned away, and Maggie stepped forward, her fists balling at her sides. "Who are you? Why are you doing this?"

When he merely ignored her and turned to leave, she took another step forward, her eyes desperately searching her cell for a weapon. "What is all this about? What have I done?"

Pausing in the lit hallway, the man turned and arched an eyebrow at her. "You know why."

"No. I don't. I haven't a clue," Maggie said honestly. The man stared at her silently for a moment, studying her face as if determining whether she was telling the truth, she supposed. After a moment he appeared convinced, but it didn't move him to explain. Giving a small shrug, he spun back to the door.

"She'll maybe explain when she comes," was all he said. Then he closed the door.

"She? She who?" Maggie called, stumbling forward to fall against the door as the lock clicked into place.

"Who?" she shrieked furiously, pounding her balled-up fists against the wood.

It was a passing fury, gone as quickly as it had erupted, leaving her to press her face to the cool surface as tears pooled in her eyes. They spilled over to trail down her face. "Who?"

She stayed there, wallowing in self-pity and frustration, until a muffled moan from Banks drew her attention. Sniffing, Maggie wiped her face with the back of one hand, then turned to move cautiously back through the darkness. When her foot brushed up against some part of him, she knelt and felt around to determine his position on the ground. She eased down next to the man and drew his head into her lap.

Murmuring reassuring words and phrases, she brushed the hair away from his face and waited for him to regain consciousness. This man had been a part of her life from the time she was born. He had been her butler, her friend, and sometimes just a grouchy old curmudgeon. He used to sit with her and talk at night after Gerald died, keeping her company in those sad, lonely hours when her mind would have turned to morbid mourning over her brother. She loved him.

She had neglected their friendship somewhat since James had come into her life, and had no idea how he had come to be here unless he had followed her here without her knowledge. She wouldn't put it past him. He'd sworn to keep her safe after Gerald's death, and he had now been hurt in the attempt.

"My lady?" His voice quavered with age and weakness.

Maggie stilled at those rusty words, her hands stiffening on his face. "Banks? Are you awake?"

"Aye." The word was almost a groan. Obviously the man was awake, and regretting it. Which answered the question she had been about to ask. He apparently had a headache, too.

"Where . . ." he asked, sounding a bit cranky.

Maggie smiled, affection rising up in her for the old domestic. "I do not know. An old abandoned building, I think." She peered around fretfully, trying to make out something — anything — in the blackness that pressed down on them from all around.

"An old abandoned house near the docks," Banks decided in a pained voice, and Maggie glanced down, forgetting she wouldn't be able to see him.

"Are we? How do you know that?"

"I . . ." He shifted, and his weight was removed from her lap. The groan that followed sounded near her ear, and she supposed he had sat up beside her. He gasped, "I followed you."

"You did?"

"Aye. I saw you sneak out of Lady Barlow's. I trailed you to Madame Dubarry's, waited, and started to follow you home when you were snatched off the street into that carriage."

"You were the one who shouted when I was grabbed," she realized.

"Yes. I tried to get to you, but I wasn't fast enough. I am getting *old.*" The word was said bitterly, and Maggie reached out in the darkness until she found the butler's hand. She squeezed his cold, wrinkled fingers gently. That drew another sigh from the man, and he continued, "I couldn't get there quickly enough. I hailed a hack and followed, but we were a ways back. Once I saw which building they took you into, I wanted to go get help, but was afraid that by the time we got back it might be too late. I paid a boy to fetch Lord Ramsey, then tried poking around, thinking that if I could just figure out where they were holding you, I might be able to break you out and . . ." His voice broke, and he was silent for a moment. "I guess in my excitement I forgot how old I am. Instead of finding and rescuing you, I ran into that scarred fellow. Next thing I knew, I was seeing lights. I am sorry."

"What for?" Maggie asked. "I am glad to have you here, and to know help is on the way."

"Aye. But no doubt finding me has warned that animal that help is on the way. It will make a rescue harder."

Maggie had opened her mouth to reassure him, when the door suddenly opened again. Light splashed into the room, bright and stabbing. Maggie shielded her eyes with one hand, blinking rapidly and hoping they would adjust. Footsteps and a shadow, then brighter light, told her someone was entering the room and bringing a lantern with him.

It seemed their time had run out.

Feeling extremely vulnerable on the floor, Maggie got shakily to her feet. She forced her eyes to open, determined to face her enemies.

"You are sure this is the right place?" James asked, peering about the deserted buildings with a frown.

Robbie — they had learned that was the boy's name — nodded solemnly. "Aye, m'lord. I live right over there, and I was playing with me mates when that old fellow waved me over."

James felt himself grimace as he took in the length of street. He found it hard to believe that anyone could live in these decrepit and deserted-looking structures. James decided he would visit this lad's parents after he rescued Maggie and see if he could find jobs for them.

Perhaps at Ramsey. The boy was too thin and pale by half; some time in the country would be good for him. James had to rescue Maggie first, though. He must not focus on anything but succeeding at that task.

"I don't see this Banks fellow anywhere," Johnstone said.

James scowled. He had been waiting and watching for the butler, expecting him to step out into the street and hail them. "Neither do I," he said. His gaze dropped to the boy. "Where was he when he waved you over?"

"Right there." The child pointed at the building their carriage had stopped before, and James scanned every nook and shadow hopefully before admitting to himself that the man wasn't to be found. He only hoped that didn't mean that they had moved and the domestic had followed.

"Which of the buildings was he watching? Could you tell?" James asked.

Robbie hesitated, then scrambled off the bench seat and made his way through the legs of the men filling the coach. He peered out the window at the buildings opposite where he claimed Banks had been. His face scrunched up in concentration as he considered the matter.

"I think he was watching that one," he decided at last, and James leaned across Johnstone to look out the window at the building in question.

"I don't suppose ye saw a woman bein' dragged into it before ye noticed the old man, did ye?" Johnstone asked hopefully.

They all sighed in disappointment when the lad shook his head. "I just come out to play when the man nipped me."

445

"All right, Robbie," James said grimly, reaching into his pocket. "Take this, and go on home now. And thank you for your help."

Robbie's young eyes brightened at the sight of the coin held out; then he snatched it up. Gasping a thanks, he scrambled out of the door James opened.

"What do you want to do, m'lord?" Johnstone asked quietly.

James pulled the door closed again. "I think we have to check all three buildings: the one the boy pointed out, and the ones on either side. She could be in any of them."

Johnstone nodded, his glance moving over the three other runners with them. "Jack, you and Bob take the house on the left; Jimmy and meself will take the middle, and m'lord —"

"No. I take the middle house," James said firmly.

Johnstone hesitated, then nodded. Glancing at the youngest of the group, he said, "Jimmy, ye'll have to take the house on the right on your own. I'll accompany his lordship."

"No," James said again, frowning at the nervous Jimmy. The boy was young and obviously the least experienced. If James was wrong and the middle building wasn't where Maggie was, if she was in the building on the right, he didn't want this fidgety pup going in on his own and possibly getting her killed. "You go with Jimmy. I can manage on my own."

"Oh, m'lord, I don't think . . ." Johnstone began, but James didn't stay to listen. Opening the carriage door, he stepped out and moved toward the building in the center, his heart pounding with rage and fear: rage that someone had dared to touch what was his, and fear that he would be too late to save her.

Maggie had thought that seeing the "she" behind these attacks would clear matters up. Much to her consternation, however, the woman hanging the lamp from the hook by the door was a complete stranger.

Maggie forced herself to look closer, sure she was missing something. Her eyes slowly absorbed the generous figure in the red dress, the blond hair piled on the woman's head, little curls free to frame her pretty face, but it didn't help. Maggie had no clue who she was.

"Who *are* you?" she asked quietly.

The blonde turned to survey her captives. Her eyebrows rose with amusement. "Come now; you don't really expect me to believe that you do not know who I am? Not the famed G. W. Clark."

Maggie stiffened, her blood running cold. "I fear you have me at a disadvantage. It also seems that you have more to blackmail me with than I have on you. I haven't a clue who you are." She thought that last bit a touch of subtle brilliance. Perhaps it would give the woman the idea of blackmailing her rather than killing her, as she feared was her captor's ultimate objective.

The woman's eyes narrowed as if suspecting a trick. "You do not recall me?"

When Maggie shook her head, the blonde's mouth twisted with disbelief. "Think! Think hard."

Maggie stared at her silently, still shaking her head until a memory exploded in her mind. Just a flash, like a bolt of lightning quickly there and just as quickly gone, but her head slowed its shaking. The woman smiled.

"You *do* remember."

Maggie hesitated, then asked uncertainly, "Madame Dubarry's? In the room I climbed into? I was putting on Maisey's mask. You were on the bed."

"There you are!" The woman smiled brightly, but Maggie still didn't understand.

"I am sorry. I saw you in Lady Dubarry's, I think. All right. Briefly, when I was trying to escape . . . but I still do not see what this is all about."

"Yes, you do. You know *exactly* what this is all about. And so do I. How long until I would have opened the *Daily Express* to find the article?"

"The article on what?" Maggie asked in amazement. "Mr. Hartwick has already published my article on the interviews I did with you women at Dubarry's."

The blonde hesitated, then frowned. "You really do not know."

It wasn't a question, rather an amazed realization the woman was voicing aloud, and Maggie felt a touch of hope tingle through her. This was all a mistake. They would let her and Banks go, because this was all a huge mistake.

"What were you doing in my room that night?"

"I climbed out of Maisey's room via the window," Maggie answered. "I'd traded my gown in exchange for hers and information on which way to go to avoid running into anyone else. She said Lady X and Lord Hastings were in the room on one side, but the room on the other was empty. She said the left was the empty room and I went that way, only to recognize my mistake when I reached that room and found it occupied. I

449

realized then that she must have meant *her* left. I had gone to *my* left, but she had been facing me through the window and her left would have been my right, so I had to turn and go back the other way. Unfortunately, by the time I made it to the right window, you were in there. Though I didn't realize that until I stopped to put on my mask and glimpsed you."

"Dear God." The woman sagged like wet cloth. "You really did not know. All this time, all this fear and . . . It was a mistake. Just a terrible, horrible mistake, and all because Maisey actually told you the right way."

"The right way?" Maggie was totally bemused. She pushed the feeling aside. What did the explanation matter? She just wanted out of here.

Waiting in that dark prison with Banks, Margaret hadn't dared reveal her fear that she might be living her last moments. That, perhaps he was, too, thanks to his loyalty to her. She had kept those thoughts to herself and suffered with them.

It wasn't death itself that frightened her, so much as the idea of never seeing James again. That very possibility caused her unbearable anguish. Now, she felt hope spring to life within her. If this was all a mistake, she might yet live to see him, might hold him in her arms and be sheltered by him once more. Trembling with this new possibility, Maggie asked, "Will you let us go?"

A bewildered expression crossed her captor's face. She seemed to struggle briefly, then shook her head unhappily. "Nay. I cannot."

"What?" Maggie stared at her in frustration. "But —"

"You could still write about all this," the woman interrupted quietly. "If you had nothing to write about before, you do now."

"No, I don't. Besides, I couldn't if I did. My fiancé has forbidden me to write as G. W. Clark anymore." Maggie almost rolled her eyes at her own words. She sounded so plaintive, like a child begging. . . . But she was begging — for her life and for Banks's.

"I am sorry," the woman said, and Maggie almost believed her. "But I cannot risk your telling."

"Telling *what*?" Maggie snapped in frustration. "I know what you look like but not who you are."

"You know I am one of Aggie's girls, and that I kidnapped you and have tried to have you removed several times," the woman said patiently.

"I will not tell," Maggie promised. Her blood was like ice in her veins as she watched a sad expression come to the other woman's face. "I wish I could believe that."

"You can," Maggie assured her. It was no use; the blonde raised a gun. Maggie's thought then was to stall as long as she could, hoping the boy Banks had paid would bring James here in time. Or, failing that, that some plan would come to her mind. "All right. At least tell me why I am dying. I deserve to know that much. Who are you?"

"I am nobody."

Maggie blinked. "What?"

"I am nobody," the woman repeated. "My name is Elizabeth Drake. I was an actress, and not a very successful one. Then I had this idea to don a mask and set myself up at Madame Dubarry's . . . or some other establishment. Always in a mask. That would lend me mystery, and mystery is a powerful aphrodisiac."

"Lady X," Maggie murmured, understanding. She never should have doubled back that night on the ledge of the brothel, at least not to avoid Lady X. She had gone the right way after all. The first room was the one that was supposed to be empty. Maisey had been in error about its occupancy.

"Yes," the blonde acknowledged.

"They say you are a lady of nobility."

"That was part of my plan. I dropped a hint or two with my first few customers. They thought what I hoped, and were quick to spread the rumors; a lady of nobility selling her body in disguise. Being naughty is as much an aphrodisiac as being mysterious. The men came in droves, reaching deep in their pockets to have just a half hour with me, hoping to figure out who I was. As Lady X I can command ridiculous sums, and often do not even have to do much to earn it. Most of them just want to talk to me in the hopes of discovering my identity — which member of the ton has fallen so low."

"Brilliant," Maggie complimented with unfeigned admiration. "As a woman who has had to make her way in the world, I admire the brilliance of your plan."

"Yes. I believe you do." Regret crossed the blonde's features. "If things had been different, I think we could even have been friends. I know you are not a snob about such things. You are friends with Agatha, after all."

"It was you at the men's club, not Maisey," Maggie realized, recalling what she should have noticed at the time. Maisey was about Maggie's own height, but the woman she had thought was Maisey that night — the woman who had locked her in the room — had been several inches shorter.

"Yes," she admitted with irritation. "I expected you to come dressed as a woman, but you dressed as a man and gave Bull the slip." Her aggravation turned to amusement. "I was livid when you arrived without him on your tail. I paid the doorman to go to my carriage and tell my driver to take him to where Bull was watching Lady Barlow's residence, and fetch him. Then I locked you in the room until he returned. It should have been easy. I did not expect you to knock him out and escape," she added dryly.

"How did you manage the letter she sent?" Maggie asked, wondering what the devil was taking James so long. "Maisey said she wrote that letter, and that there was nothing in it about meeting at a men's club. Was she lying? Did you pay her to help you?"

"I did not have to." Lady X shrugged and explained, "Maisey cannot write. I offered to write it for her."

"Ahh." The sound came out on a gust of air. She should have thought to ask. It should have been obvious the prostitute probably wouldn't have that skill. Very few of the working class did. For someone who liked to claim that she had an investigative mind, Maggie really had let a lot of details slip by.

"And how did you manage today?"

In the process of raising her gun again, Lady X lowered it once more and tilted her head in confusion. "Today?"

"I presume my disguising myself as a servant worked, else your man there would have grabbed me on the way to Dubarry's rather than on the way back. I trust he was still skulking around looking for his opportunity?"

"Yes." The blonde nodded slowly. "I have had him watching Lady Barlow's since he failed to take care of you in that fire. Your disguise did work. But there are no secrets at Aggie's, and the doorman, Ralph, was rather distraught at being reprimanded for not showing you in immediately. I was in the kitchens and heard him telling Cook about it."

"And you sent someone to fetch . . ." Maggie gestured to the scarred man, her gaze moving slowly over his blank face. There was no sign of mercy there; if anything, he appeared to be looking at her with deep dislike. She could only think that was because she had survived his various attacks and made him look bad.

"Yes." There came a click as Elizabeth Drake cocked her gun, and Maggie's attention was drawn away from such trivialities to the matter at hand: her death. She stared wide-eyed at the barrel of the pistol, her mind gone blank of any way to delay any longer. The barrel seemed to grow, filling her entire vision. She couldn't believe this was the last thing she would see in her life, the black hole at the end of a gun. And all because of poor directions.

A soft thump drew Maggie's eyes from the gun to the hallway beyond the door. She saw the shadow of a crouching figure cast on the opposite wall from the light in the room next door, and knew at once that it was James.

"What was —" Lady X didn't get to finish the question. Overcome with panic that James might be caught, Maggie leapt forward and grabbed the cocked pistol. It was an instinctive action, a desperate attempt to save Banks, James, and herself . . . and a wholly stupid move. A shot rang out, deafening her, and Maggie felt as if some invisible tree trunk had hit her in the chest to throw her backward.

"My lady!" Banks cried.

She saw James lunge through the doorway as her back slammed into the wall. Their shocked gazes met, then her legs seemed to lose their strength. Maggie began to slide toward the floor. Her last thought was that he looked terribly pale, and she wished she'd had the chance to tell him she loved him.

CHAPTER NINETEEN

James moved carefully toward the front of the building and the stairs waiting there. The first floor had a stench he didn't want to identify, and was littered with various bits of rubbish. It had also proven to be empty. He was beginning to suspect that he had chosen the wrong building and that Maggie, if she was anywhere on this block, would prove to be somewhere else. This building appeared empty and was as silent as a tomb.

He shuddered at the thought, then pushed it away. She wasn't here, he assured himself. He would not believe that her death was the reason this place felt so empty and cold. Maggie was alive. He would sense it if she were gone. The world would seem different, he was sure. It certainly had seemed different since she had entered his life.

James paused at the base of the stairs and peered up into the yawning darkness. He was really starting to think that Maggie was in one of the other two buildings and, for a minute, he considered giving up on this one and going to join the others. Then he changed his mind. He should check this building out, at least. Johnstone and his men would check the others, and he couldn't not search here, simply because of a hunch. It was just that he wanted to be the one to find Maggie, and he had a dreadful feeling that time was running out. She was in great danger. If the man who had attacked her and set her town house on fire was the same one who had her now, he would kill her; James didn't doubt that for a minute.

It was better to do a thorough check, then he could go join Johnstone and young Jimmy in the next building. With that decided, he started up the steps, walking as close to the wall as he could to avoid too much creaking of the stairs.

As he reached the last couple of steps and was able to view the long hallway at the end of it, he spotted a light. It spilled out of two rooms at the end of the long, dark corridor. James's heart squeezed painfully, then started beating at an accelerated rate. He hesitated only briefly, his hand tightening around the dueling pistol he'd taken from his aunt's library. Drawing some comfort from it, he straightened his shoulders and went determinedly onward.

He was halfway down the hall before he heard the voices. They were drifting from one of the lighted rooms ahead, and he couldn't make out what was being said. Still, he recognized one of the voices as Maggie's. He moved a little more swiftly while still trying to creep as silently as possible.

He paused at one side of the first door, took a breath, then eased around the frame for a quick peek inside. When he saw that it was empty, a beat-up chair and small rickety table the only furnishings, he relaxed. The light came from a lantern on the table, which also held a deck of cards, one dented metal cup, and a half-empty bottle of something. James supposed this was where Maggie's abductor waited. The single cup suggested there was only one man, probably the scarfaced man. Which was perfect. James would be more than happy to deal with that animal. He had been eager to meet that bastard since seeing Maggie's bruised and battered face after the fire. He wanted to return the favor and wouldn't pass up the opportunity to kill the man responsible.

His gaze raked over the table again as he listened to the murmur of voices from the next room. He couldn't hear what was being said, but the calm tones made him think that there was still time. Maybe he would hear a hint as to what to expect before he burst in to save Maggie. He wanted to be well prepared when he did so, as he had no desire to get Maggie killed by making a mistake.

The room had little else to tell. The single chair and cup suggested a single guard. The cards suggested the man had been waiting for someone — perhaps whoever had hired him. James wouldn't mind getting his hands on that person either, he decided. Easing back out of the room, he crept to the side of the next open door. His ears strained to make out the words being spoken.

"And you sent him to fetch . . ."

That was definitely Maggie speaking. James breathed a sigh of relief at the calm, strong tone of her voice. She didn't sound injured or weak, or even scared, he thought with relief. But then he heard the answering voice say, "Yes," and he stiffened. It was a woman answering her!

In all the time he'd had Johnstone looking into this mess and who might be after Maggie, he'd never considered that a woman might be involved. He'd assumed it must be one of the men she had written about, someone who had been embarrassed or ruined by one of her articles. He had never even dreamed a woman would be responsible!

James was so startled by the sound of the woman's voice that his arm jerked, the pistol he held bumping against the wall. It was the smallest sound, but seemed loud in the silence that had just fallen.

"What was —" he heard the female begin sharply; then there was a scuffling, promptly followed by a gunshot. That sound made him freeze, but the horrified shriek of "My lady!" that came directly afterward sent blood rushing through him. Horrified, James swung into the room, his pistol at the ready.

The first thing he saw were the backs of two people — a large, wide shouldered man and a petite, cloaked woman — but beyond them he caught his first glimpse of Maggie. What he saw both enraged and terrified him. She was in the process of falling backward, her pale face filled with shock and pain as blood squirted through her fingers from her chest. He watched in horror as she slid down the wall, then drove his gaze back to the couple standing between them. He had expected the man to have the gun, so he was surprised when he realized the woman held it, but that didn't give him pause for long.

Striding forward, James grabbed the weapon from her startled hands. He swung then to plow it into the face of the man. Taken by surprise, the ape stumbled backward. James pursued him, his fists flying, the heavy pistols he held inflicting more damage than did his knuckles. He didn't stop until the man was unconscious.

Chest heaving, James straightened and turned to confront the woman — only to find that she had slipped out while he'd been busy with her compatriot. He took a step toward the door, but paused when a moan drew his attention to the floor. Banks sat holding his mistress close, supporting her with one arm, the other hand pressed against her wound as if he were trying to keep more blood from spilling out into the pool already growing on the dirty wooden floor.

"Please don't die, my lady." The butler moaned, tears streaking down his old face. He rocked her gently.

Changing direction at once, James moved to kneel beside them. Banks raised sorrowful eyes to him. "She is bleeding badly, my lord. Very badly. I fear she isn't going to make it."

"The hell she won't," James answered. Scooping her into his arms, he stood and turned to the door, leaving the old man to find his feet on his own. He moved down the hall with her quickly, Banks scrambling after them, running to catch up, and promptly applying pressure to Maggie's wound from the side as he accompanied them down the stairs. Despite the awkwardness it caused in trying to descend, James didn't make him stop. He doubted the action was doing much good, but the man obviously needed to feel he was doing something.

He hardly even cared when he spotted Johnstone approaching, the woman who'd shot Maggie firmly gripped in his hand.

"What do ye want me to do with her, m'lord?" he asked as James hurried forward.

"Wring her bloody neck," he said in a cold snarl.

Johnstone jerked to a stop in shock as he recognized Maggie's pale face, then saw how she was bleeding. Alarm covered his face, and he dragged the blonde along as he followed them to the coach. "What happened?"

"That bitch shot Maggie," James answered through gritted teeth. They reached his carriage. "Her man, the scarred bastard, is upstairs. He is unconscious right now, but probably won't be for long."

"Jack!" Johnstone shouted, bringing the other man running.

"Yes sir?"

"The scarred man's upstairs. Go get him." Johnstone turned back as Crowch opened the carriage door. The driver had scrambled down from his perch on first seeing their approach, and now he held the door open as James got inside. Ramsey did his best not to jar Maggie as he did, but it was impossible not to altogether, and he winced at every little moan of pain that slipped from her lips as he settled her on his lap.

"Get us to Lord Mullin's, Crowch," he ordered. Banks clambered in after him and returned to applying pressure to her wound.

"Straightaway, m'lord," the coachman assured him, slamming the door. The carriage swayed as he hurried back up onto his seat; then the vehicle was off, leaving Johnstone to watch them go.

Crowch rode the horses full-out, careening wildly through the narrow streets in a way that would have alarmed James if Maggie weren't growing paler with each passing moment. He stared at her face, unaware that he was alternately cursing God for letting this happen and praying to him to save her. And he was begging Maggie not to die.

When the carriage at last stopped, James waited impatiently for Banks to push the door open, then scrambled out. He led the way to the door of Robert's town house, paused there, and, hands full, began kicking it. Using his free hand, Banks promptly added his imperious knock while Crowch began shouting, "Here! Here!" through his cupped hands at the windows above. Between the three of them, they were causing enough racket to disturb the whole street, and much to James's annoyance other doors began to open while Robert's stayed closed.

"It is about bloody damned time!" he said in a snarl when the door finally opened to reveal a startled and slightly annoyed butler. Furious that it had taken the man so long to answer, he pushed forward, forcing the servant back into the hall.

"What is it, Mills?"

James turned at that voice, peering over the butler's shoulder to see Lord Mullin himself standing in a room off the entry. Relief rushing through him, Ramsey quickly moved toward his friend, Banks stumbling to keep up.

"James!" Robert recognized him with obvious surprise then glanced down at Maggie whom James held in his arms. "What?

Dear God, what has happened?"

"She's been shot," he answered tightly.

Robert brushed Banks's hand away and lifted the blood-soaked cloth that was pressed to her wound. James had known it was bad — the amount of blood had told him so — but the way Robert blanched confirmed his fears. He felt his heart shrivel.

"Get her upstairs," the younger nobleman ordered, replacing Maggie's bandage. "Show them to the spare room, Mills, I'll collect my things."

James followed the servant silently, his eyes shifting back and forth between Maggie's pale face and where he was going. The clomp of footsteps on the stairs behind him signaled that Banks and probably Crouch were following, though he couldn't fathom why. They would be of little use here. He would be useless, too, he knew. Only Robert could help. There was nothing he could do for her now.

But then, he had been little use to her since they'd met, he berated himself. *Look after my sister,* was all Gerald had asked in exchange for James's life . . . and James had failed him. Miserably.

First he had mistaken the woman for a prostitute. A terribly stupid mistake. Foolish. Idiotic. Who could believe sweet, in-

467

nocent Maggie a ladybird? Only an idiot like himself. Then he had failed time after time to keep her safe. True, he had managed to pull her out from in front of one carriage, but he hadn't managed to draw her from harm's way. He hadn't saved her from being pushed in front of the second crash, or from having her hat shot, or from the fire. Dear Lord, he hadn't even protected her from himself, taking her there in his aunt's library as if she were some common strumpet. And not just once, but twice! Gerald had entrusted him with his sister. He had been foolish.

And now he hadn't protected her at this most critical moment. He had stood just feet away and let her get shot. If he had moved more swiftly, acted more quickly . . .

"You can lay her down, my lord."

James stopped his self-recriminations long enough to notice that they had reached a bedroom, and that Mills had spread a rough woolen blanket over the bed. Even now, he was brushing out the last few wrinkles so that Maggie could be laid upon it. James scowled at the sight of the prickly-looking material. "Get that off. She will lie on the sheets."

"It is to save the linens from the blood, my lord," the man explained. "Once Lord

Mullin has cleaned and sewed up the wound
—"

"Get it off!" he roared. "I shall replace the damn linens, and the damned bed, too, if I have to, but she shall not spend her last moments on that damn piece of —"

"Do as his lordship asks and take it off, Mills."

James paused midsentence, and glanced over his shoulder. Lord Mullin entered the room, his hands full of implements. He was followed by two more servants, one carrying fresh white bandages, the other dragging a bucket of steaming water.

"Lay her down, please."

At Robert's order, James turned back to the bed. Mills had whisked the ratty woolen blanket away and was now tugging the clean top linens down on the bed. Seeing the fresh white bottom linen for her to lie on, James grunted in satisfaction and laid Maggie down. He hesitated, then knelt at the bedside, taking Margaret's small hand in his own.

The doctor moved around the bed to the other side. He paused to murmur something in the ear of his butler, then tentatively lifted away the blood-soaked cloth to get a second look at Maggie's wound.

"Well?" James asked anxiously.

"I shall have to cut her gown away." Robert lifted his head, looking around at the hovering servant. "Do you wish your men to remain?"

James turned to scowl at Banks and Crowch. The two men immediately scuttled to the door, though Banks moved more reluctantly than the driver. Satisfied, James glanced back as Robert began cutting away Maggie's gown. He started at the neckline, working downward in a curved pattern that left nearly half her chest bare. Maggie moaned as he pulled the material away, that little action alone seeming to pain her. The sound drew James's eyes to her face, and he felt his heart stop beating in his chest when he saw that her eyelashes were fluttering. Then he felt her hand twitch, and he held it a little tighter. She had been so silent and still since he had lifted her, he had almost feared her already dead. These new signs, terrifying as they were, were also encouraging.

He peered at her face hopefully and whispered, "Maggie?"

Her eyelashes fluttered once again before opening. They remained open this time. "James?"

She seemed confused, and James squeezed her hand, then rubbed his thumb over her small fingers. He frowned at how cold they were. "Yes. I have brought you to Robert. He will heal you, love."

If she understood him, she didn't show it. Her eyes began to slip wearily closed; then she forced them open again as if remembering something of importance.

"James," she said softly, trying to sit up. Both he and Lord Mullin pressed her back down.

"Rest. Save your strength," Robert urged quietly.

"What, Maggie? Don't talk. Save your strength. What is it?" James murmured. Picking up her hand, he pressed it flat to his face, trying to warm the cold flesh. He wasn't even aware that he was contradicting himself, urging her to rest while asking what she wanted to say. All he could think was that she was as cold as death, and that he was losing her.

"But . . . have to . . . tell you," she got out breathlessly, then winced and sucked in a breath. Pain knifed across her face as Mullin began to probe gently at her wound.

"You're hurting her!" James shouted.

"Yes, I am," Robert said quietly, then spoke to Maggie and not him as he said, "And I am sorry for that, Margaret. But I have to get the ball out and clean the wound. It will hurt a great deal. Mills is bringing something to ease your pain, but I fear I can't wait. You have already lost a lot of blood."

"Yes." Maggie managed a grimace of a smile, then closed her eyes briefly and said, "I just . . . have . . . to tell . . ."

"Maggie." James almost moaned her name, agonizing over the pain she was suffering. He dropped his head, desperately squeezing her hand.

"I love . . . you," she managed to get out. Her voice was faint, but James heard her declaration for all that. Tears welled in his eyes, stupefying him. He hadn't cried since his parents' deaths. Shocked, he squeezed her hand and, wiping away his tears, he lifted his face.

"Mag—" Her name died in his throat as she squeezed his hand viciously and cried out. In the next moment, her grip loosened and her body relaxed, too. She fell silent.

"What have you done?" James roared, rearing to his feet.

He was about to rush around the bed and throttle Robert when a hand fell on his shoulder to stop him. James turned to see Mills standing behind him, a pitying expression on his face and a glass in his free hand. A bottle of some medicinal was caught between his arm and chest.

"She has just fainted," Robert assured him. Glancing up to nod toward the glass the butler was holding out, he said, "Now drink some of that down and go pray."

"Pray?"

"Yes, pray. She'll need it," Robert said grimly as he continued to work.

James downed a good portion of the drink Mills had poured him. His hand clenched on the glass as he lowered it, his expression turning hard. There was so much blood. She was so pale. He couldn't lose her. "You are the one who had best pray. If you let her die, I —"

James paused as Robert raised his head. He blinked in confusion, unable to believe he had been about to threaten his friend. He was obviously losing his head. Which was nothing new around Maggie.

"You have it bad, my friend," the other man announced almost mournfully. Then he turned from James's tortured face to Maggie's wound.

Ramsey winced as the other man worked, grateful now that Maggie was not conscious to feel anything. "*I* have it? What? I am not the sick one."

"Yes, you are. Lovesick. I wondered before, but this is one of the worst cases I have

473

ever seen. You have it bad." Glancing up to see his friend staring at him blankly, Robert explained, "You love her, James. It's why you're acting like such an unbearable ass. You weren't even this bad when I was working on Gerald. Now get the hell out of here and go finish that drink so that I can work on her — else you'll be loving a corpse."

James stood frozen for a minute, then staggered away from the bed when Mills urged him toward the door. His head was reeling. Was this love? Was that what this panic was? If so, the books lied. Love was not a happy, joyful feeling that made everything seem lovely; it hurt like hell and turned one into a panicked ninny. *Damn.* Love wasn't heaven; it was hell.

A moan from the bed made him pause at the door. He turned back, despite Mills's best efforts at keeping him from doing so. He couldn't leave Maggie. She needed him.

For once, Maggie found herself waking up without a headache. Unfortunately, her chest was paining her instead. Every breath seemed an effort, but she agonizingly opened her eyes, gritting her teeth as she tried to bring the room into focus. When she was finally able to make anything out, all she could do was blink in confusion. She didn't recognize the room at all. This wasn't her bedroom in her town house, she knew. And neither was it the chamber she had been given at Lady Barlow's.

She was in a small, bright yellow room, lying in a narrow bed she had never before seen. Her gaze slid over the pleasant furnishings, and she tried to puzzle out what had happened. She was still doing so when the door to the room opened moments later, and Lord Mullin stepped into the room.

"My lord." She tried to greet him, but her mouth and throat seemed terribly dry. She was unable to do naught but mouth the words.

"Ah. You are awake, I see," Robert murmured, moving to her bedside and pressing a warm hand to her forehead. "And completely fever-free."

Maggie's eyebrows rose at the combination of satisfaction and relief in his voice, but he noticed neither as he picked up a mug from a nearby table and seated himself on the side of the bed; he then helped her sit up enough to sip from it. It wasn't worth the effort, Maggie decided as pain shot through her chest. Still, she dutifully took another sip of the liquid when he pressed her, enough to wet her mouth and throat. She was thankful when Robert allowed her to lie back down again, and she sighed in relief as the pain in her chest eased.

"I imagine you feel just awful," he commented, moving to replace the mug on the table. He turned back in time to see Maggie nod. "Well, you are very very lucky to feel anything. You nearly died, Margaret. If James had not gotten you here so quickly . . ." He shook his head to finish the sentence, but Maggie understood well enough. She would have died. His words had the beneficial effect of reminding her what had brought her here. She quite suddenly recalled the dark room, the scar-faced man, Banks, and Lady X. She also vividly recalled the moment when Lady X had shot her. It was a most unpleasant memory.

She also recalled opening her eyes to find James's worried face hovering over her. She remembered being surrounded by yellow, hearing his soothing voice telling her everything would be all right. Or had that been a dream? she wondered now. His voice had seemed . . . different. It had been full of something, some emotion she had never heard from him.

"Where . . . ?" she croaked, unable to finish.

Fortunately, Robert understood. He smiled wryly before answering: "I had to throw him out."

She felt shock at that pronouncement, and it must have been evident. Robert nodded and said conversationally, "James was quite devoted. He didn't leave your side from the moment he brought you here. He held your hand throughout my work on you, then bathed you during your four days of fever — neither eating nor sleeping until your temperature lowered and the danger passed. That was last night," he added. "Of course, James was quite disruptive in his . . . attempts to help."

"Disruptive?" Maggie mouthed.

Robert made a face then explained, "He shouted a lot." When she shook her head in disbelief at that news, Lord Mullin assured her, "Yes, he did. He bellowed at me for — as he put it — 'butchering you.' Also for not healing you faster and for being . . . I believe it was a *bloodletting quack* — though I don't know why he said that; he knows that I do not agree with blood-letting."

Maggie offered an apologetic expression, but Robert wasn't finished.

"He also yelled at Mills, my butler, for being slow and lazy, at Crowch and Banks for being useless, and at you for daring to almost die on him. And he cursed Heaven too, a couple times, I believe." He grinned at Maggie's dismayed expression and patted her hand reassuringly. "He wasn't always rational. But four days without sleep or food will do that to a person. I finally had to send him home with instructions to rest and eat. I assured him I would not let him back until he had done both."

Maggie relaxed somewhat. Then Robert added, "He loves you very much."

Her first reaction was shock. It was quickly followed by hope, then doubt, then fear, and finally simple confusion as to why he would tell her something like that, and in such grim tones.

"Why . . ." she croaked, grateful when Robert once again finished the question for her.

"Why am I telling you this?" he asked. When she nodded, he sighed and admitted, "Because he didn't take it at all well when I pointed it out to him."

"You pointed it out?" she began, noting with distraction that her voice was becoming stronger.

Robert noticed it, too, and he smiled even as he saved her from speaking further by explaining, "Oh, yes; I told him that he loves you. It is rather obvious for anyone with eyes. However, he apparently wasn't ready for the knowledge, and he isn't taking it at all well. I am not sure why. I do know that he took his parents' loss poorly and has seemed to try to keep a protective distance between himself and others since then, but . . ." He shrugged and shook his head. "Anyway, he has been a bear ever since." The young nobleman looked at her with wry amusement. "Hence the reason I had him leave."

Seeing the unhappy look on her face, he patted Maggie's hand. "I thought it best to warn you up front. He wasn't ready to have such feelings thrust in his face, and I fear this moodiness shall continue until he comes to terms with them. And since he certainly won't reveal his love for you until he does . . . Well, I hoped this chat would make married life a bit easier for you to bear until then."

When she merely stared at him, her thoughts in turmoil, Robert announced, "I think it is time I take a look at your wound and change your bandages."

Maggie ignored him as he set to work, her thoughts still in an uproar. She tried to sort out all he had just said. None of it made any sense and she hoped briefly that she was still feverish and imagining this entire conversation. A stab of pain as Lord Mullin lifted the last of her bandages away and

poked at her stitches convinced her otherwise. She was awake, all right. But she was
having trouble accepting what Robert had
said, and all it meant. She had just been
told that the man she loved, loved her in
return. *By his friend.*

"Only you, Maggie," she breathed, unsure
whether to laugh or cry.

"What was that?" Lord Mullin glanced at
her in question. When she merely shook her
head and waved one hand in a vague gesture, he shrugged and went back to work.
Maggie was left to her thoughts. How could
James possibly not know he loved her until
Robert told him so? That was preposterous!
Until she recalled that it had taken a talk
with Agatha to straighten out her own
confused feelings.

All right, she reasoned, so it wasn't preposterous that he too had needed someone to
clarify his thoughts, but his being reputedly
miserable about it?

Well, that wasn't so ridiculous either, she
decided, recalling her own misery when
she'd realized she loved James and felt sure
he did not love her back. . . . Perhaps his
unhappiness was caused by the same thing.
All she needed to do was tell him that she
loved him, too, and everything would be
fine. They would be happy. Her gaze flick-

ered to Robert. "I love him, too."

"Yes, I know," he said. Robert finished cleaning her wound and began to replace her bandages. "You told him while I was first tending to you. By the way, you are doing very well. The ball missed all your vital organs. There was a lot of blood loss, but very little real damage." He glanced up and looked her in the eye. "I suppose I should tell you that Lady X and her accomplice have already been before the magistrate. They won't be bothering you — or anyone else — anymore."

Maggie nodded at that news, happy to hear it, but really more concerned with what he had said before that. "Did you say that I told him that I love him?"

"Yes," Mullin answered distractedly as he finished with her bandages. Then he offered a smile. "You are mending very well. Which means that, in a day or so, we should be able to move you back to Lady Barlow's. That ought to please James. Mind you, the house staff would probably wish it sooner. His hanging about, acting like a wolf with an injured paw, growling about this and that every few minutes, has rather put them all on edge. The sooner it is safe to pack you off to Lady Barlow's, the better. Not that your company isn't delightful," he added to soften his words.

"He's back, m'lord!"

Maggie and Robert both turned to the door. A servant stood there wringing her hands.

"Already?" Lord Mullin rose with a frown.

"Yes. Mills sent me to warn you the moment he saw the coach pull up."

"Very well." Robert sighed then glanced down at Maggie with a tired smile. "It would seem Lord Ramsey has finished resting. Let us hope his mood has improved."

CHAPTER TWENTY

"Do you, Lady Margaret Wentworth, take this man . . ." The rest of the cleric's words faded into a drone as Maggie's mind started to swim.

What was she doing? How could she marry James? Was she willing to spend the rest of her life tied to a man she loved desperately, but who felt nothing for her? Or, at least, a man who could not express the feelings he had?

Turning, she glanced over the guests at the wedding, her gaze finding Lord Mullin. The man had saved both her life and her sanity — at least up to this point. His calm, steady manner and words were the only thing, that had gotten her this far. His insistence that James loved her had helped her heal, and had kept her from calling off the wedding each time James acted as if this union were purely a matter of honor. And he'd done so many times. He had barely spoken to her since her recovery.

Of course, he had not been shouting or stomping about, either. She could have borne that. But he had been cold. He didn't seem to want her anymore — not physically, at least — and that worried her more than anything. Their passion had brought them together, and to feel its absence . . . In James's passion, she had been able to find hope that he cared for her. But he hadn't touched her since before she'd been shot. He'd even seemed to avoid her.

No, she supposed she didn't believe Lord Mullin's claims anymore. She didn't think James loved her; he didn't even seem to like her. His cold and reticent behavior these last two weeks seemed to indicate that clearly enough. If anything, he appeared to loathe her now.

What had caused this? Had it been her confession of her feelings? Perhaps it was all right for him to like and lust after her as long as her emotions were not engaged. Perhaps he was trying to let her know not to expect her feelings to be reciprocated. Would he treat her thusly for the rest of their lives? she wondered miserably. Could she bear it if he did?

"Lady Wentworth?"

Maggie peered up blankly at the minister,

aware that she had missed her cue.

"You are supposed to say, 'I do,' " James prompted. Maggie turned her eyes to his implacable expression. He did not look like a happy man. He looked stiff and cold and as if he wished himself anywhere but here with her. If she said yes, she would be consigning him to a lifetime of what he considered to be hell. And herself, too.

"No." She didn't realize the word had slipped from her lips until James's expression changed to one of shock. He looked as if she'd hit him between the eyes with a mallet.

"What?" he squawked disbelievingly. The word was echoed in horror by his aunt and all of Maggie's servants.

"I said, no," she repeated. A calm quiet replaced the fear and confusion of moments before. She was doing the right thing. She knew that. "I will not marry you, James. Not when it is going to make you miserable."

Turning away, she started back up the aisle toward the church's exit, refusing to look at the shocked guests rising from the pews.

"My lady!" Banks was the first to break out of his shock and move after her. His alarm was obvious as he hurried to her side, pleading, "Oh, do reconsider, my lady. Are you sure about this? Think of the future."

"I *am* thinking of the future," she answered sympathetically. The servant was worrying over their economic forecast, but there was so much more at stake. This once, she needed to look out for herself as well as her servants. "We shall buy a smaller home, big enough for everyone, but less expensive than the house Gerald left me. We will be fine."

"Sit down!" James suddenly roared. Maggie paused and swung around in surprise. It wasn't till she saw the way he was glaring at their guests that she realized he hadn't been speaking to her.

"All of you! Sit down! This wedding is not over," he shouted. As soon as everyone had retaken his seat, James started up the aisle toward Maggie, scowling furiously. Pausing before her, he struggled briefly until he managed a less angry expression. His voice was reasonable as he said, "Maggie, what is it that you think you are doing? You cannot refuse —"

"I just did," she interrupted quietly.

"Yes, she did," one of the nearby guests said, the comment particularly loud in the silence. A wave of murmured agreement followed.

James turned a fierce glare on the crowd

until they fell silent; then, managing to school his face into something approximating calm, he once more faced Maggie. "Think of the scandal," he implored.

Maggie did. Briefly. She was hardly aware of her foot tapping as she considered. In the end, the answer seemed easy enough. Yes. People would talk. They would whisper and twitter and so on, but if she moved to the country as she planned, all would be forgotten soon enough. Well, perhaps not so soon, but hopefully sooner than her death . . . which was how long she would suffer the misery of being married to someone who didn't love her. Straightening, she said with feigned cheer, "What is another scandal, more or less? Give them ten or fifteen years and no one will remember my name."

The comment sent another wave of whispers through the church, some agreeing that ten or fifteen years should be enough to forget the scandal, and others disagreeing. It seemed about half and half, she noted before James burst out frantically, "But we have been together! You could be with child!"

"Oh, that was grand of you to announce," Maggie snapped. It didn't look as though things would be forgotten in ten years, after all. The entire church was now talking excitedly.

"Maggie —"

"No!" she snapped. The crowd went silent again, eager to hear what came next. "I have said no and I meant it."

Spinning on her heel, she started for the door again. Banks was steadfast by her side, and the rest of her staff slipped out of the pews to march toward the back of the church in a little parade. Their show of support was heartening, and Maggie could have hugged every single one of them. She didn't see Lady Barlow give up her startled state and rush out of the front pew to hurry toward James, but she did hear her when the woman barked, "Do something, James! She is leaving!"

"You said you loved me!" he called out.

It wasn't the words so much as the betrayed sound of his voice that made Maggie pause. The murmurs in the church had grown ridiculously loud. Closing her eyes, she took a deep breath then made herself face him once more. The murmuring died at once, the air growing tense with anticipation.

"I do love you," she admitted softly, flushing at the oohs and ahhs exhaled by their guests.

"Then . . ."

James took a step forward, but she raised her hand to stop him and continued, "And that is why I will not marry you. I will not marry someone I love when the very idea of it is making him miserable."

"Who is miserable?" he asked with surprise. "I am not miserable."

"Oh, James," Lady Barlow piped up at his lame response. "I think she is referring to how cold and grumpy you have been of late."

"Aye, you been miserable lately," one guest said.

"These last few weeks at least," another agreed.

Lord Mullin stood up. "You tore a strip off your driver the other day, right in front of the club, and you never treat your servants poorly. Aye, you've acted miserable, all right, James." Robert gave Maggie an apologetic glance.

"Oh, do shut up!" James glared at his friend, then turned back to Maggie with a sigh.

"Well, perhaps I have been out of sorts of late," he admitted reluctantly. A series of snorts rose among the guests, but James steadfastly ignored them. "It is not because of this wedding, though. Or because you

489

love me. I am glad you love me. That isn't what has made me so unhappy."

"Then what has?" Maggie asked desperately. She watched a battle take place on his features. When at last it ceased and he merely looked at her helplessly, she felt disappointment tug at her. She turned toward the door again. She had managed only one step when he blurted, "Because I love you, too!"

"He loves you, my lady!" Banks called hopefully to where Maggie had stopped again.

"Harrumph. It's not decent to love your wife," a woman to Maggie's right said staunchly. "Good thing she isn't marrying him."

"Oh, do shut up so we can hear her," someone else snapped at the unhappy-sounding woman.

Maggie turned toward James, her confusion clear. "You are miserable because you love me?" she asked. Robert's words came to mind, but still she didn't understand.

"No," James answered unhappily. He moved forward until they were standing nose-to-nose. "I am not miserable because I love you; I am miserable because of how it makes me feel."

Maggie tipped her head, annoyed and

490

bewildered. "How does it make you feel?"

"It hurts and it scares me," he admitted in a soft voice. His aunt and Maggie's servants crowded closer to hear. "I cannot control or protect you, Maggie. You do what you will, when you will. When I nearly lost you, and I saw my life spreading out before me so barren without you, I —"

"What the hell is he jabbering on about?" an older gentleman asked grouchily.

Maggie glared at the rude man, then was taken somewhat by surprise when a flushed James suddenly took her arm and dragged her toward the exit. Over his shoulder he called, "Wait here. We shall return momentarily."

Much to her surprise, he didn't stop once they were out of the church, instead he continued on until they reached his coach. Waving away the temporary servant hired to watch the horses while Crowch attended the wedding, James opened the carriage door himself and helped her inside. He followed.

"This is not perhaps the best place to talk, but at least it offers a modicum of privacy," he said. Pulling the carriage door closed, he settled on the bench seat across from her.

"I —" Maggie began, but he held up a hand to silence her.

"No. Let me start," he said. Tugging at his cravat impatiently, he took a deep breath and dove in. "Maggie, I have been a complete ass these last two weeks. I love you. I realized it at Robert's after you were shot."

"Well, Robert told me that he told you that you loved me."

"Yes, he did. But he didn't have to. Not really," he added when she looked doubtful. Heaving out a breath, he confessed, "Maggie, I was half in love with you before we ever met. I think good old Robert was, too."

Maggie's eyes widened. "The letters?"

"Yes. Your letters. Gerald read them to us every time he got one. He told us a lot about you, too, of course, but through your letters we heard your voice and got to know you. You lifted us out of that blood- and muck-filled world and brought life and light with you. I couldn't wait to meet you when I returned. I was actually eager to keep my vow to look out for you. I would have done it even had he not asked me."

He grimaced slightly at himself, then said, "You see, that day you were shot, when you told me that you loved me, I opened my mouth to say it back, but then Robert started to work on you. You cried out and fainted, and I didn't have to say anything. If I had spoken, I might have convinced myself that I was just repeating the words to be polite. I'm not very . . . good at *feeling.* But I didn't have to speak. Unfortunately, Robert didn't let me off the hook. He saw how I truly felt." James sighed. "He saw that I truly love you. But what he doesn't know is *why* I love you."

"Why?" Maggie echoed, almost afraid she was dreaming.

"Yes, darling. Why. You see, I love you because of everything you were in those letters, but I love you also because of the exuberance with which you live your life. I love you because you care for your servants more than you care for yourself. I love you because you do what you believe, and go where you need to go to do what you have to do. But loving you for those reasons — you're not someone who's easy to love, Maggie. You have a wild streak. The way you live is dangerous. When I saw you lying in that bed, when I truly believed you were going to die on me, I felt such pain that . . . well, I haven't felt it since my parents died."

He looked up, and she felt herself melt in the heat of his stare. "When your brother died in my arms, it almost killed me. He was such a dear friend. I admired and loved him. But you, Maggie, have come to mean so much more than he ever did. I knew that your death would tear me apart. Losing you would hurt so —"

"But you *didn't* lose me," Maggie interrupted. She shifted from her bench seat to his, patting his leg soothingly. "I survived."

"This time," he agreed. "But I will lose you someday. I must. Either I will die or you will, and that has been tormenting me these past two weeks."

"But —"

"No, let me finish," he said quickly. "That is why I have been such an ass. But I haven't been thinking clearly at all." He laughed suddenly, self-mocking. "Obviously. Because when you said no to marrying me just now, I realized what I was doing: instead of protecting myself with my foolish behavior, I was simply causing myself to lose you even sooner than was necessary."

Taking her hands in his, he pressed a kiss to each. "An intelligent man would enjoy the time we have together, cherish every moment with you, and not waste whatever time we have on fearing the future. I haven't been a very intelligent man, Maggie, but I vow here and now that if you marry me today, I will return to being the intelligent man I used to think I was. I'll spend the rest of my life doing everything in my power to make you happy."

"Oh, James," Maggie breathed, tears welling in her eyes. "I love you and always will."

"Even when I am stomping around, grumpy and miserable?" He asked the question with gentle humor, but Maggie caught the uncertainty that flashed in his eyes.

His uncertainty should not have surprised her; his misery and grumpiness were the reasons she had just refused to marry him. Still, Maggie found herself startled by the sign of his vulnerability. Cupping his face in her hands she put all the sincerity she possessed into her words as she said, "Yes, my lord. I shall love you always no matter how grumpy and miserable you occasionally get . . . I shall just remind myself that it is caused by fear." She broke the solemn moment with a grin and added, "Then I shall remind you. That should jolly you out of the mood at once."

"Aye, it should," he admitted wryly, then chuckled and pulled her into an embrace. Hugging her close, he sighed into her hair then said, "And I love you, and always shall." Maggie was about to pull back to kiss him when he added, "Despite the fact that you tend to act without thinking, and are always managing to get yourself into trouble."

She drew back abruptly, but rather than

kiss him she offered an indignant glare. "I am not always getting myself into trouble!"

"No?" It was his turn to grin. "Who is it who was kidnapped from a brothel some weeks back?"

"*You* were the one who did the kidnapping!" she exclaimed hotly.

"Ah . . . so I was. But then you nearly got run down by that scar-faced man."

She glared at him, and he continued, "And who is it who got shot while —"

"Trying to save her future husband from being discovered and shot?" Maggie finished archly.

James stilled. "Banks said he thought that was what you were trying to do. I had hoped he was wrong."

"Why ever would you hope that?" Maggie asked in amazement.

"Ah, Maggie. Had you died trying to save me . . ." Anguish washed over his face and Maggie felt tears well in her eyes again as he said, "I must thank you for what you did, but if you ever do it again, I swear I shall —"

"My lord?"

James scowled at the interruption. "What?"

"Do please shut up and kiss me."

His scowl faded slowly, then he bent to

press a kiss to her lips. It started as a sweet kiss, a gentle brush of lips to celebrate their love, but as always happened between them, it soon became a desperate, all-encompassing embrace that left them both panting.

"Oh, I have missed you," Maggie gasped as his lips slid along her jaw and started down her neck.

James mumbled something of an agreement, then tugged impatiently at the collar of her wedding gown. Irritably he asked, "Why do they make women's clothing so damned restrictive?"

"To prevent men from doing exactly this!" Maggie laughed breathlessly, then groaned as he finally managed to get one breast free of her gown. He suckled it relentlessly. "Oh, James. Oh, oh, oh, *James!*" She squealed suddenly, pulling away as she recalled where they were.

"We are supposed to be getting married today," she reminded him, tugging fretfully at her gown, trying to get covered back up.

"We are supposed to be consummating the marriage today, too," he said in the velvety voice that always made her tingle. He began tugging at the skirt of her gown, now, trying to find the hem line to get under it.

"Yes, but I think you have it in the wrong order," Maggie pointed out with a laugh, pleased to see that the passion was back. "Do you not think we should —"

He silenced her by covering her mouth in a kiss that curled her toes. When he added to his persuasion by sliding his hand up under her skirt, Maggie gave up her arguments and melted into him.

The guests could wait a little bit longer.

"Well?"

Lady Barlow glanced from the carriage she was watching outside the church, to the woman who came to stand beside her. Agatha Dubarry. Maggie had insisted on inviting her friend, the brothel owner, and been terribly surprised when neither James nor Lady Barlow had argued. Vivian saw now that it was the right decision. The woman was dressed in a prim pink gown, her face free of makeup, and her brassy red hair was hidden by a wig. No one would recognize her.

"Ah," the madam said, noting the way the carriage was rocking. "They have made up."

"Yes. It would seem so," Vivian agreed, turning her attention back to the moving vehicle. "At least they're not in the library."

Agatha chuckled softly and when Lady

498

Barlow looked over in surprise, the woman admitted, "Maggie told me all about Lord Ramsey's love of books."

"Hmm. Love of books, love on books, love among books," she counted off humorously, then glanced over her shoulder at the wedding guests. They were all peering curiously toward them. "I suppose we should tell these people that the wedding is still on. Do you think James and Maggie will be much longer?"

Agatha squinted at the carriage, pursed her lips and shook her head. "Nay. It has been two weeks since they have been together. Besides, by the way the carriage is moving, I am guessing that things are coming to a climax."

"I hope for Maggie's sake it is two," Vivian murmured.

Agatha glanced in shock at her, then burst out laughing. When she had regained herself, she took Vivian's arm, and the two started back into the church. The brothel owner said, "Why, Lady Barlow, Maggie never mentioned what a witty woman you are. I do believe we could be friends."

"That is more than possible," the noblewoman allowed with a smile. "And please, call me Vivian."

ABOUT THE AUTHOR

Lynsay Sands is the nationally bestselling author of the Argeneau/Rogue Hunter vampire series, as well as numerous historicals and anthologies. She's been writing since grade school and considers herself incredibly lucky to be able to make a career out of it. Her hope is that readers can get away from their everyday stress through her stories, and if there are occasional uncontrollable fits of laughter, that's just a big bonus. Please visit her on the web at www.lynsaysands.net.

SOCCER

The ultimate guide to the beautiful game

CLIVE GIFFORD

KINGFISHER

BOSTON

Foreword

Soccer is a wonderful game, a sport that knows no boundaries of race, age, wealth, sex, or religion. Soccer is a sport that reaches everyone. All over the world, people young and old play it, watch it, and read about it. This book captures the international appeal, enjoyment, and excitement of this unique sport.

People often forget that for all its drama and beauty soccer is a simple game built on a set of individual skills, allied to working together as a team. Although natural ability is a gift, players are not born with these skills and understanding—they are things that must be learned. To be a success requires much hard work, patience, self-sacrifice, and a desire to study the game and improve. Most importantly it involves loving what you do. Young people will continue to play and watch soccer, and this book will help increase their enjoyment of the world's most beautiful game.

KINGFISHER

a Houghton Mifflin Company imprint
222 Berkeley Street
Boston, Massachusetts 02116
www.houghtonmifflinbooks.com

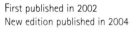

Author Clive Gifford
Consultant Anthony Hobbs
Editors Clive Wilson, Matt Parselle, Vicky Weber
Design Mike Buckley, Malcolm Parchment
Production Controller Joanne Blackmore
DTP Manager Nicky Studdart
DTP Operator Primrose Burton
Picture Research Jane Lambert, Juliet Duff
Indexer Chris Bernstein
Coordinating Editor Denise Heal

First published in 2002
New edition published in 2004

4 6 8 10 9 7 5 3

3TR/1204/PROSP/CLSN*UD(CLSN)/157MA

Copyright © Kingfisher Publications Plc 2002

LIBRARY OF CONGRESS CATALOGING-IN-PUBLICATION DATA
Gifford, Clive.
    Soccer / by Clive Gifford.—1st ed.
        p. cm.
    Includes index.
    Summary: Presents the game of soccer, including its basic rules, structure, playing
positions, needed skills, and great players.
        1. Soccer—Juvenile literature. [1. Soccer.] I. Title.
GV943.25 .G55 2002
796.334—dc21   2001038939

ISBN 0-7534-5752-0
ISBN 978-07534-5752-8

Printed in China

Contents

INTRODUCTION
The Global Game   6
From Earliest Beginnings   8
The Field and Players   10
Key Rules   12
Fouls and Misconduct   14
Ready to Play   16

THE GREATS
Great Competitions   76
Great Games   78
Great Players   84

REFERENCE
Soccer History   88
Stats and Facts   90
Glossary and Web sites   92

Index   94
Acknowledgments   96

SKILLS
Ball Control   18
Passing   20
Advanced Passing   22
Movement and Space   24
On-ball Skills   26
Tackling   28
Volleying and Shooting   30
Heading   32
Small-sided Games   34
Fancy Skills   36

POSITION AND PLAY
Goalkeeping Basics   38
Goalkeeping Choices   40
Attacking Skills   42
Opening up Defenses   44
Defending   46
Defending as a Unit   48

SET PIECES
Restarts   50
The Corner Kick   52
Free Kicks   54
Free Kicks in Attack   56
Penalty!   58

TACTICS
Managers and Coaches   60
Formations   62
Tactics   64
Tactics in a Game   66

A PRO'S GAME
A Pro's Life   68
Teams and Fans   70
Soccer Media   72
Stadiums   74

The Global Game

Goal, *gola*, *gol*! Whichever language you speak, a game of soccer provides 90 minutes or more of adrenaline-pumping action, intense drama, and breathtaking skills. Soccer is a game that can be played in a park, on a beach, or in a huge stadium watched on television by millions of people. But wherever it is played, soccer inspires powerful emotions and fierce loyalties like no other game on earth.

▲ Soccer crosses all boundaries. It is passionately followed by men, women, boys, and girls of all ages and backgrounds. Television allows even the remotest places to have access to games from around the world.

▲ Ronaldo grew up in a poor district of Rio de Janeiro, Brazil. He secured a place in Brazil's 1994 World Cup team at the age of 18. Since then Ronaldo has played soccer in Europe and has become one of the most talked-about players. He was the leading scorer in the 2002 World Cup with eight goals.

Less is more

Soccer is essentially a simple game. The aim is to get the ball into the opponent's goal without using your hands or arms. Whichever team scores the most goals wins. Of course there are many rules and regulations, but these are designed to keep the game fair and flowing. Whatever your skill level, you can enjoy the game without expensive uniforms or equipment. You don't even need a soccer field. All you need for a friendly game is a safe, open space or indoor gym, along with a ball, a few players, and something to mark out a goal.

▲ Pelé described soccer as "the beautiful game." An outstanding Brazilian player from the late 1950s to the early 1970s, he is widely recognized as the greatest soccer player in the history of the game.

"*Some people think football [soccer] is a matter of life and death. I don't like that attitude. I can assure them it is much more serious than that.*" Bill Shankly

"*Football [soccer] is like a religion to me. I worship the ball, and I treat it like a god.*" Pelé

▶ French fans celebrate their team's 3-0 victory over Brazil in the 1998 World Cup final. The game was watched by more than 600 million people around the world. In total almost 1.5 billion viewers watched games in the 2002 World Cup held in Japan and South Korea.

Big business

Big teams, such as Spain's Real Madrid, England's Manchester United, and Italy's AC Milan and Juventus, are supported around the world. These teams are run as powerful businesses that generate millions of dollars per year. Their top players are often as famous—and as well paid—as movie stars.

All over the world

From its official beginnings in Europe in the 1800s, soccer has spread to almost every part of the world. Historically South America and Europe— where the game is known as "football"—have been soccer's powerhouses. However, the rise of women's soccer in the U.S. and the emergence of great players and teams from nations in Africa, Asia, Australasia, and the Middle East have turned the game into a truly global sport.

From Earliest Beginnings

The origins of soccer are ancient. More than 2,000 years ago Chinese, Japanese, Greek, and Roman cultures all featured games that involved players kicking or carrying a ball through a goal. Later, in the Middle Ages, violent contests between two teams of unlimited numbers were often played in the streets of towns and villages. A pig's bladder or stuffed animal skin served as the ball. In the 1800s soccer became organized with official rules. By the end of the century, it had evolved into more or less the game we play today.

▲ A pig's bladder is blown up for a game of pallo. Played in Europe in the 1600s, it was an early version of soccer.

The Football Association

In 1863 representatives from 11 English "football" teams met at the Freemason's Tavern in London to form the Football Association (FA). Until then, the hundreds of schools and teams that played soccer each had their own set of rules. Some teams played by rules that allowed holding the ball or tripping, for example, while others did not. Out of this chaos the FA devised a single set of rules. Within a decade, the English FA was joined by FAs from Wales, Scotland, and Ireland. In 1882 these four created the International Football Association Board (IFAB), which attempted to rule and regulate soccer around the world.

▲ During the Victorian era the typical outfit for soccer teams, such as the Scottish international team of 1892 (above), included caps and knee breeches (long shorts).

▲ Dating from the 1500s, the annual Shrove Tuesday soccer game in the town of Ashbourne, England, has no referees and very few rules. The goals are placed at either end of the town and the teams are known as Up'ards and Down'ards.

◀ The Japanese game of kemari was developed from ball games played in ancient China more than 2,000 years ago. In kemari players had to pass the ball to each other without it touching the ground.

Explosion of interest

Toward the end of the 1800s soccer spread like wildfire around the globe, introduced first by British traders and sailors and then by travelers from other European nations. Between 1890–1910, dozens of countries, from Austria to Brazil and Hungary to Russia, formed their own soccer teams, competitions, and associations. In 1904, tired of the IFAB burying its head in the sand, the *Fédération Internationale de Football Association* (FIFA) was formed by France and six other European nations. Soccer was now a truly international sport.

◀▲ *Despite some opposition from the male-dominated establishment, women's soccer games grew in popularity from the 1880s onward.*

▶ *Until the 1940s, balls and shoes were made from heavy, unwaterproofed leather. On a wet field, both the ball and shoes would get much heavier and lose their shape.*

▲ *Shinguards were invented in 1874 by Samuel W. Widdowson, a player for the English team Nottingham Forest, and who also played for England in 1880.*

Early games and rules

Soccer games from the 1870s and 1880s onward attracted large crowds and much interest. Many of the basic rules of the game, were in place by then. Modifications to the game, such as two-handed throw-ins and penalty kicks, were introduced. For a long time, goalkeepers could be charged at and knocked over at any time; later this was allowed only when they had the ball. However, goalies could use their hands on the ball anywhere on the field. This rule changed after a flood of goals were scored in 1910 by goalies throwing the ball into the opposition's net!

▶ *The England shirt (right) was worn in the first official international game, which was against Scotland in 1872. Before this date caps were used to distinguish between teams. Caps then became keepsakes for playing for your country.*

Timeline

1848
First set of soccer rules drawn up at Cambridge University, England

1863
The Football Association formed in England

1871
Soccer's oldest surviving competition, the FA Cup, is created

1872
First soccer international game—England 0 Scotland 0

1872
Corner kicks introduced for the first time

1878
Whistles first used by referees

1885
Paying players (professionalism) legalized

1891
Penalty kicks introduced

1899
FA suggest an upper limit of £10 ($15) on player transfer fees

1905
First South American international game—Uruguay vs. Argentina

1908
Soccer's first Olympic Games won by England

1910
The first Copa America won by Argentina

1912
Goalkeepers now allowed to handle the ball only in their own penalty area

1913
"Ten-yards" rule introduced for free kicks

1926
Legendary Brazilian player, Artur Friedenreich, makes 1,000th goal in Brazilian soccer

1930
First World Cup finals in Uruguay

HUNTLEY & PALMERS
Football Wafers

1887 9

Field and Players

The field, or pitch, is where it all happens—where players pit their skills against each other and where games are won and lost. For professional games there are two teams of 11 players on a field 110–120 yards long and 70–80 yards wide. These teams play two 45 minute halves, plus injury or stoppage time.

See also

12–13 Key Rules

64–65 Tactics

Goals are 8 feet high and 24 feet wide. Corner flags are at least 5 feet tall to protect players from injury.

The penalty spot is a circle marked out 12 yards from the goal line.

Center spot—the place where a kickoff restarts the game, either after a goal or at the beginning of each half

Sideline (Touchline)

Field dimensions

Although professional fields usually are the standard 110 yards by 77 yards, a legal field can be anywhere between 100–130 yards long and 50–100 yards wide.

Center circle—at kickoffs, opponents cannot enter this circle until the ball has been played

Player positions

Soccer started off simply with players being either forwards or backs. Now with sweepers, midfield anchors, wingers, and target men, player positions have become more complicated. That said, outfield players tend to be grouped into three categories—defenders, midfielders, and attackers. Players' shirts are numbered to aid identification, and ever since the 1920s, teams have been asked to change into a second, or away, shirt if their colors clash with those of the home side.

◀ Teams have a home shirt and one or more away shirts. These are one set of Scottish team Celtic's home (top left) and away (left) shirts. Shirts tend to change every season.

Ball in play

Ball in play

Ball out of play

Goal

No goal

No goal

No goal

In or out?

The ball is only out of play when it completely crosses the boundary lines of the field—including the goal line. A throw-in, goal kick, corner kick, or goal is awarded depending on where the ball went out and which side touched it last. This applies to a ball in the air as well as one on the ground—so a clearance that curves over the sideline before landing in play will result in a throw-in for the opposition.

► *Luxembourg defender Jeff Strasser fails to stop the ball from crossing the line during a Euro 2000 qualifier.*

Midfield line—divides the field into two equal areas of play. Players have to stay in their own half before a kickoff

Penalty arc—during a penalty kick, only the penalty kicker is allowed in this space

Corner arc—corner kicks must be taken inside this area

Penalty area—known as "the box" and the area in which a goalie is allowed to handle the ball. Commit a foul in your box and your team could be facing a penalty

Goal line (Endline)—if the ball completely crosses this line, a goal kick, corner, or goal will be awarded

Goal area—known as the "six-yard box" and the area in which goal kicks must be taken

▲ *This new stadium, which has an artificial turf surface, opened in Salzburg, Austria, in 2003. It is one of four stadiums taking part in UEFA's experiments into possible replacements for turf.*

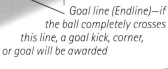

▼ *Norwegian groundsmen sweep the snow prior to a Tromso, Norway, game.*

▲ *This 1995 game between Wimbledon and Blackburn Rovers (both of England) was played in a mudbath at Selhurst Park stadium.*

The field

The rise of artificial turf in North America and in stadiums all over the world prompted ex-England manager Terry Venables to cowrite a book entitled *They Used To Play On Grass*. Yet a new century still sees grass as king, even though it requires a lot of care and preparation. A stadium's groundstaff is responsible for getting a field ready for the game. Technical advances, such as soil management and undersoil heating, have helped reduce the number of games called off due to bad weather in many countries around the world.

See also

14–15 Fouls and Misconduct

54–55 Free Kicks

64–65 Tactics

▲ A referee's signals communicate clearly to everyone watching: a direct free kick (top left), an indirect free kick (above), or a red card for a player to leave the field (left).

Key Rules

Knowing the laws of the game is not only part of becoming a soccer player, it can also give you the edge in games. If you break the rules, you may forfeit your hard-earned possession of the ball to your team's disadvantage.

Guardians of the game

Players should observe all the rules on the field, but in practice it falls on the shoulders of the referee and his assistants to enforce the laws of the game. The officials make judgements on offsides, fouls, and misconduct (see pages 14–15), whether the ball was in or out of play, and if a hand ball has occurred. They have a range of signals at their disposal to communicate their decision to other officials, players, and spectators.

▲ A corner kick is signaled clearly by the referee pointing to the corner flag.

▼ This referee is signaling for a goal kick to be taken from the goal area.

▼ There are two stages to the signals for offside. First, the referee's assistant raises his flag upright to indicate that an offside has occurred. Following this, he angles his flag to show whether the offside occurred on the far side (1), center (2), or near side (3) of the field.

◄ The referee's assistant reinforces the referee's goal-kick signal by pointing his flag level with the front edge of the goal area.

▲ The assistant signals a throw-in, pointing a flag at the goal that the throwing-in team is attacking.

◄ The assistant signals for a corner and checks that the ball is placed within the corner area by the kicker.

▲ The assistant signals that a substitution is about to take place.

Advantage rule

Referees have some flexibility in how they interpret the rules. A key part of this flexibility is the advantage rule. The advantage rule means that the referee has spotted a foul or infringement, but instead of awarding a free kick, he lets the game continue because it offers an advantage to the side sinned against. A good example of this is when an attacker is fouled, but still manages to pass to a teammate. The advantage rule reduces the number of interruptions and helps keep the game moving.

▲ There's plenty of pressure on referees to get offside and other decisions right. Here Swiss referee Urs Meier has to contend with players from the Turkish side, Galatasaray.

Offside

It's just one short soccer rule out of 17, yet more controversy is generated by the offside rule than any other. Offside is no evil plot to ruin soccer—it is in place to stop forwards from hanging around the goal waiting for a pass and then easily scoring. It helps generate exciting attacking and counterattacking play. Much of the rule's bad press comes from its seeming complexity, yet the basic gist of the law is simple:

A player is offside when—at the moment the ball is played forward by a teammate—the player is nearer to the opposition's goal line than both the ball and the second-from-last opponent.

A player cannot be offside in his own half of the field or when receiving the ball directly from a goal kick, corner, or throw-in.

Examine these words. Opponents include the goalie as well as outfield players. If you're level with the second-from-last opposition player, be it a center back or the goalie, you're not offside. The "at the moment the ball is played" part is vital, too. An essential part of attacking is to time your runs so that you're onside as the ball is played ahead of you, yet can be behind defenders to collect the ball a split second later.

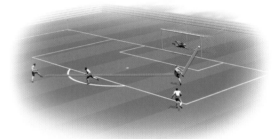

▲ When the ball was played is absolutely vital in an offside decision. Here the player who scores is clearly in an offside position when the ball is played. His "goal" is therefore disallowed as a result.

▲ The first attacker has foiled the onrushing goalkeeper by slipping the ball to a teammate. With two defenders between the goalscorer and the goal, the player is onside and the goal is allowed.

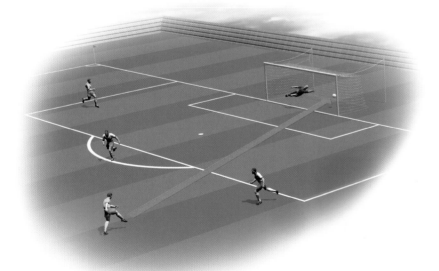

▲ Referees must judge if a player is interfering with or influencing play when offside. The player at the top left is offside, but is not considered to be interfering or actively involved in play. The player who shoots is onside when he scores, and the goal is counted.

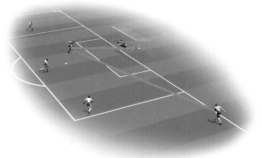

▲ You cannot be offside if you're behind the ball at the moment it is played. The scoring attacker only has the goalie in front of him. Yet he is not offside because the ball was cut back to him by his teammate.

See also

12–13 Key Rules

54–55 Free Kicks

58–59 Penalty!

Fouls and Misconduct

Act against the spirit of the game or break its laws at your own risk. It's the referee's job to penalize actions such as shirtpulling or tripping a player. If the offense is serious enough, you may be cautioned or even sent off the field.

Foul!

Tripping, pushing, or holding back an opponent are just a few of the offenses that are considered fouls. Depending on the offense and where it took place, the fouled-against team will be awarded a direct free kick, indirect free kick, or penalty. Some free-kick offenses, such as attempting to kick an opponent, apply even if the player fails to make contact. Offenses resulting in an indirect free kick include time-wasting and obstruction. For a complete list of fouls, look at a copy of the laws of the game.

No.1 Bobby Charlton

Some of the world's greatest soccer players have also been the most well behaved. During a career spanning more than 20 years and 860 team and country appearances, English soccer player Bobby Charlton was never sent off the field.

MASTERCLASS
Fouls and misconduct

Never argue with a referee. The referee's decision is final.

Never retaliate if you've been fouled. This is also a punishable offense.

Channel your aggression into winning the game, not attacking your opponents.

Always keep your cool and trust the officials to uphold the laws of the game.

◀ Thorsten Fink and Steve McManaman argue in a high-pressure Champions League semifinal encounter between Spain's Real Madrid and Germany's Bayern Munich.

▲ Dutch striker Jimmy Floyd Hasselbaink is tugged to the ground by Belgium's Eric Deflandre in the 1998 World Cup. Shirt pulling is just one of many fouls that can result in a free kick or penalty, and the offending player is shown a yellow or a red card.

▼ *Bologna's Nicola Boselli is guilty of dangerous play as he goes in high on Sporting Lisbon striker Leandro.*

Booking

A booking, also known as a yellow card or a caution, sees the referee holding up a yellow card and the player's name and shirt number being written down in the ref's book. Misconduct, including cynical, deliberate, and dangerous play, is likely to make the referee reach for the yellow card. Persistent minor infringements can also result in a booking.

Don't see red

Tempers often run high on the field but that's no excuse for a player to throw a punch or shout abuse at the officials. If you're guilty of any of these offenses, or prevent a clear goal-scoring opportunity by fouling or handling the ball, you can expect a red card. Two yellow-card offenses also mean leaving the field. The red card is no badge of honor. Players who've been given their marching orders let their team down and give the opposition a big advantage. Being sent off can also result in a player being banned from playing in one or more games.

▼ *Italian referee Pierluigi Collina is a familiar face in international soccer. He never shies away from tough decisions.*

▲ *A professional foul is committed when a goal-scoring chance is prevented by unfairly impeding an attacker or handling the ball. If the attacker is in the penalty area, a penalty will be awarded and the defending player sent off.*

Under pressure

Refereeing is a tough job. Referees have to judge a fast-moving, dynamic game for 90 minutes or more. Decisions have to be made on the spot, and referees and their assistants don't have the benefit of slow-motion replays. Officials are only human and do make occasional mistakes. Even if you feel a referee has made a bad decision, do not challenge or try to change his or her mind. The referee's decision is always final.

▼ *Officials can be subjected to verbal abuse and sometimes worse from a hostile crowd. The referee and his assistants in this Colombia, South America, game are escorted off the field by riot police, protecting them from objects thrown by spectators.*

RED-CARD OFFENSES

A second cautionable offense

Using foul and abusive language

A professional foul

Violent conduct

Serious foul play such as a deliberate hand ball

See also

10-11 Field and Players

60-61 Managers and Coaches

68-69 A Pro's Life

▲ This warm-up move involves performing a series of vigorous jumping jacks to get the blood circulating.

▲ Run and skip with an exaggerated high knee action, using your arms for balance.

▲ This exercise involves jogging along with a high backlift so that your heels almost touch your rear.

Stretching

Soccer can push your body to the limit, and stretching the muscles before a game allows them to perform at their peak, improving performance and reducing injuries. Warm up before stretching and always ease gently into and out of a stretch—never stretch too far. Hold each stretch position for five to ten seconds, and repeat the stretch several times.

▼ Perform this thigh stretch after the other stretches. Using one hand for support, pull back your leg smoothly. Hold for ten seconds and then repeat with the other leg.

Ready to Play

With seconds to go before the ref blows the whistle and the game starts, the tension is mounting. Are you ready for the game— really ready? Have you stretched and warmed up properly? Is your uniform clean and have you had enough water?

Warm-up act

Being prepared for a game involves much more than packing a spare set of socks, crossing your fingers, and jogging out onto the field. Players of all ages and abilities need to warm up and get their bodies ready for the game. Warming up can involve activities such as jogging around the field, some short sprints, jumping jacks, and other routines. Teams that have warmed up properly may have an advantage over their opponents, allowing them to react more quickly in the opening minutes.

▲ To perform a side stretch, start with your feet about shoulder-width apart. Bend smoothly to one side as far as possible, letting your arm trail down your leg. Hold and then repeat, bending to the other side.

▲ For floor splits, push your head down toward each knee and the ground, holding for five seconds.

▲ Sitting down with the soles of your feet pressed together, use your elbows to push your knees down and hold the position to stretch your groin muscles.

▼▶ *Alessandro Del Piero's silver shoes (below) feature cleats molded into the sole of the shoe. Many shoes come with replaceable, screw-in cleats (right).*

Walk a mile in my shoes

First and foremost, your shoes must be a comfortable fit. Don't squeeze your foot into a size too small or let it float around in a size too large just because it's endorsed by your favorite player. Figo, Zidane, or Rivaldo's footwear isn't going to transform you into these heroes. Forget the logos and the hype—a pair of shoes that fits well and is well made and looked after is all you need.

Good shoes are made of soft leather to let your feet "feel" the ball—regular cleaning and polishing will help keep the leather soft. Good shoes are also flexible, should offer you plenty of support around the ankle, and have a wide tongue that won't slip to one side or the other. When your shoes get wet, allow them to dry naturally instead of in front of a heat source, otherwise the leather might crack. Help them keep their shape by stuffing them with newspaper after wear.

▲ *Shinguards are required at all levels of the modern game. Get used to shinguards by wearing them during practice and practice games.*

▼ *Professional players, such as Saudi Arabian international Sami Al Jaber (pictured here), warm up and stretch thoroughly before practice or prior to a game.*

Shirts, shorts, and shinguards

Cotton shirts and shorts have been largely replaced by artificial materials. Tucking your shirt into your shorts isn't just about looking neat—it gives opponents less material to grab. Socks can be held up with small strips of material called ties. In earlier times sliding newspapers down the front of your socks was the only protection against a crack across the shins. Today's shinguards are usually made of plastic, but can prevent you from getting bruised.

▲ *Today's soccer balls are lighter in weight, waterproof, and feature the maker's logo, like this Adidas Finale ball (top).*

▼ *Drinking small amounts of liquids such as water or flat, fruit-juice-based drinks, before, during, and after a practice session or game is essential.*

▲ *The heavy cotton shirts of the past (left) have largely been replaced by clothing manufactured from lighter artificial materials (right).*

MASTERCLASS
Ready to play

Take warming up seriously, even if teammates don't.

Remember to ease your way gently through a stretch.

Clean and look after your uniform. It will last longer that way.

Wear a sweatsuit before a game to keep warm, and regularly drink small amounts of water.

▲ *The German national side, like all teams, keep warm in training and before a match by wearing sweatsuits and other practice clothing.*

See also

36-37 Fancy Skills

44-45 Opening Up Defenses

◀ For inside- or outside-foot cushioning, get into position early with your weight on your supporting leg. Watch the ball until it contacts your foot, then bring your foot back slightly to pull the ball down.

▲ Use the underside of your foot to trap the ball. Bring your foot down firmly, but don't stamp on the ball—it may pop out from under your control.

Ball Control

A long ball from a teammate is coming your way. Although you could just alter its direction with a touch of your foot, most of the time you'll want to slow the ball down and get it at your feet, ready for a run, pass, or a shot at goal. Welcome to ball control—one of the game's most essential group of skills.

The soft option

"Damping" and "killing" are terms often used to describe stopping the speed (pace) and direction of a ball. What you're actually doing is cushioning the ball. This involves following the direction of the ball with the part of your body that makes contact with it. Whichever part of your body you use for cushioning, try to stay relaxed and balanced, watch the ball very closely, and move as smoothly as possible.

◀ With a wide stance for balance, lean backward as the ball reaches your chest. This will cushion the ball. As it drops down in front of you get your foot on the ball as quickly as possible.

No.2 Ruud Gullit

The Dutch player Ruud Gullit was a superb controller of the ball. He had a wonderful first touch, which gave him plenty of time and room to deploy his other formidable skills.

Control surfaces

Almost any part of your body that's allowed to touch the ball according to the rules can be used to get the ball under control. Your thigh and the top, or instep, of your foot are two of the more difficult parts to use, but are very effective when a ball is falling steeply and sharply in front of you. Whichever area of the body you choose, try to use your arms to keep yourself balanced and aligned with the ball.

"Once you can control the ball, football [soccer] becomes a simple game."

Ferenc Puskas, former Hungarian captain

▲ *The instep cushion requires you to get your foot up, with the instep facing the ball and the toe pointing slightly down. As the ball arrives bring your foot down with the ball resting just above it.*

MASTERCLASS
Ball control

Watch the incoming ball like a hawk.

Get into position as early as you can, and try to keep your body relaxed.

Just before impact move the cushioning part of your body in the direction of the ball's flight.

Try to set the ball down as close as possible to your feet.

◄ *Spain's Deportivo la Coruna star Diego Tristan, under pressure from Paris SG's Frederic Dehu, times his jump to meet and cushion a rising ball with his foot.*

▶ *For the thigh cushion, the upper part of your leg should be almost parallel with the ground. Then pull your leg down and back as the ball makes contact. This will kill the ball's pace and should leave it in front of you.*

Practice, practice, practice

Don't wait until your side's next practice session—get out there and practice your ball-control skills whenever you can. Work with a friend and pass the ball to each other at different speeds and heights. On your own? No problem. Find an outside wall in a safe place and bounce a ball off it at varying angles to practice the full range of cushioning skills.

See also

22-23 Advanced Passing | 24-25 Movement and Space | 26-27 On-ball Skills | 42-43 Attacking Skills

Passing

Passing glues together a team's play, turns defense into attack, switches the direction of play, and creates goal-scoring opportunities. When you make a pass, you have to decide where and to whom you are passing, when to release the ball, and which type of pass to make.

▲ Pinpoint sidefoot passes can be made on the move, as Fulham's Margunn Haugenes shows.

Accuracy and weight

Accuracy is the key to good passing. The ball needs to travel in the direction that you want without being intercepted by the opposition. Your pass also needs to reach its destination in a way that makes it easy for the receiver to control it. An important factor is the speed with which the ball leaves your foot. This is known as the weight of a pass, and it varies depending on how far back you take your kicking foot and how fast you bring your foot through the ball. Only experience teaches you how to vary the weight of a pass.

"I was right-footed to start with, but I worked harder on my left, and it became better than my right." George Best

◄ Sweden's Karolina Westberg has the ball under control at her feet, ready to make a pass. She is in a good position to pass the ball with the outside of her foot or to make an instep pass (see below).

1   2   3

▲ You can use different parts of your foot to make a pass. The most common are the inside of your foot (1), which will give you the most control, the outside of your foot (2), and the instep (3)—the part of your cleats where the laces are found.

▶ Juan Sebastian Veron uses the outside of his foot to strike a powerful flick pass. The Argentinian midfielder broke the British transfer record with his $42-million move from the Italian team Lazio to England's Manchester United in 2001.

1   2   3

▲ *Striking the middle of the ball with a smooth follow-through keeps the ball low as it travels over the field. This makes it easier for a teammate to receive and control. Sidefoot passes are especially useful up to distances of approximately 65 feet.*

Sidefoot passing

The sidefoot pass, or push pass, uses the inside of the foot to strike the ball, keeping it close to the ground. You'll feel in control with this pass because a large portion of the foot makes contact with the ball, making it easier to direct the ball precisely where you want it. Your nonkicking foot should be close to the ball and point in the direction of the pass. With your body over the ball and your eyes focused on it, swing your leg from your hip through the ball. Keep your ankle firm as you make impact, and aim to hit the ball through its center.

No.3 Hidetoshi Nakata

A superb passer of the ball, Japanese midfielder Hidetoshi Nakata was voted 1998 Asian Player of the Year and has starred in Italy's Serie A for Perugia and Roma.

▼ *Place two cones or other objects 20–30 inches apart. Pass the ball between the cones. Gradually stand farther away and shrink the distance between the cones to work on passing accuracy.*

▲ *Real Madrid's Fernando Redondo displays textbook positioning and balance as he makes a sidefoot pass.*

Passing drill

Top soccer players never give up honing their passing skills. Take passing practices as seriously as the professionals. Aim for quick control and crisp, accurate passes to the receiver. The biggest single improvement you can bring to your game is to become a fully two-footed player. To do this, you'll need to work especially hard on your weaker foot in practices. Ask your coach for a range of different passing drills so that you don't get bored performing the same exercises every time you practice.

MASTERCLASS
Passing

Keep your head still and your eyes focused on the ball as you make the pass.

Aim to strike the ball with the correct amount of weight.

Move as soon as you've made the pass.

Build up passing skills with your weaker foot and practice as often as possible.

See also

20-21 Passing

26-27 On-ball Skills

36-37 Fancy Skills

Advanced Passing

Players with a wide range of different passing techniques at their disposal often control and dictate a match. While the sidefoot pass is the most frequently used, other passing techniques allow you to hit a bouncing ball, to chip the ball, or to make very long passes.

No.4 Stefan Effenberg

Veteran German midfielder Stefan Effenberg was renowned for his deadly accurate passing, which allowed him to control the movement of a game.

◄When under pressure, select a target and type of pass that you can execute accurately and quickly. Here the player makes a sidefoot pass.

▲A chip pass will carry the ball over the heads of your opponents. Aim to strike the bottom of the ball with a downward stab and a short follow-through. Your foot and the ground act as a wedge, forcing the ball up at a steep angle.

Timing

If the player you're passing to is on the move, you'll need to calculate where this teammate will be when the pass reaches his or her feet. Aim for this spot, not where your teammate is positioned when you strike the ball. Even with a relatively short pass, the player receiving the ball might have run forward several feet.

◀ The compass drill is a good way of sharpening your passing skills. As the ball is passed a player shouts north, south, east, or west. The player in the center then has to turn and pass the ball in that direction.

Instep drive

The instep pass, or drive, allows you to hit longer passes when you're standing still or on the move. With your arms out for balance, your nonkicking foot next to the ball, and your body over the ball, swing your kicking leg back then forward with your toes pointing at the ground. Your shoelaces should make contact with the middle of the ball. The follow-through should be long and smooth. By changing the angle of your foot and body, as well as the length of your backswing, you can make passes of different heights and lengths.

▶ Spanish player Gaizka Mendieta completes a lofted instep drive. His body is upright and the follow-through takes his kicking leg across his body.

▲ An instep lofted drive will send the ball quickly through the air. To make this kind of pass, plant the nonkicking foot behind and to the side of the ball. You'll need to strike the lower half of the ball, and on the follow-through your leg should swing across your body.

"Football [soccer] is a simple game based on the giving and taking of passes." Bill Shankly

Flick passes

You'll often receive the ball under great pressure, with opponents closing in on you. Inside and outside flick passes are ideal when time and space is limited. Flicks are short passes along or just above the ground. Use the toe end of your shoe in a short but firm flicking movement. If you're under extreme pressure, you can also use your toe and lower laces of your instep to flick the ball right back to the player who has just passed the ball to you.

MASTERCLASS
Advanced passing

Use the instep drive for longer passing.

Try to keep your body between opponents and the ball as you release a pass.

When making shorter passes, especially in crowded areas, use the sidefoot pass.

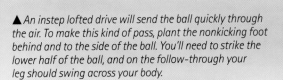

◀ In tight situations such as this you can use the outside of your foot to perform a flick pass. Try to make contact with the ball, using the little toe area of your cleats.

See also

20–21 Passing

26–27 On-ball Skills

42–43 Attacking Skills

Movement and Space

Movement and awareness of available space are vital components of any good passing team and will allow you to let the ball do the work. Crisp, accurate passing combined with decisive movements can get the ball around a field faster than a single player or covering defenders can travel. Precise passing and movement can open up even the tightest of defenses.

▲ Practice passing in triangles, with players interchanging positions, yet keeping relatively close to each other (less than 32–40 feet apart) as they move around the field.

▲ Mark out an area with cones. Three players should try to keep possession of the ball from a defender by passing and moving. If the defender gets the ball or it goes out of play, he or she should switch places with one of the other three.

MASTERCLASS
Movement and space

With or without the ball, always keep your head up, looking for opportunities to move into space.

Be aware of the positions of opponents, teammates, and the player with the ball.

Soccer is fast. Space that was there the last time you looked may have gone. Other space may have opened up elsewhere. Check first.

Pass and move

Don't rest on your laurels and stand still after delivering a pass. Get moving, and look to support the player who now has the ball. Alert players seek to get themselves quickly into a position to receive the ball again or into clear space for the second, third, or fourth pass in a move. By acting quickly after making a pass, you can catch defenders off guard and open up play.

No.5 Enzo Scifo

Belgian legend Enzo Scifo was both masterful at passing and excellent at support play, seemingly able always to find good positions in which to receive the ball.

Be a space invader

The soccer field is a big place. Even with a full set of players, pockets of clear space still exist. It's these that you should be looking for and moving into. Not having the ball is no reason to relax—just the opposite in fact. Use the time to search for an open space in a good position, invade the space, and look to receive a pass. Soccer is a dynamic game with opportunities opening up or closing remarkably quickly. Look not just for space but areas that aren't blocked off by defenders—positions that offer the on-ball player a clear, safe path to pass to you.

▼ The push-and-go calls for a weighted pass that travels past a defender's legs and allows you to run onto it quickly. Start sprinting as soon as the ball leaves your foot.

Slipping markers

A player looking to receive the ball must sometimes shake off a defender who is marking him closely. Jogging around from place to place aimlessly just won't do. Make life hard for the defender with sudden changes of pace or direction—fake a move away from your target space, then turn quickly and sprint into it to trick a marker.

▼ Luis Figo's superb ball skills are clearly displayed as he starts to perform an outside hook turn.

▲ Inside hook. Lean into the direction you want to turn and hook the inside of your foot right around the ball, dragging it with you as you turn and move away.

▲ Outside hook. Leaning in the direction you want to turn, reach across your body with that side's foot. Hook the outside of your foot around the ball, and sweep it away as you turn.

▲ For the wall pass, approach the defender, wait until he closes in on you, then exchange sidefoot passes with a teammate who plays the ball into available space.

Space behind opponents

A key area to exploit is the space behind a nearby opponent, so be on the lookout. The opponent is guarding an area of the field, so getting past him can open up opportunities. Dribbling and turning (see On-ball Skills, pages 26–27) can get you past, but so can other less-fancy techniques. One move is the wall, or return pass, where you pass to a teammate then receive it straight back on the other side of a defender. Another is the more risky push-and-go, where you approach a defender, push the ball past him to one side, and run on to collect it. The defender has to turn while you're heading the right way.

Turning

Changing direction with the ball is an important part of your game. In busy areas of the field, look to turn and change direction as soon as you receive a pass and have the ball under control. This often outwits opponents and buys you precious time to look up and make a pass or shot, or set out on a run. Always keep yourself between the ball and opponents when making a turn, and swivel on one foot, using the other to move the ball either with sidefoot or instep nudges, if you have enough room, or by using an outside or inside hook, if under pressure.

On-ball Skills

Running with the ball, protecting it from opponents, and dribbling are all techniques and skills that require good ball control and excellent awareness of the game around you.

See also

20-21 Passing

22-23 Advanced Passing

42-43 Attacking Skills

◄ *Nigerian star Jay-Jay Okocha shows good awareness as he races forward with the ball in constant reach.*

Moving with the ball

If you have the ball and see a large, promising area of open space ahead, move into it as quickly as possible. You must kick the ball far enough to allow you to maintain a good running speed, but not so far that you lose control and—even worse—possession of the ball. Using the outside of the foot allows you to keep moving at a good speed. When running with the ball, you need to have eyes everywhere, so keep glancing up at the game around you and down at the position of the ball.

▲ *Shielding requires some strength, but mostly you need skill and an ability to watch out for opponents.*

▲ *This player has the ball under control and has turned his body to shield the ball from his opponent.*

◄ *Spanish striker Raul displays excellent shielding technique as Slovenia's Darko Milanic tries to challenge him.*

Shielding

Shielding, or screening, is a valuable way of keeping control of the ball and preventing opponents from stealing possession. It involves you putting your body between an opponent and the ball and keeping it there legally, even if that means staying aware of your opponent's moves and shifting position. The difference between shielding the ball and impeding another player largely comes down to whether or not you have the ball under control. You cannot just block the path of an opponent or push or hold on to him. As soon as you start shielding you should be keeping the ball under control and thinking about your next step. This is most likely to be a pass to an unmarked teammate, although it can be a much fancier and riskier move, such as a hook and turn (see page 25) around the opposition player.

▲ *The player now has a little more time to choose his next move, which is a lay-off sidefoot pass.*

MASTERCLASS
On-ball skills

Good balance, shielding, and awareness are needed when you have the ball.

———

Think about the result of your on-ball move—where, when, and to whom are you going to pass?

———

One-on-one drills and small-sided games are the places to hone your on-ball skills.

———

Always look for the simple option.

▲ *The player running and dribbling the ball is about to be closed down by a defender. The dribbler drops his right shoulder and leans a little in one direction.*

Dribbling

A skill guaranteed to get crowds on their feet, dribbling calls for good balance, superb control, and plenty of confidence. Keep the ball in front of you and close to your feet, but never under them or you may overrun the ball. You can use your instep and the outside and inside of your foot to nudge the ball forward and to each side. Dribbling is a high-risk move and even the very best players surrender the ball on occasion. This is why you should only dribble when away from your defensive-third of the field, and always be on the lookout for a safe pass. A good dribbler knows where he is heading, when to release the ball, and how to avoid getting cornered by two or three defenders.

▲ Practice dribbling at walking speed, then build up your speed. Using slalom courses can help you keep your balance and control while changing direction as this young player demonstrates.

Dribbling deception

Unless you're blessed with outstanding speed, dribbling without deception is a surefire way of losing the ball. Deception can take the form of tricks such as feinting—pretending to move past an opponent in one direction, only to go the other way—or sudden changes in pace, from sprint to walk to sprint again. Feinting requires exaggeration and confidence to really convince the defender that you will head left, when you intend to go right. In all deception moves accelerate away from the opponent you have just deceived, keeping yourself between the ball and player as much as possible.

▲ For this dribble and tag game, each player is given a ball and must stay within the center circle. If you touch a player with your hand, you gain a point. If you are tagged, you lose a point; and if you lose control of the ball or dribble outside the circle, you forfeit two points.

No.6 Harry Kewell

With the ball seemingly stuck to his feet at times, Australian Harry Kewell terrifies defenses. But Kewell also knows when to release the ball, either with a telling pass or a deadly shot.

▲ The body movement by the dribbler tricks the defender into believing his opponent is going to head one way. The defender follows through in that direction.

▲ As the defender follows through in the wrong direction the on-ball player is able to swerve around his opponent in the opposite direction and dribble away.

See also

46–47 Defending

48–49 Defending as a Unit

1 2 3 4

▲ *For the front block tackle, the tackler (in white) approaches the on-ball player (1), getting his bodyweight over his foot and striking the ball firmly (2). The tackler concentrates on dispossessing his opponent (3) before moving away quickly with the ball under control (4).*

Tackling

When the opposition has the ball, there are a number of ways to win it back. You can try to intercept a pass or you can challenge the opponent with a tackle. Although tackling can leave you open to being dribbled around, it is a key part of the game. Tackling isn't just for defenders, it's a skill required all over the field.

▲ *This ill-timed lunge from behind doesn't make contact with the ball, and so it is a foul. The player may be booked or sent off, and a free kick or penalty will be awarded to the opposition depending on where the foul was committed.*

The front-block tackle

The block tackle is the most commonly used tackle. For this tackle, you'll usually be facing an opponent from the front. Plant your nontackling foot firmly on the ground and lean forward into the tackle. This will give you a solid base. Use the inside of your foot to make strong, firm contact with the middle of the ball. Often this will be enough to remove the ball from your opponent.

No.7 Franco Baresi

Franco Baresi, one of Italy's finest-ever sweepers, was a superb tackler. Along with Marco Van Basten and Ruud Gullit, he played a major role in AC Milan's successes.

Tackling tips

The timing of a tackle really comes only with experience and practice. Try to make your move when your opponent is unbalanced, looking down at the ball, or playing it too far in front. Aim to tackle from the front or side, staying on your feet whenever possible. This enables you to steal the ball, or if you're unsuccessful in the tackle, to chase after the ball. Determination and confidence are very important—if you don't fully commit yourself to a tackle, your challenge is probably going to fail, and you are more likely to hurt yourself.

Sliding tackle

Sliding tackles are sometimes the only way to deflect or clear a ball. Although sliding tackles look spectacular, if they're executed badly there can be a high risk of injury or being penalized with a free kick or penalty. Make sure you bend your supporting leg at the knee as you slide in on it. As you make contact with the ball you need to transfer your bodyweight to your tackling leg and foot. Although they usually just clear the ball, some tacklers try to hook their foot around the ball to keep possession.

◄ *Sometimes players have to challenge when the ball is in midair. Here England's Karen Burke and Scotland's Michelle Barr compete for the ball.*

► *England's Tottenham defender Sol Campbell times his sliding tackle to perfection as he wins the ball from England's Arsenal player Robert Pires. In 2001, Campbell joined Pires playing for Arsenal.*

▲ *England midfielder Steven Gerrard challenges Brazilian striker Rivaldo from the side. He puts his weight on the tackling leg and bends the supporting one for extra stability as he makes the tackle.*

See also

36-37 Fancy Skills

42-43 Attacking Skills

44-45 Opening up Defenses

Volleying and Shooting

To get the ball past the goalkeeper and any defenders, your shot has to be struck with the right combination of power and accuracy. When the ball is off the ground, you'll need to make a volley. As well as attempts on goal, volleys can also be used for quick passes and long clearances.

No.8 Marco Van Basten

Dutch center-forward Marco Van Basten was a magnificent striker of the ball with some spectacular goals to his credit. These include a memorable volley against the U.S.S.R. in the 1988 European Championships.

1

2

3

The volley

A volley is made when the foot and ball connect in midair. Because you can get the full weight of your body into a volley, it's one of the most powerful shots you can make. When a volleyed shot comes off, it can be spectacular, but you'll need to keep your eye on the ball and accurately judge its speed as it comes toward you.

▲ *Volleys can be used in both attacking and defensive situations. Here French central defender Marcel Desailly performs a clearance volley to get the ball out of danger.*

▲ *For a side volley, lean back a little from the incoming ball (1) and swing your leg up and around, making contact with your instep (2). Make sure your foot is over the ball to keep it down, and follow through smoothly and firmly (3).*

Sidefoot volleying

Using the side of your foot, you can perform two types of volley. The first is a gentle, slightly-cushioned pass to a nearby teammate who is in a better position. This is called a layoff volley. You'll need to meet the ball early, and your foot should make contact with the middle, or just above the middle, of the ball. The sidefoot volley can also be used as a close-range shot to steer a bouncing ball toward the goal.

▲ *Whatever type of shot you make, always follow through with your foot pointing in the direction of the ball's path.*

1   2   3

◀ For a front-on instep volley, prepare to lift your knee and point your toes down (1). Keep your head in front of the knee of your kicking leg (2). Look for a clean contact to send the ball in the direction you want (3).

▲ For a half volley, the ball should be hit as soon as it touches the ground. Stretch your ankle so your toes point down and keep your knees bent.

Shot placement

The instep drive is the basis of the shooting technique you'll most frequently use. Unlike using the instep for a long, lofted pass, the key to shooting is to get your body over the ball and to keep the shot low. If you have the time and space to pick an exact place to shoot, aim low into the corners of the goal. It takes a goalkeeper longer to dive low than to dive and stretch high. If you're at one side of the goal, try to aim for the corner of the goal not covered by the goalie.

▶ English legend Dixie Dean, who scored 60 goals for Everton in the 1927–28 season, lines up a shot using the instep drive to power the ball forward.

Shot selection

Long-range shots require a volley or instep drive to generate enough power to trouble the goalkeeper. If you have learned how to bend or swerve the ball, you'll be even more effective. From close range, many players prefer accuracy over power and hit the ball firmly with the sidefoot. If the goalkeeper has advanced off the goal line, a chip kick or lob may be the best shot to make.

▲ Marked-out squares on a wall make excellent targets for shooting practice. One player passes the ball and calls out a square that the other player then attempts to hit.

▲ Japan's Naohira Takahar plays a lob volley in an attempt to lift the ball over the Uruguayan goalkeeper.

See also

42–43 Attacking Skills

44–45 Opening up Defenses

46–47 Defending

52–53 The Corner Kick

Heading

A soccer ball can spend as much time in the air as on the field, so heading is a skill that all players—not just central defenders and strikers— need. Heading doesn't hurt—or rather, it shouldn't. Heading is painless as long as you use your forehead to make contact with the ball.

▲ A power header from a running position involves a player leaping off his front foot to create maximum thrust as the ball is met. Bending the knees helps keep the player balanced on landing.

Eyes wide open

Usually when you make a header you'll be directing the ball horizontally or down. Try not to shut your eyes as you meet the ball, but watch it right onto your forehead. Your body position should allow you to get over the ball. The exception to this is when clearing a ball from defense. In this case, you still need to use your forehead, but position yourself underneath the ball to send it up and forward.

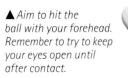

▲ Aim to hit the ball with your forehead. Remember to try to keep your eyes open until after contact.

▲ Corner kicks often create good heading opportunities. Excellent control is needed to guide the ball away from the goalkeeper's hands.

Meeting the ball

Only jump to head the ball when absolutely necessary. Heading with your feet on the ground gives you a more stable, balanced base. Try to get into position early and meet the ball, rather than just let the ball hit your head. You also need to keep your neck muscles taut just before you make contact in order to support your head and provide maximum control.

▶ Midfielder Allan Nielsen makes a spectacular diving header for Tottenham Hotspur against Coventry City, both English teams. His arms are extended to help break his fall.

Power heading

To put more force into a header, arch your back and thrust your upper body and head forward and through the ball. For even more speed and distance you can spring off the ground to meet the ball in midair. Timing is essential. Ideally you want to connect with the ball at the top of your jump. You can generate extra force by driving your arms backward to help propel your head firmly through the ball.

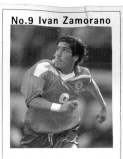

No.9 Ivan Zamorano

At a far-from-towering 5'10", Chilean striker Ivan Zamorano has proven for many years that you don't have to be the tallest player on the field to be an excellent header of the ball.

▲ *French defender Laurent Blanc makes a header upfield. Defenders, like Blanc, who are very good in the air often join the attack during free kicks or corners.*

▼ *Defensive headers require both height and distance. Here the defender meets the ball at the top of his jump and angles his head to clear a dangerous ball.*

Other headers

The cushioning header is similar to the basic header, but as the ball reaches your forehead you should recoil smoothly back and down, killing the speed of the ball and leaving it at your feet. The flick-on header tends to be used from a long clearance, a nearpost corner kick, or a goal kick from your goalie. Flick the ball behind you, hopefully in the direction of a strike partner. It is one of the most difficult headers to master.

▲ *This effective heading drill begins with one player using an underhand throw to lob the ball at a headable height to a partner 15 feet away. The header should be aimed down toward the thrower's feet for him to practice ball control. After ten headers, swap positions.*

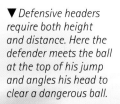

MASTERCLASS
Heading

Don't be scared of the ball.
————
Make sure your body is both balanced and relaxed.
————
If you can, keep your eyes open while heading the ball.
————
When jumping to head the ball, you can use your arms for balance, but keep your elbows down to avoid fouls or injuries.

See also

20-21 Passing

24-25 Movement and Space

30-31 Volleying and Shooting

Small-sided Games

Playing small-sided games is not only fun, it can also help improve your skills for regular games. Millions of people play small-sided games during their breaks from work, in fun afterschool sessions, and in competitive evening and weekend divisions.

▲▶ *Soccer players of all ages and skill levels can take part in and enjoy small-sided games, as these former stars playing in a veterans' five-on-five illustrate.*

Why smaller games?

In games with 11 players on each side you may feel uninvolved and far from the action for long periods of the game. The advantage of small-sided games is that they don't allow you to hide for long. Players see plenty of the ball, have to make more contact with the ball and playmaking decisions, and will practice certain skills and techniques more than they would in a regular game. There are also fewer stoppages and less reliance on set pieces. This forces players to be constantly prepared for action.

▼▶ *Five-on-five has different rules to the regular game. Playing the ball over head height (right) and entering the goalie's area (below) are both banned.*

Walled five-on-five

Five-on-five games allow players of all ages to compete in indoor or outdoor games, from informal lunchtime sessions to seriously contested divisions. Five-on-five rules vary, but usually ban the ball from traveling above shoulder or head height and ban outfield players from entering the goalkeeper's area. Many fields feature low-height goals and walls instead of sidelines. These help keep the ball in play and encourage players to play passes off the walls to beat opponents.

▶ *The walls surrounding five-on-five fields offer a handy way of beating opponents. Here the on-ball player's path to the left and straight ahead is blocked. He opts to play the ball against the wall, running around the other side of his opponent to collect it.*

Small-sided games for young players

More and more youth and children's coaches are turning to small-sided games as a key way of developing young players' skills. Small-sided games place an emphasis on technique and movement, not height or physique, and so are ideal for players who are still growing. There aren't the large fields or strict team formations found in the full-sized game, so everyone gets the chance to hone their attacking and defending skills. Small-sided games encourage attacking play. Players learn that a two or more goal deficit can be overcome quickly with fast, precise passing, movement, and low shots. The quick pace of the action also means there's no chance to worry about mistakes.

▲ ▶ *Smaller fields and looser formations give these youth players (above) and these future stars of Italian team Perugia Calcio (right) greater opportunity to work on their skills.*

Futsal

Futsal is a form of five-on-five soccer approved by FIFA in 1989 and increasingly played all over the world. There are no walls around the edge of the field, and the junior-sized ball can travel above head height. Played on a roughly basketball-sized court and with rolling substitutes, Futsal games have two 20-minute halves, but the clock is stopped whenever the ball goes out of play. One rule states that if a team makes six serious fouls in one half, the ref will award a direct free kick no more than 40 feet from the goal, with no defensive wall allowed.

◀ ▲ *Small-sided games can be played in a wide variety of locations. This inflatable court allows five-on-five action to spring up almost anywhere.*

▲ *This picture is from a playground in Buenos Aires, Argentina, but there are similar sights in parks, backyards, and areas of open land all over the world. Players improve their skills with simple pickup games, playing keeping the ball up, or games of headers and volleys.*

On the streets

Soccer can be played almost anywhere as long as it is away from traffic, windows, and other hazards. All top soccer players can fondly recall practicing either on their own or with a few friends in the streets, backyards, and parks of their towns or cities. Many pros believe that their superb close skills came from kicking around a tennis ball or other small ball. The smaller ball demands excellent touch and close control.

Beach soccer

Beach soccer is a fun and popular pastime played by many that has recently grown into an organized sport. It features a number of prestigious tournaments, including Umbro's Pro Beach Soccer series, starring players who were formerly top internationals such as Italy's Lodovico Costacurta, Portugal's Adelino Nunes, and England's John Barnes.

◀ ▼ *Many stars, such as Claudio Gentile of Italy (among those pictured left), now play in beach soccer tournaments. Brazilian maestro Zico (below) grew up playing Futsal and credits this for developing his remarkable skills.*

See also

30-31 Volleying and Shooting

34-35 Small-sided Games

"Football [soccer] is about glory . . . doing things in style . . . doing them with a flourish."

Danny Blanchflower

Fancy Skills

Spectacular overhead kicks, aerial side volleys, long-distance shots . . . breathtaking to watch—especially when executed by a Best or a Pelé or a Figo. You are more likely to make use of slightly less ambitious, but extremely valuable skills such as the back heel pass or dragback.

◄ *The back heel is a good way of changing the direction of the ball and tricking your opponents. With your nonkicking foot level with the ball, strike through the center of the ball with your heel or the sole of your cleat.*

◄ *An aerial side volley is a spectacular way of dealing with a high, rising ball.*

Getting airborne

Overhead kicks can be made with one foot on or just off the ground and the ball hooked back over your head toward the goal. But the top-of-the-range bicycle kick will have you launching yourself off the ground and leaning far back as you swing your kicking foot back over your shoulder to hit the ball. Only ever try this on very soft ground or sand, never on artificial turf or a hard field.

Just for show

Skills such as the back heel and dragback are valuable techniques that can be used sparingly by all players. Other tricks, such as catching the ball on the back of your neck or the flick-up, are more for show and unlikely to be used during a game—but they can be fun to practice.

▲ *Clever Chala of Ecuador performs an excellent overhead kick. He gets his foot over the top of the ball to keep the ball's height down.*

► *For the flick-up, place one foot in front of the ball and trap it between the toes of your back foot and the heel of the front (1). Lift your back foot up to roll the ball over your heel (2), then flick the ball up (3) and over your head (4) so that it lands at your feet.*

1   2   3   4

You've been nutmegged

Few things are more embarrassing for a player than being nutmegged. A nutmeg means kicking the ball through the open legs of an opponent, either for a teammate to receive the pass on the other side or for you to run around the startled, nutmegged player and collect the ball. Nutmegs are risky, but when they work they can be extremely effective.

▲ *Faouzi Rouissi of Tunisia (left) nutmegs Congo's Kibemba Mbayo (right), playing the ball straight through his legs.*

1

2

3

4

Self-restraint

Although you can practice fancy tricks such as overhead kicks to sharpen your skills and to impress your friends, you probably won't have many opportunities to use them in a real game. Only use these skills when it gives your team an advantage—rather than simply for the entertainment of other players and spectators.

▼ *Zinedine Zidane (below right) displays his excellent ball control skills, using the outside of his foot to bring the ball down while on the move.*

No.10 Rivaldo

The Brazilian player Rivaldo has a dazzling array of skills. They've helped the midfielder become the top scorer in the Spanish League and won him FIFA's World Player of the Year.

▲ *The dragback is a way of catching an opponent off guard. You look as if you're going to play the ball in one direction, but instead you stop the ball (1), drag it back (2), and pivot (3) before heading off in another direction (4).*

◄ *Claudio Reyna of the U.S. balances a ball on his head during a practice session.*

▲ *Colombia's maverick goalkeeper René Higuita has a unique method of clearing the ball from his goal area. This technique, which involves flicking his feet over the back of his head, has been dubbed the "scorpion kick."*

See also

16-17 Ready to Play

40-41 Goalkeeping Choices

46-47 Defending

▶ Drills in which players stand a short distance away from the goalie and kick or throw the ball at varying heights and speeds make vital practice routines.

"The goalie has to be one of the fittest, most agile, quick-thinking, and determined players in the team." Gordon Banks

Goalkeeping Basics

Goalkeeping is a unique skill and one that holds a lot of responsibility. The only player allowed to handle the ball (inside his penalty area), a goalkeeper is the last line of defense. A sloppy goalkeeping performance can cause a strong side to lose a game, whereas an inspired performance can secure a memorable win. More hinges on the goalie than any other single player.

▲ Swedish goalie Magnus Hedman displays a good stance, making any goalkeeping move possible.

Stance

Maintaining a good stance whenever the opposition is attacking is a straightforward yet vital part of goalkeeping. The basic stance is with the legs shoulder-width apart, the arms in front, head straight, and bodyweight slightly forward. Two of the most common mistakes are too wide a stance, which makes it hard to change direction, and staying flat-footed, which makes it almost impossible to move quickly. The goalie should be up on the balls of his feet whenever the ball is in a dangerous position.

▲ To gather in a ground-level ball, get down on one knee, get your hands behind the ball, and scoop it up with your knee and foot forming a barrier.

1

2

◄ This goalie adopts the basic stance (picture second left) from which he can move to collect a ball to his right at waist height (far left) or perform a high diving save (left and below).

▲ The above-head-height catch can be used to cut out high balls from the penalty area.

Communication and positioning

Goalkeeping is all about preventing attacks from becoming goals, and many attacking chances can be snuffed out using nothing more spectacular than concentration, good basic positioning, and good communication. A well-placed and alert goalkeeper can often see the game in front of him better than teammates and should relay advice to them. At set pieces, such as free kicks, the goalie should be in charge of his goal area. Instructions to players should be clear, brief, and calm.

Simple saves

Many shots and loose balls can be gathered in without resorting to a dive. The secret is quick footwork and a sharp eye to get in line with the incoming ball so that your body is fully behind the ball as you collect it. Try to cushion the ball on arrival. Goalkeepers do this by taking the ball early, giving them room to bring their hands back as the ball impacts, thus killing its speed. Remember: soft hands equal safe hands. Shots, loose crosses, stray passes, and knockdowns come at different heights, so goalies need to practice a range of ball-taking skills at waist, chest, ground, thigh, and head height.

MASTERCLASS
Goalkeeping basics

Maintain a good stance on the balls of your feet and with your head up, ready for action.

Get your body in line with an incoming ball, and always watch it all the way into your hands.

If you decide to go for a ball, shout loudly and be positive, determined, and decisive.

▲ With his arms 8–12 inches in front of his body, the goalie gets his hands behind and to the sides of the ball with his fingers spread out.

No.11 Gordon Banks

Gordon Banks was one of the finest goalies of his or any other era. Career highlights included a stunning save from Pelé in the 1970 World Cup and winning the 1966 World Cup with England.

3

◄ With the attacker clean through on goal, the goalie comes off his line to narrow the angle (1). Staying upright as long as possible (2), the goalie performs a smothering save, diving at the feet of the attacker, spreading himself out, and gathering in the ball (3).

Goalkeeping Choices

The best goalkeepers are good communicators and know how to concentrate. A goalkeeper has to also make many decisions quickly and calmly throughout a game. A goalie has a number of different goal-stopping techniques to master, including punching the ball and diving saves. Dealing with back passes and distributing the ball to teammates are also essential skills.

See also

22–23 Advanced Passing

38–39 Goalkeeping Basics

58–59 Penalty!

MASTERCLASS
Goalkeeping choices

If a player in your half isn't free, kick a long ball upfield.

Good, clear communication can prevent many defensive errors.

Put any mistakes you make behind you, and concentrate on the rest of the game.

Remember, the three B's of goalkeeping—be positive, be the boss, be first.

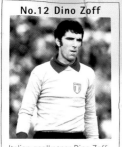

No.12 Dino Zoff

Italian goalkeeper Dino Zoff was a fine goalie and very calm under pressure. He once went a record 1,143 minutes without allowing a goal. He played at international level until the age of 41.

▶ *A dramatic leap to deflect the ball is sometimes the only way of preventing a goal. When tipping the ball over or around the goal, the goalkeeper must be alert for rebounds off the goal posts.*

Punch or deflect?

Although a two-handed catch is the ideal save to make, it's not always possible to get both hands fully on the ball. Sometimes punching or deflecting are the only options. To punch a ball, use both fists placed close together and angled slightly inward. With wrists firm aim to punch just below the middle of the ball with a short but strong jabbing action. On other occasions you'll be at full stretch and the only way of preventing a goal will be to deflect or tip the ball around the post or over the bar.

◀ *Sometimes a goalkeeper can be too ambitious. Colombian goalkeeper René Higuita threw caution to the wind when he tried to dribble the ball past Cameroon's Roger Milla during the 1990 World Cup. Milla scored and Cameroon went on to win the game 2–1.*

◀ *Moving across the goal from the basic stance (1) this goalkeeper launches himself off of one foot (2) and gets his hands behind the ball (3). He uses his body and arms to prevent the ball from popping out as he lands (4).*

1   2   3   4

Diving

Every goalkeeper has to make diving saves. The ball should be caught in front of the body and always followed into the hands. Gather the ball in as quickly as possible to prevent it from bouncing out. One of the most difficult dives for a goalkeeper is the low drop onto the ball. To respond to a shot fired low and near your body, push your legs away and get your body down and behind the ball.

▶ *French goalkeeper Fabien Barthez performs an underhand throw. With his front foot pointing at his target, he releases the ball and follows through smoothly.*

Distribution

You've saved the ball—what now? You have to decide whether to distribute the ball either by foot or by hand. Throws tend to be more accurate, although kicking the ball, usually using an instep volley or half-volley, can cover more distance. There are three ways of throwing the ball: the underhand rollout, which is good for accuracy; the overhand throw for distance; and the javelin throw; where the ball is thrust forward using a bent arm. The javelin throw is often the quickest way of distributing the ball.

◀ *For an overhand throw, the arm should be kept relatively straight as it swings over with a bowling motion. A wide stance helps provide balance.*

◀ *Barthez releases the ball from his hand and connects with it on the volley using his instep. Hit hard enough and with enough height, the ball will reach players in the other half of the field.*

Back pass rule

The back pass rule was introduced to cut down on timewasting. The rule says that a throw-in or intentional pass back to the goalkeeper cannot be handled. If it is, an indirect free kick will be awarded to the other team. Don't try to be smart and attempt some fancy dribbling when the ball comes back to you. Hit a back pass cleanly and immediately, or if you have plenty of time and space, cushion and control the ball before launching it upfield. If you're under pressure, it's far better to give away a throw-in rather than a possible scoring opportunity.

▲ *Using his arms for balance, legendary Danish goalkeeper Peter Schmeichel hits another big goal kick with the instep of his cleat.*

See also

24-25 Movement and Space | 26-27 On-ball Skills | 20-21 Passing | 22-23 Advanced Passing

Attacking Skills

Attacking is not just the role of two or three forwards. Counterattacks are often started by defenders and driven forward by midfielders, while many crosses come from fullbacks out near the sideline. Every outfield player can take part in attacking moves and should develop the key skills involved.

▲ As he approaches the defender the wide player with the ball passes to his teammate.

▲ With the defender indecisive, the wide player makes an overlapping run down the line.

▲ The wide player receives the return pass and now has time and space to make a cross or cut infield.

Overloads and overlaps

Attacks that use plenty of a field's space, its width and depth, can stretch defenses thin and lead to goalscoring chances. Giving your attack depth means staggering your positions up the field. This not only allows the on-ball player to make a safe pass backward, it also makes it very difficult for a defender to set up and play the offside trap against you. Width is very important because the defense tends to concentrate in the middle of the field, and an overlapping run by a wide player down the touchline can lead to a great crossing opportunity. Always be on the lookout for an overload. An overload occurs when the attacking side has more players in the attacking-third of the field than the defending side. This requires fast running and support from teammates.

"Football [soccer] should always be played beautifully; you should play in an attacking way; it must be a spectacle." Johan Cruyff

▲ Giving your attack depth gives you more options. Here a pass has been made to the player on the far left who is making a late run into the area, staying onside and joining the attack at the last minute.

MASTERCLASS
Attacking skills

Always look to support an attacking teammate with the ball, offering him passing and laying-off options.

Aim to cross the ball with accuracy and speed—don't just punt the ball into the area.

Split up into groups of defenders and attackers when working on attacking moves during practice.

Opening up spaces

Sometimes attackers break away from a defender or find space to receive the ball. On other occasions they move to create space for others to exploit. Attacking without the ball is very important, and it often involves an attacker making a quick change of direction or speed to take a defender with him. As the defender moves to cover his opponent, space that another attacker can run into appears.

▲ A diagonal run across and into the defense, as done by the player in yellow on the left, can cause hesitancy among defenders. They may be unsure whether to follow him, opening up space for another attacker, or to leave him be.

▶ Most crosses have to be hit when a player is on the move, so practice crossing by running with the ball for approximately 30 feet before hitting it into the penalty area.

▲ Bordeaux's Corentin Martins prepares to swing a cross into the penalty area. Use an instep drive to add speed to the ball.

Crossing the ball

A cross is simply a pass from out wide into the penalty area, but it can be deadly if hit with accuracy. Players work hard on their crossing and tend to use the instep-drive pass to hit the ball quickly into the target area. Aimless punts into the goal box are easily defended. Make sure you glance up to locate a target before you make a cross. You're looking to get the ball onto a teammate's head or in front of them for a snap shot. Hitting the byline means crossing from close to the end of the field. A cross from this position is harder for a goalie to defend because the ball tends to be moving away from him.

No.13 Gianfranco Zola

As well as having scored some classic goals, the skillful Italian also has the vision to pick out teammates in better positions than himself with unerring accuracy.

See also

12-13 Key Rules

30-31 Volleying and Shooting

42-43 Attacking Skills

Opening up Defenses

Many attacks break down as a result of slow or lazy thinking. Defensive techniques such as offside traps, where the entire defense move up in a line to catch forwards out, prey on sloppy attacking. Quick, accurate movement and passing can open up even the strongest of defenses.

▲ *Blessed with incredible pace, vision, and skill, the Ukrainian star Andri Shevchenko has managed to keep his goalscoring touch in the toughest defensive league in the world—Italy's Serie A, in which he plays for AC Milan.*

Attacking passes and through balls

The closer you get to the opponent's goal, the less time and space there tends to be. A top-quality attacking pass should be placed and timed so that the receiver can do something with it when they first touch the ball. Passes for attackers to run on to must be carefully weighted so that they don't speed too far ahead of the receiver and get intercepted. Passes behind defenders, often known as "through balls," catch those defenders off guard, but they require expert timing and teamwork between players.

▶ *This attacker deceived a line of defense into thinking he was going to play a through ball. As the offside trap was set and the defenders moved up, the attacker continued dribbling and broke through the defense.*

▲ *The attacker on the left drags a defender out of position, just enough for a through ball to be played between the two defenders. The attacker on the right times his run to stay onside and collects the ball behind the defense.*

Swerving passes

Swerving or bending the ball through the air is a technique often used when taking free kicks, but that is not its only value. During attacking moves the ability to swerve the ball can be very useful. Swerving the ball (see page 57) involves kicking through one side of it with a long follow through. This action puts sidespin on the ball, which sends it off on a curved path. Inswinging and outswinging passes can clear opponents to find a teammate in a good position. Swerved shots can get around a defense and fool the opposition's goalie.

Scoring goals

A good attacking move doesn't guarantee a goal. For that you need a decisive finish from whoever receives the ball in a goalscoring position. The role of other attackers at this point is also crucial. In fact, following up a goalbound header or shot is vital because many goals at all levels come from rebounds off players or the goal. Good awareness is a vital quality in a forward because he or she must judge quickly which teammate is in the best position to attempt a goal.

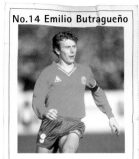

No.14 Emilio Butragueño

The winner of five league titles in a row with Real Madrid, Butragueño, a Spanish striker, was nicknamed "the vulture" for his lightning reactions and awareness in the penalty area.

▲ The on-ball player has a choice. He can cross the ball to the player on the right-hand side of the area using an outswinging swerved pass. Or he can simply send a short, straight pass to another free teammate.

▲ The player in yellow at the bottom of the picture gets into position, but at the last moment passes to a teammate at the top of the illustration who is in a much better position to tuck the ball away.

▼ Aston Villa forward Julian Joachim (center) threads a ball past the outstretched foot of Leicester City's Matt Elliott, both English teams, for strike partner Stan Collymore (right) to run on to.

Defending

See also

28-29 Tackling

48-49 Defending as a Unit

62-63 Formations

"Strikers win you games, but defenders win you championships."

John Gregory

When the opposition has the ball, it's time to defend. Defending is sometimes seen as the least glamorous side of the game, but a goal prevented by a watchful, expert defense is just as valuable as a spectacular strike by your side. Skilled defenders are prized assets on all teams.

MASTERCLASS
Defending

As a team you should close down space and reduce attacking options for the opposition.

Delay an opponent on the ball as much as you can by jockeying.

Never dribble out of your own penalty area when attackers lurk nearby. Look to pass the ball to teammates in plenty of space.

If in doubt, kick it out!

Regaining possession

Defending has two prime aims—to stop the opposition scoring and to regain possession of the ball. Regaining the ball can sometimes involve tackling, but there are other ways, such as jockeying and delaying an opponent, pressuring him into making a mistake. One vitally important method is closing down space. This involves you and your teammates getting into goalside positions, working together to cut out space for opposition attacks, and tracking attackers who run into dangerous positions.

▲ Arsenal's Sylvain Wiltord avoids the challenge of Queen's Park Rangers' Clarke Carlisle, both English teams. Tackling is a vital part of defending, but isn't the only way to regain possession.

Jockeying

Getting in the way of an attacker with the ball is a vital part of defending known as jockeying. When an opposition player with the ball approaches, close in on him. Don't close in too much—or he may find it easy to get around you—but enough to cut out open space in front of him. Get into a defensive stance with your body weight over your knees, standing on the balls of your feet, with your arms out for balance. Move with the player, keeping at a similar distance and staying goalside of him. By holding up the attacker, you are buying time for teammates to get back into stronger defensive positions.

◄ German striker Jürgen Klinsmann tries to jockey Pavel Pardo of Mexico, proving that it's not only defenders who have to use defensive skills.

Forcing a weaker position

Apart from delaying a player, jockeying is about forcing the attacker into a weaker position while staying goalside of him. One option is to try to guide him out toward a sideline—a less threatening position where he will have relatively little space and few options.

▲ Pressure from Germany's Bayern Munich forces Real Madrid's Jose Mari Gutierrez to lose track of the ball.

From this position it may be easier to challenge him. If your opponent has his back to the goal when receiving the ball, you are in a strong jockeying position and your main task is to prevent the player from turning to face the goal without giving away a foul. Done well, jockeying may force a mistake, or at least a pass back and away from your goal. Stick with the attacker if he attempts to turn and run into open space behind you.

▲ Wolverhampton Wanderers' George Ndah jockeys Mark Patterson of Gillingham, both English teams, away from goal.

◀ Albania's Geri Cipi takes the full force of England's Michael Owen's powerful shot.

No.15 Bobby Moore

The captain of England's 1966 World-Cup-winning side was a superb tackler and a great reader of the game. Pelé described him as, "the best defender I ever played against."

Get rid of it!

Great defenders such as Germany's Franz Beckenbauer were excellent at playing the ball skillfully out of defense before hitting an accurate pass to a teammate to set up an attacking move. However, even the very best defenders know that if the ball comes to them when under pressure, they should think safety first when clearing the ball. This can mean safe passing into space, or when under severe pressure, getting plenty of height and distance on the ball to take it well away from the danger zone and your goal.

▲ The defender in blue clears while under pressure from the attacker in yellow.

See also

14-15 Fouls and Misconduct

28-29 Tackling

32-33 Heading

▼ *French defender Marcel Desailly clears the ball while under pressure from Australian Mark Viduka.*

Defending as a Unit

Preventing an opposition attack leading to a goal is key to defending and the reason why teams defend as a unit. Attackers shouldn't expect the back four or five players and the goalkeeper to do the work. Defending is the responsibility of all 11 players. There are different roles for different player positions, but many of the basic rules of defending apply to all.

Defending from the front

Intelligent, committed defending begins at the front line and goes all the way back. The attackers' role in defense is an important one. They are the front line of defense, looking to restrict the opposition's space, chase down passes between opponents, and force these players to make mistakes. Good defensive work by attackers can put the opposition player on the ball under pressure. This can result in him making an aimless punt forward for your side to collect, or even an interception and immediate attacking chance.

MASTERCLASS
Defending as a unit

Don't dive in to intercept the ball or make a challenge until you have cover behind you.

Communication is vital when defending, especially at set pieces such as corners or free kicks.

Don't get distracted when marking—keep positioned to watch your opponent first and the game second.

Interception

Stealing the ball from the opposition as it travels from passer to receiver can be a clean, efficient way of regaining possession. It can also leave you with room to move away quickly and start an attack. Intercepting a ball simply requires immediate speed and calls for quickness of thought, awareness of where players are, and judgment of the ball's speed and direction. In short you need to decide whether you can get to the ball before the opposition. A failed interception leaves the ball with your opponents and you out of position and out of the game.

▲ *The blue midfielder has spotted an underhit pass and is about to make an interception. The farther from goal you are, the less risky this move becomes.*

◀ *A zonal defense system. When a forward enters a defender's zone (marked out by the dotted lines), defenders usually move in to mark that player. As an attacker moves out of one zone, the neighboring defender can pick him up.*

► *A player-to-player marking system used in your side's defensive-third of the field relies on additional players to act as spare defenders, putting the attacker on the ball under pressure.*

▼ *Marking is about getting relatively close to an opposing forward and not giving him the time or space to receive the ball. Try to stay goalside of your opponent and in a position to see the game developing in front of you.*

"The goalkeeper is the jewel in the crown and getting to him should be almost impossible. It's the biggest sin in football [soccer] to make him do any work."

Ｇｅｏｒｇｅ Ｇｒａｈａｍ

Defensive systems

There are two main ways in which a team works defensively as a unit. The first is by marking player-to-player, where defenders mark one player and stick with him whenever the opposition is on the attack. The second system is zonal defense, where players are responsible for certain areas, or zones, of the field that all overlap, providing some cover. These zones can move up and down the field as the play dictates. Teams often mix systems, for example, playing a largely zonal defense, but giving one defender the task of player-marking a particularly dangerous attacker.

▼ *Vaclav Budka of Czech side FK Jablonec positions himself by the post ready to defend a corner and make a goal-line clearance if necessary.*

▼ *Marking at set pieces, such as corners, is essential. The blue team have used their central defenders to mark the tallest attackers. Other players are positioned by the posts and the edge of the area.*

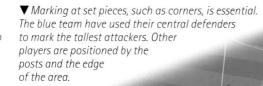

See also

24–25 Movement and Space | 36–37 Fancy Skills

48–49 Defending as a Unit

▲ *A kickoff opens a game between Atletico Madrid of Spain and Borussia Dortmund of Germany during a 1996 UEFA Champions League encounter. The player who kicks off is not allowed to have the second touch of the ball.*

Restarts

Play can be stopped during a game for a number of reasons. These include when the ball leaves the field, a goal is scored, or a foul is committed. The way play is resumed depends on the kind of stoppage. For example, when the ball crosses a sideline, the officials will signal a throw-in. Corners, goal kicks, free kicks, kickoffs, and drop balls are other types of restarts.

The kickoff

Every game begins with a kickoff. This set piece is also played whenever a goal is scored and at the start of the second half. The ball has to be moved forward over the halfway line by the kicking off team, while the opposition must stay in their half—but not enter the center circle—until the ball has been kicked. Many teams play the ball back after it has been tapped forward. Others launch a wide pass out to a flank, hoping that a winger can collect the ball and immediately attack the opposition's goalmouth.

◀ *Your hands should be spread around the back of the ball so that your thumbs almost touch. Too far around the sides and the ball can become harder to control.*

▶ *Placing your hands too close together around the back of the ball can lead you to lose your grip as you make your throw.*

◀ *With feet firmly planted on the ground and ball behind your head, arch your back and thrust your upper body and arms forwards. Release the ball just before your arms come over your head.*

▲ *This is a foul throw for three different reasons: the front foot is completely over the sideline, the trailing foot is off the ground, and only one hand is on the ball when the player makes the throw-in.*

Throw-ins

Throw-ins have to be taken from close to where the ball crossed the sideline. Officials usually penalize players who persistently try to gain extra ground before making the throw. Players of all standards are often penalized for foul throws. There are a few key rules you need to remember—your feet need to be behind the sideline, the ball brought back behind your head, and both hands have to be on the ball. Both feet have to be touching the ground as the throw is made and the ball is released. If you commit a foul throw, the opposing team is awarded the throw-in.

◀ For this throw-in, the receiver plans to pass the ball back to the thrower who, once on the field, can control and play the ball.

◀ In this decoy move, one player draws an opposition player toward him. In the meantime the ball is thrown over their heads into a space where an unmarked player can receive the ball.

▲ Here the receiver moves toward the thrower, drawing the marker forwards. The receiver then cuts back sharply to lose the opposition player and collect the ball.

Longer throws

Long throws can get a ball directly into an opponent's penalty area. Even if you can't propel the ball that far, longer throws give you potentially more teammates to aim for and can be helpful for clearing the ball upfield. Take several quick steps up to the sideline and pull the ball right back behind your head. Arch your back as much as possible, then uncoil your back and arms to catapult the ball forward. Keep most of your weight on your front leg and follow through with your hands and fingers to direct the ball.

Don't throw it away

Treat throw-ins like you would any other set piece and practice a range of different throw-in moves. Avoid giving the ball away easily with a foul throw or a halfhearted throw that can be easily intercepted by the other side. Try to throw to a teammate who is unmarked and at a height that allows him to control the ball quickly and easily. Aim to throw to your teammate's feet, thigh, or head for a flick-on to another member of your side. A ball that bounces waist high in front of a player can be extremely difficult to control.

◀ Tranmere Rovers' Dave Challinor, of England, holds the world record for the longest throw-in, a distance of 152 ft. It came, according to Challinor, "after 29 dreadful attempts."

▲ A drop ball is given by a referee when there has been a temporary break in play, such as when a player has been accidentally injured. One player from each side contests the ball, which can only be kicked when it has hit the ground.

See also

32-33 Heading

44-45 Opening up Defenses

48-49 Defending as a Unit

The Corner Kick

When a ball crosses a team's goal line and was last touched by a player from that team, the referee signals a corner kick. A corner is a dangerous situation for the defending team and a great opportunity for the attacking side.

Corner advantages

Corners are similar to crosses in open play, but with some big advantages—the ball isn't moving and you choose when to hit it. There are other pluses as well. Defenders have to be at least 10 yards away from the ball, you can have plenty of teammates in the penalty area as targets to aim for, and the offside rule doesn't apply. But there's also one disadvantage— defenders will be closely marking your side's players.

No.17 Luis Figo

Portuguese striker Luis Figo is well known for the accuracy and power of his corner kicks. In 2000 he was bought by Spain's Real Madrid for what was then a record fee of over $65 million.

◀ *Teams practice different corner kicks in training. Here the player signals to his teammates what type of corner to expect.*

The art of a good corner kick

Good corners are hit with speed and accuracy—they should arrive in the target area a little above head height. Slow, high, looping corners are easily cleared by defenders. When you take a corner, you should feel completely balanced on your nonkicking foot and strike through the middle or just below the middle of the ball. The kicking leg follows through and across the body as the body turns into the cross.

▲ *For a corner from the left-hand side of the field (from the attacking team's viewpoint), this is where you should place the ball if you're right-footed.*

Aiming long

Most corners are taken long and hit with enough power to reach the six-yard box or even closer to the goal. The classic target area is a point just in front of the near or far post. Inswinging corners swerve toward the goal, outswinging ones away from the goal. Both can be lethal.

◀ *This is where you should place the ball if you're left-footed. Using the left foot from this position can create an outswinging corner.*

▶ An inswinging corner usually bends into the six-yard box. Some inswinging corners have enough power and bend to hit the back of the net without being touched by another player.

◀ Near-post corners allow a flick-on header by a teammate (yellow arrows). Deeper corners toward the far post can give a teammate a chance to strike behind the goalie (red arrows).

Speed and accuracy

Another advantage of a corner hit with speed is that it is harder for defenders to clear, and a mistake or deflection can easily lead to an own goal. When a corner is driven hard, teammates in the area may only need a touch rather than a power header or full-fledged shot to redirect the ball over the line.

▼ ▲ David Beckham's corners (below) led to many goals for England's Manchester United. Few were more important than Ole Gunnar Solskjaer's, also of Manchester United, in the 1999 Champions League final (above).

Short corners

Taken quickly, short corners to a teammate a few feet away can allow the cross to come in from a different angle. They can catch the defending side off guard, with unmarked players in the box. But taken sloppily or slowly, they just waste a golden opportunity, leaving you or your teammate stranded in the corner.

See also

22-23 Advanced Passing

24-25 Movement and Space

56-57 Free Kicks in Attack

Free Kicks

If a team commits an offense, they can expect the referee to blow his whistle and award a free kick to the other side. In a free kick the ball is placed on the ground at the point where the offense was committed, while the opposing team is forced to retreat at least ten yards (30 feet). Not every free kick offers an attacking chance, but all give a side valuable possession in time and in space.

▲ One exception to the ten-yard rule occurs when a team is awarded an indirect free kick inside the opponent's penalty area. The defenders are allowed to stand on their goal line, even if it isn't ten yards away from the free kick.

▲ Direct or indirect, a quickly taken free kick in the middle of the field can open up large amounts of space and lead to attacking chances. Here Raul of Real Madrid is showing the key trait of a quick free-kick taker, keeping his head up to view the options around him before kicking the ball.

◀ Brazilian star Sissi is a renowned free-kick taker in the women's game.

◀ Referee Graham Barber signals that an indirect free kick has been awarded. His arm will remain in the air until the kick is taken and has either touched another player or gone out of play.

Turn defense into attack
Wherever you are on the field, a free kick gives you the great gift of possession—so don't waste it. Quick free kicks can open up attacking opportunities, but only if you and the receiver are alert, the free kick is hit accurately, and no opponent can intercept it. When awarded a free kick deep in your own half, aim to get the ball out of your danger zone and move possession farther upfield. Don't put your side in danger by hitting a lazy ball or playing the ball to a teammate who's not expecting the pass. Be aware and look around for a free player.

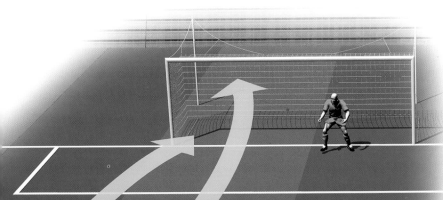

Indirect free kicks

An indirect free kick is so called because you cannot score directly from it—instead the ball must be played by one other teammate before a goal attempt can be made. Indirect free kicks are given for less serious offenses in soccer, including charging or obstructing a player who isn't on the ball or receiving the ball in an offside position. Goalkeepers can incur indirect free kicks if, for example, they hold on to the ball for more than the allowed six seconds or handle a deliberate back pass.

▲ *An English experiment, which began in 1999, gave referees the power to move a free kick ten yards toward the defending goal if defenders failed to retreat the correct distance, delayed the kick, carried, threw, or kicked the ball away, or showed dissent— disagreement with the ref.*

MASTERCLASS
Free kicks

Rehearse your free kicks as a team hard and often. Split up into defenders and attackers to create as realistic a situation as possible.

Keep your free-kick moves simple and effective. A move that requires more than three touches exposes it to more possibilities to break down.

Vary free kicks during a game to keep opponents guessing.

▲ *The arrows show some of the options possible from this direct free kick—bending the ball around one side of the wall of defenders, a shot up and over the wall, or rolling the ball out to the side for a teammate to strike.*

Direct free kicks

For the more serious offenses, including pushing and tripping, or a goalkeeper handling outside of his area, teams get a direct free kick. This is where the first touch can, but doesn't have to, be a direct shot on goal. Direct free kicks in central positions in the attacking-third of the field can offer many options and are very difficult to defend against, even with a wall in place. Players and teams practice their free-kick moves long and hard to try to turn the threat into a goalscoring reality.

▶ *Peruvian star Nolberto Solano, shown here playing for England's Newcastle United, has his head over the ball and his body well-balanced—the perfect stance from which to deliver a deadly free kick.*

See also

30-31 Volleying and Shooting | 52-53 The Corner Kick | 54-55 Free Kicks

▲ Communication between the goalie and his defensive wall is vital. Here Borussia Dortmund's Stephane Chapuisat (left) and Paulo Sousa (right) look for instructions.

▲ For long-range or wide free kicks, a two- or three-man wall is frequently used. When the free kick is central and close to goal, teams build a five- or six-man wall.

Free Kicks in Attack

Free kicks give you one touch of the ball without being challenged and with the opposition some distance away. In an attacking position this is a priceless commodity. Many games are decided on the results of free kicks, so the attacking side needs to take advantage of it, and defenders have to be alert and vigilant.

Defending a free kick

As soon as the ref gives a free kick to the opposition, get back into a defensive position. Be alert for a quickly taken free kick—if it doesn't come, get organized, and listen to teammates' instructions. It's vital to get players behind the ball, covering the spaces where a goalscoring chance might be created. If the free kick is likely to be a cross, taller defenders should mark good headers of the ball, while other defenders look to cut out knock-downs and pick up attackers making late runs into the box.

▲ A sidefoot pass can change the angle of attack and give the receiver the chance of a shot without the defensive wall blocking his way.

Surprise and disguise

Some element of cunning and surprise is often required for free kicks to be successful. Don't let it be obvious what you plan to do to the opposing side—it'll make the free kick easy to defend. Fake and decoy runs by players can cause confusion and mask the planned free-kick attempt. Attackers can form a wall in front of the real wall to hide the ball. One ploy is for several attackers to join the end of a defensive wall. This can block a goalkeeper's view, and by peeling off just before the kick is taken, can create a sudden gap for the shot to pass through.

Bending the ball

A useful skill to have on the field during open play, the ability to bend or swerve the ball accurately can be deadly at free kicks. Expert free-kick takers, such as David Beckham, Roberto Carlos, and Jay-Jay Okocha, all have this skill. It's a complicated technique that requires much practice and perseverance, and some players find they're better at hitting inside swerves or outside swerves. Both types of swerve involve hitting the ball low through one side and finishing with a long, relaxed follow-through.

▲ *To hit an inside swerve (left), strike the ball with the inside of your cleat, using a straight follow-through. For an outside swerve (right), use the outside of your cleat—the follow-through should take your foot across your body.*

Fast or wide

The quickly taken free kick isn't only used in the middle of the field to put the ball into space. A rapid move, such as a snap shot from a direct free kick, can catch a goalkeeper and his defense off guard—just ask the England team about Dietmar Hamann's speedy strike that won a 2002 World Cup qualifier for Germany. Wide free kicks can also offer more options than just a simple, immediate cross. An overlap down the wing can send in a cross from a more threatening angle, and a ball infield to a late-arriving runner can offer a shooting chance.

▼ *The options from this position include bending the ball in for a cross, passing the ball infield, or playing it down the wing for a wide player to cross from the goal line.*

▶ *Players on the attacking side peel off from the defensive wall, causing confusion among their opponents as the free-kick taker attempts a shot on goal.*

MASTERCLASS
Free kicks in attack

Listen to your goalie and other players when forming the defensive wall.

When defending, stay alert to the possibility of a sudden, surprise free kick.

Work hard on learning how to bend the ball. It will assist your free kick and corner taking as well as your long passing and shooting in open play.

▲ *All successful sides, from local or school teams right up to Holland's Euro 2000 national side pictured here, work on their free-kick moves during practice.*

No.18 Roberto Carlos

Brazilian World Cup winner Roberto Carlos is perhaps best known for scoring a stunning, swerving, and dipping free kick from more than 82 ft. out against France in 1997.

Penalty!

A penalty kick is a free shot on goal taken from the penalty spot. Any foul where a direct free kick would normally be awarded becomes a penalty if the foul was committed inside the box. To give a penalty, referees have to judge where the foul was committed—not where the fouled player ended up. For the attacking side, a penalty is a goal in the making.

See also

12-13 Key Rules

14-15 Fouls and Misconduct

30-31 Volleying and Shooting

▲ When a penalty is given, only the referee, goalkeeper, and penalty taker are allowed in the penalty area until the penalty taker has made contact with the ball. A referee can order a penalty to be retaken if any other players from either team enter the area.

▲ The penalty taker starts his run up, noting the goalie's position. Most penalty takers have decided what sort of penalty they intend before they move toward the ball.

▲ This player has approached the ball as if he is going to kick it toward the right side of the goal as he views it. The goalie commits early and starts to move in that direction.

▲ The penalty taker wraps his foot around the ball and uses a firm, low sidefoot pass to place the ball into the opposite corner of the goal.

The mental game

Zico, Platini, Baggio—these and dozens more star players have all missed penalty kicks in crucial situations. So how do high-caliber players miss such a clear chance on goal? In a single word—pressure. In a few more words—pressure and plenty of time for a player's thoughts to get the better of him. The good news is that at all levels of soccer if you can stay relaxed and focused, the task in front of you is relatively simple. You're just 11 yards away from the goal, with only the goalie to beat. The odds are certainly stacked in the penalty taker's favor.

Chip, blast, or place

For professional players, the choice of penalty shot to use is great. Some players prefer the simple chip over an early-diving goalie into the back of the middle of the net. Many choose to blast the ball as hard as possible or aim a driven shot into a corner. Add the possibility of feints and fakes during the run up and the pregame preparation, which involves studying rivals' penalty takers and goalkeepers, and it soon becomes a confusing array of options. The placed penalty is the most popular choice for amateur players. This is a relatively simple shot made with the side of the foot, hitting the ball firmly but under control into one of the goal's four corners.

No.19 Matt Le Tissier

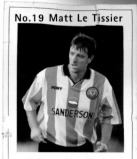

Matt Le Tissier retired in 2002, but he will always remain a legend at Southampton, in part due to his success with penalty kicks. In 1999–2000 he scored 48 penalties from 49 attempts.

▲ *The 2001 Champions League final saw the German team Bayern Munich and the Spanish team Valencia compete in a penalty shootout. Bayern ended up winning—their goalie Oliver Kahn (above) saves a penalty.*

The goalie's view

As a goalie facing either a normal penalty or a penalty shootout, you should be calm and relaxed. A goal from a penalty is expected, but if the opposition push or blast the penalty high or wide, you'll be delighted; but if you actually save their attempt, then you're the top dog. It is very much up to you as a goalie what you do at a penalty. Goalies are allowed to move along their line, but not off of it, before the penalty is taken. Some goalies, just like penalty takers, decide in advance which way to go and dive at full-stretch as the kick is taken, or choose instead to remain standing. Others try to read the taker's intentions, or if they've come up against the taker before, try to recall the most likely direction.

▼ *Practice penalties using a goal and two cones each placed 3 feet in from the goalposts. Aim to send your kicks between the cones and the goalposts.*

MASTERCLASS
Penalty!

Decide early where you intend to put the penalty, and don't change your mind in the run up.

Keep your head down and your body balanced as you take the kick.

Stay alert and aware after taking a regular penalty for a second chance following a save. Other players should follow up after the kick has been taken to both attack and defend.

▲ *The goalkeeper as heroine—U.S. goalie Briana Scurry made the save that saw the U.S. win a tense shootout with China, 5–4, and collect the 1999 World Cup.*

▼ *Paraguay goalkeeper Jose Luis Chilavert is famous both for taking free kicks and penalties and for saving them.*

▲ *Italian Roberto Baggio blazed his 1994 World Cup final penalty over the crossbar, handing the trophy to Brazil. Baggio did, however, score two spot kicks at the 1998 World Cup.*

Penalty shootouts

Many knockout competitions use penalty shootouts to decide the outcome of a game when the scores are still even after overtime. A shootout usually calls for five players on each side to take alternate penalties, and if the score is even after those ten kicks, more players, one from each side, continue until there is a winner. Although labeled as cruel on individuals, penalty shootouts are pure theater, and many believe a fairer way of deciding the outcome than drawing straws or flipping a coin.

▲ *Stuart Pearce made up for a miss at the 1990 World Cup with a successful spot kick in the Euro '96 shootout with Spain. The image of him celebrating is an enduring memory of the tournament.*

"You must believe you are the best and then make sure that you are."

Bill Shankly

▲ *Spain's Real Madrid manager Vicente Del Bosque (far right) stands in front of his team's substitutes' bench, watching the game intensely.*

▶ *A passion for the game and the ability to motivate players are hallmarks of successful managers such as Liverpool England's legend Bill Shankly, who transformed his team.*

Managers and Coaches

No one feels the pressures of soccer more than the person in charge of shaping the team, selecting the players who will play and in what positions, and choosing the tactics. At some teams this responsibility is split between a director of soccer, who oversees the team's development and is involved with transfers, and a first-team manager or coach, who works with the players. At other teams it's all down to one individual, usually known as the manager.

◀ *Many ex-pros move into management. Others, such as Paul Power, head of England's Manchester City's youth development, are employed behind the scenes to work with a team's younger players.*

Head of a team

Although they usually receive most of the attention, modern-day managers and coaches tend to be part of a large team of backroom staff. They frequently employ a second-in-command, an assistant coach who helps with the day-to-day running of the first-team squad. There are often additional coaches in charge of the youth and reserve teams as well as scouts who scour regions, countries, and even continents on the lookout for fresh talent. Fitness trainers, physical therapists and other medical staff, uniform assistants, and sometimes sports psychologists, who help to focus the players mentally, complete what is a good-sized team, all working behind the scenes for a team.

▲ *Sometimes league managers and coaches assist the national team. Here two of England's up-and-coming managers, Peter Taylor and Steve McClaren, help the England team.*

Pressure cooker

Despite being part of a team, the manager or coach of a team can often find himself under immense pressure, particularly at top teams for whom success is expected. Managers' reputations stand or fall on their player selections, their transfer wheelings and dealings, and by the tactical decisions they make in individual games or over a season. But above all managers are judged on their team's results. It can take only a handful of disappointing scorelines for managers to be criticized in the media and by fans and owners. Continued failings inevitably lead to speculation over their future employment. In the past many managers spent decades at the same team. Today with the financial stakes much higher and the pressure to deliver trophies far greater, the managerial merry-go-round sees managers in and out of work quicker than ever.

▲ England's Arsenal chairman, David Dein, raises the FA Cup while manager Arsène Wenger parades the Premiership trophy for the fans after Arsenal won the Double in 2002.

▲ Team officials at Real Madrid welcome Zinedine Zidane in 2001 after he was signed for a world-record fee of over $75 million.

◄ Argentina coach Cesar Luis Menotti controversially left the rising star Maradona out of his 1978 World-Cup-winning squad.

A manager's duties

An excellent soccer brain, top-notch people and decision-making skills, and a vision of how the team will develop and should play are vital requirements for the modern manager or coach. A manager's tasks include structuring the players' coaching and practicing, dealing with the media, working on specific skills, playing styles, and set pieces, and checking out upcoming opponents and possible transfer targets. In addition a manager has to assess the form and ability of new players, youngsters, and players returning from injury, deciding when to play them and in what position.

◄ Manager Ottmar Hitzfeld celebrates with his triumphant Bayern Munich team moments after they collected the 2001 Champions League trophy.

▲ Some well-known international managers together, including in the back row from left, Arsène Wenger, Sir Alex Ferguson, Fabio Capello, Rinus Michels, and Gérard Houllier, and in the front row, Dr. Jozef Venglos, Andy Roxburgh, and Roy Hodgson.

Team and country

With soccer teams a big business, particularly in Europe, a manager's ability to wheel and deal profitably in the transfer market is considered a major asset. Some managers have earned themselves excellent reputations for their uncanny knack of buying players cheaply and selling them on at a later date for a much higher fee. An astute transfer swoop can invigorate and inspire a team and bring them honor. Replacing valued players with underperforming ones, on the other hand, often leads to being fired. National team managers don't have the pleasure of dealing with transfers, but instead they must endure the major headache of selecting a successful team from a much wider base of players. They must also be able to cope with the phenomenal pressure and the expectations of an entire nation. Be it team or country, all managers fear failure and dream of the glory and satisfaction that comes with success.

Formations

All soccer teams need a structure with players organized into a basic shape called a formation. Formations tend to be described in terms of the numbers of outfield players, from the defense forward. So 4-4-2 describes a system of four defenders, four midfielders, and finally two attackers. The following are some of the most important formations and systems in soccer history.

"Football [soccer] is self-expression within an organized framework."

Roger Lemerre, French national coach

Major William Suddell of Preston North End (England)

2-3-5

Preston North End coach Major William Suddell was just one of many managers to adopt the first commonly used formation 2-3-5. It featured five forwards with three midfielders, known as halfbacks, and just one pair of fullbacks defending the goal. The key player was the center-half, who played in the middle of the field and was the main playmaker in attack, but also had to get back to mark the opposition team's center-forward. While sides in Europe and South America toyed with a variety of different formations, most teams in the U.K. stuck with 2-3-5 until the mid-1920s.

W-M (3-2-2-3)

Changes to the offside law for the 1925–26 season initially saw teams struggle to contain a five-man attack. After a 7-0 defeat to another English team, Newcastle United, Arsenal manager Herbert Chapman decided to pull his center-half back into defense and move two of his forwards back into midfield. Arsenal beat West Ham (England) 4-0 with this new formation two days later. It was called "W-M" because the forwards formed a "W" shape, the defenders an "M" shape. Many other sides adopted this system, and for a quarter of a century it was used all over the world.

Arsenal manager Herbert Chapman (England)

4-2-4

Brazil, under the management of Vicente Feola, arrived at the 1958 World Cup finals with two secret weapons: a 17-year-old attacker we now know as Pelé and a system designed to counter the old W-M formation. The 4-2-4 system saw a strong defensive line of four players, with two midfielders controlling and directing play for a pair of wingers and two central strikers. Although this formation proved successful for Brazil and some other teams, it is rarely used in the modern game because it places too much emphasis on the midfield players, who may be outnumbered.

Vicente Feola (Brazil)

Catenaccio (1-4-3-2)

Italian for "big chain," *catenaccio* means creating a defensively strong side, often at the expense of the attack. Central to this formation is the role of the sweeper, who plays behind the defense, mopping up loose balls and covering challenges. Under Helenio Herrera, coach of the highly successful Inter Milan team of the 1960s, *catenaccio* frequently stifled opposition attacks. Teams playing this system often relied on fast breaks by small numbers of attackers to score.

Helenio Herrera, coach of Inter Milan (Italy)

4-3-3

From the 1960s onward, soccer tactics became increasingly defensive. Even the most attack-minded of international sides, such as Brazil, withdrew one of their forwards back into midfield to play with a 4-3-3 formation. Brazil won the World Cup in 1962 and 1970 with this system. 4-3-3 is still used to this day—often, ironically, as an attacking alternative for a team that's behind, with time running out. One of the forwards, usually with excellent dribbling and crossing skills, takes up a wide position in attack and may switch from side to side, searching for openings.

Aymore Moriera led Brazil to glory in 1962

4-4-2

4-4-2 dispenses with wingers in favor of a four-man midfield. One of the first to use it was England manager Sir Alf Ramsey, whose "wingless wonders" won the 1966 World Cup, despite initial criticism of their playing style. Its strengths are that it provides two waves of four players to defend and close down the opposition. Its weakness is that the two strikers need to cover a lot of ground and must receive support from the midfielders to launch meaningful attacks. It is one of the most commonly used formations in the modern game.

England manager Sir Alf Ramsey

3-2-3-2

Inspired by Dutch coach Rinus Michels, "total football [soccer]" saw a team's players interchange positions and roles fluidly, a system that required every player to be comfortable on the ball. It is rare to see "total football" today. More common are 4-4-2 and the 3-2-3-2, or wing-back, formations. The two key features of this latter formation are the three center-backs, one of whom may be asked to man-on-man mark an opposing striker and the two wide players—the wing-backs. Wing-backs have to cover the entire length of a field, linking up in midfield and attack, as well as defending.

Rinus Michels (Holland)

Tactics

Within the chosen basic formation a manager or coach has plenty of room to try out different tactics, systems, and ploys. Over the last 50 years there have been a great number of innovations in tactical thinking that have seen subtle alterations to certain formations. There has also been a development of moves and tactics within these formations.

► Sweepers such as Italy's Gaetano Scirea (left) can play defensively— rarely straying ahead of fellow defenders—or can move up to attack.

▲ An Argentinian defender challenges Dutchman Johan Neeskens. Modern wing-backs need to get forward as well as perform similar defensive duties.

Options and systems

There are many variations and options within each formation. For example, sweepers can be used defensively or as a potential attacking weapon (see illustration top left). The same is the case for a system featuring wing-backs *(left)*. Wing-backs can be instructed to stay back, creating a five-man defense. Alternatively they can move back and forth, helping out in defense and attack, or they can surge forward, becoming wingers and creating an overload up front.

Another option in midfield and attack is called the diamond system. This involves four midfielders, or three midfielders and a striker, forming a diamond shape on the field. At the head of the diamond, farthest upfield, is an attacking midfielder or striker who makes late runs into position and links the midfield with the attack. Because the diamond system creates a great deal of depth up front, it can be hard for teams to defend.

◄ The diamond formation offers plenty of options for the team going forward.

In the hole

Many sides play a pair of attackers or just a lone striker in the most forward position with another player positioned behind the front line. This player plays in what is called "the hole" and can be a massive threat to the opposition. He stays onside and can prompt attacks by precise passing and through balls, or if defenders back off, he can advance and unleash a long-range shot.

◄ Juventus' (Italy) Didier Deschamps (center) shields the ball from Marc Overmars of Ajax (Holland). Deschamps often played as a midfield anchor, sitting in front of the defense and breaking up attacks.

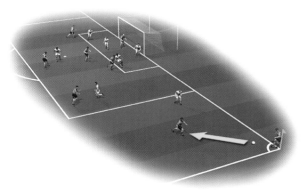

▲ There is always a risk involved in playing the offside trap, and that applies even when an attack develops from a short corner, as is the case in the above illustration.

◄ Arsenal's (England) Tony Adams (right) and Sol Campbell attempt to catch Roma's (Italy) Gabriel Batistuta offside.

► To play the offside trap, the defense, on a signal, move up quickly at the same time and in as much of a straight line as possible, just before a ball over the top is played (yellow arrow). Timing is crucial.

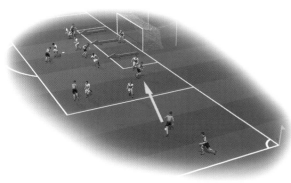

▲ The attacker shapes to pass to a teammate (yellow arrow). Most of the defense has moved upfield but the defender marking the likely receiver keeps him onside.

The offside trap

When an attacker is offside, possession passes to the defending team, so many sides adopt a defensive tactic known as the offside trap to make this happen as often as possible. The offside trap involves the back three or four players maintaining a straight line across the field as they suddenly move upfield to catch an opponent offside. Performed well, the offside trap can be infuriating for the opposition, but it does carry the risk of being sprung, leaving no defensive cover during an attack.

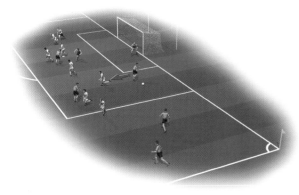

▲ The defender must step up before the ball is played to force the attacker offside. If the defender is not quick enough, the attacker would have a good chance to score.

▼ Norway use the long throw to get the ball quickly into thier opponent's (Yugoslavia) penalty area during a Euro 2000 qualifier.

► Long-ball teams often use a target man. Here John Fashanu formerly of England's Watford (left) plays that role.

The long-ball game

Some teams prefer to build attacks patiently with the emphasis on keeping possession and switching the direction of play to probe an opposition defense for an opening. A contrasting tactic is rapid and direct. A long-ball pass out of defense or midfield to an advanced attacker can quickly open up a game. The role of this target player is to get to the ball first and then control it. From there he may either turn and attack the goal himself or hold on to the ball long enough to open up a teammate who has arrived in support. For a defender it is possible to largely bypass the midfield and send long balls up to the strikers.

▲ A fourth official holds up his electronic board to indicate a substitution.

Tactics in a Game

Once the game starts managers have to hope that their formation, tactics, and player selection all conspire to bring their side victory. But it doesn't always work out that way. Opposition teams can spring tactical surprises, decisions and luck can go against a team, and certain players can be lacking certain skills. In order to react to such events, managers can make extra changes to their side's tactics and play throughout the entire game.

Assessing the game

From kickoff onward managers and their coaching staff study the action, checking out the opposition's tactics and looking for weaknesses or mismatches on either side. For the players involved in the game it can be hard to assess how things are going beyond the scoreline. Managers are far better positioned to judge both the game and how individuals are faring. Is a player slightly injured and not performing to his best? Is a defender getting pulled out of position by one particularly tricky attacker? Is the opposition's offside trap weak and liable to be sprung? These and a dozen other questions will be occupying the manager or coach's thoughts.

▲ In large squads players, such as John Hartson of the Scottish team Celtic here coming on for Henrik Larsson, have to accept a role on the bench.

> **MASTERCLASS**
> A winning attitude
>
> Prepare for every game as if it were the biggest of the season.
>
> As a substitute warm up well before coming on. This will help you get up to speed in a game.
>
> Don't ease up when your side is ahead. Too many games swing back the other way.
>
> Accept the manager's decision to substitute you or play you in a different position.

◄ Substitute Teddy Sheringham prepares to enter the action in the 1999 Champions League final. It was an inspired decision by manager Sir Alex Ferguson (right) with Sheringham grabbing a vital goal (above).

Substitutions

Substitutions are a vital part of a manager's armory. He can replace a player who is injured, not performing, or just needs a rest. A manager can also sacrifice a player in order to bring on another type of player. Two common substitutions are to bring off a striker when your team is winning by several goals or to replace a defender with an extra attacker when your side is behind.

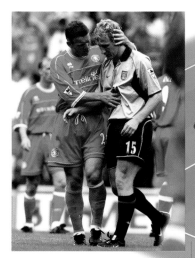

▲ Middlesbrough's (England) Dean Windass (left) consoles Ray Parlour of Arsenal (England) when Parlour is sent off.

▲ A 5-3-2 team reorganizes after a midfielder is sent off. They pull one wing-back into defense, push the other into midfield, and play one striker behind the other as a link between midfield and attack.

Changing tactics

Some coaches toy constantly with tactics during a game; other coaches prefer to leave things pretty much as they are. But they all want their sides to get and maintain possession, to look secure in defense, and to be effective in attack. As a game develops managers spot weaknesses in both teams and look to fix their own while exploiting those of the opposition. For example, a manager may pull a midfielder back to track and guard a dangerous opposition attacker who plays deep.

► Encouraging teammates, as German goalkeeper Silke Rottenberg (top right) is doing, helps maintain confidence. The Korea Republic side (right) build morale as they huddle just before kickoff. Listening to the advice and support of teammates is important for strong team spirit.

▲ Communication is vital in marshaling a team, as Fiorentina's (Italy) Daniele Adani demonstrates.

A winning attitude

The best coaches in the world won't succeed unless their players have the right attitude. Coaches and managers seek to instill a winning attitude in their teams so that even when things are going against them, the players continue to work hard to turn things around. But what is a winning attitude in practical terms? It involves keeping your confidence when your side is being overrun. It means not picking on your own teammates when they make a mistake, but encouraging them. Above all, it means concentrating and working not as individuals, but as a team.

"You can play any style that you like, the important thing is to create a strong group."
Cesare Maldini

▲ *Spectators watch a youth game in Victoria Park in East London, England. Talented young players can give themselves a better chance of making the grade through hard work.*

A Pro's Life

Throughout the world millions of children, teenagers, and amateur adult players turn out for their local teams every week. Of these it's a fairly safe bet that most, if not all, of them dream of one day getting paid to play soccer and eventually reaching the very top of the professional game.

A long, long road

Gifted youngsters may be the best midfielders or strikers in their school, area, or even region, but they face a long, uphill path before they can join the top ranks. Many never make the grade and others falter after joining a soccer team as a youth player, never completing the step up to the reserves and the first team. Disappointment is rife, but some players are lucky enough to be given a second chance.

► *Dutch club Ajax is renowned for the quality of its youth academy, which has produced Johan Cruyff and Patrick Kluivert, among many others. Here former Holland star Arnold Muhren works with some of Ajax's youngsters.*

▲ *A team with a rich crop of youngsters has a greater chance of a rosy future. Manchester United's (England) youth team of the early 1990s, pictured here after their 1993 FA Youth Cup final win, was captained by Gary Neville and also contained Paul Scholes, Nicky Butt, and David Beckham—now star players on the first team.*

Pro health

Top players are expensive assets, and teams strive to keep them as healthy and fit as possible. The days of eating greasy food prior to a game are long gone. Diet and bodyweight are monitored carefully, and foods packed with carbohydrates such as vegetables, pastas, and rice are typical fare. Minor injuries or tiredness often result in a player losing form and possibly his place in the team. The biggest fear of most professionals is a major injury that can keep them out for many months, or even end their career.

► *Players receive immediate attention when they get injured during a game. Here Korea Republic's Woon Jae Lee is treated for a head injury during his side's 2001 Confederations Cup game against Australia.*

◄ *Injured professionals, such as Gary Ablett (left), spend hours working out, strengthening their bodies.*

▲ *Midfielder Luis Figo attends a glamorous function with his wife, Helene. Particularly in Europe, top stars are major celebrities.*

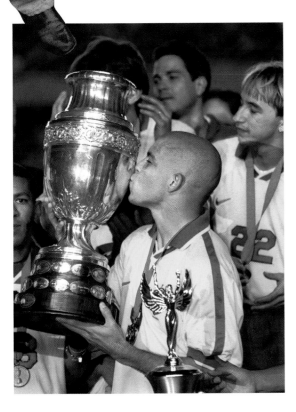

◄ *George Best, Britain's original soccer superstar, was one of the first to employ a business manager, pictured next to Best along with Best's secretary and chauffeur.*

Playing for a living

The majority of professional soccer players earn a fraction as much as Rivaldo and Beckham. With relatively short playing careers and the threat of injury always present, more and more players use agents to negotiate good contracts and transfer deals on their behalf. Agents and certain freedom of work laws and court rulings have helped engineer far more player movement between European teams than ever before.

Rewards and responsibilities

The rewards for making it to the top are huge. Massive salaries, measured in tens of thousands of dollars per week, are just the start. Sponsorships and endorsements of a company's products can quickly make star players multimillionaires, and that's before money from personal appearances, media work, and cuts from a transfer deal. All this comes at a price, however. The pressure to perform and media intrusion are two of the negative aspects of a pro's life.

▲ *Rivaldo collects his 1999 FIFA Player of the Year trophy at a glitzy awards ceremony held in Brussels, Belgium.*

◄ *The money is great, but most players dream of the glory of lifting a major trophy more than anything else. Here Ronaldo kisses the Copa America trophy, which Brazil won in 1997.*

▶ *England internationals Rachel Brown and Karen Walker sign autographs for eager fans after a game.*

Teams and Fans

Especially in Europe and South America, the bond between fans and their team is powerful and passionate. Fans may chant for a manager to leave, or be unhappy with certain players or the current team, but their love of the team itself remains. Many fans travel the world to show their undying support for their team.

▼ Team mascots often entertain the crowd before the game. This cartoon cat, called Gatton Gattoni, is Vicenza's mascot, the griffin bird is Perugia's both Italian teams.

An emotional rollercoaster

Whether it's your national team, your favorite professional team, or a local amateur team you support, soccer games generate a range of intense feelings. From the dreadful low of seeing your team knocked out of an important competition to the incredible high of watching a spectacular winning goal by your team, the emotional rollercoaster ride you can experience is addictive—which is why most fans support the same team for their entire life.

FINAL

Arse

FA CUP SEMI-FINAL
STOKE CITY
v ARSENAL
Villa Park, Saturday April 15th 1972, 3.00pm
Official Programme 10p

OFFICIAL PROGRAMME
SEASON 1936-7

▲ The game day program is essential prematch and halftime reading for many fans.

▶ This full stall outside Rome's Olympic Stadium is selling merchandise to passing Roma fans.

All dressed up

To be a lifelong fan of a soccer team is like being part of a close-knit tribe. In Europe and South America fans learn their own team's chants and songs, wear the team colors, and buy many team-related products known as merchandise. Merchandising has become an important money-maker for professional sides with sales of shirts and other items often exceeding the money made by ticket sales.

▼ Paris St. Germain fans proclaim their support for their team with a sea of banners and flares during a Champions League encounter with Italian giants AC Milan.

The big game

Many fans get excited long before the start of a new season or before an important game. Derby games, where a side plays their local rivals, tend to produce the most intense atmospheres. Derbies between Spanish rivals Real Madrid and Barcelona, Italian giants Internazionale and AC Milan, and the Scottish "Old Firm" games between Celtic and Rangers are among the biggest clashes in Europe.

◀▼ *Fans can generate an incredible atmosphere, few more so than the supporters of the Reggae Boyz (left)—the nickname of Jamaica's national team. International games are an occasion to celebrate your country, as these face-painted U.S. fans show (below).*

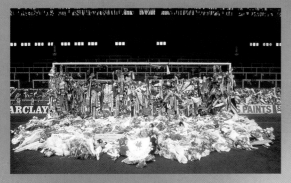

▲ *Floral tributes left at Anfield stadium in England, home of Liverpool FC. The tributes were in response to the 1989 Hillsborough tragedy in which 96 Liverpool fans died.*

▲ *Team stores sell shirts, clothing, souvenirs, and other memorabilia to devoted fans. This is the team store of Japanese J-League side Yokohama Marinos.*

Trouble and tragedy

Throughout soccer's history there have been incidents of violence, accidents, and tragedy. The intense passion of some fans can overstep the mark, turning to hatred, abuse, and violence toward players, officials and, in particular, fans of rival teams. Outbreaks of hooliganism and crowd trouble have blighted the game in Europe and South America, but more intelligent policing and the use of video cameras has led to many arrests. Up to 1990, many stadiums had a combination of standing and seating areas, but after a number of tragedies—including people being crushed as crowds of standing fans surged forward—many stadiums have become less-crowded, all-seater venues with more attention paid to safety.

Soccer Media

Playing soccer and watching it live in a stadium are only two of the ways in which fans can immerse themselves in the game. Reading about soccer in newspapers and magazines, surfing the Internet, picking up scores from the radio, or watching highlights on television all allow people to follow the sport they love.

◀ Fans have a variety of options to choose from when it comes to finding out more about the game, such as magazines, newspapers, and sports shows on TV.

The press

Newspapers in South America and Europe have back pages devoted to sports news, interviews, results, rumors, and gossip with soccer tending to dominate on a day-to-day basis.

▶ Web sites, including this official site for Italian side Roma, allow fans to keep up to date with their team.

Some publications are often criticized for being too harsh on players, unsettling them with rumors of transfers, and seeking to inflame disagreements and generate scandals. However, there's no doubt that the press stirs up enthusiasm and interest in the sport, allowing fans to obtain game reports and features on famous players and managers. Some fans of teams, players, or a particular competition produce publications for other fans. Known as fanzines, these publications are independent of teams and offer ordinary fans the chance to put their often critical opinions in print, thus reaching a wider audience.

▲ The first television filming of soccer came in 1936 when the British Broadcasting Corporation (BBC) filmed a demonstration game featuring Arsenal and Everton players.

▶ Television coverage of the game has greatly advanced since the early days, with viewers in Europe now able to access a huge array of statistics.

◀ TV cameras on cranes can provide great aerial views of the stadium and the game.

◀ *Almost every angle is covered by TV cameras, including the bird's-eye view offered by this Goodyear blimp.*

Television coverage
Television, more than any other media outlet, is responsible for the explosion of interest in soccer. In Europe, South America, and the Far East broadcasting soccer is a sophisticated operation, involving many camera angles, commentators, and a host of behind-the-scenes technical staff. The U.S. showed its soccer broadcasting capabilities during the 1994 World Cup.

New views and choices
Soccer has pushed television technology to provide new and improved ways of covering the game. The image-capture quality of cameras has increased, allowing crystal-clear slow-motion replays of even the fastest action. Cameras have also shrunk in size, so they can now be fitted into the back of the goal and other unusual places. The arrival of subscription and pay-per-view television via cable or satellite means that fans have to pay larger sums to watch chosen games, but in return more viewing options are being provided. Instant replays and different camera angles can be selected, and game statistics can also be accessed, just by pressing buttons on a remote control.

▲ *Fieldside cameras help viewers feel even closer to the action and their heroes.*

▲ *Up in the commentary boxes, commentators call the game, explaining the action and who it involves.*

▶ *Giant screen technology shows instant replays of goals and other highlights to spectators.*

Other media
Although in Europe television dominates, many fans in other countries rely on other forms of media to follow games. In most of the world fans can listen to live radio commentaries, just like listening to a baseball game in the U.S. In other countries, including the U.S., fans can keep up-to-date with results via the Internet. The Net has thousands of official and unofficial websites dedicated to teams, competitions, and individual players. Such is the demand for up-to-the-minute soccer news and results that in Europe cellular phone users can receive the latest updates through text messages!

◀ *In England soccer is taken seriously, as can be seen by the press turnout when Terry Venables was appointed manager of the national team in 1994.*

◀ *Fieldside reporters often grab short interviews with players and managers before, during, and after a game.*

The press conference
In countries where soccer is popular the players, managers, or chairman of the team frequently hold press conferences. This allows newspaper, TV, radio, and internet reporters to have the latest information on transfers, new appointments, and resignations—not to mention opinions on the game results—to share with the fans.

Opened in 1903, Hampden Park was home to the world's biggest crowds for the first half of the 1900s. The stadium underwent major refurbishment in the 1970s and 1990s.

Super Stadiums

Just a place for spectators to watch soccer? Think again. Stadiums—particularly in Europe and South America—are the temples of soccer and each has its own special atmosphere and unique history.

Hampden Park (Scotland)

One of the first great stadiums, the home of the Scottish national team, but built for and still used by the professional team Queens Park. Until the 1950s Hampden Park was the largest capacity soccer arena in the world. The 149,415 people who watched Scotland play England in 1937, when stadiums had seating and standing areas, is still a U.K. official record attendance. Now as an all-seater stadium, Hampden's capacity is 52,000.

Almost 200,000 people tried to cram into Wembley stadium for the 1923 FA Cup final between West Ham and Bolton. Its original capacity of 126,000 was recently reduced to 80,000.

Wembley (England)

Built in just 300 days in 1923, the two towers of north London's Wembley stadium were a stirring sight for visiting fans for over three quarters of a century. Wembley has been home to the England national side, the FA Cup final, and perhaps most famously of all, host to the 1966 World Cup final in which England beat West Germany 4-2. Wembley was closed in 2000 for major redevelopment.

San Siro (Italy)

The Giuseppe Meazza stadium, better known as the San Siro, is home to two Italian Serie A giants. The San Siro started life in 1926 as the 35,000-capacity home of AC Milan. Milanese rivals Internazionale left their own stadium, Arena, to make the San Siro their home in 1955. The 85,000 all-seater ground has hosted two European Cup finals and games from the 1934 and 1990 World Cups.

▲ *The 1990 renovations to the San Siro cost more than $75 million and added a third level of seats to the stadium, supported by 11 massive cylindrical towers.*

Maracana (Brazil)

Based in Rio de Janeiro, Brazil, and home to the Brazilian national side, the Maracana is a huge arena. Opened in 1950 for the World Cup finals, the stadium holds the official world record attendance when 199,854 spectators came to see Brazil play Uruguay. It also holds the world record local professional team attendance of 177,656 for a game played in 1963 between Brazilian sides Flamingo and Fluminense.

▼ *The Maracana, also known as the Maracane and Estadio Mario Filho, now seats 120,000 spectators.*

▲ *Home to one of the world's biggest clubs, FC Barcelona, the Nou Camp, which means "the new ground," hosted the opening of the 1982 World Cup.*

Nou Camp (Spain)

The magnificent home stadium of Spanish team, Barcelona, the Nou Camp was opened in 1957 with a 90,000 capacity. This was later increased to a maximum capacity of around 115,000. Uniquely, the Nou Camp is connected via a walkway to a 16,500-seater stadium. This smaller stadium is where Barcelona's reserve or nursery team plays in the lower divisions of the Spanish league.

Stade de France (France)

Built specifically for the 1998 World Cup finals, the Stade de France is a state-of-the-art sports stadium. Le Grand Stade, as it is popularly known, features a retractable lower level, 36 elevators, 43 cafés and snack bars, 670 bathrooms, 17 stores, and 454 floodlights. Built at a cost of more than $400 million, the stadium holds up to 80,000 spectators.

▼ *The 45,409-capacity Nagai stadium in Osaka, a major venue for the 2002 World Cup, was renovated in 1996.*

▶ *The crowd at the Stade de France use cards to spell out* Coupe de Monde *(World Cup) during the opening ceremony of the 1998 World Cup finals. France went on to win the final against Brazil.*

Nagai (Japan)

Nagai stadium, one of a record 20 stadiums involved in the 2002 World Cup cohosted by Japan and South Korea, is the home of Japanese J-League team, Cerezo Osaka. Major international competitions such as the World Cup provide a major impetus to build new playing fields and upgrade older ones such as Nagai stadium.

Great Competitions

Hundreds of different competitions, from youth five-on-five events to international tournaments for professionals, take place worldwide. Many competitions feature the best national or local teams all vying for a highly prestigious trophy.

Marco Tardelli, Italy

▲ *Uruguay win the first ever World Cup.*

◄ *Maradona, clutching the 1986 World Cup, is held up by Argentina fans, while Marco Tardelli (far left) celebrates scoring Italy's second goal in the 1982 final against West Germany. Italy won 3–1.*

World Cup

Simply the biggest soccer competition of them all, the World Cup was the brainchild of Frenchman Jules Rimet. Since the first tournament in 1930, the World Cup has provided a global stage, normally every four years, for the national teams that make it through qualifying. This procedure sees more than 150 nations play in groups, usually against rivals from their own continent, for the right to attend the finals. So far only seven teams have won the World Cup—Brazil (five times), Italy and Germany (three), Argentina and Uruguay (twice), and England and France (once). Germany, who will host the 2006 tournament, will hope to avenge their defeat by Brazil in the 2002 World Cup final.

National professional leagues and continental competitions

Almost every soccer-playing country has its own national league made up of a number of professional teams competing against each other for the league title. Some of the world's most famous and competitive leagues include the German Bundesliga, the Spanish La Liga, the Italian Serie A, the Brazilian Serie A, and the English Premiership. The best-placed teams in many countries' leagues often enter a continent-wide team competition, such as Europe's UEFA Champions League or South America's Copa Libertadores. Continental competitions also exist for national teams. Surprisingly, given soccer's long history there, Europe was the last major continent to get such a competition. Since its first final in 1960, the European Championship has been very prestigious and popular, attracting huge TV audiences around the world.

◄ *France's Marcel Desailly (left) and Marco Delvecchio of Italy during Euro 2000.*

▼ *Rivaldo (far left) and, next to him, Ronaldo are part of the throng of Brazilian players enjoying their 1999 Copa America success. Surprisingly, this was only the sixth time Brazil had won.*

Copa America

The first continental competition for national teams began in 1910 and was named the Copa America—the South American Championship. A mere 8,000 spectators watched Argentina beat fierce rival Uruguay 4–1 in the final. Uruguay took their revenge in the second competition, held six years later in 1916, as they defeated Argentina to lift the trophy. Between 1959 and 1987 the tournament was usually played once every four years. In the years on both sides of these dates the tournament tended to take place every two years. Argentina and Uruguay have dominated, with 15 and 14 wins respectively. Brazil, Peru, Paraguay, and Bolivia have also been winners. Host nation Colombia beat Mexico in the final of the 2002 competition.

African Nations Cup

The African Nations Cup started in 1957 with just three teams—Egypt, Ethiopia, and Sudan. Egypt emerged as the winner. Since its small-scale beginnings, the competition has grown in size and importance. South Africa was readmitted into African soccer in 1992, and in 1996 the number of teams contesting the trophy was increased from 12 to 16. Twelve different nations have won the tournament, Ghana and Egypt being the most successful with four victories each. Both the 2000 tournament, cohosted by Ghana and Nigeria, and the 2002 tournament, held in Mali, saw narrow victories on penalties after extra time for Cameroon's Indomitable Lions.

▲ Cameroon's Lucien Mettomo receives the African Nations Cup after his team beat Nigeria in the 2000 final.

Asian Cup

The Asian Cup started in 1956 and has boomed in quality and popularity since its early days. The 12 founding teams of the Asian Football Confederation have now expanded to some 45 countries—more than half of the world's soccer-playing peoples. Recent tournaments have involved major tussles between Far Eastern nations, such as China and Japan, and teams from the Middle East, such as Kuwait, United Arab Emirates, and Iran. The 2000 Asian Cup final, held in Lebanon, saw Japan clinch a tense 1–0 victory over a strong Saudi Arabian team.

▲ Japan line up with the Asian Cup trophy after their narrow win over Saudi Arabia in 2000.

▶ Cameroon's Joel Epalle (left) and Puyol of Spain chase the ball in the 2000 Olympics final.

Olympic Games

Soccer was played at the first modern Olympics, held in Athens in 1896, and it remained a demonstration sport at the Games until 1908. Before being overshadowed by the arrival of the World Cup in 1930, it was the only global soccer competition around. From 1952 to 1988 nearly every winner came from Eastern Europe. The 1990s saw the introduction of women's soccer at the Games and the emergence of African nations, with Nigeria in 1996 and then Cameroon in 2000, both winning the final.

▲ Tiffeny Milbrett (left) of the U.S. and Norway's Goeril Kringen at the 2000 Olympics.

▼ Canada's Josa De Vos and Craig Forrest (left) with the 2000 CONCACAF trophy.

CONCACAF Gold Cup

In 1941 a tournament for the soccer-playing countries of Central America was devised. Now known as the CONCACAF Gold Cup, it has been held in various formats and guises and has occasionally involved invited guest teams such as Brazil. At times teams from North America have been included as well. In 1991, for example, the U.S. recorded its first victory in the competition, beating Honduras on penalties in the final. With ten wins—a tally that includes victories in eight of the first 11 competitions—Costa Rica have lifted the trophy more than any other nation. In recent times Mexico has dominated, winning three tournaments in a row between 1993 and 1998. Canada were the victors in 2000, beating Colombia 2–0 in the final and notching up their first international tournament win since the 1904 Olympic Games.

"They were simply a great team and they took us apart."

Sir Stanley Matthews about the 1953 Hungary team

Great Games 1

England 3 Hungary 6, friendly, 1953

Despite England's lackluster performance in the 1950 World Cup (the first time they entered the competition), many people still believed they were one of the best teams in the world. A friendly match at Wembley against a gifted and tactically brilliant Hungarian side, headed by the attacking genius of Ferenc Puskas, quickly shattered that illusion.

▲ *An England cross is cut out by Hungarian goalkeeper Gyula Grosics.*

▶ *Hungary's number ten, Ferenc Puskas, turns to the crowd to celebrate another goal for his team.*

Magic Magyars

From the first minute, the England side, boasting stars such as Stanley Matthews, Billy Wright, and Tom Finney, were outclassed and outplayed. The fluid Hungarian side, dubbed the "Magic Magyars," launched wave after wave of ferocious attacks. The rigid English tactics couldn't handle the sublime skills and movement of Kocsis and Puskas or those of the midfielder Nandor Hidegkuti, who scored a hat trick.

◀ *England's goalkeeper Gil Merrick comes out to block a shot from the foot of Sandor Kocsis.*

A class act

If Hungary hadn't eased up in the last 20 minutes of the game, the six goals they scored against England might have reached double figures. The Hungarian victory at Wembley was no fluke. Six months later an England side with seven changes traveled to Hungary for a rematch. England were thumped 7–1.

Real Madrid (Spain) 7, Eintracht Frankfurt (Germany) 3. European Cup Final, 1960

One of the finest exhibitions of soccer ever seen between two teams hell bent on winning the European Cup was watched by 127,621 people at Hampden Park in Glasgow, Scotland. Eintracht Frankfurt, who had demolished their semifinal opponents Glasgow Rangers, opened the scoring and dominated the first quarter of the game. Real Madrid then burst into life with their two outstanding players Alfredo di Stefano and Puskas running rings around the German team. The great vision, swift movement, and superlative ball skills captivated the crowd and took Real Madrid from one goal down to 7–3 in style. Di Stefano completed his hat trick in the 74th minute, just two minutes after Puskas had hit his fourth goal.

◀ *Puskas scores Real Madrid's fourth goal with an effortless kick from the penalty spot.*

▲ *Real Madrid celebrate their sensational 7–3 victory over Eintracht Frankfurt to win the European Cup.*

Nonstop action

Eintracht's commitment to attacking was as much a factor in this spellbinding match as the Spanish side's dazzling play. The German side didn't give up easily—in the second half they hit the goalposts twice and twice put the ball in the back of the net. But it wasn't enough to prevent Real Madrid's onslaught.

◄ *Real Madrid goalkeeper Dominguez makes another save as Eintracht Frankfurt try to get back in the game.*

Brazil 4, Italy 1. World Cup final, 1970

The 1970 World Cup in Mexico, the first to feature red and yellow cards and substitutes, was a wonderful display of high-class soccer and epic games. It culminated in a final that saw what is considered the finest team display by an international side. That side was Brazil. Their opponents, Italy, were in top form as well. Although Italy had beaten the West German side in the semifinals 4–3, the talents of, among others, Pelé, Rivelino, and Jairzinho proved just too much for them.

◄ *Jairzinho makes a run behind Italian player Giacinto Facchetti. Jairzinho scored in every round of the World Cup, including the final.*

Pelé scores first

Pelé opened the Brazilian account with a superbly-taken header in the 19th minute. But a sloppy Brazilian back pass was exploited by Boninsegna who equalized for Italy. In the second half Gerson put Brazil ahead again with a superlative individual effort. Picking up the ball 115 feet from goal, he changed direction to beat one defender before unleashing a precise and devastating shot.

▶ *Pelé celebrates after scoring the opening goal for Brazil. It was the last international game in which he played.*

On top of the world

The remainder of the second half was a one-sided display of outstanding soccer, with the Brazilians dominating the game and scoring twice more. The final goal was pure genius. With five minutes to go, a wonderful series of passes by the Brazilian forwards resulted in Pelé rolling the ball out to his right. Timing his run to perfection, Carlos Alberto connected with the ball the first time, thundering a shot into the Italian net. It was a fitting climax to the game. Satellite broadcasting, used for the first time during this World Cup, allowed millions of people around the world to watch one of the greatest of all international games.

▲ *Carlos Alberto seals Brazil's 4–1 victory with a stunning drive beyond the reach of Italian goalkeeper Albertosi.*

Great Games 2

Congo 3, Mali 2. African Nations Cup final, 1972

Soccer in Africa is not a recent phenomenon. Although the World Cup and Olympics exploits of teams such as Nigeria and Cameroon during the 1990s are well known, African soccer has a long history. The African Nations Cup, which started in 1957 and is the equivalent of the European Championships, has produced some classic games. One of the greatest is the 1972 final, held in Cameroon, between two very strong sides—Congo and Mali.

▲ François M'Pelé, who scored for Congo in the final, played for the French side Paris St. Germain during the 1970s.

▲ A Mali defender wins a challenge for the ball with M'Pelé. As runners up this remains Mali's highest achievement to date in the African Nations Cup.

No let up

Mali dominated the first half. Only a series of acrobatic saves from Congo goalkeeper Masima kept Mali at bay, although they managed to take the lead right at the end of the first half. Congo surged forward in the second half with M'Bono scoring two goals in two minutes. M'Pelé added a third, and the game looked over until Mali scored their second with 15 minutes to go. Despite a grandstand finish with both sides playing wonderfully fluid soccer, the score remained 3–2 to Congo.

West Germany 2, Holland 1. World Cup final, 1974

Although billed as a battle between Dutch maestro Johan Cruyff and brilliant German tactician Franz Beckenbauer, the game was in fact a fascinating and highly-skilled encounter between two teams at their peak. The game began explosively, with Cruyff brought down in the German penalty area soon after kickoff. The penalty was converted by Johan Neeskens. The Dutch continued to dominate the game with elegant and fluid movement focused around Cruyff, Neeskens, and Johnny Rep.

▲ With under two minutes on the clock, Johan Cruyff (on the ground, right) is brought down by Uli Hoeness. The resulting penalty, scored by Johan Neeskens, is the fastest goal in a World Cup final.

Enter "Der Bomber"

Superb defending and outstanding goalkeeping from Sepp Maier prevented Holland from netting the vital second goal. The Germans made the Dutch pay for their lack of killer instinct by equalizing with a penalty. Then in the 43rd minute the German striker Gerd Müller, nicknamed "Der Bomber," scored a second goal for his side with a glorious individual effort.

Dutch pressure

The Dutch pressed furiously for an equalizer, but Sepp Maier, the goalkeeper of the tournament, continued to thwart them. As more space opened up West Germany also had their chances—with Müller particularly unlucky when he had a goal disallowed for offside, although replays confirmed he was onside.

▶ Despite giving away a penalty, West Germany and Bayern Munich forward Uli Hoeness, just 22 years old at the time, played an important part in the German victory.

Revenge

The 2–1 final scoreline meant that West Germany were crowned world champions. Unfortunately for the Dutch fans and players, they had to wait 14 years for victory over the Germans. Their Euro '88 side, boasting legendary players such as Ruud Gullit and Marco Van Basten, finally put to rest painful memories of their 1974 World Cup loss.

◄ *The Dutch defense crumbles as Gerd Müller displays dazzling footwork before firing the ball home with his right foot.*

► *French midfielder Alain Giresse (right) formed a magnificent partnership with Jean Tigana, Luis Fernandez, and Michel Platini throughout the tournament.*

France 3, Portugal 2. European Championships, 1984

This enthralling semifinal was the game that put the European Championships on the map. The French midfield of Jean Tigana, Alain Giresse, and Michel Platini controlled much of the game with a wonderful display of passing and movement. At halftime the much-favored French team were 1–0 up thanks to Domergue. During the second half the French couldn't consolidate their lead. Attack after attack was repelled with the Portuguese goalkeeper Manuel Bento making some great saves. Then in the 73rd minute Rui Jordao equalized for Portugal, shocking the 55,000 crowd packed into Marseille's Velodrome stadium.

► *Michel Platini makes one of his trademark runs through the Portuguese defense. Platini's haul of nine goals in the tournament remains a European Championships record.*

▲ *French defender Maxime Bossis falls to the ground. The French victory in the finals helped ease memories of Bossis' missed penalty, which had lost France their World Cup semifinal against West Germany two years earlier.*

At the last minute

Extra time came and the game opened up further with wave after wave of attacks by both sides. Portugal took the lead with striker Jordao scoring again, but France pulled back with a goal from Domergue. Another dreaded penalty shootout looked inevitable. Then in the very last minute of extra time Jean Tigana played a cross into the penalty area. It was met by Platini who struck it sweetly into the back of the net, securing victory seconds before the final whistle. Four days later, France beat Spain in the final 2–0 to win their first-ever international competition. Platini was made player of the tournament.

Great Games 3

Argentina 2, Nigeria 3. Olympic final, 1996

Inspired attacking from both sides made for a thrilling match, full of goalmouth incidents. The game began badly for Nigeria. With less than two minutes on the clock, poor defending allowed Argentina's Claudio Lopez plenty of space to head home the opening goal. But Nigeria wasn't a team to give up easily. In a dramatic semifinal against Brazil they had come from behind to beat the South Americans 4–3, and now in the final they fought back with great determination and flair.

▲ Gifted Argentinian forward Ariel Ortega turns to control a loose ball during his side's shock 3–2 defeat by Nigeria.

▲ Nigerian midfielder Jay-Jay Okocha challenges the Argentinian player Bassedas. Okocha has played in Nigeria, France, Turkey, and Germany.

On the attack

Celestine Babayaro's equalizing header was as impressive as his celebration—a spectacular double somersault. However, the Argentinians struck back with a penalty taken by Hernan Crespo. With 15 minutes to go, Amokachi latched on to the ball and flicked it over the Argentinian goalkeeper. The final appeared to be heading for extra time when Nigeria was awarded a free kick wide out on the left.

Going for gold

The Argentinian defense tried to catch Nigeria offside, but Emmanuel Amunike beat the trap and volleyed home the winning goal in the 89th minute. The final whistle was met with wild celebrations. Nigeria had become the first African nation to win a major international cup competition.

◀ Celestine Babayaro gets the ball away from Argentinian defender Javier Zanetti. Babayaro played a major role in Nigeria's victory.

China 5, Norway 0. Women's World Cup semifinal, 1999

Along with the eventual winners—the U.S.—Norway and China were far and away the most-favored sides in the 1999 World Cup finals. This semifinal clash was a contrast in styles between the determined and defensively strong Norwegian team and a Chinese side that relied on speed and close-range passing. China ran riot. The blistering speed and superb movement of their team proved far too much for a tough Norwegian side, who started the game as favorites in many commentators' eyes. China made a fairy tale start to the game when striker Sun Wen scored in the third minute.

◀ Ying Liu, one of China's talented strikers, shows she's equally adept at defending as she makes a robust sliding challenge on the veteran Norwegian captain Linda Medalen.

Unstoppable

Liu Ailing doubled the lead with a blistering right-footed volley 11 minutes later. Ailing, superb with either foot, scored her second goal, a left-footed volley, after a corner wasn't properly cleared by the Norwegian defense. Norway threatened the Chinese goal on a number of occasions in the second half but one of the best goalkeepers in the women's game, Gao Hong, pulled off three spectacular saves to foil them. China retaliated with a fourth goal in the 63rd minute from yet another volley, this time by defender Fan Yunjie. Sun Wen's 72nd-minute penalty made her joint top scorer for the tournament, along with the Brazilian Sissi, and completed the 5-0 victory, equaling Norway's worst ever defeat.

▲ The Chinese players celebrate another goal in their devastating 5–0 victory over Norway.

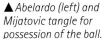

▲ Abelardo (left) and Mijatovic tangle for possession of the ball.

▼ Slobodan Komljenovic (right) celebrates a 2-1 lead six minutes into the second half with goalscorer Dejan Govedarica.

▲ Alfonso (left) tackles Yugoslavian defender Sinisa Mihalovic.

Incredible strikes

Early in the second half Yugoslavia took the lead again. Dejan Govedarica, a halftime substitute for Vladimir Jugovic, powered a superb strike from the edge of the penalty area. A minute later Pedro Munitis eclipsed Govedarica's goal, firing in a wonderful curling shot. With the game poised at 2-2, it appeared the turning point had come in the 63rd minute when Jokanovic was sent off the field. Spain now had the advantage.

Last-minute thriller

In an earlier group match against Slovenia, Yugoslavia had made an incredible comeback from being down 3-0, again with only ten men. True to form, against the Spanish side, Yugoslavia scored next when a goalmouth scramble saw Komljenovic slam the ball home. Yugoslavia fought desperately hard to protect their lead and appeared to have secured a wonderful victory. The game was into injury time and the Spanish looked to be heading home, before a disputed penalty, converted by Mendieta, appeared to have created the fairest of results—a 3-3 draw. But this epic game had yet more drama when in the dying seconds Alfonso volleyed home the winner for Spain. The Yugoslavs were downcast, but it turned out that both they and Spain advanced to the next stage.

Spain 4, Yugoslavia 3. Euro 2000

This pulsating contest proved the undoubted highlight of Euro 2000 and a contender for the best-ever European Championships game. It started as an important group encounter with neither side certain of qualifying for the next stage. Spain looked to be the sharper side at first, carving out a number of attacking chances, but were hit by a classic counterattack that saw Savo Milosevic head the first goal in for Yugoslavia. Spain pressed forward in numbers, and Raul's darting run let Alfonso equalize.

"The difference between heaven and hell is one minute."

Josep Guardiola after the Spain vs. Yugoslavia match.

▲ Alfonso scores the winning goal for Spain with a well-hit volley in the dying moments of a thrilling game.

The Great Players I

Alfredo Di Stefano [born 1926, Buenos Aires, Argentina]
Di Stefano (right) joined his father's old team, River Plate, as a teenager and soon became part of an extremely successful forward line known as "La Maquina"—The Machine. In 1953 he moved to the legendary Spanish team Real Madrid, which dominated European soccer in the 1950s and early 1960s. A center-forward, Di Stefano was also brilliant at defending, tackling, creating chances for other players, as well as scoring many superbly taken goals himself. Real Madrid player and coach Miguel Munoz summed up his contribution to the game—"The greatness of Di Stefano was that with him in your side you had two players in every position."

Lev Yashin [born 1929, Moscow, former Soviet Union. Died 1990]
Just slightly better than Gordon Banks, Lev Yashin (left) is still regarded as soccer's greatest goalkeeper. Nicknamed the "Black Panther" for his incredible agility and awesome saves, he had an almost supernatural anticipation of where the ball would next appear. During his 20-year career at Moscow Dynamo (where he had originally started out as the team's hockey goaltender) the team won the Supreme League title six times and the Soviet Cup twice. He also won 78 caps for the Soviet Union. Records are sketchy, but Yashin is believed to have saved more than 150 penalties in his illustrious career. In 1968 he was awarded the Order of Lenin, at that time the Soviet Union's highest honor.

Pelé [Edson Arantes do Nascimento, born 1940, Tres Coracoes, Brazil]
If any player deserved a ten out of ten over a long career, it has to be the man who always wore that number for his main team, Santos, and for his national team, Brazil. Pelé had it all—speed, strength, creativity, breathtaking vision, and skills to match it all. At the age of 17 he became an instant celebrity, scoring six goals for Brazil's 1958 World-Cup-winning team. It was the first of three World Cups that Pelé helped to win for his country. The last, in 1970, featured some of his finest moments—outrageous fakes, flicks, passes, and shots few others would have attempted. Pelé played 93 internationals for Brazil, with a remarkable tally of 77 goals. When Pelé retired from Santos in 1974 after 18 years, the team removed the number ten shirt from their team as a tribute. He later came out of retirement to help promote professional soccer in the United States, playing for the New York Cosmos before retiring for good in 1977. In 1994 Pelé was appointed Brazil's Minister of Sport.

Eusebio da Silva Ferreira (born 1942, Lourenço Marques, Mozambique)

Eusebio played his early soccer in Mozambique, at that time a Portuguese colony. Although groomed to play for the famous Portuguese team Sporting Lisbon, he was snapped up by their great rival Benfica. He scored more than 300 goals in his 15-year career at Benfica, and the team won major honors in all but two of those years. Blessed with an explosive right foot, there was a good deal more to the "Black Pearl's" game than powerful shooting. Wonderfully skilled in all areas of attacking play, he was also admired for his sportsmanship even in the tensest encounters. In 1965 he was voted European Footballer (soccer player) of the Year. The following year Eusebio was the leading scorer in the World Cup with nine goals to his credit.

Franz Beckenbauer (born 1945, Munich, Germany)

An outstanding defender, Beckenbauer revolutionized the position of sweeper. Originally the sweeper was an ultradefensive position, but he made it into an exciting way of turning defense into attack. In game after game for Bayern Munich and his national side, West Germany, the player nicknamed "Kaiser Franz" had a game-winning impact, creating hundreds of scoring opportunities for his teammates. He didn't hold back from making shots on goal himself and put away 44 goals for Bayern. Beckenbauer was capped 103 times for West Germany, and under his captaincy the team triumphed in the 1974 World Cup. He was appointed manager of the national team in 1984 and steered them to victory over Argentina in the 1990 World Cup final. In 1977 he was converted to midfielder when he came to the U.S. to join the Cosmos for $2.8 million over 4 years.

George Best (born 1946, Belfast, Northern Ireland)

One of the most extravagantly gifted players to grace the game, George Best shared with Pelé attacking vision, brilliant goal scoring skills, and an eye for the unexpected or outrageous. Superb with both feet and a fearless tackler, Best was a supreme dribbler of the ball. He was also a deadly finisher with 137 goals for England's Manchester United, the team he joined as a teenager. He was instrumental in United's European Cup victory over Benfica in 1968. His national side, Northern Ireland, never made it to the World Cup finals. Although he made a number of comebacks in both Britain and North America, the player dubbed "the fifth Beatle" was never the same after he sensationally quit Manchester United in 1973. The pressure of fame and being Britain's first soccer playing superstar had sadly taken its toll.

The Great Players 2

Johan Cruyff [born 1947, Amsterdam, Holland]
One of the greatest of European players, Cruyff *(left)* was a key player in the Dutch revolution known as "total football." This involved players changing positions with breathtaking speed and effectiveness. Cruyff, three times European Footballer of the Year, displayed sublime ball skills and, although a center-forward, he was equally effective in midfield or on the wings. He enjoyed huge success at the Dutch team Ajax, where he was instrumental in the team winning three European Cups. In 1973 he moved to Barcelona where he helped the Spanish team win a number of league and cup titles. Cruyff returned to Ajax and then Barcelona as manager, taking both teams to victory in European cup competitions.

Michel Platini [born 1955, Joeuf, France]
One of the most effective midfielders the game has ever seen, Platini *(below)* captained the French side to the 1982 World Cup semifinals and to victory in the 1984 European Championships. Supremely creative, Platini was dazzling in attack or hovering around the midfield, hitting deadly accurate 130 foot passes. Playing for the great Italian side Juventus, he was Serie A's leading scorer and was crowned European Footballer of the Year in 1983, 1984, and 1985. In 1992, five years after retiring, he became manager of the French national side and later headed France's successful bid to host the World Cup in 1998.

Diego Maradona [born 1960, Buenos Aires, Argentina]
A superb goalscorer with beautiful technical skills, Maradona was *the* player of the 1980s. Highlights of his career include winning two Italian league titles with Napoli and his performance in the 1986 World Cup, when he transformed a solid Argentinian side into the world's best. During the tournament Maradona provided a serious contender for the greatest goal ever—against England during the quarterfinals (earlier in the same game he infamously used his hand to score a goal). Despite leading Argentina to the 1990 World Cup finals, where they finished as runners-up after losing 1–0 to West Germany, Maradona's later years were sadly dogged by failed drug tests and numerous disappointing comebacks.

George Weah (born 1966, Monrovia, Liberia)
Born in the small African nation of Liberia, Weah played for
four teams in Africa before Arsène Wenger, then the manager
of Monaco, brought the 22-year-old forward to Europe in 1988.
Weah proved instrumental in Monaco's 1991 French League
championship win. He transferred to Paris SG, and helped them
win the league title in 1994, and then he moved to the celebrated
Italian team Milan. Both powerful and graceful, Weah was also
a devastating finisher. In 1995 he won a unique triple feat—
African Player of the Year, European Footballer of the Year,
and FIFA Player of the Year. He has invested much of
his earnings into helping charities and developing
the game back in Liberia.

Mariel Margaret "Mia" Hamm
(born 1972, Alabama, U.S.)
The most famous player in women's
soccer, Hamm was the youngest-
ever American international when
she debuted in 1987, at the
age of 15. She dominated
the 1990s as the game's
most inspirational and
devastating attacker, with
more than 100 goals to her
credit, helping the U.S. win
both Olympic and World Cup
titles. She was voted U.S. Soccer's
Female Athlete of the Year an unprecedented five
years running from 1994 to 1998. Usually playing
as a forward, Hamm took over in goal during the
1995 Women's World Cup, after the regular
goalkeeper, Briana Scurry, was sent off.

Zinedine Zidane (born 1972, Marseilles, France)
The son of Algerian immigrants, Zidane has captivated spectators around
the world with his brilliant performances. He helped France win the 1998 World
Cup (including two goals scored in the final against Brazil) and the 2000 European
Championships. Blessed with a delicate touch and quick acceleration, "Zizou," as he
is known to his fans, is at his best when making space for himself in a crowded
midfield or on the edge of the opposition's penalty area. He made his name playing
for the French team Bordeaux, where he won France's Player of the Year award
in 1996, before moving to the Italian team, Juventus. Voted World Footballer of
the Year three times, Zidane is one of the most highly sought-after players in
the game. In July 2001 he went from Juventus to Real Madrid for a
world-record fee of $72 million.

Soccer History

Many fans from other countries are not aware that the United States boasts as long a soccer history as theirs—in some cases longer. From its origins in the 1600s, it has flourished into one of the nation's fastest-growing team sports and now features the first-ever professional league for women.

Early history

Soccer, or a very basic form of the game we know today, was brought over to the U.S. by British settlers in the 1600s. The early academic colleges of the northeastern United States occasionally played "soccer." For example, from 1827 onward classes at Harvard played a once-a-year contest that was closer to a crowd brawl than a real sport, so much so that the event became known as "Bloody Monday." As the game developed into a codified sport in Britain it started to be organized and played in the United States as well. The first team with a roster of players in the U.S. is believed to be the Oneida team. Based in Boston and playing from 1862 onward, it is considered to be the first organized soccer team outside of Great Britain.

"Football" was the name given to both the sports we know today as soccer and rugby. The kicking-only game became known as "association football," which was abbreviated as "assoc.," which led to "soccer"—the name that stayed in the U.S. Soccer was played in a number of colleges, but in the 1870s a split occured between soccer, football, and rugby. Soccer declined as a sport of privileged Americans. New immigrants to the U.S. kept the soccer flame alight, and by 1884 a group of ex-British soccer lovers formed the American Football Association. The AFA ran a cup competition, the American Cup, from 1885 to 1898 and also organized the first national side, which in 1885-86 played two games against Canada—the first a 1–0 defeat, the second, a 3–2 win.

In 1894 the first attempt was made to establish a completely professional soccer league. It came from a group of baseball team owners, looking for a way to fill their stadiums outside of the baseball season. The league didn't make it through an entire season. However, other leagues sprung up, including the National Association Football (soccer) League and the Southern New England Football (soccer) League.

In 1921 the American Soccer League was founded. The wealthier teams in other leagues, such as Bethlehem Steel and Fall River, left their own leagues that were struggling to attract big enough crowds, and joined the ASL. Backed by big business, the ASL was fully professional and started on a strong foot. Crowds often reached five figures, and in 1925 two additional teams the New Bedford Whalers and the Boston Wonder Workers joined. The Fall River Marksmen, founded by businessman Sam Mark, became one of the most dominant teams in U.S. soccer history. They won five championships in eight years and three cup competitions. Sam Mark aided this achievement by signing top players from Europe, particularly the U.K., such as Tec White, Charlie McGill, and Harold Brittan.

Although soccer was booming, disputes arose between the league, teams, and other authorities. By the time these were resolved the Wall Street crash had occurred and with it the onset of the Great Depression. The ASL never regained the heights it reached in the mid-1920s and disbanded in 1933. The second American Soccer League (ASL2) was started in 1933 with more modest aims and a completely new roster of teams. Based in New York, New Jersey, and Philadelphia, the league kept players at a semiprofessional level. The Kearny Scots was the first dominant team in the ASL2, winning five league titles in a row between 1937 and 1941.

A truly professional soccer league

In the boom years of the 1950s onward, sports participation and spectating rose like never before. Baseball, basketball, and football went through a renaissance. The rise of television coverage and the related advertising revenues was part of the success. Increased recreational time and rising standards of living were other reasons. The ASL2 was still in existence, along with many amateur and some semiprofessional teams, but a brand-new professional league became a possibility. It seemed natural to capitalize on the great interest shown in soccer by some communities in the United States and to reflect the massive worldwide interest in "the beautiful game." Yet almost from the beginning the professional league concept was plagued with problems and dogged by controversy.

Two competing organizations were formed in the 1960s, both with the aim of establishing soccer on a similar level to the big three: baseball, basketball, and football. The United Soccer Association was sanctioned by FIFA, but the National Professional Soccer League was not, and the two argued over many things, including player transfers. Neither attracted the necessary large TV audiences, and in 1968 the two leagues merged to form the North American Soccer League (NASL).

Of the first 17 teams in the NASL, only five were in business by the third season. All looked bleak. But the teams managed to attract enough local interest to keep going, and slowly additional teams joined. The most notable of these new teams was the New York Cosmos, who rocked the entire soccer world with one new signing. Pelé, the world's greatest player, had retired in 1974, but came out of retirement in 1975 to perform in the NASL.

Pelé's arrival saw attendances in the NASL rocket, media attention go into overdrive, and many more of the world's great players, such as Dutch maestro Johan Cruyff, West German captain Franz Beckenbauer, and the gifted Irishman George Best, arrived to play in the U.S.

Sadly, lacking a national TV deal and with rising player costs, some teams struggled to compete and stay in the NASL, which led to the league's demise in 1984. But interest in soccer was now at an all-time high in the U.S., particularly as a participation sport that was easy to play, required little equipment, and caused relatively few injuries.

U.S. national teams

There had been friendly games before, but the U.S. men's national team was only recognized by FIFA in 1916. The first officially sanctioned national team drew 1–1 with Norway and beat Sweden 3–2. Because of World War I, the U.S. national team did not play again until the 1924 Olympics. The team competed in the 1928 Olympics as well and were one of the handful of nations to attend the first ever World Cup, held in Uruguay in 1930. The U.S. team beat Paraguay 3–0 and followed up with the exact same score against Belgium to reach the semifinals where they lost to Argentina. They competed regularly in World Cup qualifiers and finals, and in 1950 created one of the World Cup's greatest shocks, defeating England 1–0. Joe Gaetjens scored the winning goal.

The U.S. men's team made it to the 1990 World Cup finals and covered themselves in glory the following year by winning the CONCACAF Championship. By now, leading U.S. players were plying their trade at teams in Europe, and in 1994 the U.S. hosted the World Cup for the first time. Drawing a record 3.6 million spectators, averaging 67,000 per game, the World Cup was a major success.

The finals featured plenty of attractive soccer, exciting games and shocks, such as the U.S. beating favored Colombia in the first stage before falling narrowly to the mighty Brazil in the second stage. The U.S. team impressed—players such as Tab Ramos, Cobi Jones, Claudio Reyna, and Alexi Lalas became household names. They followed up their World Cup exploits in the 1995 Copa America, reaching the semifinals before losing to Argentina.

The U.S. men's team reached the 2002 World Cup held in Japan and South Korea. Given little chance of making it beyond the group stages, the U.S. side beat Mexico and tied with eventual surprise semifinalists South Korea to make it to the quarterfinal match with Germany. A close game, with the U.S. taking more chances, Germany narrowly won 1–0. Partly as a result of their World Cup performance, the U.S. team entered FIFA's top-ten world rankings for the first time in 2002.

The women's national team, only formed in 1985, features stars such as Michelle Akers, Tiffany Melbricht, and the incomparable Mia Hamm and is one of the top teams in women's soccer. Winners of many tournaments, including the 1991 and 1999 World Cups, the national team has been credited with raising interest and bringing in crowds not just for women's games in the U.S., but for men's games as well. Soccer has been the fastest-growing team sport for women in North America for a number of years now.

21st-century professional leagues

Buoyed by the excellence of U.S. women's soccer and by the massive success of the 1994 World Cup, the MLS was launched in 1995. The question was, could soccer work at a professional level in the U.S.? It had been over ten years since a professional soccer league existed in the U.S., so did it stand a chance against the large array of other team sports present in the United States? Would it hook fans in large enough numbers, and would the press, radio, and, most importantly, the television companies give it the necessary coverage and publicity for it to flourish? The answers for the first season, starting in 1996, were positive. Good public relations and the positive memories of World Cup 1994 saw just over three million spectators pay to see the games in the flesh, while many more watched games or followed the news and results on television. Starting with ten teams, the 1998–99 season saw the MLS grow to twelve as teams from Miami and Chicago joined.

Entering the fray in 2001 was the first fully professional league for women soccer players to be found anywhere on the planet—the WUSA. Around $40 million was raised by a number of sponsors and board members, and the WUSA was able to import the cream of international stars from China, Brazil, Norway, and Germany. Unfortunately the WUSA suspended its operations in September 2003, due to debts related to difficulties in attracting corporate sponsors. However, the profile of women's soccer was raised earlier in 2003 when FIFA approved the U.S.'s bid to stage the 2003 FIFA Women's World Cup. This last-minute arrangement occurred after the outbreak of the SARS virus in Asia—China was no longer able to host the world championship as was originally planned.

Stats and Facts

Statistics and records are a vital part of the game for fans, commentators, and even managers, and these days you can buy whole books dedicated to all kinds of facts and figures. Below is a selection of some of the most important and fascinating soccer stats available.

National Association Football (soccer) League (NAFL) winners

1895 Bayonne Centerville
1898 Paterson True Blues
1907 West Hudson
1908 Paterson Rangers
1909 Clark A. A.
1910 West Hudson
1911 Jersey A. C.
1912 West Hudson
1913 West Hudson
1914 Brooklyn F. C.
1915 West Hudson
1916 Alley Boys
1917 Jersey A. C.
1918 Paterson F. C.
1919 Bethlehem Steel
1920 Bethlehem Steel
1921 Bethlehem Steel

American Soccer League I (ASL1) champions

1922 Philadelphia FC
1923 J. & P. Coats
1924 Fall River Marksmen
1925 Fall River Marksmen
1926 Fall River Marksmen
1927 Bethlehem Steel
1928 Boston Wonder Workers
1929 Fall River Marksmen
1929 Fall River Marksmen
1930 Fall River Marksmen
1930 Fall River Marksmen

1931 New York Giants
1932 New Bedford Whalers
1933 Fall River FC

American Soccer League II (ASL2) champions

1934 Kearney Irish-Americans
1935 German-Americans
1936 New York Americans
1937 Scots-Americans
1938 Scots-Americans
1939 Newark Scots
1940 Newark Scots
1941 Newark Scots
1942 Philadelphia Americans
1943 Brooklyn Hispano
1944 Philadelphia Americans
1945 Brookhattan
1946 Baltimore Americans
1947 Philadelphia Americans
1948 Philadelphia Americans
1949 Philadelphia Nationals
1950 Philadelphia Nationals
1951 Philadelphia Nationals
1952 Philadelphia Americans
1953 Philadelphia Nationals
1954 New York Americans
1955 Uhrik Truckers (Philadelphia)
1956 Uhrik Truckers (Philadelphia)
1957 New York Hakoah
1958 New York Hakoah
1959 New York Hakoah
1960 Colombo

1961 Ukrainian Nationals (Philadelphia)
1962 Ukrainian Nationals (Philadelphia)
1963 Ukrainian Nationals (Philadelphia)
1964 Ukrainian Nationals (Philadelphia)
1965 Hartford Football Club
1966 Roma Soccer Club
1967 Baltimore St. Gerards
1968 Ukrainian Nationals (Philadelphia)
1968 Washington Darts
1969 Washington Darts
1970 Ukrainian Nationals (Philadelphia)
1971 New York Greeks
1972 Cincinnati Comets
1973 New York Apollo
1974 Rhode Island Oceaneers
1975 New York Apollo
1976 Los Angeles Skyhawks
1977 New Jersey Americans
1978 New York Apollo
1979 Sacramento Gold
1980 Pennsylvania Stoners
1981 Carolina Lightnin'
1982 Detroit Express
1983 Jacksonville Tea Men

North American Soccer League (NASL) winners

1967 Los Angeles Wolves
1967 Oakland Clippers
1968 Atlanta Chiefs
1969 Kansas City Spurs
1970 Rochester Lancers
1971 Dallas Tornado
1972 New York Cosmos
1973 Philadelphia Atoms
1974 Los Angeles Aztecs
1975 Tampa Bay Rowdies
1976 Toronto Metros-Croatia
1977 New York Cosmos
1978 New York Cosmos
1979 Vancouver Whitecaps
1980 New York Cosmos
1981 Chicago Sting
1982 New York Cosmos

1983 Tulsa Roughnecks
1984 Chicago Sting

National Professional Soccer League winners

1992 Detroit Rockers
1993 Kansas City Attack
1994 Cleveland Crunch
1995 St. Louis Ambush
1996 Cleveland Crunch
1997 Kansas City Attack
1998 Milwaukee Wave
1999 Cleveland Crunch
2000 Milwaukee Wave
2001 Milwaukee Wave

Major League Soccer (MLS) winners

1998 Chicago Fire
1999 D. C. United
2000 Kansas City Wizards
2001 San Jose Earthquakes
2002 Los Angeles Galaxy
2003 Chicago Fire

U.S. Open Cup Championship games

Listed are the results since World War II. In some seasons the competition was played over two games. The score of the second game is in parentheses.

1945 New York Brookhattan 4 (2), Cleveland Americans 1 (1)
1946 Chicago Vikings 1 (2), Fall River Ponta Delgada 1 (1)
1947 Fall River Ponta Delgada 1 (1), Chicago Sparta A & BA 1 (2)
1948 St. Louis Simpkins-Ford 3, New York Brookhattan 2
1949 Pittsburgh Morgan SC 0, Philadelphia Nationals 1
1950 St. Louis Simpkins-Ford 2 (1), Fall River Ponta Delgada 0 (1)
1951 New York German-Hungarian 2 (6), Pittsburgh

Heidelberg 4 (2)

1952 Pittsburgh Hamarville 3 (4), Philadelphia Nationals 4 (1)

1953 Chicago Falcons 2 (1), Pittsburgh Hamarville 0 (1)

1954 New York Americans 1 (2), St. Louis Kutis 0 (0)

1955 S. C. Eintracht 2, Los Angeles Danish Americans 0

1956 Pittsburgh Hamarville 0 (3), Chicago Schwaben 1 (1)

1957 St. Louis Kutis 3 (3), New York Hakoah 0 (1)

1958 Los Angeles Kickers 2, Baltimore Pompei 1

1959 San Pedro McIlvane Canvasbacks 4, Fall River SC 3

1960 Philadelphia Ukrainian Nationals 5, Los Angeles Kickers 3

1961 Philadelphia Ukrainian Nationals 2 (5), Los Angeles Scots 2 (2)

1962 New York Hungarians 3, San Francisco Scots 2

1963 Philadelphia Ukrainian Nationals 1, Los Angeles Armenian 0

1964 Los Angeles Kickers 2 (2), Philadelphia Ukrainian Nationals 2 (0)

1965 New York Ukrainians 1 (3), Chicago Hansa 1 (0)

1966 Philadelphia Ukrainian Nationals 1 (3), Orange County 0 (0)

1967 New York Greek-American 4, Orange County 2

1968 New York Greek-American 1 (1), Chicago Olympic 1 (0)

1969 New York Greek-American 1, Montabello Armenians 0

1970 S. C. Elizabeth 2, Los Angeles Croatia 1

1971 New York Hota 6, San Pedro Yugoslavs 4

1972 S. C. Elizabeth 1,

San Pedro Yugoslavs 0

1973 Los Angeles Maccabee 5, Cleveland Inter 3

1974 New York Greek-American 2, Chicago Croatia 0

1975 LA Maccabee 1, New York Inter-Giuliana 0

1976 San Francisco A. C. 1, New York Inter-Giuliana 0

1977 Los Angeles Maccabee 5, Philadelphia United German-Hungarian 1

1978 Los Angeles Maccabee 2, Bridgeport Vasco de Gama 0

1979 Brooklyn Dodgers 2, Chicago Croatian 1

1980 New York Pancyprian Freedoms 3, Los Angeles Maccabee 2

1981 Los Angeles Maccabee 5, Brooklyn Dodgers 1

1982 New York Pancyprian Freedoms 4, Los Angeles Maccabee 3

1983 New York Pancyprian Freedoms 4, St. Louis Kutis 3

1984 New York A. O. Krete 4, Chicago Croatian 2

1985 San Francisco Greek-American A. C. 2, St. Louis Kutis 1

1986 St. Louis Kutis 1, San Pedro Yugoslavs 0

1987 Washington Club Espana 1, Seattle Eagles 0

1988 St. Louis Busch Seniors 1, San Francisco Greek-American 0

1989 St. Petersburg Kickers 2, New York Greek-American/Atlas 1

1990 Chicago A.A.C. Eagles 2, Brooklyn Italians 1

1991 Brooklyn Italians 1, Richardson Rockets 0

1992 San Jose Oaks 2, Bridgeport Vasco de Gama 1

1993 San Francisco CD Mexico 5, Philadelphia United German-

Hungarians 0

1994 San Francisco Greek-American 3, Milwaukee Bavarian Leinenkugel 0

1995 Richmond Kickers 1, El Paso Patriots 1 (pens 4-2)

1996 Washington D. C. United 3, Rochester Rhinos (A-League) 0

1997 Dallas Burn 0, Washington D.C. United 0, (penalties 5-3)

1998 Chicago Fire 2, Columbus Crew 1

1999 Rochester Ragin' Rhinos 2, Colorado Rapids 0

2000 Chicago Fire 2, Miami Fusion 1

2001 Los Angeles Galaxy 2, New England Revolution 1

2002 Columbus Crew 1, Los Angeles Galaxy 0

2003 Chicago Fire 1, NY/NJ MetroStars 0

U.S. Women's Open Cup

1998 Los Angeles Ajax 5, Dallas Lightning 0

1999 San Diego Auto Trader 14, Patrick Real Wyckoff 0

2000 Los Angeles Ajax 2, Detroit Rocker Hawks 1

2001 Detroit Rocker Hawks 1, Southern California Blues 0

2002 Southern California Blues 5, Peninsula (New Jersey) Aztecs 0

Women's Premier Soccer League winners

2000 San Diego WFC
2001 Ajax Southern California
2002 California Storm
2003 Utah Spiders

Top league goalscorers (1950-2000)

1950 Joe Gaetjens 18
1951 Nick Kropfelder 17

1952 Dick Roberts 19
1953 Pito Villanon 12
1954 John Calder 19
1955 Jack Ferris 20
1956 Gene Grabowski 19
1957 George Brown 13
1958 Lloyd Monsen 22
1959 Pasquale Pepe 17
1960 Miguel Noha 22
1961 Herman Niss 17
1962 Pete Millar 18
1963 Ismael Fereyra 14
1964 Walter Czychowich 15
1965 Herculiano Riguerdo 7
1966 Walter Czychowich 27
1967 Yanko Daucik 20
1968 John Kowalik, Cirilo Fernandez 30
1969 Kaiser Motaug 16
1970 Kirk Apostolidis 16
1971 Carlos Metidieri 19
1972 Randy Horton 9
1973 Warren Archibald, Ilja Mitic 12
1974 Paul Child 15
1975 Steve David 23
1976 Derek Smethurst 20
1977 Steve David 26
1978 Giorgio Chinaglia 34
1979 Giorgio Chinaglia 26
1980 Giorgio Chinaglia 32
1981 Giorgio Chinaglia 29
1982 Ricardo Alonso 21
1983 Roberto Cabanas 25
1984 Steven Zyngul 20
1985 Josue Partillo 8
1986 B. Goulet 9
1987 J. Mihaljevic 7
1988 Jorge Acosta 14
1989 Ricardo Alonso, Mirko Castilo 10
1990 Chance Fry 17
1991 Jean Harbour 17
1992 Jean Harbour 13
1993 Paulinho 15
1994 Paul Wright 12
1995 Peter Hattrup 11
1996 Roy Lassiter 27
1997 Jaime Moreno 16
1998 Stern John 26
1999 Stern John, Roy Lassiter, Jason Kreis 18
2000 Mamadou Diallo 26

Glossary

Advantage rule   A rule that allows the referee to let play continue after a foul if it is to the advantage of the team that has been fouled against.

Anchor   A midfielder positioned just in front of and given the job of protecting the defense. An anchor player can help allow other midfielders push farther forward.

Assistant referees   Formerly known as linesmen, these officials assist the referee with his decision-making during the game.

Bicycle kick   An overhead volley, usually a shot on goal.

Blind side   A position on the opposite side of a defender from the ball.

Box   The penalty area.

Cap   Recognition given to a player for each international appearance made for his country.

Caution   Another word for a yellow card.

Chip   A ball lofted into the air, either as a pass from a player to a teammate or as a shot. Also known as a lob.

Clearance   Kicking or heading the ball out of defense.

Counterattack   A quick attack by a defending team after it regains possession of the ball.

Cross   Sending the ball from the side of the field toward the opposition's penalty area.

Direct free kick   A kick awarded to a team because of a major foul committed by an opponent. A goal may be scored directly from the kick.

Direct play   A method of attacking, using long passes from defense that tend to bypass the midfield and go straight to the forwards.

Dribbling   Moving the ball under close control with short kicks or taps.

Drop ball   A way of restarting play involving the referee releasing the ball and a player from each team competing for the ball once it has touched the ground.

Feinting   Using fake moves with the head, shoulders, and legs to deceive an opponent and put him off balance.

Formation   The way a team lines up on the field in terms of where the defenders, midfielders, and forwards are positioned.

Hand ball   The illegal use of the hand or arm by a player.

Indirect free kick   A kick awarded to a team because of a minor foul or offense committed by an opponent. A goal cannot be scored directly from the kick, but instead has to be played to a teammate first.

Laws of the game   The 17 rules of soccer as established and updated by FIFA.

Lay-off   A short pass made by a forward to a teammate who is to the side of or behind him.

Libero   Another term for a sweeper.

Marking   Guarding a player to prevent him from advancing the ball toward the net, making an easy pass, or receiving the ball from a teammate.

Narrowing the angle   A goalkeeping technique involving the goalie moving out toward the on-ball attacker to narrow the amount of goal the attacker can aim a shot at.

Obstruction   When a defensive player, instead of attempting to win the ball, uses his body to prevent an opponent from playing it.

Overlap   To run outside and beyond a teammate down the sides of the field in order to create space and a possible passing opportunity.

Professional foul   A foul committed intentionally by a player, stopping an opposition attacker from a clear run on goal.

Set piece   A planned play or move that a team uses when a game is restarted with a free kick, penalty kick, corner kick, goal kick, throw-in, or kickoff.

Shielding   A technique used by the player with the ball to protect it from a defender closely marking him. The player in possession keeps his body between the ball and the defender.

Square pass   A simple pass made by a player to a teammate running alongside him.

Stamina   The ability to maintain physical effort over long periods. All players require good levels of stamina to stay effective over an entire game.

Stoppage time   Time added to the end of any period to make up for time lost because of a major halt in play, such as treating an injured player. Also known as injury time.

Sudden death   A type of extra time period where the first goal scored by a team ends the game and gives that team the victory. Also known as "golden goal."

Sweeper   A defender that can be played closest to his own goal behind the rest of the defenders or in a more attacking role responsible for bringing the ball forward.

Tactics   Methods of play used in an attempt to outwit and beat an opposition team.

Target man   A tall striker, usually the player farthest upfield, at whom teammates aim their forward passes.

Through ball   A pass to a teammate that puts him beyond the opposition's defense and through to goal.

Volley   Any ball kicked by a player when it is off the ground.

Wall   A line of defenders standing close together to protect their goal against a free kick.

Wall pass   A quick, short pair of passes between two players that sends the ball past a defender. Also known as a one-two.

Weight   The strength of a pass.

Zonal marking   A system in which defenders mark opponents who enter their particular area of the field.

Web sites

The Internet abounds with thousands of web sites devoted to particular teams, players, or aspects of soccer. Below we've detailed some of the most interesting and informative web sites currently available.

www.360soccer.com
A strong international look at the global game with sections on each continent's soccer news and reports. Packed with links to sites focused on soccer in specific countries.

www.allsports.com/mls
Up-to-date news and results from the MLS provided by the Allsports news and picture agency.

www.clivegifford.co.uk
The author's web site that, under the In-Print section, features regularly updated soccer tips and links to other web pages.

www.thecoachingcorner.com/soccer/ index.html
A good, thorough grounding in the rules and tactics of the game.

www.countrylife.co.uk/worldsoccer/ index.htm
The on-line version of *World Soccer* magazine, this site has news about all the major competitions, plus exclusive player profiles, interviews, and features, as well as the latest fixtures, results, and tables.

www.fifa.com
FIFA's official site is huge and takes time to surf around. But stick with it because there's tons of data, helpful fact sheets, and the latest version of the laws of the game. There are also links to the governing bodies for soccer in each continent.

www.mlsnet.com
The official web pages of the MLS league are a fabulous, packed collection of history, team data, statistics, news, and opinions. Also included are the rules of the game and coaching advice.

www.precision-goalkeeping.com
Great web site devoted to the art of goalkeeping and featuring legends, goalkeeper news, and plenty of tips and techniques.

www.soccerclinics.com
Text, graphics, and animation that explain all aspects of coaching the game of soccer.

www.soccerhall.org
The web page of the National Soccer Hall of Fame is crammed full of the great soccer players to have played the game in the U.S. and beyond.

www.ussoccer.com
The official home on the Internet of U.S. soccer in all its many and various forms. It includes news and results from inside the U.S. leagues and also of U.S. players playing abroad.

www.worldstadiums.com
As its name suggests, this is a site devoted to the venues in which the game of soccer is played all over the world. It is a massive site searchable by country or stadium name.

www.youthsoccer.org
The official site of the U.S. Youth Soccer Association, featuring news about young players and their coaches, as well as a list of upcoming competitions and a calendar of events.

Index

A

Abelardo 83
Ablett, Gary 68
AC Milan 28, 44, 49, 71, 74, 87
Adams, Tony 65
Adani, Daniele 67
African Nations Cup 77, 80
Ailing, Liu 83
Ajax 64, 68, 86
Al Jaber, Sami 17
Albania 47
Alberto, Carlos 79
Albertosi 79
Alfonso 83
American Soccer League 88, 89
Amokachi 82
Amunike, Emmanuel 82
Ardiles, Osvaldo 89
Argentina 20, 35, 61, 64, 76, 82, 86
Arsenal 29, 46, 62, 65, 67, 88
Asian Cup 77
Aston Villa 45, 88
Atletico Madrid 50, 88
attackers 42-45
attacking systems 64
    crossing 43
    defensive role of 48
    depth and width 42
    free kicks 56-57
    long-ball game 65
    off the ball 43
    opening up defenses 44-45
    opening up spaces 43
    passing 44
    through balls 44
Australia 7, 27, 48
Austria 9

B

Babayaro, Celestine 82
back heel 36
backward pass 42
Baggio, Roberto 58, 59
ball control 18-19, 37
ball games 8
Banks, Gordon 38, 39, 84
Barber, Graham 54
Barcelona 71, 75, 86
Baresi, Franco 28
Barnes, John 35
Barr, Michelle 29
Barthez, Fabien 41
Bassedas 82
Batistuta, Gabriel 65
Bayern Munich 14, 47, 53, 59, 61, 85
beach soccer 35
Beckenbauer, Franz 47, 80, 85
Beckham, David 53, 57, 68, 69
bending ball 44, 57
Benfica 85
Bento, Manuel 81
Best, George 20, 69, 85, 88
bicycle kick 36
Blackburn Rovers 11
Blanc, Laurent 33

Blanchflower, Danny 36
Bolivia 76
Bolton Wanderers 74, 89
Boninsegna 79
bookings 15
Bordeaux 43, 87
Borussia Dortmund 50, 56
Boselli, Nicola 15
Bossis, Maxime 81
Brazil 29, 57, 75, 84
    Copa America 69, 76
    formations 62, 63
    vs. Italy, 1970 79
    World Cup 6, 7, 76, 84
Britain, Great 88-89
    foreign players 89
    managers 88
    Premiership 89
    statistics 90-91
Brown, Rachel 69
Budka, Vaclav 49
Burke, Karen 29
Busby, Sir Matt 88
Butragueño, Emilio 45
Butt, Nicky 68

C

Cameroon 40, 77
Campbell, Sol 29, 65
Canada 77
Canizares, Santiago 59
Capello, Fabio 61
caps 8, 9, 91
Carlisle, Clarke 46
Carlos, Roberto 57
cautions, see bookings
Celtic 10, 66, 71
center circle 10, 50
center spot 10
Central America 77
Cerezo Osaka 75
Chala, Clever 36
Challinor, Dave 51
Champions League 14, 50, 53, 59, 61, 66, 70, 76
Chapman, Herbert 62, 88
Chapuisat, Stephane 56
Charlton, Bobby 14, 88
Chelsea 11, 88
Chilavert, Jose Luis 59
Chile 33
China 8, 77
    women's team 59, 82-83
chip 22, 58
Cipi, Geri 47
clearing the ball 47, 48
coaches 60-61
Collina, Pierluigi 15
Collymore, Stan 45
Colombia 15, 37, 40, 77
communication 39, 40, 48, 56, 67
competitions 76-77, 90-91
CONCACAF Gold Cup 77
Confederations Cup 68
Congo 37, 80
Copa America 69, 76
Copa Libertadores 76
corner arc 11
corner flags 10
corner kick 11, 32, 33, 52-53

defending 48, 49, 52
    in- or outswinging 52, 53
    marking up 49
    pace 53
    placing ball 52
    referee's signal 12
    short 53, 65
Costa Rica 77
Costacurta, Lodovico 35
Coventry City 32
Crespo, Hernan 82
crosses 43
Cruyff, Johan 42, 68, 80, 86
Cup-Winners' Cup 88
cushioning ball 18-19
    goalkeeping 39
    header 33
    instep cushion 19
    side-foot cushion 18
    thigh cushion 19

D

De Vos, Josa 77
Dean, Dixie 31
deception moves 27
defending 46-49
    attackers' role in 48
    clearing ball 47, 48, 65
    communication 48, 56
    defensive header 32, 33
    defensive systems 48, 49
    defensive tactics 64, 65
    forcing weaker position 47
    free kicks 48, 56
    interceptions 48
    jockeying 46-47
    regaining possession 46, 48
Deflandre, Eric 14
Dehu, Frederic 19
Dein, David 61
Del Bosque, Vicente 60
Del Piero, Alessandro 17
Delvecchio, Marco 76
Denmark 20, 32, 41
Deportivo la Coruna 19
Derby 88
Desailly, Marcel 30, 48, 76
Deschamps, Didier 64
Di Stefano, Alfredo 78, 84
diagonal run 43
diamond system 64
Domergue 81
Dominguez 79
dragback 36, 37
dribbling 26-27
drives 23, 31, 43
drop ball 51

E

Effenberg, Stefan 22
Egypt 77
Eintracht Frankfurt 78-79
Elliott, Matt 45
England 9, 29
    coaches 60, 88
    formations 63
    vs. Hungary, 1953 78
    women's team 29, 69
    World Cup 39, 47, 76
    see also league, English

Epalle, Joel 77
Eriksson, Sven-Goran 88
Ethiopia 77
Europe 7, 8, 9, 71, 76, 91
European Championships 30, 59, 65, 76, 81, 83, 87
European Cup 74, 78-79, 85, 86, 88
Eusebio (Eusebio da Silva Ferreira) 85
Everton 31, 72

F

FA Cup 61, 74, 88-89
    statistics 90-91
Facchetti, Giacinto 79
fancy tricks 36-37
fans 69, 70-71, 72, 73
fanzines 72
Fashanu, John 65
Feola, Vicente 62
Ferguson, Sir Alex 61, 66, 88
Fernandez, Luis 81
field 10-11
FIFA (Fédération Internationale de Football Association) 9, 35, 37
Figo, Luis 25, 52, 69
Fink, Thorsten 14
Finney, Tom 78
Fiorentina 67
five-on-five games 34-35
FK Jablonec 49
flick-on header 33
flick pass 20, 23
flick-up 36
Football Association (FA) 8
    see also FA Cup
formations 62-63, 64
Forrest, Craig 77
fouls 14-15, 28
    foul throw 50
    professional 15
    shirt-pulling 14
    see also misconduct
France 7, 9, 75, 76, 81, 86
free kick 14, 33, 54-57
    defending 48, 56
    direct 12, 14, 55
    goalkeeping 39
    in attack 56-57
    indirect 12, 14, 41, 54, 55
    quickly taken 54, 56, 57
    referee's signals 12, 54
    ten-yard rule 54
front-block tackle 28
Futsal 35

G

Galatasaray 13
Gentile, Claudio 35
Germany 17, 47, 57, 76, 79, 80-81, 85
Gerrard, Steven 29
Gerson 79
Ghana 77
Gillingham 47
Giresse, Alain 81
Glasgow Rangers 78
goal area 10, 11, 39
goalkeeper 38-41, 49, 67, 84
    catching ball 39
    communication 39, 40

defending penalties 59
deflecting ball 40
distribution 41
diving 41
offenses 55
punching ball 40
rules 9, 41, 55
stance 38, 39
throw outs 41
goal kick 11, 12
goal line 11
goalscoring 11, 45
Govedarica, Dejan 83
Graham, George 49
great games 78–83
great players 84–87
Gregory, John 46
Grosics, Gyula 78
Guardiola, Josep 83
Gullit, Ruud 18, 28, 81
Gutierrez, Jose Mari 47

H
halfway line 11
Hamann, Dietmar 57
Hamm, Mia 87
Hartson, John 66
Hasselbaink, Jimmy Floyd 14
Haugenes, Margunn 20
header 32–33
    cushioning 33
    defensive 32, 33
    diving 32, 33
    flick-on 33
    power 32
health and fitness 68
Hedman, Magnus 38
Hereford United 89
Herrera, Helenio 63
Hidegkuti, Nandor 78
Higuita, René 37, 40
Hillsborough tragedy 71
Hitzfeld, Ottmar 61
Hodgson, Roy 61
Hoeness, Uli 80
hole, playing in 64
Holland (Netherlands) 30, 57, 63,
    64, 80–81, 86
Honduras 77
Hong, Gao 83
hook, inside and outside 25
Houllier, Gérard 61
Hungary 9, 78

I J
injury 68
Inter Milan 63
interception 48
International Football
    Association Board (IFAB) 8, 9
Internazionale 71, 74
Internet 72, 73
Ipswich Town 89
Iran 77
Italy 40, 43, 49, 59, 64, 76, 79
Jairzinho 79
Jamaica 71
Japan 8, 31, 75, 77
Joachim, Julian 45
jockeying 46–47

Jokanovic 83
Jordao, Rui 81
Jugovic, Vladimir 83
Juventus 64, 86, 87

KL
Kahn, Oliver 59
kemari 8
Kewell, Harry 27, 89
kickoff 10, 50
Klinsmann, Jürgen 46
Kluivert, Patrick 68
Kocsis, Sandor 78
Komljenovic, Slobodan 83
Korea Republic 67, 68
Kringen, Goeril 77
Kuwait 77
Larsson, Henrik 66, 89
Law, Denis 88
laws, see rules
Lazio 20
Le Tissier, Matt 58
league, English 88, 89
    play-offs 89
    statistics 90
leagues, national 76
Leandro 15
Lee, Woon Jae 68
Leicester City 45
Lemerre, Roger 62
Liberia 87
Liu, Ying 82
Liverpool 60, 71, 88, 89
long-ball game 65
long throw 51, 65
Lopez, Claudio 82
Luxembourg 11

M
McClaren, Steve 60
McManaman, Steve 14
Maier, Sepp 80
Maldini, Cesare 67
Maldini, Paolo 49
Mali 80
managers 60–61, 88
    game tactics 66
Manchester City 60
Manchester United 7, 20, 53,
    68, 85, 88
Maradona, Diego 61, 76, 86
marker, slipping 25, 43
marking 48, 49
    player-to-player 49, 67
    set pieces 49, 56
Martins, Corentin 43
mascots 70
Masima 80
match preparation 16–17
Matthews, Sir Stanley 78
Mbayo, Kibemba 37
M'Bono 80
Medalen, Linda 82
media 6, 7, 69, 72–73, 79, 89
Meier, Urs 13
Mendieta, Gaizka 23, 83
Menotti, Cesar Luis 61
merchandising 69, 70, 71, 89
Merrick, Gil 78
Mettomo, Lucien 77

Mexico 46, 77
Michels, Rinus 61, 63
Middle East 7, 77
Middlesbrough 67
midfielders 64
Mihalovic, Sinisa 83
Mijatovic 83
Milanic, Darko 26
Milbrett, Tiffeny 77
Milla, Roger 40
Milosevic, Savo 83
misconduct 14–15
Monaco 87
Moore, Bobby 47
Moriera, Aymore 63
Moscow Dynamo 84
M'Péle, François 80
Muhren, Arnold 68, 89
Müller, Gerd 80, 81
Munitis, Pedro 83
Munoz, Miguel 84

N
Nakata, Hidetoshi 21
Napoli 86
Ndah, George 47
Neeskens, Johan 64, 80
Neville, Gary 68
New York Cosmos 84
Newcastle United 55, 62, 89
Nicholson, Bill 88
Nielsen, Allan 32
Nigeria 26, 77, 82
North American Soccer League
    (NASL) 88
Northern Ireland 85
Norway 11, 65, 77
    women's team 82–83
Nottingham Forest 88
Nunes, Adelino 35
nutmegging 37

O
offside rule 12, 13, 52, 62
offside trap 42, 44, 65
Okocha, Jay-Jay 26, 57, 82
Oldham Athletic 11
Olympic Games 77, 82
on-ball skills 26–27
O'Neill, Martin 88
Ortega, Ariel 82
overhead kick 36
overlaps 42, 57
overloads 42
Overmars, Marc 64
Owen, Michael 47, 89

PQ
Paisley, Bob 88
Paraguay 59, 76
Pardo, Pavel 46
Paris St. Germain 19, 70, 80,
    87
Parlour, Ray 67
passing 20–23
    accuracy 20, 21
    advanced 22–23
    attacking 44
    practicing 21, 23
    swerving 44

timing 22
weight 20
Patterson, Mark 47
Pearce, Stuart 59
Pelé (Edson Arantes do Nascimento)
    7, 39, 47, 62, 79, 84
penalty arc 11
penalty area 11, 58
    indirect free kick in 54
penalty kicks 9, 11, 14, 15,
    58–59
penalty shootout 59
penalty spot 10
Peru 55, 76
Perugia Calcio 21, 35, 70
Pires, Robert 29
Platini, Michel 58, 81, 86
players
    earnings 69, 89
    foreign 89
    great players 84–87
    positions 10
    professional 68–69
Portugal 52, 81
Power, Paul 60
practice
    dribbling 27
    free kicks 57
    goalkeeping 38
    heading 33
    passing 21, 23
    passing and moving 24
    penalties 59
    sessions 17, 61
    shooting 31
    throw-in 51
Premiership 89
Preston North End 62
professional game 68–69, 89
program, game 70, 72
push and go 25
push pass, see sidefoot pass
Puskas, Ferenc 19, 78
Puyol 77
Queen's Park 74
Queen's Park Rangers 46

R
Ramsey, Sir Alf 63
Rangers 71, 89
Raul 26, 54, 83
Real Madrid 14, 21, 47, 52, 54, 60,
    61, 71, 78–79, 84, 87
records 91
    attendance 74, 75
    longest throw-in 51
red card 12, 15, 67
Redondo, Fernando 21
referees 12–13, 14, 15
    signals 12, 54
regaining possession 46
    interception 48
Rep, Johnny 80
restarts 50–51
Reyna, Claudio 37
Rimet, Jules 76
Rio de Janeiro 75
Rivaldo 29, 37, 69, 76
Rivelino 79
River Plate 84

Robson, Bobby 88
Roma 21, 65, 70, 72
Ronaldo 6, 69, 76
Rottenberg, Silke 67
Rouissi, Faouzi 37
Roxburgh, Andy 61
rules 7, 8, 9, 12-13
   advantage rule 13
   back pass rule 41
   ball out of play 11
   five-on-five 34
   fouls 14
   offside rule 13, 52, 62
   ten-yard rule 54
   throw-in 50
Russia 9, 84

S

Santos 84
Saudi Arabia 17, 77
Schmeichel, Peter 41
Scholes, Paul 68
Scifo, Enzo 24
Scirea, Gaetano 64
scorpion kick 37
Scotland 8, 9, 74
   women's team 29
Scottish Cup 91
scouts 60
screening, see shielding
Scurry, Briana 59, 87
sending off, see red card
Shankly, Bill 7, 23, 60, 88
Sheringham, Teddy 66
Shevchenko, Andri 44
shielding 26
shooting 30-31
short corner 53, 65
shot placement 31
shot selection 31
Shrove Tuesday games 8
sidefoot pass 20-21, 22, 56
Sissi 54
six-yard box 11
sliding tackle 29

Slovenia 26, 83
soccer
   as business 7, 61, 89
   origins of 8
   spread of 7, 9
Solano, Nolberto 55
Solskjaer, Ole Gunnar 53
Sousa, Paulo 56
South Africa 77
South America 7, 71, 76
Southampton 58
Soviet Union, see Russia
space, using 24-25, 42, 43, 46
Spain 23, 26, 76, 83
stadiums 74-75
   Anfield 71
   Hampden Park 74, 78
   Highbury 72
   Maracana 75
   Millennium, Cardiff 89
   Nagai 75
   Nou Camp 75
   safety 71
   San Siro, Milan 74
   Selhurst Park 11
   Stade de France 75
   Wembley 74, 89
stance 38, 39, 46, 55
Stein, Jock 88
Strasser, Jeff 11
street soccer 35
stretching 16-17
striker 64
substitution 12, 66
Sudan 77
Suddell, Major William 62
support play 24
supporters see fans
Sweden 38
   women's team 20
sweeper 63, 64, 85
swerving ball 44, 57

T

tackling 28-29, 46

tactics 64-67
Takahar, Noohira 31
Tardelli, Marco 76
Taylor, Peter 60
teams 7, 69, 70-71
Thijssen, Frans 89
through ball 44
throw-in 9, 11, 50
   foul throw 50
   long 51, 65
   referee's signal 12
   rules 50
Tigana, Jean 81
"total football" 63, 86
Tottenham Hotspur 29, 32, 61, 88, 89
Tranmere Rovers 51
transfers 61, 69, 89
Tristan, Diego 19
Tromso 11
Tunisia 37
turf, artificial 11
turning 25

UV

Ukraine 44
uniform 8, 9, 10, 17
   home and away 10
United Arab Emirates 77
Uruguay 31, 76
U.S. 7, 11, 37, 71, 77
   women's team 59, 89
Valencia 59
Van Basten, Marco 28, 30, 81
Venables, Terry 11, 73, 88
Venglos, Dr. Jozef 61, 88
Veron, Juan Sebastian 20, 89
Vicenza 70
Viduka, Mark 48
Vieira, Patrick 89
Villa, Ricky 89
violent conduct 14, 15
volley 30-31
   aerial side 36
   half 31, 41

instep 31, 41
lay-off 30
lob 31
sidefoot 30

W

Walker, Karen 69
wall, defensive 56, 57
wall pass 25
warming up 16-17
Weah, George 87
Wen, Sun 82, 83
Wenger, Arsène 61, 87, 88
West Germany, see Germany
West Ham 62, 74
Westberg, Karolina 20
Widdowson, Samuel W. 9
Wiltord, Sylvain 46
Wimbledon 11
Windass, Dean 67
wing-backs 63, 64
Wolverhampton Wanderers 47
women's soccer 7, 9, 54, 69, 77, 89
World Cup 6, 7, 14, 39, 40, 47, 57, 59, 61, 62, 63, 74, 75, 76, 79, 80, 82-83, 84, 85, 86, 87
Wright, Billy 78

YZ

Yashin, Lev 84
yellow card see booking
Yeovil 89
Yokohama Marinos 71
youth players 35, 60, 68
Yugoslavia 65, 83
Yunjie, Fan 83
Zamorano, Ivan 33
Zanetti, Javier 82
Zico 35, 58
Zidane, Zinedine 37, 61, 87
Zoff, Dino 40
Zola, Gianfranco 43
zonal defense system 48

ACKNOWLEDGMENTS

Photographs in this book have been supplied by Empics, except the following:
Key: b = bottom, c = center, l = left, r = right, t = top

4 bl Still Pictures; 5 tr Popperfoto, br Rex Features; 8 tl The National Football Museum, cr The National Football Museum, br Corbis, bl The National Football Museum; 9 t The National Football Museum, tl Robert Opie Collection, cl The National Football Museum, c The National Football Museum, cr The National Football Museum, bc The National Football Museum, br The National Football Museum; 10 bc www.umbro.com, bc www.umbro.com; 11 bl Allsport U.K. Ltd./Gary M.Prior, bc Colorsport; 17 c www.umbro.com, c The National Football Museum, cr The National Football Museum; 30 bl Colorsport; 33 tr Popperfoto; 35 c Wall 2 Wall Futbol, cr Wall 2 Wall Futbol; 51 br Allsport U.K. Ltd.; 57 br Colorsport; 61 c Colorsport; 62 cr Colorsport, bl Hulton Getty; 63 tr Hulton Getty; 68 tl Hulton Getty; 69 tl Popperfoto/Ray Green, cr Popperfoto/Yves Herman; 70 cr Robert Opie Collection, cr Robert Opie Collection; 71 tl Popperfoto; 72 cl Hulton Getty, cr www.asromacalcio.it/sito-ufficiale/index.html, br pictures courtesy of Sky Sports; 73 c Colorsport, br Colorsport; 74 tl Popperfoto, cl Allsport U.K. Ltd.; 75 tr Allsport U.K. Ltd./Jamie McDonald; 76 t Popperfoto, tl Colorsport, tr Popperfoto; 78 c Colorsport, cr Hulton Getty; 80 tl www.psg.fr, tr www.psg.fr.
The publishers would like to give special thanks to Jen Little at Empics.

Every effort has been made to trace the copyright holders of the photographs. The publishers apologize for any inconvenience caused.